This is a work of fiction. Names, characters, places, and incidents either are the product of the author's imagination or are used fictitiously. Any resemblance to actual persons, living or dead, events, or locales is entirely coincidental.

First paperback edition March 2024

First digital edition March 2024

Cover design by Fiona Jayde Media

ISBN 979-8-9891199-1-2 (paperback)

ISBN 979-8-9891199-0-5 (ebook)

Published by ScarabSkin Books

www.scarabskinbooks.com

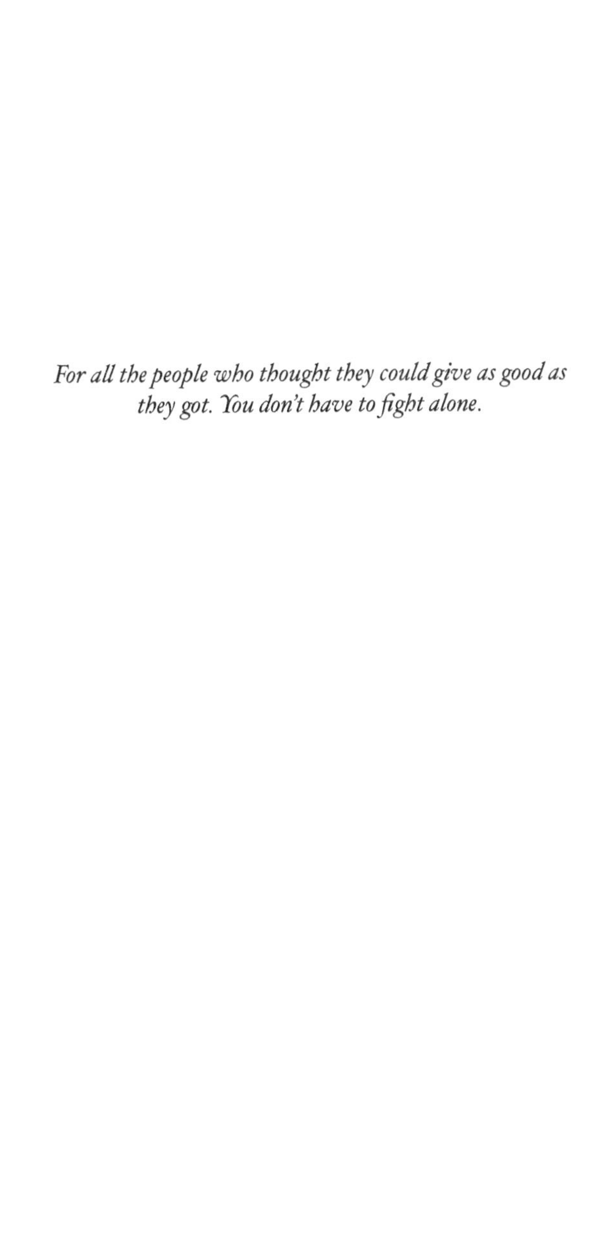

For all the people who thought they could give as good as they got. You don't have to fight alone.

WHEN THE BLOOD IS UP FINALE

EDIE CAY

CAST OF CHARACTERS

Jane Laurent, viscountess, mother of Lord Andrepont, sister to Lady Lorian
Emma Laurent, the eldest daughter
Matthew Wallingford, Lord Andrepont father of the current viscount, husband to Lady Andrepont.
Gareth Somerset, youngest son of Lord Lorian, a commissioned officer in His Majesty's Armed Forces.
Vasily Nikolaevich Kuznetsov, friend to Gareth Somerset, former revolutionary, nicknamed Vasya.
Mary Renwood, niece of the Andrepont housekeeper, wife of Vasya.

Martha Foraker, a maid at the Aberscomb townhome, later a housekeeper.
Hope Miller, Jane's lady's maid and mother of Margaret Miller by Matthew, Lord Andrepont.
Mr. Barton, the longtime butler for the Andrepont home.
Mrs. Thorne, housekeeper at Meadowpond, the favorite country estate of Lord Lorian.
Mrs. Renwood, housekeeper of the Andrepont townhome.
Mr. Vernon, butler of the Andrepont townhome.

Mr. Dendrum, the stable master of the Andrepont townhome.

Mrs. Houseman, a midwife and herb woman from Chilton who teaches young Jane her craft.

Mr. Laurent, Jane and Emma's father. An investor who lost most of his fortune in the credit crisis of 1772.

Aunt Diana Fraser, sister to Mr. Laurent, aunt of Jane and Emma. Married in London to a much older man, she is now a widow with social connections.

Lord Lorian, the earl and father of two sons. Holds the title of the viscount Aberscomb, which is given to the heir of the Lorian title.

Percy, Lord Aberscomb, eldest son and heir of Lord Lorian, older brother of Gareth

Mr. Eier, the coroner

Mr. Breaverton, the magistrate

The Children:

William Somerset, the oldest son of Gareth and Emma Somerset.

James Wallingford, son of Matthew and Jane, heir to the Andrepont title. Cousin to William, Lydia, and Agnes

Lady Lydia, eldest daughter of Gareth and Emma, first cousin of James.

Lady Agnes Somerset, youngest daughter of Gareth and Emma.

Margaret Miller, half-sister to James Wallingford, daughter of Matthew, Lord Andrepont, and a Hope Miller, Jane's lady's maid.

Lord Hackett, a lord who looks up Andrepont and follows his lead into vice.

Lord Denby, a lord who looks up Andrepont and follows his lead into vice.
Lord Tottingham, a lord who is well into vices.
Lord Beecher, a lord who is well into vices.
Lady Haglund, a baroness, friend of Emma and later Jane, thrower of parties.
Sir Frederick Haglund, a baron, thrower of parties.

CHAPTER 1

NOW

NOW - 1801

The Russian's broad shoulders filled the doorway into the drawing room. His expression, as much as Jane could see of it given the dark beard on his jaw, was unperturbed. "The coroner will likely be here in the morning," he rasped.

Martha Foraker let out a shaky breath and looked to Jane. They all looked to Jane—even Jane's older sister, Emma, and Emma's husband, Gareth, who occupied the chaise by the fire. Jane was the woman of the house, and with this murder, she had become the leader of their strange family. The dark smudges under Martha's eyes, so prominent on her pale, freckled face, spurred Jane. But as Jane opened her mouth, the grandfather clock boomed three, making them all jump.

Jane hated that clock. She hated this room. This prison Matthew had kept her in for all these decades. She kept every knickknack on display, every gift, everything that was only hers, as if to showcase her cell. And that clock was meant to remind her that her time had been his. A wedding present. A reminder of his control.

Not anymore. Jane waited for the clock to finish its business. She would relish burning that thing in the garden. But not now. "We all need some sleep," she said.

Martha scooped up the small, forgettable teapot that sat on the table between them. "I'll dash this on the stones in the garden before I rest."

Jane's hand shot out, gripping Martha's wrist. "You shan't do anything of the sort. Put it back. Nothing shall change. Nothing can change until the coroner calls."

"But we already know his lordship is dead." Martha glanced at Vasya, still in the doorway, still as wide as a piano case, still unperturbed.

Vasya inclined his head. His dark eyes bored into hers. The man she'd dreamed of. The man she'd hoped could be hers. The man who helped in her husband's debauchery, and helped her with his murder.

"Wash it thoroughly and tidy it away by morning," Jane said, snapping her eyes away from Vasya. "Nothing should be missing or out of place." She let go of her housekeeper. "And get some sleep. We must look as if it is merely any other day."

Emma stood, followed by Gareth. Emma's guilt was a shroud, a bloody, pulpy mass of grief and anger and shame. But the time for Emma's apologies was over. All of it was over, as far as Jane was concerned. She was free. But it didn't feel like freedom. It felt like a new cage. Perhaps that would change once their actions started bearing consequences.

"We will also go," Gareth said, nodding at Vasya to have the carriage brought around.

Jane flinched at the command. Hadn't Vasya done

enough? Hadn't Gareth claimed that despite Vasya being a servant by title, that he was a friend first?

"A late night of cards, then?" Gareth stood, offering his hand to Emma.

Jane stood as well, wishing to pull her sister into an embrace as if they were children again, as if their only worry was the missing lid to her paint pot. But this night was too far. Another night to mark *we will never be the same again* in Jane's imaginary diary. Perhaps now that her husband was dead, she would have the courage to start anew. She refused to look at Vasya now. She couldn't, not with the mixture of violence and hope she felt. Instead, she looked to her sister. "I will write you with news in the morning."

Emma laced her arm through her husband's—the only sign this evening of their affection for one another. Jane knew they were careful not to touch in her company, as if their love would cause Jane pain. Emma was right, naturally, as she often was. Their happiness did hurt Jane—it was a happiness she would never have. A happiness she had unwittingly discarded through her own naivete. Her own mistakes. But that was in the past. And tomorrow she would embark on a new life as the widow Andrepont.

BEFORE - 1780

"You're supposed to say 'tell me everything' in a breathless voice and flounce down on my bed in a desperate bid for attention," Emma scolded Jane.

Jane looked up from her book of pressed flowers, which held more botanical information than a typical young lady's book of pressings. Her father indulged Jane's hobby, allowing her a flower press and paper, with which she'd made a compendium of their village's plants and their uses. Jane had argued that having the knowledge to physic for a vast household would make her all the better a *grande dame* someday.

"Tell me everything," Jane said evenly.

"That's hardly breathless."

"I'm very fit. It takes quite a lot to leave me breathless." Jane dipped a quill and carefully lettered the plant's name on the page. Her calligraphy was passable, at least.

Emma rolled her eyes, which Aunt Diana had absolutely forbidden her to do. "Well, this man would have left even *you* breathless."

Jane's eyebrow arched, as if that were argument enough. Her interest in the male of the species would be enhanced if they also had pollen and attracted bees. Emma contemplated her sister. Jane was objectively prettier, but most people seemed to believe that Emma was. Jane was angles and wide, curving eyes with sharp brows that expressed far more than the typical emotional range. Emma, by contrast, was rounder, both in face and in body. She appeared more maternal while Jane, if she were not careful, would be construed as a seductress due to the contrast of her dark hair, her bright green eyes, and her naturally plump, cherry-colored lips.

"I'm very interested to know if this swain made *you* breathless," Jane said.

Emma lifted her chin, imperious as the elder, more worldly sister. "Of course he did."

Jane's head was still bent over her book, laboriously lettering in Latin, which was so easy to misspell. She lifted her head to glare at Emma. "You are a terrible storyteller."

"I am not. You are a terrible listener, which makes me not want to tell the story."

Jane sighed. "There. Breathless. Tell me everything."

Emma couldn't help but huff out a laugh. "Fine, you ungrateful wretch." Emma leapt off the bed, stood next to where Jane sat on the floor, and looked out the window. "There I was, dressed in my finest—"

"You're standing in my light." Jane squinted up at her, a teasing grin barely suppressed.

Emma nabbed a pillow from the windowsill and bopped her sister on the head.

"Watch the inkpot!" Jane cried, muffled by the pillow.

Emma clutched the offending weapon and retreated, allowing Jane's precious sunlight to fall across her page. "Watching everyone was reward enough for getting trussed up last night. The patterns, the clothes—everyone was dressed so beautifully. And the jewels!"

"The magpie strikes again!"

Emma shot Jane a withering look. "I didn't take anything. Nor would I. But how could anyone not appreciate the richness on display?"

Jane smiled as she finished her lettering on the page. "I can only imagine."

"It will be your turn soon enough." Emma sighed.

Jane preferred not to think about that. Their father had never fully recovered from the '72 financial crisis, though he was happy to remind them of how dire it had been, with banks closing in London and Scotland. While not terribly vain, their father hated to be wrong. Pointing out how the entire world— from Amsterdam to the colonies—had also been affected made losing all their money less his fault. Even if his daughters would be the ones to regain his fortune.

At the doorway to the room, Emma called down to the housekeeper, asking if there were any bouquets or visitors. The housekeeper assured her it was still much too early in the day to expect such things. Their aunt and father weren't even up yet.

The ball had gone so late that the sun was rising as the carriage arrived home. It had awoken Jane, who helped release Emma from her gown and stays before they both fell into bed. Emma only slept a few hours before she was awake again, wanting to tell Jane every detail. Even though Jane didn't particularly care.

Noise from the street began to pick up, and Emma drifted back to the window. There was likely something to see. It was London, after all. Something of note seemed to happen on every street corner, if the newspapers were to be believed. But the window was always sooty, and the smell of people wafted in through every crack and seam of the house. Jane sighed, laying down her quill pen.

"What's wrong?" Emma asked.

"Aside from you standing in my light again?" Jane teased, sanding the page to help the ink dry. "I hate it here. I want to go back to the country. To the woods. I want to feel the grass beneath my feet, smell the clean, bracing air. Work on my book. I haven't even started on the fungi."

The lines in Emma's forehead appeared. Jane knew what she was thinking: *perhaps Jane could find some country gentleman, happy to indulge a wife's interest in local botany.* Or perhaps she could parlay her interest in cataloging into some kind of art. Her watercolor representations were quite competent, if she did say so herself.

"Watch out, little sister, or someone will accuse you of witchcraft." Emma meant it in jest, but Jane's expression froze. It was a joke she'd heard often and hated, aimed at any woman who physicked in the village. But then, the massive front door of their townhouse creaked open. The front door! Not the back door for deliveries! Jane hoped Emma would get bouquets and suitors and gifts and requests for strolls through the park. She wanted her sister to get her heart's desire.

Emma pulled her wrap around herself and ran to the stairs. Jane couldn't help but put aside her work and run after her, arriving just in time to see Aunt Diana's butler accepting a man's hat and gloves! The visitor in question was hidden around the column, but Emma shouldn't appear too eager. They glanced at each other, holding their breath, hoping to hear voices.

The visitor would be taken upstairs to the drawing room in moments if he was there for Emma or her aunt. But if he was there for their father, they wouldn't know his identity until supper.

"You can't very well be seen lurking on the stairs," Jane whispered.

"But—" Emma stood on her toes, as if that would somehow make the man more visible.

"Your poor curiosity. So neglected." Jane pulled Emma back into her bedroom.

"I'll throw another pillow at you." Emma huffed while she paced. Jane took up her lap desk and resumed her Latin.

"Fiddlesticks."

"Which imaginary argument are you having now?" Jane asked, not looking up from her work.

"Should I go to the drawing room without Aunt Diana? Or should I wait until she calls for me?"

"If you busy yourself with embroidery, should you not be safe?" Jane suggested, dipping her quill carefully.

"So level-headed," Emma teased.

"One of us has to be." Jane looked up at Emma, waiting for her sister's decision.

"Join me?" Emma pleaded.

Jane's shoulders sagged.

"Please?"

Jane nodded at last, looking around at her mess. The lap desk, the inkpot, her wet quill, the penknife, the book stuffed full of plant specimens. "But you'll have to help me carry everything."

"Of course." Emma rushed to help, but paused.

Jane knew what Emma was thinking, that sudden confrontation with the idea that Emma might not be the prettier sister. But Jane knew she was. Besides, Jane was too young to be married off. So it didn't matter if she was in the drawing room, hoping to finish her Latin without misspelling any words. And petty jealousy was unbecoming.

❧

VASYA ENJOYED FETCHING WATER FOR HIS ROOM. Flirting with the landlady was perhaps his new favorite pastime. She was an older woman, still handsome despite the lines on her face. He preferred older women—they didn't have expectations of marriage or princely gifts that Vasya could not afford. He also preferred early mornings, a time when everything was still and the clamor of the world hadn't yet invaded his thoughts. There was a knock on his door, and while Vasya might hope that Mrs. Hatcher was coming to offer him something more than a breakfast tray, he knew it wouldn't be.

Upon opening, he found his friend Gareth Somerset, looking like he'd been trampled by a horse and then tossed in a river. They had indulged last night, a smaller gambling hell that didn't have the frills of the higher-end places, but it was frequented by serious players. Despite the high bets they placed, liquor had flowed freely and at no cost to them.

Gareth blinked up at him, eyes red and dry. "You must be joking."

Vasya cocked his head. "I don't understand." He had said nothing; there was no joke present. Was this an English thing? A verbal tic he'd not yet encountered?

"My head feels like a pig's bladder that's been kicked around by an entire village's worth of dirty children."

Vasya considered his words. "How do you know they are dirty?"

Gareth chuckled, but then raised his hands to his head. "Why don't you look as if an entire cavalry battalion has trampled you?"

Vasya raised his thick black eyebrows. He'd had his share of alcohol last night, but he would not have considered it to be over-imbibing. He was, after all, playing to win. But apparently Gareth had taken too much. There could be only one explanation. "I am Russian."

"Not helpful." Gareth turned to return to his room.

But Vasya was not done with his friend. Gareth had saved Vasya's life years before. He'd found the Englishman's easy manner and enjoyment of the world a balm when Vasya was spiraling into despair. Gareth had been on a "Grand Tour," apparently a British term for drinking in all the worst places across the Continent. Perhaps not every man would consider this to be a savior, but Vasya did. The debt was not easily repaid. But a good shave on a morning when Gareth's hands would be unsteady? This he could do. He lifted the bowl that sat on his dressing table, following his friend into the hallway.

Gareth opened his door, and they both went into his room. "Where did you get warm water?"

Vasya prepared Gareth's shaving instruments as Gareth stumbled into the chair. "I went down to the kitchens," Vasya said. "They give you much if it means they do not have to carry it. Water is very heavy." He wasn't about to share Mrs. Hatcher's virtues with Gareth, who was fair-haired and blue-eyed, and much better with women. Aside from which, he knew his friend was lovestruck by someone else. A woman who was his better match, being clearly of privileged means.

Gareth relaxed, arranging a towel around his neck and scooting the chair closer to the window for better light.

There would not be many shaves in the future. Gareth's father, the earl, had purchased a military commission for Gareth, and he would be dispatched to the unruly American colony shortly. It surprised Vasya, as he had not seen Gareth as a soldier, but it would give them something in common after he returned from the war.

"Will you try to see her?" Vasya rumbled, lathering the soap in a bowl. Gareth had insisted on them renting rooms in this boarding house rather than staying with his brother, Percy, Lord Aberscomb. Gareth claimed his virtuous brother would look down upon their gambling. And perhaps any woman Vasya might find himself entangled with. But if there was one thing to raise his friend's spirits with, it was the prospect of his lady love.

During their long travel days, Gareth had regaled Vasya with the old English tales of love from afar. It seemed wasteful. Why love from afar when loving from very, very close was more pleasurable?

Gareth shook his head. "Why? We haven't been introduced, and there's no way she'll remain unmarried until I return."

"Marriage before you leave?" Vasya suggested. "A wedding night at least."

Gareth gave him a look of disappointment. Was he angry that Vasya would suggest this? His young lady love was a breathtaking beauty. Dark hair with highlights of auburn, arresting blue eyes. This is what Gareth had told him, sighing like a maiden. "Uncalled for, Vasya. You speak of a respectable young lady."

Vasya lowered his head in silent apology. There were times when he didn't understand why a man was allowed to say his lewd ideas about one woman but not another. He understood castes better than Gareth, but he'd heard many men say these things about women of higher rank. Better to be respectful of all than try to learn the rules.

Yet, with Gareth's father's and brother's connections, should Gareth's heartbreak not bear an easy solution? Perhaps it was part of Gareth's practical fatalism. Instead of winning the girl, Gareth would don his uniform, step onto a boat, and make his way to North America. Hopefully, Vasya's friend would sail back home again in one piece.

But with most wars, soldiers returned home to find all the desirable women snatched into matrimony by elderly titled bulls, happy to orchestrate wars that kept young men out of reach.

Vasya lathered Gareth's face. Being near Gareth meant they had the best soaps, the best brushes. Vasya kept the blades razor-sharp, which made shaving more enjoyable. "There is still time before you leave. Why not enjoy good wine while you can?"

Gareth squinted at him. "Are you telling me to drink when my body already contains more alcohol than blood?"

Vasya picked up the honed straight razor, letting it glint in the light from the window. "If there is a place where you may admire this girl, and it happens to serve fine wine and good food, why should you not attend?"

"I can't get you a ticket. You're unknown here. I can't vouch for your rank. There's no proof."

The razor scratched along Gareth's cheek. "Call me your driver. Whatever you like. Then I can sneak into the kitchens and help myself to that good food." Vasya wiped the blade and took it to Gareth's skin again. Perhaps there was a maid or a cook who enjoyed foreign men. Men whose English came out in rumbled consonants?

"Is this plan for my benefit or yours?"

"Why not both?"

⁂

Jane watched Emma straighten her posture, fidget with her dress, and check her hair in the looking glass as if she were caught in some sort of mad dance. This man must be quite the Adonis to ruffle her practical sister in this way.

Personally, Jane did not believe in love. It seemed much more likely that she would be set up in marriage with someone of a like mind. A man whom she could respect, and who could respect her in turn. Was that not how the vicar told them it would be? Helpmeets and all that nonsense?

Jane would prefer to be a spinster like Mrs. Houseman. There had never been a Mister Houseman, but after a certain age, the village had granted her the appellation. She had no good things to say about men or marriage, and so there was not a chance she would change her mind. Mrs. Houseman was the midwife, the best and least expensive option for healing, and she wasn't given half the amount of credit for her work.

While a surgeon-apothecary might be called in from the next village over, he would harrumph and *hmm* over the symptoms while never directly touching the ill patient. He didn't feel a distended belly or the sweaty temples that gave sign to a thousand sicknesses, but he earned twice the money with a quarter of the efficacy. But Mrs. Houseman would sweep in, all smiles and old lady charm, handing out tisanes of peppermint and ginger for the distended bellies, willow bark tinctures for the fevers, and reassurances for the rest of the family.

That was what Jane wanted to do. She wanted to sweep in like Mrs. Houseman, giving relief to a household on tenterhooks when they were scared of losing a child or wife or husband to forces they could not control. Emma had joked that Mrs. Houseman was a witch, and there had been talk of it all over the village for as long as Jane could remember. But instead of turning on her, they all felt that Mrs. Houseman was *their* witch and was therefore safe from persecution. Mostly.

Jane followed Emma into the drawing room. Moving her botanical journal—which Mrs. Houseman had recommended for her learning—was terribly inconvenient, but her sister's need seemed important. Besides, this might be her first look at a brother-in-law! And a handsome one, at that.

Emma picked through the darning basket while Jane set up her journal and portable writing desk once again. She'd hoped to improve her watercolor work, which she would then paste into her journal as well. It was a way to learn species down to the smallest, most intimate level. For now, though, copying names and bits of information she remembered from Mrs. Houseman's bedside lectures was enough. She was so engrossed in her project that she didn't notice when Aunt Diana came to sit with them.

"Oh! Good morning, Aunt," Jane exclaimed when she looked up to find Aunt Diana glaring at her.

"I addressed you multiple times, girl. You must pay better attention."

Jane wanted to protest that her work was

important, but she knew better. Aunt Diana was trying to make them into marriageable young ladies so a kind, handsome, wealthy man might scoop them up and take them off their father's hands, giving relief to all. As if a woman's quest for well-being ended after matrimony. Jane had wondered before how different their lives would have been if their mother had lived. Her father bumbling through his raising of daughters, never sure of his rules, never sure of the world's rules.

A footman appeared carrying a tray laden with summer stone fruit and ratafia. It was already quite a warm day, and refreshment was welcome. Jane would have to put aside her project if she wished to eat—she couldn't risk a juicy plum ruining a page of *Taxus baccata*.

Her aunt's butler strode into the room, bending to confer with Aunt Diana. Her aunt's eyes widened with pleasure, darting to Emma. Perhaps the mysterious stranger was, in fact, Emma's handsome viscount.

To think, her sister would be an officious aristocratic wife, birthing a litter of bluebloods for King and country. Jane chuckled. The idea that Emma—who loved to doze in the green lawns at the edge of the woods—would become a viscountess! It was almost as absurd as Jane becoming one. Though, admittedly, slightly less. Emma worked very hard on her lessons—she danced better than Jane and could set a table to rival a grand house in London. Emma could even play the pianoforte with passable ability.

"Put away your books, Jane!" Aunt Diana bade her, flapping her hands, as if she could wave away Jane's botanical interests.

Jane was proud of herself for not making a smart comment back or making a face as she capped her inkwell. She could do all this work tomorrow. Or the next day. Thank goodness she wasn't the one who had to attend parties and assemblies and dinners and frivolous games with other young ladies who vied for the same few titled men.

Suddenly, the door swung open and her father walked in, followed by a handsome stranger. Emma made a strangled sound and dropped her mending. This must be her viscount. His jaw was square in a way that made Jane think of old oaks being shorn into boards. But his nose was fine and straight, and his eyes were a dark, bottomless black, like the woods after sunset. Dangerous and comforting, all at once.

His mien was confident—no, that wasn't merely confidence. There was something else that made his spine so straight, his shoulders so broad, the tilt of his chin bordering arrogance.

"My sister, Mrs. Fraser, and my daughter, Miss Emma Laurent, whom you've met." Her father gestured across the small but comfortably appointed drawing room. The women rose, and Jane slowly got to her feet.

The viscount bowed low, and he centered his gaze on Emma in a way that made Jane uneasy. Her stomach flipped. Was this how men looked at women? Like they were a freshly whipped cream? Jane felt the buzz in the room, but she didn't understand it. She felt it from both her sister and from the viscount. What was happening?

"And this is my youngest daughter, Miss Jane Laurent. This is the viscount, Lord Andrepont."

His gaze flitted over her, and she curtsied as prettily as she could. He didn't look at her like a custard, and she was relieved in a way, but also disappointed. Surely she was custard-worthy?

The viscount sat, as did her father, flipping the tails of their coats out behind them. Jane gathered a shirt from Emma's basket of mending and started in, trying to keep busy as there would be no reason for her to speak during the viscount's visit. But it didn't stop her from looking.

Emma stayed flushed, which made her blue eyes stand out in greater contrast. Indeed, she was quite pretty, and the pale blue ribbon she had threaded through her frock's scooped neckline lent her the air of the mythical sort of dairymaid. Not an actual one, for they knew those girls—the twins from the Brewer family—were hale and hearty in a way that didn't lend so much to frolicking as an outright wrestling match.

Emma poured cups of ratafia, the viscount watching her with fascination. Oh, that was good, wasn't it? If they were to be married, he already loved her. That was something. Jane felt happy for her sister. Fate had stepped in, or perhaps God or Providence, or whatever mysterious hand guided their simple lives, and delivered the answer to her father's prayers: a rich, titled husband for Emma, and Emma's prayers besides: a handsome husband who loved her.

Jane returned to her mending, no longer listening as the rest of them bantered. All was well, and she would return to the country and finish her informal apprenticeship to Mrs. Houseman. Good.

CHAPTER 2

BEFORE

"Walking in the uniform will help with the comfort of the fitting," Vasya advised.

Gareth squirmed and almost danced in the uniform's white pants. He also wore the lobster-red jacket of British soldiers, and Vasya was glad it was Gareth and not him: the white pants put a man's testicles on full display. At least, if they were of any decent size.

Gareth's bollocks appeared well-formed, but still, this seemed like information a man might want to keep to himself.

The boots were stiff as well, making creaking sounds as the men walked across the parks of London. They'd have to break them in before Gareth had to spend any time in them. Vasya slid another glance over to see if his friend was dancing once again, but no, Gareth had squared his shoulders. He couldn't be seen slouching when he might be a leader. Gareth's father was proud of buying his son's commission—the idea of which seemed strange to

Vasya. Allowing men to buy a rank instead of earning one seemed a dangerous way to form an army.

"What makes you the expert on uniforms?" Gareth challenged Vasya.

"I served my country. In a sense." Vasya had joined the ranks of farmers and boys, old men and laborers. They were starving, tired of serfdom, tired of rules made by those who had never once lived off the land. Vasya stared off into the distance of Rotten Row, where the finest fashions paraded about. Wide skirts, embroidered coats, and tall wigs were all on display. How had he gone from tall grasses and the wide banks of a clean, clear river to this absurd parade of wealth?

Gareth looked at him sharply. "When was this?"

Vasya returned his gaze. "You think I appear only when you seek me? I lived before I sat at your gambling table."

"I bet you did. I've always thought you had the air of a man on the run from something." Gareth's boots creaked. "Damn these new boots. I'll have blisters on my shins come tomorrow."

"Better to have the blisters now than when you must reload muskets on the American frontier," Vasya growled, watching the parade of finery before them. He'd never had new leather boots, so he couldn't empathize with this rich man's plight.

The two of them joined the promenade of Rotten Row, talking of gambling dens, coffeehouses, and taverns with the best meals. Vasya didn't like speaking of his past, nor of war. They rarely spoke of important things or politics or war. Chief amongst their discussions was their next meal.

They were speaking of a new place to play cards when Gareth spotted his girl. His breath caught and his spine stiffened. He was still such a boy when it came to this lady. He hadn't been like that with the tavern girls or the whores they'd encountered over the last few years. But this one—when he spoke of her, he looked so wistful. The pining was something Vasya knew.

Gareth's lady was still far away, so there was no shame in his gushing. "She has an air about her, doesn't she? How she walks, the way she seems to take in everything in front of her, as if watching the world unfold before her." Gareth elbowed Vasya.

"I see her," he rumbled. It was all he could do to not roll his eyes.

"I should have worn the sword," Gareth said.

Vasya agreed. He'd tried to insist on it earlier, but Gareth had thought it silly—they both had defended themselves handily with fists plenty of times. Vasya had told Gareth he would feel more like a soldier if he'd had the sword, but it was too late now. Gareth straightened again, as if he could gain another inch of height in the next few minutes as their paths approached one another. The absurd scarlet coat would have to be enough, Vasya thought, for it was brighter than a peacock. Another thing Vasya found unfathomable about the British military.

"I need an introduction," Gareth complained. "I can't just walk up to her."

Vasya grunted again. This was indeed a strange land. He'd already heard the joke: *What do two Englishmen talk about when stranded on a desert island? Nothing. There is no one to introduce them.*

Vasya had no time for such idiocies, and knowing his friend, he'd come prepared.

As the parties approached each other, Gareth openly gaped at her. Vasya wanted to shut his friend's mouth for him but didn't since it would only draw attention to his foolishness. Gareth's young lady was with a girl who was clearly her sister, the resemblance obvious, and an older woman holding a parasol to shade her against the fading late afternoon sun.

The older lady glared at both Gareth and Vasya, as well she should, guarding the virtues of those two ripe beauties. And then they passed one another. That was it. The encounter was over. Vasya wanted to laugh. Was it everything Gareth had hoped it to be?

Gareth stopped in the middle of the path, clearly disappointed that no magic had occurred. It was a nearly sunny day in London, so Vasya considered that magic enough.

"I need to do something. What should I do?" His wide, watery eyes made him seem like a panicked horse.

He shouldn't tease a man in love, but Vasya couldn't help it. "Why? You leave so soon."

Gareth groaned. "I hate you, you know."

Vasya decided to change the subject. Gareth was the son of a nobleman. There were so many strings to be pulled in his favor. The boy should be able to figure it out himself. "There's a coffeehouse nearby that has good roasts."

Gareth gritted his teeth and glanced at the retreating women, bouncing on the balls of his feet, clearly wanting to take action.

Vasya sighed and took pity on his friend. He pulled a scrap out of his waistcoat pocket and dropped it onto the ground.

"What is that?" Gareth demanded, but Vasya only smiled.

"I should have been a great general, but alas, I cannot follow orders so well." Vasya gestured to the ground, hoping his ruse was obvious to his friend. "You should retrieve your lady's handkerchief."

Jane loved their walks along Rotten Row. While the path boasted the trees and shrubbery of England, Jane was sometimes able to spot a foreign tree or flower planted in someone's front garden. The British Empire was vast enough that people could bring home all sorts of fascinating plants from across the globe.

The activity was a pleasure to all of them, though Jane knew that it was the latest fashions, the peacocking gentlemen, and all the hubbub that charmed both Emma and Aunt Diana. Indeed, Aunt Diana rarely spoke when they took their stroll, a constitutional that she felt very strongly about. She believed that stirring the blood in the late afternoon kept a woman slim of figure and quick of wit.

Jane looked over at her relations. She knew Emma was worried about that last part—being slender—as Emma had inherited their father's rounder face. Emma also seemed to believe she was somehow larger than other women, even though she wasn't. It was her pleasing, motherly roundness that made her seem so. Far more appealing than Jane's hard angles and peaked cheekbones.

Besides, the ideal was so hard to understand, as some preferred women to be small and plump, others long and slender. Were women to be lithe and nymph-like or round and goddess-like? Either way, the consensus seemed to be that women were to be otherworldly and not human at all.

And Emma wanted to be perfect. It was sometimes exhausting to watch Emma attempt to meet every standard set before her. Being present for Lord Andrepont's call had been more than Jane could stomach, watching as Emma sat stunned and mute for the entire visit, unsure of what to do or say.

The man was decidedly handsome, there was no question. But Emma went positively breathless when he looked at her. Jane would not want to be such a fool for a man. It seemed humiliating.

Not to mention that it was very strange behavior for Emma, who prided herself on her conversational skills and encyclopedic knowledge of etiquette and proper topics for young ladies. Their family library back in Chilton contained more than a few manuals for young ladies, from which Emma had large passages practically memorized.

A soldier, resplendent in his red coat, walked past. He and his companion spoke intently, and she wondered if they were discussing military secrets. Perhaps being a soldier and a debutante were similar: they drilled and practiced for the real event, but nothing prepared one adequately for war. Or courtship. Or . . . marriage.

Jane stopped their procession. "Do you see that bird, Emma?" Emma looked in the boughs of the oak tree nearby. Jane had instantly spotted the drab little wren amongst the shrubbery. She hadn't seen one since Chilton, and it made her feel somehow closer to home.

"*Mademoiselle*!" Called a man from behind them.

They all turned, Aunt Diana's face already in a scowl, prepared to do battle against impertinence.

It was the soldier in the crimson coat. Jane liked his face. He had an amiable, open expression with sparkling blue eyes and smooth skin. He seemed . . . kind. He presented a beautifully embroidered handkerchief to Emma. Jane slid her eyes over to Emma, who already had color high in her cheeks. She seemed to like the look of him also.

Jane examined the soldier's companion. Only a remarkably handsome man could compete with a man this size for attention. The companion looked large enough to pull an oxcart and not be winded by it. His hair was dark as midnight, and he sported an impressive beard. The beard was well-kempt and tidy, the same blue-black midnight color as his head, which made it seem not unfashionable but exotic.

His dark eyes slid to hers, holding her gaze steady. It wasn't that custard-devouring look she'd noticed between Emma and Lord Andrepont, but it was incisive, insightful. As if he had opened her soul like a book and was perusing at his leisure. She shifted the weight on her feet, feeling a need to run.

"What is this?" Aunt Diana sniffed at the soldier and the handkerchief.

"I believe one of you may have dropped this. I was walking opposite you, and forgive my impertinence, but it seemed too lovely to keep your property." The soldier performed a charming bow.

Emma stifled a giggle at his gallantry, letting her smile mirror his infectious one. Aunt Diana turned to her. "Is it?"

"Pardon?" Emma said, not following.

"Your handkerchief. Is it one of yours?"

The soldier was daring and dashing, the exact inverse of the dark and intimidating Lord Andrepont. Emma reached out tentatively. "May I?"

The soldier waved it about theatrically and then brandished it before her. "But of course."

Emma took it from him. Jane noted that his gloves were pristinely white and his uniform neatly pressed. His shave was close and he smelled of soap, not of tobacco or coffee or spirits. That was pleasant, and a good sign. Emma turned the handkerchief over in her hands, Jane peering over, trying to seem unobtrusive. It was not one of theirs—while the embroidery was well done, it lacked Emma's signature white X in the corner or Jane's line of three white dots. They both marked all darning and embellishments so neither girl could claim the other's work for her own. They'd devised the system after too many arguments about who did chores and who lazed about.

Emma always accused Jane of shirking because Jane preferred to be out in the woods gathering supplies, and Jane accused Emma because she would hold a piece of darning in her hands for well over a half hour while daydreaming, not putting in a single stitch.

Emma glanced at Aunt Diana, who didn't know of their system. Aunt Diana was looking intently at the soldier, as if trying to place him. However, the soldier only had eyes for Emma, and the large oxcart man stared into a tree when a loud songbird again trilled its call.

"It's a wren," Jane said to him. His startling eyes once again went to hers, and he nodded.

"A wren," he said, the R sounding somehow trilled, just like the bird. Jane couldn't help but smile.

Emma turned the handkerchief over, as if she were still inspecting it. "Yes," she said, looking boldly at the soldier, as if they now shared the charade. She was accepting his attentions. Jane thought it wasn't that much different than birds, really, presenting a pretty trinket to a potential mate. "Thank you ever so much for returning it to me, soldier."

The soldier swept off his tricorn hat and bowed deeply before her. "Captain Gareth Somerset, at your service."

Next to him, the large bearded man cleared his throat.

"And this is Vasily Nikolaevich Kuznetsov," Captain Somerset announced. The other man swept into a bow that Jane thought was rather elegant for such a large man, but Aunt Diana ignored the foreigner completely.

Aunt Diana narrowed her eyes. "Isn't your father an earl? Lord Lorian?"

Captain Somerset rewarded Aunt Diana with a gallant smile, and Jane had to admit that she wouldn't mind having him bestow such a blinding expression upon her as well. He was rather handsome, if one liked fair-haired, amiable sorts. "I am his lordship's second son."

Jane glanced at Emma, her eyebrow cocked as if to say, *This one too? How many do you need?* Aunt Diana gave an appreciative hum in response to Captain Somerset's parentage.

"Have we seen you at any of the local assemblies?" their aunt questioned.

"Very few as of yet. As you can see, I'm set with my commission. I leave for the colonies in a matter of weeks." Captain Somerset tucked his hat under his arm. "But I am hoping to attend the next assembly, though I admit I don't remember when it is. I've been so focused on my career, I haven't the head for this Season's parties."

"Tomorrow evening," Aunt Diana told him. "I'm sure you and your brother are on the guest lists of everyone in Town."

"Undoubtedly," Captain Somerset said. "May I inquire after your names, then? In hopes of finding you for the next round of dancing?"

"As long as you don't wear those boots," Jane said. They shone bright as a mirror but were so stiff he wouldn't be able to dance well.

Mr. Kuznetsov chuckled, but Aunt Diana *tsked* her. Jane didn't mind because she'd made Mr. Kuznetsov laugh, and that seemed like reward enough.

Captain Somerset grinned at Emma. "I'm an excellent dancer. But I will endeavor to wear softer shoes in case I grow suddenly clumsy."

Emma was practically glowing from his attentions

and allusions to her dancing with him. Would Jane somehow become this silly?

"I am Mrs. Fraser, aunt to Miss Emma Laurent and her sister, Miss Jane Laurent."

"A pleasure to meet you all. I hope we may converse the next we meet." Captain Somerset returned his hat to its perch atop his head.

"Thank you for returning my handkerchief," Emma said, catching his eye once more.

He inclined his head. "At your service."

The words seemed more than just a polite idiom, and even Jane understood the intent. She had not made herself known in public, so this fascinating exchange was at an end for her, but that was fine. Emma would tell her every single detail anyway, whether Jane wished to know it or not.

The soldier and the foreigner took their leave, and the women resumed their walk. None of them spoke, and Emma tucked the found handkerchief in her bodice, rather than up her sleeve. Jane wondered if it was wicked to do so—something he had touched so close to her heart, to her breast.

Jane wondered what Lord Andrepont would make of the scene had he been nearby. Besides a single visit, Lord Andrepont had not set any intentions; therefore, Emma needed to keep herself available. Even Aunt Diana would agree—at least, Jane thought she might.

❦

AFTER – DAY ONE

The coroner and magistrate appeared at the front door early in the morning, telling poor Mr. Afreé that they would wait for Jane to ready herself, no matter how long it took. By the time Jane made herself ready for this dreadful day, the coroner and the magistrate were attempting to bring something into the house.

"What is this?" Jane demanded, coming down the stairs.

Both men immediately ceased bickering with her butler to sweep hats off their heads and bow to her.

"My apologies, my lady," said the taller, paler of the two strangers. "We come bearing horrific news. Might we find somewhere comfortable?"

"Of course." Jane gestured to the drawing room. "But what is that outside the door?"

The other man waved off the men outside, and grumbling emanated from the open door.

"Mr. Afreé, some tea, please," Jane said to her butler before turning to her guests. "Come along, gentlemen."

She tried to remain regal and unconcerned. This was just another day. A normal day. Her heart pounded so loudly she was almost surprised that neither man commented on it as they took the seats she gestured to in her feminine drawing room. The damned grandfather clock still rang on the half hour. It set her teeth on edge. She would enjoy smashing that thing to bits.

They introduced themselves as Mr. Eier, the coroner, and Mr. Breaverton, the magistrate. Jane narrowed her eyes at them but said nothing. Which clearly made them nervous. She knew her silences were powerful—as they ought to be. She'd honed them enough over the years. Both men fidgeted and glanced at one another, wanting the other one to do the job.

"We regret to inform you, my lady . . . that is, ah —" Mr. Eier took a big breath. "That is, unfortunately, we found Lord Andrepont, your husband, that is."

"Oh?" Jane raised her eyebrow at his stalling.

"Which brothel did you pull him out of this time?" Matthew didn't believe in brothels. But it was a good seed to plant in their minds right then.

Mr. Breaverton winced at her harsh words.

"That isn't it, at all, my lady." Mr. Eier looked like he wanted to run away. Run very far away indeed. "No, we pulled him from the Thames early this morning, down by Wapping."

"Wapping?" Jane didn't need to pretend the confusion she felt. "But that's . . ."

"Not a good area," Mr. Eier supplied.

"It's far," Jane said.

"That too," Mr. Breaverton added, as if he needed to be a part of the conversation.

"Why was he down there?" Jane asked without thinking, grateful they would assume *he* meant Matthew, although she meant Vasya.

"My lady," Mr. Eier said gently, scooting to the edge of his seat. "Do you understand what we mean?"

"Wapping. The Thames?" she repeated.

"Your husband is dead," Mr. Eier said.

Jane blinked at him. She'd thought she would need to act at this point. But it didn't feel real at all. The idea that Matthew would never darken this doorway. That Matthew would never come home. He would never again receive odious visitors to his study, which lurked next to her son's music room.

"When we say that he was pulled from the river, we mean that he is, ah, deceased." Mr. Breaverton said, for no apparent reason at all, except to take up more air.

"It appears he was robbed, and I would judge this a homicide. Therefore, we will have an inquest. The body is in a cart outside, covered, of course, ready to put in whatever room you deem appropriate."

Jane shot to her feet. She hadn't anticipated that.

Not even Gareth had anticipated that, though they should have. "No," she said. "No."

The men glanced at each other. "Lady Andrepont, it is customary to—"

"I will not have his body here. I will not have people tromping through my home to examine his corpse. I won't." Jane closed her eyes, seeing in her mind what the river might do to a person. She opened them again.

The men looked at each other. "There is a nearby inn that has taken bodies for an inquest before. Shall we ask them?"

Jane felt her head might shake off her head with how firmly she nodded. "I'll pay anything, I don't care. Just—"

"She's overcome," Mr. Eier murmured to Mr. Breaverton, as if Jane could no longer hear. But let them think that. Let them believe she was helpless. Mr. Eier looked to her now. "I shall make the arrangements."

"Now remember," Mr. Breaverton said, sounding more like a kindly schoolmaster than a man who delivered news of the dead. "It'll be three days for the inquest, and your staff and your family will need to be available for interviews. We can do the interviews here or at the inn, whatever your leisure. We'll do our best to accommodate a woman of your sensibilities."

They didn't make accommodations for poor women. Or women who worked. Just for noblewomen, such rarefied and fine captives.

"We will take our leave now, my lady," Mr. Eier said, taking a step towards the door. "But we shall return in the afternoon to interview your staff ourselves. Should we deem anyone worth speaking to, they'll be summoned to tell their story to either a magistrate or a jury, depending on what we find. But we have no time to lose."

Jane nodded, swallowing past the lump in her throat. "Of course." She rang for Mr. Afreé, who escorted the men down. Jane sank into her chair, grateful for the tea tray that had appeared courtesy of a footman. This was merely another lock before her door to freedom opened. They could do this, get through this. Three days was nothing.

She scribbled her note to Emma, delivering the news of Andrepont's death. There was so much to do, and yet she felt like she couldn't move. Stuck, as it were, in a day she'd often thought of but never dared believe would happen.

When the horrid grandfather clock struck three, the men returned and commandeered her drawing room, calling up servants one at a time and questioning them. Jane took Martha Foraker's advice and had her continually serving them coffee and replenishing the seedcakes, hoping to glean a murmur of their thoughts. Jane knew they wouldn't leave until the seedcakes stopped arriving. There were few good things she could say of her husband, but one of them was that he employed the finest cooks. France's lost pastry chef was England's gain.

Mr. Breaverton made no effort to disguise his delight in the seedcakes. He took no notes and, indeed, did not bother to even look at each servant that sat in the chair opposite him, sweating as they answered simple questions about their role in the household.

Jane sat motionless in a chair next to the interrogation seat, lending her support and what little protection she could offer. Mr. Eier's pallor had not rosied since his early morning call, and now that Jane had time to think on it, she found he resembled his Germanic name. Not that Jane knew much German, but enough to know that his last name translated as *eggs*, which seemed fitting. His blond hair was thinning, and soon a bald head would truly fit his moniker.

Mr. Eier drank the coffee steadily but rarely touched a seedcake, scratching notes into a small notebook with a roughly sharpened pencil. Those implements were precious, and Jane couldn't help but wonder if they came with the appointment or if he bought them himself with his wages. He started methodically with the lowest-tier servants—the chambermaids, of whom they had the highest turnover. Then he moved on to the footmen.

When Mr. Eier dismissed the last of the footmen, he said, "It's all in the name of being thorough, Lady Andrepont."

"I understand." Jane didn't feel like she could move. Her hands felt as heavy as stone, no doubt giving the impression of true grief. But how could she do anything? She'd been numb for so long, resigned for even longer. Happiness was a foreign idea; even relief seemed unobtainable.

"I don't believe your husband was in the wrong place at the wrong time, as some might think when discovering a body floating face down in the Thames. One must be thorough for a member of the House of Lords. After all, we have but three days to investigate any wrongdoing." Mr. Eier looked up from his notebook, examining her.

He was testing her, the oaf. No need to be indelicate, but she supposed this was his way of interrogating her. Leaking small details, hoping to see if she gave anything away. But she did nothing, said nothing.

"You don't seem surprised by any of the statements." He tapped his pencil on the paper. "You were so overcome this morning—I'm surprised you've been able to withstand this."

Jane hadn't the effort to feign surprise. "My

apologies, Mr. Eier. This is all quite a shock, as it must be for my staff as well. I want to project strength for them." It was the truth. How long had she prayed for her husband's death? Dreamed it? Plotted it? And how long had she tried to look strong, seem strong for those around her?

"I would like to speak with your personal servants now, Lady Andrepont. Your . . . what is he? Not the stablemaster, Mr. Snyder—we've spoken with him—but I suppose he is your coachman, is that right?"

Jane raised her eyebrow. She liked making this efficient, thorough egg-man trip over Vasya's name and duties.

"A Mister Vasily . . ." Mr. Eier stared at Martha's ledger containing every servant's name, duties, and wage. "Nikolaevich Kuznetsov?"

Though Mr. Eier stumbled on the Russian name, Jane had known he would be next. Martha, too, had anticipated Mr. Eier's wishes, and Vasya appeared in the doorway. Jane's heart flipped. This man had protected her when no one else would. In another life, she would have picked him. That was not this life. Jane focused on the interrogation chair.

This was the man who had flipped a nobleman's body into a dirty river. A thankless task. And a task she'd asked him to do. What gave her the right to ask this of him? But he had done it, just as he had always done as she'd asked. A sudden veil of shame lowered over her as Vasya sat down so near to her, not looking at her.

Vasya settled his bulk into the chair, staring down Mr. Eier, expressionless but somehow martial in his bearing.

"I am Mr. Eier, the coroner. I'm sure you have heard by now that your employer, Lord Andrepont, has been found dead." The man's eyes drifted over to Jane again, as if measuring for the umpteenth time how upset she might be by repeatedly hearing this news.

"One would be deaf to not know of it." Vasya deepened his Russian accent, causing Jane to push away the smile that threatened. He only did this when he was set on annoying the person he was speaking with.

"Quite," Mr. Eier said, his eyes still on Jane. "To begin, er, what is your position in the household?"

"I drove his lordship." Vasya kept his hands on his knees as the chair arms snugged up against his wide bulk. Jane knew this bulk wasn't the man's softness, but rather, the impressive size of a man who could perform unprecedented physical tasks. Without help, he'd once righted a carriage with a broken wheel.

"Do you drive for Lady Andrepont as well?" Mr. Eier questioned after ticking something off in his notebook.

"She prefers walking."

"Lord Andrepont did not?"

"His lordship could not always walk at the end of an evening."

"What does this mean?" Mr. Eier asked in a clipped tone that seemed to show an accent as well. Jane surmised that Mr. Eier might have grown up in one of London's immigrant enclaves and might have also something to prove.

"His lordship was fond of . . . drink."

Drink had not been Matthew's true preference, but he had been fond of all forms of hedonistic pursuit.

"And were you with him last night?" Mr. Eier asked, scribbling more in his notebook.

"For some of the evening. He asked me to drive him to his . . . club, then to Lord Carlisle's estate. He planned to stay overnight, or at Lord Denby's estate, also in Mayfair. The three of them are often together."

"What time did you take him to Lord Carlisle's?"

Vasya shifted in his chair, which Jane recognized as an affectation. He shifted as if he was hoping to spare her. That would allow for some details to not be so firm in the coroner and magistrate's minds. Though none of them had truly believed there would be any questioning. Jane thought her word as his long-suffering aristocratic wife would be enough to put off any sort of inquiry. But perhaps Mr. Eier was not willing to overlook a single thing. Annoying, but not impossible.

"Do you not remember?" Mr. Eier asked, observing Vasya's discomfort.

"I do not wish to say with the lady present," Vasya said.

Mr. Eier's forehead creased, giving the impression that he was much older and much balder than he actually was. "I fail to see why the time might disturb Lady Andrepont. She has proven herself to be resilient today."

"There was . . . a stop taken before Lord Carlisle's house. I fear for Lady Andrepont's natural delicacy." Vasya's accent thinned, and Jane wondered if he actually meant it.

"Of course. Lady Andrepont, I realize this is your drawing room, but would you please excuse us? I'm sure you have other matters to attend. I will notify you when we have finished our interview. Please do not leave the premises; there are still discrepancies we must discuss."

"Discrepancies?" She echoed, but the man didn't see fit to look at her, let alone answer her question. Her feet felt heavy with sand, but she stood anyway, the men standing to bow their respects. "Of course,

Mr. Eier, Mr. Breaverton." She dared not look at Vasya. Dared not say his name.

The numbness was ebbing away, giving rise to something she didn't know how to name. She had more messages to write, including the one she dreaded writing to her son, James. The boy was the new Lord Andrepont. How awful it would be for James to hear his father's title out of everyone's mouth, knowing it now referred to him. To be a viscount so young, while still in school, not quite a man.

She didn't know how to ease the pain for James. Fortunately, he'd taken after her side of the family more than his father's. Still. Did a monster's urges perpetually lurk below the surface, or did they rise with age? Should she expect James to metamorphize into his father at some point, or would remain as he'd always been: her affectionate, sensitive boy whose love of art and music surpassed his interest in all other things?

CHAPTER 3

Emma gasped as she entered the ballroom. As inured as she had become in the past few months, attending glittering parties and the Queen's Ball, this one took her breath away. It was lavish. Bright garlands festooned the walls, hothouse flowers of every color dotting the greenery. Gold and silver baubles accented gold-painted leaves.

They were announced, and Aunt Diana guided them over to their hosts, Sir Frederick and his wife, Lady Haglund. Sir Frederick was younger than her father, but not by much, in Emma's estimation. Lady Haglund, on the other hand, was only a bit older than Emma. Excitement came off the young noblewoman in waves. Her hostess had powdered her hair, which was piled high upon her head and studded with small pink roses.

"It will be an utter triumph, don't you worry," Aunt Diana said to Lady Haglund as Emma's father chatted with Sir Frederick.

Captain Somerset made his way to them, clearly watching arrivals. He was handsome in his blue and silver coat, his black shoes polished to a high shine with a silver buckle for contrast. He hadn't worn his uniform, but Emma preferred him looking like a regular citizen. It kept the idea of his upcoming service at bay. Aside from which, Emma was happy to live in a time when she could admire a man's shapely calves, for Captain Somerset had excellent calves.

He greeted them, but he looked only at Emma as he spoke.

"My father and brother are here tonight as well," he said, gesturing vaguely to the adjoining rooms where card tables were set for gambling. "I'd be happy to introduce you to the earl, if you like."

"Most gracious of you," Emma's father said.

The dancing master called a form and the musicians tuned their instruments.

"It's the first dance of the evening," Captain Somerset said, looking at Emma.

Part of her felt like she was removed from the situation, shocked by her fortune to be in that room, being asked to dance by a man with calves like those and eyes like that—a man who was clearly in love with her. How did she get so lucky?

She nodded, glancing at Aunt Diana for permission. Aunt Diana graciously assented and Captain Somerset presented his arm to Emma. She took it, doing her best not to seem as eager as she truly was.

"You look beautiful," he said. "I mean, you always look beautiful, but I think saying it as often as I think it is perfectly acceptable, is it not? You may tell me to stop any time you wish."

"Thank you." Emma stifled her amusement. She didn't want to seem like some simpering idiot, but he was charming and funny, and she felt like her insides were nothing but air. "I don't think I'll ever want to stop hearing it."

"I'm glad to hear it, because I don't think I'll ever stop wanting to say it."

Emma blushed, and Captain Somerset beamed at her. They stood facing each other as the dance began. They moved through the steps, faster and faster as the musicians sped up, laughing as they moved, the dancers all young and spritely. It was a delight to feel so winded, and Emma collapsed into Captain Somerset, laughing as she did so. It was the closest they'd been.

"Emma," he whispered, using her given name for the first time, gambling with his forthrightness.

She nodded, encouraging him. She liked the woman she was with him—carefree and laughing. He felt right. Would he ask her father for permission tonight? Was this when it would all happen? Was this when life would begin?

"Miss Laurent," called a voice from behind her.

She straightened and turned to find Lord Andrepont holding out his hand. His dark eyes glinted, reminding her of wolves in the woods. "May I have the next dance?"

"Of course," she said without thinking. Though she knew it to be dangerous to turn one's back to a wild animal, she swung back to Captain Somerset. "If you'll excuse me."

His expression was conflicted, but he let her go to Lord Andrepont with no hesitation, as manners dictated. Andrepont glared after the affable captain with undisguised disdain. Emma wondered if they had history with one another or if it was a sign of the viscount's possessiveness. She had not mentioned any other suitors to him and didn't think it worthy of discussion.

The next dance was slower and statelier, fitting the status of the grander and older dancers who took to the floor. Emma felt almost guilty for having danced with Captain Somerset, though she knew she was in the right. One dance meant very little. That was politeness. And Captain Somerset had made no claims on her, nor had Lord Andrepont.

Andrepont's dark eyes bored into her, as if he could see through her somehow. Her stomach fluttered under his attention, and her mental acuity seemed to dissolve when their palms touched. It seemed as if he wanted to consume her.

"Miss Laurent," he said, his voice low and guttural. "May I call you Emma?"

She swallowed hard. This felt very different from how Captain Somerset had whispered her name. "Yes."

He smiled, or at least, she would have said that he did, but it wasn't an expression of happiness—it was a different sort. A dangerous emotion that she couldn't parse, hadn't the experience to name.

"I've asked your father for his permission to marry you. He told me that he wouldn't sign any nuptial contract until you gave your acquiescence."

Emma nodded dumbly. The words "marry" and "acquiescence" circled in her mind. She couldn't think. This was what she wanted, wasn't it? But the way he'd said it sounded so formal and business-like. And he was aloof, so didn't it make sense that he would speak in such a way? Nothing would come out of her mouth, as if her voice had abandoned her along with her sense.

The music ceased, and the other dancers shuffled and reordered.

"Let me escort you back to your aunt," Lord Andrepont said, smoothly moving her through the crush to the safety of her chaperone.

Earlier that evening, Emma had told Jane that marrying the viscount meant safety and security. She would be taken care of when she said yes, as would her entire family. She would be an utter ninny to say no to wealth, status, and power.

Her father looked at her, wide-eyed and expectant, as Andrepont returned her to him. Even Aunt Diana seemed enthusiastic, her eyes shining with what Emma would call ambition but might just be the ratafia if she'd had more than three cups. The mildly upturned corners of her mouth were certainly a change from her regular suspicion of any man Emma stood next to. Her father glanced from her face to Andrepont's. Clearly impatient, he demanded, "Well?"

"I—" she stuttered. She had not given an answer, and no announcement could be made until she officially agreed to Andrepont's proposal. She looked to the viscount again. What could possibly go wrong? He was handsome, wealthy, and titled. What were the other qualifications? Love? That would come in time, as everyone had said, if it was needed at all.

"Yes," she said, first to Andrepont and then to her father and aunt. "Lord Andrepont has asked to marry me."

Her father clapped his hands, then clapped Andrepont on the shoulder. Aunt Diana pulled Emma into an embrace. She would be a viscountess. Even Jane should congratulate her on this excellent match. She was elevating their family and ensuring their security when her father died. Her children would be members of a storied family of the British Empire. There was no downside. So why did she feel suddenly dizzy?

"Some ratafia?" She asked, hoping for something to occupy her before she fell over.

"Of course," Andrepont said, disappearing from her side.

"Good work, my girl," Aunt Diana said. "You made it seem easy."

Emma smiled weakly. It *had* been easy. All she'd had to do was stand there, dance a little, and be agreeable. That didn't sit well with her. Shouldn't there have been more for her to do? To say?

Andrepont returned with cups for both her and Aunt Diana. Hopefully Aunt Diana wouldn't have a fainting episode, given how the room was heating with so many bodies in it.

"Let's get a drink, my lord, and we can settle a time to sign the contract," Emma's father said.

"I can call tomorrow morning, if you like," Andrepont said. He was calm and cool—not at all exultant, but rather, darkly satisfied.

"Tomorrow?" Emma said, finding her voice. "Doesn't the solicitor need to draw up the documents?"

Her father snorted dismissively. "They've been prepared for weeks now. I just needed your acceptance. Your mother swore me to it, you know."

Emma frowned. Her mother had died not long after Jane was born, but everyone spoke of her as if she had been extraordinary. Not just beautiful but also intelligent and able to engineer anything she wished, including her own marriage. Clearly, she'd thought ahead on the matter of her daughters. But Emma's father had executed this match in a way that felt contrary, underhanded somehow. The discussion had circumvented Emma entirely. But she supposed that happened to many of the women in the room. At least, the women who came from money. Still. She didn't care for the feeling.

The two men left together, presumably going to the card tables where they could smoke without the company of women. Emma turned to Aunt Diana and said, "Did you know of this?"

Her aunt's searching expression told Emma that she'd absolutely been a party to it.

"What of your encouraging me with Captain Somerset?" Emma demanded.

"Watching his lordship wax and wane in his attentions made it clear he needed a rival. Captain Somerset provided that." Aunt Diana sniffed. "It isn't unheard of. And any man with an ounce of sense would understand why you've agreed to become a viscountess. What could he offer you? A second son? Nothing near so valuable as an actual title."

Emma let her eyes wander over the crowd, not wanting to feel the sense of betrayal that came. She finally understood that she existed in a world of layers that she couldn't possibly see. Everyone had been moving her like a chess piece, and she had dumbly believed she'd had a choice. Her eye caught on Captain Somerset, whose mouth was flattened to a straight line. It was as if he'd already known of her engagement.

"Mrs. Fraser, Miss Laurent." He bowed as he arrived next to them.

"How fortunate you are here, Captain Somerset," Aunt Diana said, shooting a stern glance at Emma. "Miss Laurent has agreed to become the next Viscountess Andrepont. Is that not stunning news? We shall have to announce before we go into dinner. Such a coup."

Captain Somerset's face crumpled. Emma liked that he wasn't stern and formal like Andrepont. That sometimes, an emotion escaped through his amiable exterior. "May I offer my deepest congratulations, Miss Laurent. I wish you the utmost happiness."

"Thank you, Captain Somerset," Emma whispered. She couldn't bring herself to look him in the eye. It wasn't that she was embarrassed so much as that she felt guilty for disappointing him. Just ten minutes prior he'd whispered her given name, and it had been a heady experience. And now—now she had agreed to let another man be bound to her in front of God.

"Where is Lord Andrepont? I must offer my felicitations to him as well." Captain Somerset clicked his boots together like some kind of Prussian mercenary.

"He and my father have gone off to discuss whatever it is men discuss at a time like this." Emma hated that her future husband had wandered off. He'd no doubt be back to escort her into dinner, and she should use this time to make more friends as she'd now insured that she would return for next year's Season. A viscountess must be social to secure her husband's social standing.

A lump formed in her throat, and for all the world, she couldn't imagine why.

⚜

AFTER – DAY ONE

Martha Foraker brought a tray up to the music room for Jane. If it hadn't been for James, they would never have had a room for music, let alone an instrument to put inside it. Jane hadn't the patience to practice the pianoforte. That had been Emma's talent. Jane had been too busy with her hands in the dirt. And, she supposed, she was metaphorically doing the same, all these years later, what with a murder investigation occurring under her roof.

"Are they still speaking with Vasily Nikolaevich?" Jane asked Martha.

The housekeeper's mouth thinned into one slim line as she nodded. "He's a smart man, but he's a foreigner and freely admitted he was with his lordship last night."

Jane knew the risks. They'd all known the risks. With no one else in the room, she could wring her hands and twist her rings to her heart's content. But she wouldn't. Her hands were at rest, as cool and calm as marble. That's what she'd told herself she'd have to be to protect herself, her family, her Vasya.

She'd always felt his dark eyes on her, watching, observing. Just as she used to observe her plants from shoots to full-fledged and leafy, so Vasya had watched her from her first days as viscountess until now. But she didn't know how to finish that metaphor, as she would never consider her growth to be like blooming; rather, it was surviving in spite of everything.

Vasya would be the first suspect for Mr. Eier, given his accent and his status as a member of the servant class. Gareth had once said Vasya could have been known as a gentleman, if he'd wanted to be. That the Russian had chosen this alternate life. She'd wondered if he had done so for her. Not that she had ever asked. Or ever would.

To ask questions was to invite answers she might not want to know. Matthew had drained that desire out of her long, long ago. She'd felt such relief when Matthew's eyes weren't fixed on her that she certainly didn't want to know what he was up to when he was out of her sight.

Matthew had plenty of enemies, and any number of men and women from all over London wanted him gone for a variety of reasons. Only novelists created the chaotically evil who inflicted pain and death upon strangers. No, to hate someone enough to kill them, one needed a personal acquaintance.

"I think Mr. Eier is also a foreigner, which might help Vasily," Jane said. She noted that the teapot on the tray was the fat brown one from the north. None of the beautiful decorative teaware today. Serviceable, steady, somber. They were a household in shock, and ostensibly grieving. It was odd to still be wearing her dark gray day dress, the only frock that was appropriate after this morning's news as she had no black at the ready. Tomorrow she would be required to don mourning attire. Her beautiful gowns were already being dyed a flat black shade to serve as her widow's weeds, which she would wear for at least a full year.

Mourning for that man. Or perhaps mourning for a life unlived. A life that could have been hers with Vasya, in the country. A gentleman farmer, perhaps? She, an avid gardener and herbwoman. Children?

No.

That had not been her life. And she did have a child. James. Without Matthew, there would be no James, and she could not discard her love for her son because she hated his father. James was blameless in all things, and she'd tried—oh how she'd tried—to raise him with respect for his fellow man. And others, besides.

Martha put her hands on her hips. "And that Mr. Breaverton. He'll eat Cook out of a week's worth of butter at this rate!"

"I'd rather them happy and gone than suspicious and lingering." Jane did her best not to rub her eye. Though perhaps she ought to, given that rubbing would redden it. Tears might be required in her performance for Mr. Eier. She needed to stay focused on the task at hand.

A footman opened the door, announcing Emma and Gareth.

"Darling, I came as soon as I could," Emma cried, rushing into the room and crushing Jane into an embrace.

"You needn't be here," Jane said.

Emma immediately released her, color ripening in

her cheeks. "Good practice nonetheless. Is the coroner in another room?"

"Questioning Vasya." Jane glanced over at Gareth, who had been friends with the man first. Gareth's expression grew taut.

"He's got a good alibi." Gareth's hands fisted.

Emma touched Gareth on the chest. "Of course he does. And he will use it. If not for himself, then for Jane. Right, Jane?"

She didn't rightly know. No one had told her of his alibi. She only knew that it had been "taken care of," meaning all was in place. That she needn't worry.

Indeed, it was how she had operated for years, depending on Vasya despite the fact that he had always kept his own counsel. While he may have once been close to her, it had been years since they'd really spoken. Even then, he'd changed the subject if she asked him questions about the past, and he was purposefully vague when she asked him questions about his future. He lived in one moment: the moment he spent with her, making each of those moments precious and jewel-like. "Let's hope he can protect himself," Jane added.

Jane gestured to the tea tray, extra cups at the ready. "Mrs. Foraker, if you wouldn't mind?"

Emma gave a frown at Jane's sudden formality but said nothing. All Jane's hostess graces were needed that day. She couldn't slip up, not even once. More lives were on the line, for Vasya would do whatever he could to protect her. She knew that much to be true.

BEFORE

Jane woke the morning after the Haglund ball surprised to see the sun streaming through the windows. She usually woke when Emma arrived home from a soiree, but for some reason, she hadn't. Their bedrooms were separate here in this house but directly next door to one another. Jane could hear Emma's every sigh, every brush of her hair, even when she turned over in bed.

As much as Jane wasn't interested in suitors and dresses, she still enjoyed Emma's retellings of the events. Emma's enthusiasm was infectious and made the evenings sound magical, even if Jane would have been bored silly. She stared at the wall between the two rooms. No sounds. Not even the soft, deep sighs of sleep. Jane frowned.

Emma had believed last night's ball would be significant. Jane didn't know how her sister knew it— perhaps one developed a sixth sense for this sort of thing when one began courting. Jane hoped to never find out.

She separated herself from her tangled counterpane and pulled on her wrapper and slippers. Her hair was tied in loose curls, as per Emma's instruction. She was going to try some new styles on Jane in the hopes of figuring out if she wanted to try them on herself. That was to be today's game after they had their morning chocolate. Jane crept into the hall, avoiding the part of the floor that creaked, and scratched at her sister's door. No sound from inside, so Jane swung it open to find a perfectly made-up bed.

Jane frowned. This didn't feel right. Something wasn't right at all. She padded down to the dining room to see if perhaps Emma was already at breakfast or had stayed up all night, too exhilarated to sleep. But when she arrived in the dining room, there was no one there. Not even a footman setting up kippers.

She padded back up to the drawing room, which she also found empty. Was no one here? Or perhaps her father and aunt weren't awake yet? But her father always woke with the dawn, regardless of what time he'd come home the night before. He would sometimes doze on the couch in his study to make up for the sleep he'd missed.

The door to his study was open, and she peeked around the corner to find him at his desk. Head in his hands, he still wore his rumpled evening clothes.

"Papa?" she asked, hating that she still sounded like a child when uncertain.

His head snapped up, and his alertness faded when he realized that it was only Jane. "Come in, child." His voice was scratchy and exhausted.

She padded into the chilly room. The fire had gone out ages ago, and it wasn't because it had been banked. A woolen blanket lived on the back of his chaise, so she swooped it around her shoulders before sitting in the cold leather chair across from her father. "You seem out of sorts."

His eyes were bloodshot. His wig sat at the end of his desk like some kind of drowned sheep washed up on a beach. He said, "Did Emma speak to you about leaving?"

Again Jane frowned. What a perplexing morning. "Only that when she was married, she and I would live separately. I wasn't listening very well, if I'm honest."

Her father shook his head, staring down at the paper in front of him. Jane's confusion turned to dread. Something momentous had happened while she slept.

"Is she . . . is Emma not here?" Jane asked, a cold stab of fear striking her.

Papa shook his head, his tightly downturned mouth the only thing keeping in the tears threatening to roll down his cheeks. "She left the ball at some point before the supper. No one has seen her. Andrepont is livid. As he should be."

Jane took in what her father had said. Sitting with it, turning it over in her mind. She didn't like to speculate or jump to conclusions, and Emma was quite capable. She certainly wasn't the type to be carried off by brigands, nor was she silly enough to go with someone who might hurt her. So where could she be?

"As he should be," Papa whispered again, staring at the paper before him.

Jane stayed quiet. To find a wild animal, one had to think like one. To find a plant, one had to know its proper environment. So, she needed to think like Emma. There were two men she favored: Lord Andrepont and Captain Somerset. Andrepont was aware Emma was missing and upset by it. "Have you spoken to Captain Somerset?"

"Who?" Papa looked up, distracted.

"Her other suitor. His father is an earl, I believe. Aunt Diana knows him. He approached us in the park, and I know she's danced with him on several occasions."

Her father waved his hand. "Oh, that lad. He has nothing to do with this. He danced with her last night but happily went on his way once Andrepont claimed Emma."

Jane tried not to squirm, but she detested the idea of a man claiming her. As if she were a coat left behind on a park bench.

"I hate to steal your sister's glory, but Andrepont offered for her, and she accepted. We were to announce it as we went into supper."

Then the answer was obvious. Jane wanted to shake her father. There could be no doubt that Emma had run off with Captain Somerset. Didn't he see? Something had happened—whether Emma suddenly became scared of becoming a viscountess or Captain Somerset was particularly charming—and Emma had chosen the other man. "Papa," she said, trying very hard not to have that tone in her voice that he'd warned her would only cause trouble for her future husband.

"I don't have time for your lectures, Jane. I'm sure whatever foraging outing you want to go on is safe, but not now. I can't have both my girls missing." Her father propelled himself up from his chair and paced next to the windows.

"Papa, send word to Captain Somerset's father. Aunt Diana knows which one he is. If you want to find Emma, she'll be with the captain."

"That doesn't make sense," Papa said, shaking his head. He gestured at the desk behind him. "I have the contract right there."

Jane sat up and leaned over to read the paper. Sure as anything, that was a marriage contract. Jane was excellent at reading upside down since Emma always hogged their few books.

If Papa had ever really paid attention to Emma, he would have realized a marriage contract drawn up before she'd consented would have spooked her. Her father was really quite blind when it came to the inner workings of people. He wanted them to behave like dolls, with behavior prescribed by other people, or like characters in moralistic novels. Which Emma usually did. She tried so very hard to please him, but she couldn't change who she was on the inside.

Just as Jane couldn't change herself. Like healing an illness, Jane liked to fix things, and in this case, she needed to fix her family most of all. But she was glad Emma had run away with the captain. The dreamy, faraway look Emma had when recounting his conversation made it obvious that she could really love him. Besides, Jane liked how hard he'd tried when they met him and his large companion in the park.

"I'll wait. I have utmost faith that Andrepont will find her." Her father put his hands on his hips, his decision finalized in his head.

Oh dear. The viscount was looking for her sister. That wouldn't end well. "Excuse me, Papa. You should ring for your valet. Try to get some sleep. It will make you feel better."

"I can't sleep. How could I sleep when Emma is missing?" Papa's voice was thin and wheedling.

"At least let him shave you. It'll do you some good." Jane left her father there and practically ran up the stairs. She had a few coins set aside from her apprenticeship work with Mrs. Houseman. It wasn't much, but it was enough to get a note to the earl. She just had to figure out which earl he was. Of course, Aunt Diana had a copy of Debrett's hidden in the drawing room. She'd manage, of course, to fix what wasn't broken, just out of alignment.

Jane was in the drawing room with Aunt Diana when the butler delivered Lord Andrepont. Her sister's jilted groom looked as tidy as he always did, his garments perfectly tailored and his shoe buckles somehow still gleaming despite the dirt of London. She noted that the white embroidery on his dark jacket was especially intricate and fine, which was very expensive. Emma would have noticed that, praised it even.

Jane was working on her watercolors. She was attempting to expand on her botanical book but didn't want to paint directly in it. Not yet. She was not an accomplished artist, though she rather enjoyed the act of painting. Emma would say it was because she spent too much time in the woods and not enough time practicing the arts. Which was true. But the woods were so invigorating! Jane honestly didn't understand how people could survive cooped up in a house all day. It was unnatural.

"My lord," Aunt Diana said, rising to her feet, holding her hands out to him as if Emma had died.

Jane stood as well, knowing she should have thought to do so before Aunt Diana, kicking herself for it. At this rate, Jane would have to marry well since Emma had . . . done whatever Emma did.

Jane sent a footman to deliver a note to Lord Lorian's home, hoping she would receive some kind of answer back, but none was given, and the footman said he hadn't heard any word among the servants of a young lady in residence.

But Jane wasn't the sort who was prone to panic, and she was sure Emma could take care of herself. Goodness knew that Emma had spent much of their lives taking care of everyone else. Emma had taken on the role of the lady of the house at a young age. Even though it was only the three of them to feed, and Emma and Jane should have been taking meals in the nursery, Emma planned meals with Cook. Their father said it was too lonely to eat by himself, so they dined with him every night even though Jane was not quite ten years old.

When Jane did an awkward curtsy, she was glad Andrepont didn't directly witness it. She would have to practice. There was much for her to learn.

"Mrs. Fraser, is there any word of my beloved?" Andrepont asked.

Jane started at the word *beloved*. He'd never used such flowery language before. What had changed?

"None." Aunt Diana's eyes were red. She had wept, that was true. And Jane believed it was in earnest, not out of what she might have lost having had a connection to a viscount. Aunt Diana was absolutely prone to panic and worst-case scenarios. "We know not if she lives or dies!"

Jane watched Aunt Diana collapse into her chair. It was quite a performance. A quick glance at Andrepont showed he thought so, too.

"Perhaps I should ring for something to invigorate you, Aunt? Perhaps tea?"

Aunt Diana wailed and trilled as Jane made her way to the bell pull. Jane felt Andrepont's dark eyes on her as she moved. Sort of like when she'd been in the woods and felt the wolves watching her. Waiting. Weighing. To see if she was worth the trouble.

When the footman appeared, Jane instructed him to fetch a heartily brewed black tea and some honeyed oat cakes, which always seemed to put Aunt Diana to rights, no matter what the crisis.

"My apologies, my lord," Jane said, crossing the room again, acutely aware of Andrepont's gaze. "It is very trying to have no word from my sister."

"It is likewise trying for me, though she is no relation of mine. Not yet."

There was something in his words, the way he'd said *not yet*, that made her pause. As if he could mean so many things all at once. She went to sit, and since Aunt Diana was still pretending to be in her faint, Jane gestured for Andrepont to sit as well, playing hostess. He sat with one leg extended forward, the other back. She knew it was the most comfortable way to sit when wearing heeled shoes, but it also displayed his legs to the greatest advantage.

Emma had been correct—Lord Andrepont was a very handsome man. Excellent tailoring, new stockings, and a clear visage went a long way. But even more than that, there was something darkly alluring about him.

"To keep the worst thoughts at bay, may I inquire about what you are working on?" Andrepont asked, his tone light but curious.

"I have an interest in botanicals. At home, there is

a wooded area near our property, and all sorts of medicinal plants are there for foraging. I've learned a great deal from the women of the village. I'm making this book, a compendium of sorts. How to identify which plants are helpful, and for what sort of ailment. I want to make them like the botanical studies coming out of the Royal Society, but I admit my watercolor skills are lacking."

"How fascinating," he said, scooting to the edge of his chair. "May I?"

Jane hoisted the book into his outstretched arms, and he weighed it with a charming smile. "You've done quite a lot of work."

Jane nodded. "It is my passion, you might say."

He looked at her thoughtfully. "Education for all people. For the good of an entire village. How kind you are, Miss Laurent."

She basked in his praise, even knowing she shouldn't. Feeling that it was somehow wrong to do so, what with Emma being missing.

"Are these all your entries? And drawings?" He turned the pages, examining each one carefully.

She nodded. "I learned from Mrs. Houseman, the midwife in our village, but the phrasing is mine."

"And your watercolor attempts? May I see?" Andrepont held out his hand expectantly.

"They are still wet." Jane handed over her latest few, wondering why she was doing so. She hadn't wanted to show these to anyone, and yet, here she was displaying them to a learned man. He would think her foolish.

He nodded. "I have some expertise in art. I studied it for some time."

Interest sparked her. "I had no idea."

"I don't tell just anyone." He glanced over at Aunt Diana, who now seemed fully recovered and was back to her mending, staying as silent as a mouse.

"I would adore any kind of direction you could give me. There aren't many watercolor instructors that would come to a village as small as ours."

"You are in London now, Miss Laurent. The world is your oyster." Andrepont smiled at her, and once again, Jane was reminded of the wolves in the woods as twilight took the sky.

CHAPTER 4

The coroner returned, this time with no sympathetic Mr. Breaverton. At least the household seedcake supply would be safe. James hadn't written, not that there had been time for the post to bring a response to her first letter. Jane wasn't sure her son would come home before the holiday break, and she could only hope he would return to her for it. The burial would be soon, after the coroner released his findings or any potential jurors looked over Matthew's body.

The bloated, slowly decaying body was housed at a nearby inn. Jane hadn't been able to bring herself to visit it. And why should she? To gloat? There was nothing to gloat over when justice was served. She could always claim her delicate aristocratic sensibilities for not visiting a corpse. The thought of it made her stomach turn over. She couldn't bear to look at him. All the promises the word *husband* had held. All of Matthew's threats that had never come to pass.

She couldn't blame their son for keeping his distance, if he decided to do so. More than once,

James had said he wouldn't return to pay respects to his father after death, saying, "I don't think I could refrain from spitting on his grave."

For which Jane couldn't blame him. It would be difficult for her to behave decorously, but she had ample practice in pretending. So much pretense.

Jane received Mr. Eier in the drawing room. A tea tray was delivered before he could sit down.

"May I pour you a cup?" Jane asked.

"Thank you," he said. "I shan't be long. I wanted to keep you informed on the progress of the inquest."

Jane gave him a small widow's smile. Or at least, what she assumed would be the sort of smile a woman would give if she had actually liked or respected her dead husband. "Thank you for your thoroughness."

"We can't have the Peers of our Realm being murdered. It would not do." Mr. Eier drew himself up, as if it were he delivering justice to the people of the country.

"And what have you discovered?" Jane poured herself her own cup, willing her hands not to shake. She was in her full mourning attire now, voluminous black skirts that hid her antsy feet. She'd been tempted to order red satin dancing slippers for the occasion but thought better of it.

"I spoke with several of his lordship's friends, including Lords Beecher, Denby, Hackett, and Tottingham."

Jane made a noncommittal noise that could be construed as either acknowledgment of Mr. Eier's thoroughness or her dislike of the men. She thought it was remarkably economical of her. She despised those men. They were her husband's cadre and informants. Of all those men, she thought Hackett might be the least of her worries. He was young and remarkably stupid. He had the common affliction of believing that all people found him charming.

Mr. Eier flipped back through the pages in his small notebook, pencil scratches smearing with the number of times he'd referenced them. "Lords Beecher and Tottingham were together, on their own business—"

A gentleman's word for whoring.

"—and Lords Denby and Hackett were together with your husband on the night he was killed, though they could not remember the exact times."

Imagine that. Jane knew Matthew had preferred the company of Denby and Hackett to the other two as they were more malleable. Beecher and Tottingham were by no means men to be idolized, but they were the same age as Matthew and not as easily led. Already satisfied with their lifetimes of debauchery, they felt no need to push the limits of decency. Denby and Hackett, on the other hand, adored Matthew. He was exciting, powerful, influential. All the things both men aspired to.

Jane sipped her tea, leveling her gaze at Mr. Eier as she returned the cup to her saucer. Matthew had not been with Hackett or Denby. The lords were lying in case whatever might be revealed was too detestable. "And what activities were they engaged in?"

Mr. Eier at least had the wherewithal to squirm under her gaze. "Gambling, my lady."

Jane dropped her eyelashes. "Come now, Mr. Eier. We both know that when that group gambled, it wasn't just gambling."

The man blushed, turning red as a beet from the top of his head down his shirt collar. "There were, er, some, well . . ."

Jane watched him writhe in polite discomfort. "Some drinking?"

Mr. Eier cleared his throat and nodded, clearly grateful for the out she had given him. "Yes. A great deal of spirits."

"Scottish whisky? French wine?" Jane supplied him. Matthew hadn't cared about liquor. He drank, but that was not his favored hedonistic pursuit. He liked his mind sharp: far easier to manipulate those around him that way. That is, until he thought he'd won. Then opium was his preferred release. Apparently it was the same for these fellows.

"Likely," Mr. Eier said, his face back down in his notes. The blush receded and he regained control of himself. "According to his companions, his lordship typically left their gatherings sometime around three or four in the morning. That bit is not well-known in the minds of those present. They claim the details of the night in question are hazy in their recollections."

Opium, likely.

"I see. Does this bring you closer to finding the perpetrators of this heinous crime?" Jane's heart pounded as she asked. Is that not what a grieving woman would ask? Would she not hold ill will in her heart?

Mr. Eier snapped his notebook shut and scrutinized her. He was struggling to retain control of this conversation, and having been on that end of an encounter so many, many times, Jane found that she did enjoy having the upper hand. She could see why Matthew sought out this sort of situation. Except, Jane wouldn't go to the lengths he did. Or punish those who might outwit him.

"I only meant to keep you up to date on my information. I cannot bring a man to justice if the man cannot be identified."

"Of course," Jane said, bowing her head, an act of submission, but here, now, it didn't feel like submission. It felt quite the opposite. "Do keep me apprised of when I may make burial arrangements."

He stammered, clearly thinking he would be here longer, not wanting to be dismissed. "Naturally, but if I may, Lady Andrepont, I—"

The drawing room door opened and Mr. Afreé announced a visitor. "Your sister, Lady Lorian."

Jane looked at Mr. Eier as blandly as she could. He was struggling, she could see. She debated sending him away, but if she did, he would only return. This way, she would at least have an opportunity to cut short the interview should he start to ask difficult questions. "Mr. Afreé, please ask my sister to wait in the music room. Send for refreshments. I shall attend her shortly."

The butler bowed, and Jane turned back to Mr. Eier. "You had some questions, did you not, Mr. Eier?"

He gave her a smile that made him appear to be wincing. "Yes, thank you. I questioned your staff, but I came to realize that perhaps you yourself might be the holder of the best information."

Jane forced both eyebrows up in a look of surprise. "Oh?"

"What were you doing that night?"

"On nights that my husband is out, I invite my sister over. He does not enjoy her or her husband's company."

Mr. Eier scratched the answer into his notebook. "And why not?"

"Ancient history. My sister snubbed him during a courtship and ran away with Lord Lorian."

Mr. Eier looked up, clearly shocked. "I had no idea."

"It wasn't the sort of thing we wanted to publicize, of course. Especially since everything worked itself out." Jane choked on those last words. If only they'd known. If there had been a way to look into the future and see what would become of them all. But they had muddled through, just as everyone must, hoping to keep the damage to a minimum.

"Is there animosity from Lord and Lady Lorian towards him?"

More than you can imagine. "Of course not."

"Should I interview them? Particularly Lord Lorian?" Mr. Eier looked almost frozen, a paralysis of indecision.

"I should think not. Once Lorian inherited, there was not much either man could do but get along for the sake of the House of Lords."

"No, of course not. An earl would never . . ." Mr. Eier glanced down at his notes. "Were there any messages? Any notes carried to you that evening?"

"A ransom note? Of course not. His driver came home, knew that I was still entertaining my sister, and came up to inform me that my husband was safe and staying out all night. I had no reason to believe otherwise."

"Do you always keep an accounting of Lord Andrepont's whereabouts?"

I had to. "Only when he would stay out all night. I worry, after all. It seems my worry was not misplaced."

Mr. Eier nodded. "Thank you, Lady Andrepont. This has been most helpful."

"Has it?"

"I can see that you are a fine lady grieving the loss of her husband, as is only right. I was worried there might be something sordid I might uncover, and I didn't wish for the newspapers to descend upon you."

"I've never paid attention to gossip."

"Of course. Such is beneath you." Mr. Eier stood up. "Thank you for your time. I can see myself out."

Jane kept herself tame and bland as the man left the room but exhaled sharply after he left. Time for Emma. Jane went down to the music room. She wondered if Emma might be playing the piano Matthew had bought for James. Emma had played well on harpsichords and virginals, and this pianoforte was an excellent instrument. But Emma was not in the music room.

Matthew's study door gaped open. Cold, biting fear shot through her. Her hands shook. It was irrational. Matthew couldn't be lurking in there, lying in wait for her. He hadn't summoned her before him for yet another humiliation. Still, her stomach gripped into a fist, just as it had every time he'd done it. But it couldn't be.

This open door terrified her, but Jane willed herself to peer around the doorframe. Emma was there, going through the papers on Matthew's desk. He had not always been tidy. Emma's color was high as she sorted through the sheaves of paper on his desk.

Cold sweat pricked under Jane's arms. She was cold and hot all at once. She couldn't step over the threshold. She stood in the passage, gazing from afar. Her sister was the bold one, just charging in here like that. But then again, Emma didn't know what had happened in this room.

"What are you doing?" Jane managed to gasp between pounding heartbeats.

"Looking for evidence of further misdeeds," Emma said, not looking up and not seeming to understand how terrible the trespass was for Jane.

"Get out." Jane's temper frayed.

"But—" Emma said, finally looking up. Finally seeing Jane. Not her sister, not the little girl she left all those years ago for her own great love and adventure.

"Get out," Jane repeated, her voice louder than it ought to be. Tears pricked her eyes.

Emma held up her hands and left. Jane pulled the door shut, releasing a gasp of relief when the latch clicked into place.

BEFORE

The Haglund's kitchen maid was perhaps too young for Vasya, giggling as she set another cake in front of him. He thanked her, daring to put his large hand over her fingers as she flirted with her pretty blue eyes. The kitchens at the Haglund townhome were perhaps his new favorite place in London. Decent tea, even for the servants, which he already knew was rare, and excellent beer, the rarest of all in England, in his opinion. He'd been spoiled by those months in Flanders, doing hard labor for the monastery. They'd provided meals and plenty of their brew to anyone who needed it. Lodging for those who worked hard. Which Vasya always did.

But while the monks' beer was good, none of them had a fine rump like Mary's, and none of them slid him sweet honeyed oatcakes while he looked his fill. He sat at the wooden bread-making table, where the bread was still in its long rise, and thus this small corner was a safe spot to perch himself.

Echoes of the party were still being felt down here, with leftover food needing to be eaten before it spoiled—which Vasya was offered—and special dishes still being polished before being stowed away, making the next event less of a chore for the staff. And this was the best place to sit for gossip. The highlight being, of course, Miss Emma Laurent's disappearance during the party two nights ago.

To be clear, Vasya did not gossip. Largely considered a woman's trade, Vasya felt that gossip was largely the same as military intelligence. So he listened. Vasya had been told by many a woman that he was an excellent listener, and the benefits of such a compliment were obvious. He was no fool. There were other services to be offered with his mouth than talking. Especially when not talking allowed those services to be rendered.

"It was a mess, it was," Cook said, her ample hips swaying as she threw a towel over her shoulder. "Frederick, you were up there then, weren't you?"

A tall boy, obviously a footman, as they were hired for their height and their strength, pulled back around the corner. "Yes ma'am. In the very room."

Cook leaned against the countertop on the opposite side of the room. Mary gravitated towards Vasya, as if to reassure him that she didn't favor Frederick. "Well, go on boy, tell us what happened," Cook prodded.

"The one all in black, the viscount, comes sliding in, all smooth as can be, asking where Miss Laurent is."

Across the room, a young maid at the servant's dining table put down her mending. She began to furiously wipe at her cheeks as Frederick told his story. Vasya couldn't help but note her distress and wonder at it.

"But no one could find her. Even her family there began asking questions, and the whole dining room began whispering, assuming she slipped off with some other bloke."

In truth, Miss Laurent *had* slipped off with another bloke. Vasya knew because he'd driven away with them.

The maid at the dining table stood, her cheeks flaming red, tears in her eyes. "Don't you say a word poorly about Miss Laurent! Don't you say one word!" And the girl fled.

That had Vasya's attention. More had happened last night than even what he knew. Gareth had boarded a ship that very morning, so Vasya couldn't ask him. Perhaps he could sniff around Gareth's brother's townhouse, where they'd installed the girl, to see what he could find out.

It always surprised Vasya that noblemen undervalued their staff. The vast network of servants consisted of many people working together, many outside of the aristocracy. He knew more about the men he gambled with by virtue of talking in kitchens like these, flirting with kitchen maids and cooks, than anyone in London knew about him. It never occurred to those drunk arses in gaming hells to befriend their footmen and gardeners.

And now, he knew that Miss Laurent had a staunch defender in the Haglund household.

⚜

JANE'S FATHER WAS LIVID. HE WAS ROARING through the household like the lion trapped in the Tower of London menagerie. He burst into the drawing room where Andrepont had been showing her how to angle her brush for a better distribution of paint.

The viscount's hands were large, covering her own. It wasn't entirely unpleasant, though Jane didn't feel the way heroines in novels would have felt at his nearness. He smelled of lavender, no doubt in his wig, and his clothes were freshly steamed. Jane liked that. He was clean, and he'd chewed parsley before coming to call so his breath had a hint of sweetness to it. He was a man who understood manners, and Jane respected that.

When her father burst in, Andrepont shot to his feet, as if Aunt Diana hadn't been sitting in the chair next to them watching the whole painting lesson.

Jane's father shook the letter in his hand, his face red with rage. "That wretched girl is perfectly well!"

Aunt Diana looked at him in alarm. Jane stood, mostly to see around Andrepont's coat to properly get her father's attention.

"Isn't that a good thing?" Jane asked. She'd known it. Of course Emma was perfectly well. Emma was smart and practical, even if she had that romantic streak.

"She's married that Captain fellow!" Her father stomped around the room. Eloping wasn't rare, but it did look suspicious for unseemly behavior. It did not reflect favorably on the rest of the family. Jane would have to work extra hard for a good match.

"I believe he is shipping off to the colonies just today," Aunt Diana said. "The entire regiment is leaving. It was well-known last night. Many ladies reserved dances for the poor officers who would be leaving proper civilization."

"How did she marry so quickly?" Jane asked. She wasn't entirely ignorant, but weren't banns supposed to be read for three Sundays before a couple married?

"Special license from the archbishop. Must've been his father."

"Lord Lorian," Jane supplied, since she'd found the Debrett's. "He's an earl."

The silence as they all stared at her made her feel that perhaps her contribution was not all that welcome. Or necessary.

"Lord Andrepont, my deepest apologies for the behavior of my daughter. Truly, I did not raise her to be such a . . . a . . ." Jane's papa shook his head.

Andrepont put a fist over his heart. "It does pain me. I thought Miss Emma and I had an understanding, one that we would have the pleasure of deepening over the course of a lifetime."

Aunt Diana stood now, her mending put aside. "My dear Andrepont, do not despair. Perhaps Emma was the wrong sister for you."

Once again, all eyes were on Jane. Heat flushed her face.

"I cannot think on such a matter now, Mrs. Fraser. Perhaps I may call again? And Miss Laurent, I would love to see how you do with your brush technique until then."

Jane dropped into a curtsy as Andrepont left the drawing room. The three of them stared at the beautifully tailored coattails as he left the room, listening as the front door snicked shut behind him.

Her father stared at Aunt Diana. "Have you lost your mind?"

"Did you not see them when you walked in?" Aunt Diana hissed. "His lordship's arm around her, and she, receptive and giggling, as if she were ripe on a tree, ready for plucking."

"I beg your—" Jane sputtered.

"Hush girl. I saw it all."

"He was helping me with my painting!" Jane blushed even more furiously. It was only for technique! But Aunt Diana was too conniving to believe otherwise. She'd never believed Jane's interest in botany was anything more than a ploy—a ploy for what, Jane couldn't figure out.

"We have the contract drawn up. The same settlement could apply." Her father scratched at his chin.

Jane stared at him. She didn't dare accuse him of going mad, but she could think it. Emma had been missing from their lives for a mere day and they were already thrusting Jane into her place? Was she not her own person? She was not an interchangeable replacement for her sister when Emma was too inconvenient. But Jane kept her mouth shut. Now was not the time to protest. Emma had ruffled their feathers far too much.

AFTER – DAY TWO

Dinner might have seemed meager to some in the finer echelons of Society, but it was all Jane could manage at the moment. And her ascetic approach to dining would be lauded as appropriate restraint given her circumstances.

As if this household was in mourning. This house had held its collective breath for decades, wincing in anticipation of one man's violence. Now, the relief was palpable. She'd actually heard laughter coming from the garden at one point. It turned out, it had been her.

She joyously cultivated the mint leaves that would be dried for teas to soothe an upset tummy, snipped anemic lavender from the garden to fill a poultice for an anxious heart. Simple tonics, nothing complicated as her mind and body rocked and swooped as though on rough seas in these odd days.

While dinner was a simple plain broth, chicken cutlets in a wine sauce, and the end of summer berries for dessert, Jane still drank from one of her husband's finer bottles. For when one was a member of these finer echelons, one must have the best libations even when company no longer graced your despicable doorstep.

Jane was determined to drink them all. And indeed, this dark ruby Spanish wine was delicious. Sharing it with Emma and Gareth seemed only reasonable. They ate in almost silence. Despite believing the footmen were loyal to her, she didn't want to discuss Matthew so overtly.

Once they'd all retired to the drawing room, they switched to a delightful port complete with caramel flavors and woodsy aromas. Matthew was the worst a man could be, so how on earth had he gotten such excellent vintages?

Jane had ordered that horrific clock to be hauled out to the garden just before dinner. She'd find time to take an axe to it at some point. Without its looming presence, the drawing room was looking more and more how she preferred it. Sparer, less crowded, more elegant. She would swap out the portraits of Matthew's family members for some less fraught idyllic landscapes. No dairymaids or pucks, just simple, restful landscapes.

She swallowed the last mouthful of her golden-brown port and leaned forward to pour herself another glass. Emma was gazing at Gareth. She looked improved, Jane's sister. Matthew's death had lifted a weight from her shoulders, a weight that Jane had felt entitled to but didn't wear.

Drowsy and relaxed from the wine, Jane didn't want to think about Matthew. She much preferred thinking of Vasya. There was a thought she'd dared over the years—taking his hand and guiding him up the staircase. No words passed between them, only knowing looks. Matthew was gone now. She was suddenly free, and Vasya could become the lover she craved: kind, gentle, attentive. She'd never imagined what would happen if they actually got to her bedroom because she couldn't imagine him in that room. It didn't make any sense to her. She only imagined the way he would dare to look at her in that moment. That was enough.

Jane's stomach flipped, but she poured more port anyway. She caught Gareth's eye and raised the decanter, silently offering him more. He slid his empty glass over the tabletop. She poured it—possibly overfull, but was such a thing possible on a day such as this?

"That's plenty," Gareth said, holding up his hand.

Jane slid a look at Emma's glass, still half full from the first pour. Emma hadn't had much wine, either, come to think of it. Who needed to imbibe when one glowed like the moon? How positively irritating.

"One more day?" Gareth asked.

Jane nodded, scooping up her glass and cradling it close, as if it were a fire and she a lonely street urchin. Sometimes she hated her sister. There. She'd thought it outright.

"One more day for what?" Emma asked.

"Until the coroner must put aside his investigation," Jane said, hearing how the last syllable of the word slurred into one chewed, digested piece.

"I don't think he'll have anything to find," Gareth said. "Vasya gave his alibi. I didn't know if he would."

"What is his alibi? I don't remember." Jane had never known it. They hadn't discussed plans like that. At least, not with her. She wasn't sure who the mastermind had been—not anymore. The intent had simmered for so long that she could no longer track each branch of desire, each person's involvement, all wanting a hand in Matthew's erasure.

Emma and Gareth exchanged a look. Jane didn't like what that meant—this shorthand between the two of them. The looks that lifelong friends gave each other when words spoken aloud were redundant.

"His alibi was that he was having his wedding night." Gareth said the words gently, as if he were approaching an untamed horse.

Jane blinked, feeling the air leave her body of its own volition. "His wedding night?" These syllables didn't form words that made any sense, and she repeated them to see if she could find clarity in her own voice. Wedding. Vasya married. Taken from her. Or rather, abandoned her outright. "Who would he have married?"

"Mrs. Renwood."

Jane made a face that Aunt Diana would not have sanctioned, lo those many years ago. "Mrs. Renwood was a hundred years old when I moved into this house. She's a foot and a half in the grave if she's not already lying in it. You can't be serious."

Emma winced, embarrassed by Jane's outburst. "A different Mrs. Renwood, but related all the same. She's a bit younger."

"Methuselah would be a bit younger," Jane bit out.

"As you say," Gareth said, agreeing just to be agreeable, no doubt. Jane hated that he managed her. She didn't want to be petted and managed and kept in the dark. "But it is not her that he has married anyhow. A cousin or a relation of some sort. I honestly couldn't keep track."

Vasya had married another woman! How could he be so cavalier? How could he *leave* her? Not now. "But —" she sputtered. "He can't be marrying women he doesn't know!"

There was another look between them. Jane tried to calm herself, but she could feel the heat high in her cheeks.

"It isn't what you think," Jane said, sounding like an absolute child.

"I don't think anything," Emma said, almost like that was her response to any accusation. That must be what it was like to have daughters.

Jane clenched her fists. She didn't need to be managed. This was all happening in *her* house, to *her*, and any outrage she felt about not being informed was perfectly legitimate.

"Is there anything else you'd like to tell me?" Jane

asked, sounding terribly bitter. She squeezed her eyes shut, trying to shove aside all those emotions that had flown free the minute of Matthew's death.

"I'm sure you know all. We don't keep anything from you—all you have to do is ask." Gareth gave her a sympathetic look.

Was this how Gareth behaved in Parliament? If so, Jane could see why he was a successful politician. He made even the most outlandish thing seem so very moderate.

"I have a headache," Jane said, wanting them to leave. Her statement wasn't a lie. It had come on suddenly, a descending of all she had done, all she had lived through, only to find herself with an empty house. Her son was gone. Vasya was gone. She was alone with Matthew's ghost.

CHAPTER 5

Vasya enjoyed wine. And the smuggled Scottish whisky. And the smiles from the painted whores who lounged in the corners, eyeing the Faro players. But more than anything, Vasya loved winning against arrogant Englishmen who didn't realize that the entire room was set up as a distraction. Smoke curled thick in the air. Tobacco and cheroot, ambergris and tallow. Sweat of desperation and triumph.

It was a surprise when Lord Aberscomb found him there. Gareth's brother was known to dislike gambling. Nor did he seem to engage with women found in these types of gambling hells. Out of respect, Vasya stubbed his cheroot out, as he pulled in his winnings, keeping one eye on his money and the other on the lord.

"Mr. Kuznetsov."

Vasya got to his feet and gave a bow of respect. He hated doing it for men who were, in the English terms for it, a wanker. But for Gareth's brother, a bow was no hardship. "Lord Aberscomb."

The lord glanced at the other men around the table, his lip curling in distaste. "I need to speak with you privately."

Gareth had left on his ship, surely it had not sunk? Anxious to hear his news, Vasya swept his winnings in his big hands and stuffed them in his pockets, not bothering to count it. They stepped away from the table, while the other players grumbled. Vasya ignored them. He'd take more of their money another time.

"Is your brother—?" Vasya rumbled as they stepped into a quiet room.

"Gareth is fine as far as I know. It is his new wife." Aberscomb's mouth settled into a tight, thin line.

Vasya frowned but waited for what the trouble could be. She seemed an easy enough woman.

"You know the viscount Andrepont?" Aberscomb continued.

Vasya grunted. The servants didn't like him. Gareth despised him. There were rumors he'd killed his older brothers to obtain the title. But rumors meant very little. If there was one thing the Russians and the English had in common, it was love of a good story.

"He broke into my townhome, knowing Mrs. Somerset would be there. He threatened her. Fortunately, I was called, and was able to assist. But this cannot happen again."

Vasya's hands curled into fists. Threatening women was unacceptable. Especially if she had spurned his advances. The lady had made her choice. "What do you ask of me?"

Aberscomb looked as if he had swallowed a lemon. "As of now, all I can ask for is protection, despite what I'd like to do to that bastard."

Vasya inclined his head, trying to signal the other

man that he'd had experience in the bloody arts. He was willing.

"I'd like to hire you on as my stablemaster. Unfortunately, I have no horses there at the moment, but that is easily rectified. I will pay you, of course, since I can't have you spending your time here, if you are needed to safeguard Mrs. Somerset."

Vasya grunted. He was happy to protect Gareth's wife, but it did grate that he would no longer have the freedom of his time at his disposal. But surely, this would only last until Gareth returned. From what he'd heard, the war was supposed to end soon. But then, everyone believed wars ended sooner than they actually did.

"She's my sister now. It is my duty to protect her when Gareth cannot. And you are clearly a man that would intimidate Andrepont. Should he break in again, do not hesitate to think him a low-life brigand. Deal with him accordingly."

Now, cleared out from his boarding house and the lovely Mrs. Hatcher, Vasya looked around his new home. It was smaller than the rooms he and Gareth had rented in the past, but cleaner. A new bed, a small stove for warmth, a well-polished dressing stand with an unchipped porcelain ewer and bowl for bathing. This untouched flat was perched above a carriage house that likewise sat empty and unused. This was a new area of London, where only the wealthiest opted to stay, and this townhome belonged to Gareth's brother, Percy Somerset, the Lord Aberscomb and heir of the Lorian earldom.

He wondered why they could not think of some other occupation for him since his spotless home was far from the rooms of the woman he was charged with protecting. He put his arms out and couldn't touch both walls. At least the rooms were spacious. He checked the coal chute, which was full and ready.

He opened the stove, which was clean enough that he could eat from it. He shook his head at the outlandish wealth. This had stood empty for how long, waiting for a stablemaster and horses to come along.

At least being stablemaster made sense for Vasya's talents, which was perhaps what Aberscomb had meant when offering this position. Vasya was an excellent horseman. Where he was from, horses were part of every day, from travel to warfare. And he was good at both. He did not mind long days, the horse cantering to keep good time. Discomfort rarely even registered with him. Which was how he had felt when Gareth found him at the faro game on the outskirts of Paris, in a town whose name was so unimportant that no one seemed to know it. Discomforted. Poor. Not nearly drunk enough. Ready to die.

Lord Aberscomb's skeletal staff included an affable, pious butler, Mr. Wellman, and a fiery-headed maid, Martha Foraker. Both of them informed Vasya that Aberscomb kept the house for a mistress, but the man was so pure of heart that he'd never taken one. Clearly, both of them were also loyal to a fault, something Vasya noted with interest. More staff would be taken on in the event of a tenant, which surely would be handled now that the new Mrs. Somerset was settling in.

But she wasn't settled, as Gareth's brother complained. Andrepont had broken in threatened her, and probably would have accosted her if Aberscomb hadn't been nearby. So now Vasya would be nearby.

Vasya put down his one small carpetbag. He would find the kitchens, make friends, and learn the house. There was much to do—at least he assumed there would be. Helping the others with the regular household tasks would endear him to them as well as let him keep an eye on every corner of the house. His bulk fit the narrow stairway exactly. He couldn't indulge in too many more delicacies if he was to fit through the passageway. Why did they make everything so small here?

The confined space recalled the feeling of his home's open plains during the peak of summer when the river was swollen and all was green and hot and open. Not cold and damp and cramped.

Suddenly, it occurred to him—was this the English way of asking him to kill the lord? Should he trespass a second time, was Vasya to hurt him? Or was his position one of protection only? He had killed before. Would he be expected to do such a thing again?

❦

LETTERS CAME FROM EMMA, BUT HER FATHER refused to hand them out. He shook with fury, not bothering to open the one Emma wrote to Jane before throwing it into the fire. Jane watched the flames lick the edges of the paper. She understood her father's anger but was so very disappointed not to have word from her sister.

It had been a matter of days, but it felt rather like a year since she'd last seen Emma. Lord Andrepont had called daily, commenting on Jane's artwork each time, giving her more instruction. Despite enduring Aunt Diana's outrageous beliefs that Jane had somehow angled for the viscount's attention, Jane liked his input. He was knowledgeable about the effects of watercolors and how to render objects in a realistic manner—not the stylized art that might be employed when painting portraits or landscapes.

"You'll not do this to me," her father said, looking at her, his face still purpled from anger.

"No, Papa." Jane could definitively say she wouldn't jilt one man to run after another. It wasn't in her nature. But could she say that it was in Emma's pragmatic nature? Neither of them was prone to flights of fancy. Nor were they particularly changeable creatures. If a fortuneteller had predicted such an event at the county fair last summer, Jane would have refused to pay and laughed in her face.

Aunt Diana's pull of a thread was particularly audible. How could a person sew loudly? But Aunt Diana could. "There's an easy solution." She *tsked* as if she were a person beset upon by fools.

"The girl's too young," her father said, but he still eyed Jane with an appraising eye.

"Wouldn't be the first time," Aunt Diana said, her eyes flicking between them.

"First time for what?" Jane asked, knowing full well they meant her marriage.

"For a young girl to marry an older man." Aunt Diana cast her eyes back down to her mending, a ploy to seem all the more innocent, Jane was sure. "I myself had the span of fifteen years between myself and Mr. Fraser."

Jane's father was back at his desk, looking over the marriage contract. "It isn't his age I'm worried about. It's Jane's. I could stipulate some assurances."

Aunt Diana nodded. "I would worry for her health if she carried a child at this age. She's so small."

Despite being talked about like a breeding cow, Jane's only stipulation was that if she married, then her family would welcome Emma back with open arms. If that condition was met, Jane had no qualms whatsoever. Andrepont was titled and handsome and rich, and she wouldn't have to attend the ridiculous matchmaking parties and dinners that Emma had done the last few months. Besides, Andrepont would likely be amenable to helping her progress her botanical book. At least, the artwork portion of it.

"Assurances for your well-being, of course." Her father thinned his lips. "I'll bring this to his lordship."

"And if I agree, you'll let Emma come back to the family? No disgrace?" Jane speared him with her gaze. Papa shifted uncomfortably.

"In good time, yes." He cleared his throat. He was a man of hard-won loyalty and lasting grudges. Emma was testing both ends of that candle.

"And all will be forgotten," Aunt Diana chirped, as if their lives were as tidy as her stitches.

"And forgiven," Jane insisted, but neither of them said anything to that.

৩৵৩

IT WAS NOT LONG AFTER MRS. SOMERSET ESCAPED London to join Gareth in America that Vasya heard about the banns that had been read. He learned of it from Mary, the kitchen maid at the Haglund house. That staff attended church services en bloc, as many households did. Vasya, as a foreigner, did not attend the Anglican church services. Nor the Catholic services, much to the relief of Mr. Wellman.

Vasya had seen enough of religion, the clash between the Old Believers and the new church in Orenburg, the way in which God was wielded as a club to bring peasants like himself to heel. Aside from which, heavy incense wafting through dark, drafty buildings made him sneeze.

Though, from what Vasya had heard, this English God was much blander than what he'd known. What was the point if the mysticism was stripped away? That King George was somehow the appointment of God on Earth? That made Vasya laugh heartily. There was no magic in England that he could see. It was all watered-down belief with no fullness, no strength, no curse, the way his life in Orenburg had been.

Until the banns. He heard the news for the second time from Martha Foraker, who'd heard from another, and so on—the line of women talking to one another as if they were their own postal system. But it provided Vasya with information, and because he knew Gareth, he rendered his resignation to Lord Aberscomb.

Gareth's brother protested, but the man quieted when Vasya told him the banns had already been read twice.

"By all means, then." The lord tugged on his waistcoat and gave a frustrated noise. Vasya did not like noises like that. They suggested powerlessness, and indeed, in this case, powerlessness was accurate. "I'm happy to offer a reference."

And then Vasya found the curse here in England. He found the bleak struggle that felt so much like his life before he left his hometown. It turned out he had spent too much time with Gareth, too much time with a good man. Orenburg was not full of bad men, no, but opportunistic men. Men who did not care how many lies they told to get to an ending they desired. And now, in London, Vasya had found the evil he hadn't known he was waiting for—just that he would recognize it when he saw it. And it was unmistakable.

Vasya debated going to Mr. Laurent, the bride's father, but instead decided it would be better if he went straight to Andrepont himself. He presented himself at the kitchen entrance and was questioned by the housekeeper, Mrs. Renwood, the butler, Mr. Vernon, and the stablemaster, Mr. Dendrum. They were all far older than both Vasya and the viscount who paid their wages. Clearly holdovers from another time. Mr. Dendrum in particular looked as if Death had already stopped and tried to collect him once or twice.

Mr. Vernon seemed to note the age difference as well. He took the reference, promised to speak to his lordship, and asked Vasya to return the next day, which he did. That was when he met Lord Andrepont, his new employer.

"You're good with horseflesh?" Andrepont asked, his head bent over his desk. The study was meant to be imposing, serving as a partial library. Its bookcases were built from heavy oak, floor to ceiling, shoved full of precious tomes. Vasya could read, of course, but reading in English was very difficult for him. The books didn't interest him so much as they were an overt display of wealth. It took resources to own so many books.

Vasya shrugged in response to the viscount's question. "I am Russian. I have been on a horse a very long time."

"Tell me, were you a Cossack?" Andrepont asked, lifting his dark eyes. He stared, unwavering and bold, his look a challenge.

Vasya knew the man was looking for any information, a way to weasel into Vasya's confidence and find his weakness. But Vasya also knew he would never let this man into any knowledge willingly. So he shrugged again, thickening his accent, which put off many a high-ranking bureaucrat. "I am Russian."

Andrepont harrumphed but let the matter drop with a wave of his hand. "I value loyalty above all else. Why did you leave your last post?"

"The occupants left. I prefer to stay in London." This was the truth, and he hoped that Andrepont found him so insignificant that he wouldn't associate him with Mrs. Somerset. Lord Aberscomb had signed the recommendation letter, but in an illegible fashion.

"Can you race a curricle?" Andrepont asked, a light shining in his dark, empty eyes.

Vasya inclined his head.

"Please, demonstrate." The viscount stood from behind his massive oak desk, gesturing Vasya out the door.

So they went to the stables, where Vasya bridled the recommended horse—a beautiful Arabian, Vasya could admit. They hopped into the small racing curricle, and Vasya turned them toward Rotten Row.

"Not there," Andrepont directed.

Vasya sat shoulder to shoulder with the man. Until now, there had never been a moment when he'd truly been uncomfortable touching another person unless it had to do with the strength of the touch— for Vasya had been in his share of brawls. But Vasya did not like this man. Even the smell of him was wrong.

The viscount directed him to the outskirts of London, where the fields were still untilled. There, Vasya learned the horse's capabilities and the curricle's turning radius. He cornered them at speed, taking the vehicle to its shaking point, threatening to break a wheel but always pulling back before damage was done.

At the end, Andrepont clapped him on his back, which Vasya did not care for. "Well done, sir. You shall be my personal driver. I like your handling, and you're big enough to serve as a footman all at once. Fewer people in my way, the better."

Vasya bowed his head, at once happy and disgusted.

He moved into Andrepont's servants' quarters. His room was smaller than the cozy flat he'd had at Lord Aberscomb's townhome with Mrs. Somerset. And previously occupied. But at least he was in the house, close at hand. He sat at the table with the servants and hoped to find gossip, but each of them kept their eyes downcast. And for a great house, there didn't seem to be enough staff. Particularly maids. There was an adequate number of footmen, and the houseboy served as the scullery maid when Cook's rheumatism acted up. But this group didn't speak much, didn't raise eyes much. And Vasya had enough experience with petty tyrants to recognize the signs of one's reign.

A week later, deliveries started showing up. Extra butter, eggs, flour. Linens, dried fruits, expensive cuts of meat. After that came the servants with fresh flowers, fruits, and vegetables. A French man-cook arrived, looking his nose down at white-haired Cook. Vasya was incensed that Cook let this newcomer treat her like that, but he said nothing, as all the servants kept their heads down and mouths shut. All the temporary servants treated them that way.

Vasya knew every animal possessed a threshold where they broke. Just because humans had two legs and not four didn't mean they couldn't also become broken and biddable. The Andrepont servants were just that.

He knew how to recognize it because his parents had been broken. Until Pugachev, the false tsar. It seemed every person in Orenburg knew the man they followed wasn't the dead tsar, Peter. But they liked him talking about abolishing serfdom. About letting them take the benefits of the Cossack ranks at the very least. Letting them be freedmen who no longer had to beg a noble for permission to take a shit.

Vasya was young when he'd been a part of Pugachev's ranks, full of fire and ideology. He was barely able to grow a beard yet he was in the great man's circle, ready to kill on the false Peter's behalf. And he did. There was something about that day he couldn't forget. The humidity of the air, the smell of sweet, tall grass, the sticky-hot wetness of another man's blood flowing over his hands. It came back every so often, when a smell was near enough to that grass. When he found honey between his fingers.

But then, as now, he fought against downcast eyes. Which is why he'd had to flee to escape the consequences. He'd be damned if he'd let that kind of abuse happen again. There were no serfs in England. Slaves, yes, but that was calling serfdom by its true name, Vasya thought. And there weren't that many of those.

Soon, a wedding day arrived—the reason for the extra butter, the extra linens, the French man-cook. Vasya and the other permanent servants lined up outside the front of the house to welcome the bride. When she stepped out of the carriage, he felt as if he'd been thrown from a horse.

He felt everything in that moment—the pebbles beneath his shoes, the air on his cheeks, the strain of his coat on his shoulders. He could barely breathe.

It was her—the same young lady he'd seen in the park with Mrs. Somerset. But though it had been only a few months, those months had aged her. She was breathtaking. She had dark hair and green eyes, her dress a silver silk gown with dark green accents that caused her eyes to glow like blades of spring grass on a sunny afternoon. She was fresh and untarnished in the ways of the world, and that held a sweetness for any man.

He was ashamedly besotted. She was but a girl, and he was a man who had felt blood between his fingers. She was beautiful, but he'd known many a beautiful woman in his time. Why was she different? Because she likely did not know what mire she was walking into. This was Gareth's sister by law, and she clearly needed help in a house such as this. He would kill himself before he allowed her eyes to cast downwards.

But no, he must maintain his control, his firm grip on what was achievable. He was a man while she was on the brink of womanhood. He could find her beautiful, but he would not touch her, of course. Not only was she the lady of the house and married to another, she was barely out of childhood, and that made his chest ache for her. She did not deserve the man she had married. She would not know how to handle him.

Perhaps the viscount would not behave in the ways he'd heard whispered while he accepted deliveries, at least not to his lady wife. Perhaps.

The young viscountess greeted Mrs. Renwood and Mr. Vernon and allowed them to make the introductions. When they got to him, Vasya did not smile, did not allow that they had met before. Her eyes widened in surprise, recognizing him, but she said nothing.

His chest ached badly enough he wanted to rub it. She knew him. And he hoped she realized that she had a friend in the house. That he was there for her. It was what he could do to make a difference in this world. And he would do the best he could.

❧

JANE THOUGHT THE WEDDING CEREMONY HAD GONE rather too quickly. Wasn't something so momentous meant to be longer, somehow? And how could something so momentous happen without Emma there to witness it? Jane had begged and pleaded to invite her sister only to find out she was on a ship to the colonies. To a war!

Jane missed Emma so much. Her silvery gown was plain with dark green accents, which suited Jane fine, but she wished Emma had taken a crack at it, wished they'd stayed up late together to embroider. She didn't even care about the gown, just the time they might have spent together on it. Laughing and joking and teasing as they sewed. But no. Emma was gone.

Marrying this man would allow Jane to have Emma back whenever she returned. Jane knew that in war, nothing was guaranteed, but she also knew that worrying helped no one. So she resolved to believe that Emma was returning, no matter what the newspapers said. She had no opinions on colonies or land seizures or politics. She wanted her sister; whatever grand treaty might wink into existence to make her sister return to England, that was what Jane craved.

So when the bishop had asked if she would obey the man standing next to her, she agreed that she would. Her hair was finely done; it had been curled and swirled and pinned and powdered. The joining of two people, the bishop had said. The joining of her father and Lord Andrepont in money, and the returning of Emma to Jane. It had nothing to do with Jane and Andrepont. Matthew was his name? She was not entirely sure, but she thought it to be true? If she had to wager, anyway.

She fixated on the things she wanted: Emma. Painting lessons. A house in the country. She could endure whatever was needed for that.

Glancing at her *husband* as he escorted her down the aisle of the church after having been officially announced as this man's wife, she admitted he was handsome. That was helpful. But his dark eyes still unnerved her. She couldn't read him as she could read Emma, or her father, or even Aunt Diana. He wore a silver brocade suit and a powdered wig befitting his status.

They must have made quite the pair; the entire

church seemed to be in awe of them as they promenaded out to the carriage. They rode to his townhome in silence. She didn't mind. What was there to talk about, really? *Sorry my sister ran off with another man. You'll get over it. Chin up.*

He handed her up into the carriage. It was a nice carriage. That was something. She watched the chairmen out the window as they carried the well-to-do from place to place in sedan chairs. All strong, large men holding aloft both men and women. What feats of everyday strength these men committed.

What feats of strength could she commit? Strength of character? Strength of marital bond? Strength of vow? Of course. These things were expected. So expected that they weren't considered a feat. She glanced across at her husband, who was likewise preoccupied. He gave her an acknowledging smile but didn't speak.

They arrived at the townhome, a grand new construction of pale stone. The house was massive and modern, and she would be the lady of multiple floors, impressive grounds, and an army of servants. Many of whom were lined up outside the front door, ready to receive her.

They pulled to a stop and Andrepont—should she ask to address him by his Christian name?—jumped out of the still-swaying carriage to hand her down. He seemed solicitous, which was nice, and she spared his fine figure a second glance. He was dashing, anyone could see that. He brought her to the man and woman who stood at the center of the servants, then introduced her to Mrs. Renwood, the housekeeper. She was a woman another generation older than Aunt Diana, and Jane wondered if she was up to the task for much longer. But perhaps she wasn't as old as she looked.

Andrepont also introduced her to Mr. Vernon, the

butler, who was equally ancient. She knew her youth made everyone seem old, but truly, these two seemed as old as the King's Forest. They might have been childhood friends with Robin Hood. Or heard about a funny little thing called the Magna Carta. But Jane smiled politely instead and tried to seem as ladylike as possible.

Mrs. Renwood introduced her to the rest of the servants, one at a time, but as much as Jane tried to remember individual names, she failed. Until she came to the last man on the pecking order. "Vasily Nikolaevich Kuznetsov."

The only thing Jane could think was *oh dear.* Because he was large and imposing, with a dark black beard that was well-trimmed but out of fashion. Because he gave her a serious gaze that clearly didn't recognize her rank. Because he was handsome in a way she could not define. And she knew she would spend empty nights trying to puzzle out the reason she felt the hand of the Fates pushing her at him. She recognized him, the friend of Captain Somerset, whom she and Emma had met in the park one morning. How could that same man be standing in the ranks of her staff? But it was clearly him—she'd never met another person like him. He was unmistakable.

Andrepont guided her away, back toward the house, issuing orders for tea and readying the house for the wedding breakfast they would be hosting. Jane couldn't help but look over her shoulder at the giant man. His impertinent eyes bored into hers.

In a matter of moments, Jane was ensconced in the drawing room, a tea tray brought by a footman settling on the table in front of her. This felt foreign. She'd hoped her husband would understand that she was not a bride who was terribly good at all the hostessing duties a viscountess would be called upon to perform.

Her husband, relaxing on the settee across from her, dismissed the footman and Mrs. Renwood, who had been hovering nearby. Once the door closed behind them, Jane felt strangely trapped.

"Would you pour us tea?" he prompted in a voice that sounded less like a request and more like a demand.

Jane, who'd never feared her father nor any other authority figure, suddenly felt unnerved. She glanced up at him, now very aware that he was examining her as a pupil and not as a wife. What an idiot she'd been not to realize she was still a child to him. She wasn't to be a proper wife for some time yet.

Her father, at Aunt Diana's urging, had put language in the contract stating that they would not consummate the marriage until her eighteenth birthday. And her husband had agreed. That meant she had just shy of two years of being his wife without being his lover. Would Andrepont manage such a thing?

He turned his head, looking as if he could read her mind. The light changed his face; it was now all hard planes, like a statue planted in front of a royal building. Would *she* be able to wait until she was eighteen to discover the mysteries of the marriage bed?

"Well?" He prompted.

She grasped the teapot's handle. It wasn't as if she'd never poured anything in her life. Obviously, she had poured tea before. But there was something about his gaze, about his judgment on their wedding day, that made this seem somehow difficult.

"Cream?" she asked, glancing up at him.

A very wicked expression that she did not understand flickered across his face. "No, thank you."

She nodded and picked up the teapot. It was heavier than she was used to, and tea splashed all over the tray. She winced and poured a cup for him, still managing to let the spout dribble down the front of the pot. She poured herself a cup as well—no cream.

"Sugar?" she asked, pleased that there was, in fact, sugar available. Not everyone could afford such luxury.

"No, thank you."

She nodded, but dropped a lump into her own teacup. Sugar for tea! Such a luxury she could get used to. She picked up his cup, wiped it on the cloth napkin so the spill would not drip, and held the cup out to him.

He looked at her. "Was that the best you can do?"

She shook her head.

Without warning, he hit the teacup from her hand. The cup shattered as it hit the wood floor. Dark liquid sprayed away from him in an arc, landing on her dress. She gasped.

"Do it again."

She stared at the porcelain fragments on the floor. No one she'd ever known had behaved in such a beastly manner. She looked at him, his face calm. He didn't seem to be angry. "But—"

"Was it the best you've done?" He stared at her with those black eyes.

"Of course not. I said—"

"Then do it again."

Jane nodded. Swallowing hard, she looked down at the tea tray. There were more cups. Jane had assumed they were for guests that would be arriving soon. She wiped down the teapot.

Obediently, she picked up the teapot and glanced at him, but he remained expressionless. The pot wasn't as heavy this time, and it didn't slosh as she lifted it above the cups. She poured a fresh cup.

When she looked at him, he said nothing. So she picked it up and held it out to him.

"You didn't ask me for cream or sugar," he said flatly, his face unreadable.

"Because you—"

He hit her hand this time, knocking the cup from her. Her knuckle smarted where it had made contact with his, and the tea sprayed onto her hand, uncomfortably hot.

"Jane. I am your husband. You are to serve me, yes?"

Jane frowned. They had servants to serve, didn't they? There was a passel of them within earshot. What did it matter if she served him or not? "I suppose—"

"No, Jane. Your supposition doesn't matter. I am your lord and husband, am I not?"

She nodded. That was the general way of things, but no need to be such an arse about it.

He gave her a pitying smile, as if she were stupid. Tears pricked at her. She wasn't stupid. She wasn't. And her lessons in etiquette weren't due to start until next year. She was supposed to have another two years before she was ready to enter into something like this! It wasn't fair to judge her on something she hadn't been taught.

"Your behavior reflects upon me. You are a viscountess now. While I have agreed to forego my marital rights for two years, I will not let you be idle during this time. You will grow into a viscountess I can be proud of. You want that, don't you, Jane?"

She nodded, feeling very stupid and childish.

"Good. I want to be proud of you."

She was going to cry. Right here, in her new home, in front of her new husband. She was supposed to be his helpmeet. That's what Mrs. Houseman had spoken of when discussing what it meant to be man and wife. Of course, she meant regular people, not nobility.

"Pour another cup."

"Yes, my lord." With shaking hands, Jane lifted the teapot again. "Cream?" she remembered to ask just before she tilted to pour. Her heart thudded in her chest.

He gave her a smile. "Good girl. No cream."

She nodded and poured. The tea didn't dribble down from the spout, and Jane felt such relief. "Sugar?" she asked.

"One lump," he said this time.

Relief flooded her, and a little pride that she had managed to remember all the steps properly. Even if it was just pouring a cup of tea. This wasn't a terribly difficult task. At least, it shouldn't be. She extended her hand, willing it not to shake as she held out his teacup for him.

He stared at her for a moment. Cold dread dripped down her insides. But then he smiled and accepted the teacup.

"Thank you, Jane."

"You're welcome, my lord." Jane turned to her cup, but before she could pick it up, he interrupted her.

"You cannot just leave this mess on the floor. The tea will stain the wood." Andrepont looked at her, again in a condescending way. "Ring for the servants."

She nodded, looking around for the bellpull. It was near the fireplace, so she went to it and pulled. Moments later, the door opened to admit the footman. She opened her mouth to speak, but her husband spoke instead.

"Fetch a bucket and mop. My new wife is clumsy and would hate for a maid to have to clean on a day when there is so much to do. She'll be happy to do it herself."

Jane felt her eyebrow raise in the way Emma had said would get her into trouble. But it was her wedding day, after all. Shouldn't she get to relax and play at being a great lady? Yet, Andrepont was likely not wrong about servants being busy. And it wasn't as if Jane was averse to cleaning things, but her pretty dress was already spotted with tea, and this would make it worse. She still needed to change. And she hadn't had any tea yet, nor any of the delicious-looking honey seedcakes.

"My lord," the footman said, earning a withering look from his master. "The clock is here."

"Ah!" Andrepont clapped his hands and seemed pleased, which was a relief to Jane. "Bring it up, then."

The door shut as the footman went to fetch the cleaning implements and whatever clock her husband was excited about.

"Why—?" Jane started to ask, but she stopped when she saw the darkness that gathered in his eyes.

"This is your first day of learning consequences, Jane. You've been a child until now. I may not rule your bed for another two years, but I am your husband. You will obey me or suffer the consequences. Is that clear?"

Jane nodded, feeling as if her mind was somehow not in her body. She wasn't sure why. It would be easy enough to clean the mess, change her clothes, and have plenty of time before guests arrived. All would be well. He was right, after all; he was in charge. But did he need to be so monstrous?

CHAPTER 6

BEFORE

The days went by quickly and pleasantly enough. A modiste came with a trunk full of fabrics and little dolls dressed in the latest fashions. Andrepont—for Jane was still unsure of what to call him and did not yet feel comfortable asking him for permission to use his given name— insisted she spend whatever she liked.

Her teatime was filled with cream and butter and sugar, so clearly, no expense was spared. Jane worried for a moment that she might grow fat, but she took exercise in the park every day in the form of long walks with her new maid, Hope.

Hope had been hired solely for Jane, and she was eighteen to Jane's not quite seventeen. Hope was a pretty girl with straw-blonde hair and large gray eyes, only a shade taller than Jane. Each day, they would practice a hairstyle to keep Hope's skills at the ready and figure out what would suit Jane should she ever be presented to Society.

It wasn't long until the two were laughing and giggling together over nothing of importance, and Jane began to feel at home. There was a routine and a friend, and all her needs were met. She dined with her husband in the evenings, and he listened as she prattled on about the flowers she had seen in the park or something amusing Hope had said.

Andrepont encouraged her in all things, and slowly, Jane began to feel lucky. She had a handsome, wealthy husband, not to mention a title, which would give her access to a glittering world, should she wish it. Suddenly, she felt grateful to Emma for running off with her captain, leaving Andrepont available for her.

To be sure, it hadn't been all perfect, as their wedding day had shown. But as long as she asked permission for her activities and didn't question his judgments, he was an amenable husband.

Hope looked at Jane in the mirror. "How is this one?"

Jane held up the hand mirror to view the back of her head, which was adorned with braids and extra hair pinned on to make the style seem fuller. "It's nice."

Hope frowned. "You don't like it."

"None of them feel right," Jane said. "I can't explain why."

Hope squeezed her shoulder. "Your wigs will be arriving today or tomorrow. We can work on those together. Maybe that will help you feel more yourself."

Jane sighed. Wigs. "I'm not really one for adornment."

Hope smiled, and Jane saw depths in her friend's expression. "'Tis a gift to be simple."

The phrase stuck in Jane's mind for a moment before she recognized it and finally put the pieces together. Her maid's name, Hope. Her simplicity, her urging for Jane to assert herself as more of her husband's equal. "Hope. You're a Quaker."

The girl met her eyes in the mirror. "I grew up as one. But we've left the community."

"Why?" Jane loved the Quakers even though she knew next to nothing about them. She loved that they urged women to pursue academics and have more authority over their own lives, and, of course, she admired their extreme outspokenness for abolishing slavery.

Hope sighed, and Jane couldn't help but notice how very lovely the girl was. She was sweet and kind and amiable-looking in all the ways Jane was not. "The leader of the women's community did not . . . like my mother. She made it rather hard on us, so we left. And here I am, in service."

"Why did she not like your mother?" Jane knew, as soon as the question was out of her mouth, that Hope's vague words had been meant to signal the end of the conversation. But Jane couldn't help it.

"My mother is very beautiful, and that woman's husband coveted her." Hope's mouth thinned into a straight line.

Jane could see through Hope's beauty that her mother must also share those traits. "I'm sorry."

"Beauty is . . ." Hope trailed off, searching for words. "Transcendent. Worth more than money, and yet a curse all the same."

Jane wanted to fold her friend into an embrace, but she didn't. That was not their relationship. They were not to be equals.

Hope sighed and straightened. "Speaking of beauty, has his lordship considered a ball to celebrate your nuptials?"

Jane started. "Why would we have a ball for that?" As far as she was concerned, it was a contract, one that made her live here instead of at her father's house.

"To celebrate," Hope insisted. "To let you meet other ladies of rank."

Two months after being wed, Jane sat in the dining room with her husband. The table was heavy walnut and pillar candles burned in the center, surrounded by fragrant, freshly picked bouquets from the garden, arranged in a pleasing shape. The chandelier was likewise lit, an expense Jane didn't think was necessary for just the two of them, but she was told not to worry about such things, so she put it from her mind.

The room was wallpapered with a dark print, making it seem darker in the evening. And now that autumn was in full effect, the light disappeared earlier. There was a sense of oppression to it, but Jane ignored it.

Andrepont sat at the table opposite her, calmly eating the fish course. He was in his usual dark colors, accented by black with gold buttons and the gold signet ring he wore. Noticing her watching him, he put down his utensils. "Do you have a question, Jane?"

Her hands were in her lap. She was too nervous to eat, and her fish had remained untouched. "I was wondering something."

Andrepont raised his dark brows, his inky black eyes staring her down. Oh, it was so much harder to speak to him when he watched her like this. "Do tell."

She licked her lips, her nerves drying her throat. That gesture seemed to appease him, as he gave a sort of predatory smile. She tried to smile in return. "I was wondering if we would ever entertain?" Her voice went up at the end, as if she were asking a question. She hated when she sounded so young, so uncertain, so indecisive.

"Whom would you like to entertain?" he countered.

"I'm afraid I don't know anyone to invite." She felt so very stupid. Of course he would ask who would come.

"Having dinner guests is all well and good, but if we haven't anyone to invite, that does make the dinner party much smaller."

Jane squeezed her eyes shut. She was so stupid. There was nothing to do but stare at her hands until the embarrassment of her request abated. "Of course. Apologies, my lord." She felt him staring at her, as if his eyes could heat her scalp from across the table.

"However," he said, "since you don't know anyone, we could host a Michaelmas ball for anyone still in Town. Unless you'd like to retire to the country and hold one there."

Jane looked up. "The country?"

Andrepont smiled. "Indeed. I have several estates both to the north and to the south. Whichever you prefer."

Jane's heart leapt. She adored the country—there was space, and gardens, and forests, and manageable villages. As a great lady, she could visit the tenant farmers, bringing them balms and goods from the estate. That would be so much better than walking along Rotten Row with Hope every morning.

"I would love to see them all. Whichever you deem best."

He gazed at her, studying her, a gentle smile playing at his mouth. "You like the country?"

"I adore the country," Jane said.

"No French modistes in the country."

"I don't care." There would be woods where she could look for wild onions and mushrooms, things she knew and understood. She could take off her boots and stockings and feel real earth beneath her feet. She felt almost starry-eyed with longing for it.

He considered her. "I suppose you haven't had the true London experience either. I haven't had time to take you out to the opera or any concerts. Perhaps we should find entertainment here first."

Jane blinked. First he dangled the countryside in front of her, and now he was saying they would stay in Town? "Whatever you desire, my lord."

He smiled again at her, sizing her up. "I'll let you know what I decide. Have your new gowns come in yet?"

She nodded. "Two so far. She is working on the rest."

"Brilliant. Have one ready tomorrow evening. I shall take you out."

She smiled for him, even as disappointed as she was. She didn't want to go out to London entertainments, not when there was a country house just waiting for her arrival. "Thank you, my lord."

Andrepont picked up his utensils and went back to the fish. Jane picked up her own, hoping her stomach might stop somersaulting. She nibbled at the rich cream sauce. How had he managed to turn the conversation around on her so easily? She'd asked about entertaining people at the house, and the next thing she knew, they would attend the opera the following evening. But then, he always turned her in circles.

She'd asked about painting lessons, but she ended up with a pair of riding boots and a horse. She'd asked for a garden but was told to go for walks with Hope every morning. It wasn't that she didn't appreciate the walks, or the horse, or the boots, but it wasn't what she'd wanted. Worst of all, she couldn't figure out how she'd ended up agreeing to forego what she desired because he had agreed to everything she asked for. So how did she not have any of what she wished? He gave her place holders, hoping she might forget her actual needs.

Andrepont was finished with his fish, so the footman cleared her plate as well and returned with the next course. Jane didn't care anymore about the food. She was accustomed to it now—everything worked on his schedule, to his desires. Which, if she thought about it, was the right thing. He was the master of the house. He was the one who worked hard in Parliament, bettering the country for everyone. And then, after dinner, he went to his club, where he further worked—she knew because he told her about talking with other gentlemen in the House of Lords.

His life was difficult, full of conflict and compromise, and all he wanted was to come home to a smoothly run household and an agreeable wife. She could do that much, couldn't she? The housekeeper, Mrs. Renwood, took care of the menu planning and the staff, so Jane didn't have to worry about such things.

The drawing room was full of her things to remind her of their home, and when she had friends, she would be able to receive them there. Jane should be grateful for how generous he was. New dresses, the finest foods, and imported teas. It certainly wasn't his fault that she hadn't any friends outside of her lady's maid.

But perhaps that would change when they went to the opera. There would be other fine couples he could introduce them to, and she would find friends. They might be older than her, given how young of a bride she was, but still. It didn't matter. At this point, anyone would do.

Vasya disliked this viscount. Typically, Vasya refrained from judging another person. It was not his place, nor his business. If anything, watching a man go about his day would give Vasya enough insight to beat him at cards. Was he a man who bluffed? Was he a man who stayed sober? What did his face do when he lied?

But this man, this viscount, was not a man Vasya could respect. The meticulous dark coat, his starched white stockings, the shining buckle on his shoes—they all pointed to a certain type of wealthy man. Vasya knew better than most that neither money nor clothes made for an honest ethic.

With Andrepont, it was not one thing that scratched at Vasya's irritation, it was many. For instance, the man had asked Vasya to help pick a new horse for Lady Andrepont as a gift. Vasya was delighted that he wanted to bestow such a rich present on his new bride, regardless of the sting of envy. Vasya wanted to be a man who could buy a woman a horse on a whim—but he wasn't, and that was his lot. So he had chosen a very pretty dappled gray mare with a pleasant disposition. The viscountess was young and athletic, but clearly not an experienced horsewoman. She needed a mount that could be forgiving and mild. Vasya could picture her in the saddle, cantering down Rotten Row, a satisfied expression on her face.

Lord Andrepont, however, brushed off Vasya's expert opinion and instead picked a horse much too big for the lady: a sleek chestnut mare that stood too high. If the viscountess fell off such a creature, she would surely break a bone, if not her pretty neck. Vasya said as much, but the lord scoffed at his warning. This mare was headstrong and fast, far more than Lady Andrepont could likely control. Again,

Vasya voiced his concerns for the lady's safety, and again the man rejected them.

The worst part of the experience was that when the purchase time came, Andrepont bullied and threatened the seller into much less than was deserved. Vasya was embarrassed by the man's impudence. It didn't matter if he was a nobleman; that horse was a prize and deserved to be sold at its value.

After an hour of poor behavior, Andrepont received ownership of the mare, and Vasya transported her back to the stables, soothing and feeding the animal. When the lord retrieved the viscountess, Vasya could read the surprise on her face.

But the unwanted gift gave Vasya the opportunity to see her. She was a child still, her limbs lithe and beautiful the way any unpicked flower was. Vasya was a vulgar man by nature, prone to looking at a person's walk to assess the realities of their world. And she was still naïve in it. She did not think to be wary of him, or of her husband. She had no concept of whether the tilt of her head was attractive to them or not. Some women were born to such pretexts—or perhaps were pushed into them so early they couldn't remember a time without them.

That day, the viscountess wore a pinkish sort of color—Vasya was not good with names of hues and shades—but she was vibrant and unselfconscious in the ways of youth. It was obvious to anyone with eyes: she did not need or want a horse, let alone one of this size. It was a waste to coop up this animal in Andrepont's in-town stables. But Vasya was not a man who would or even could complain. It made him ache for her. For what she would become under the rule of a man like Andrepont.

Vasya sat with her image in his mind, ill at ease. He was discomfited by his attraction to her. He couldn't even tug himself with her in mind. She was on the cusp, and it was as if all the men in London could smell her. She was ripe. She was almost ready to be plucked.

Andrepont had the right of first taste, and the thought of it turned Vasya's stomach. Vasya knew him to be depraved because of all the half-dead opium-addicted whores he preferred. The opium-eaters were mostly nonsensical as Andrepont carried them back to the carriage from the dockside brothels and ordered Vasya to drive them to his friends' manors. These were not women who could even remember to be paid for the use of their bodies. One of them, Vasya was fairly certain, would never exit Lord Denby's property. She had been too far gone in her love of the drug, and Vasya had noted the bruises and blood on the other women when he returned them to their hard-eyed madams.

But Vasya said nothing. What could he say? What would he say? He would not survive accusing a noble of murder, let alone impropriety with women who sold their bodies. Driving bleeding, dead-eyed women was hard on his conscience, but he did it because he knew he couldn't help them. There was other work to be done, and the young Lady Andrepont needed a protector, for she hadn't had any other one. If Gareth had been in London, he wouldn't have allowed the marriage.

Watching after Lady Andrepont was the only thing Vasya could do. And for all the gods in the world, the old ones and the new ones, none had mercy enough to deliver the beautiful young Lady Andrepont from her husband. Vasya's big heart ached; he knew what would befall her next and was powerless to stop what had already been set into motion.

JANE'S CREAM-COLORED GOWN HAD A RED RIBBON that threaded along the extremely low neckline of her bodice. Her bosom pushed up against the rigid stomacher. This was not the dress she had ordered. It had come this morning, along with a note from her husband saying this was the dress she should wear.

Hope had aired it out as soon as it arrived, and both of them had stood frowning at it, wondering why a modiste would have made it. It was something for a courtesan.

"You could put on something else," Hope suggested, eyeing the red ribbon.

But Jane couldn't. If her husband wanted to her to change, he would tell her, so she had no choice but to leave her room and show him the gown. Then he would tell her to change. Perhaps they would laugh over the mistake?

She tried to breathe steadily as she left her room. Andrepont looked at her with approval as she descended the stairs of their home. Her hand was clammy as she clutched at the dark wooden banister.

"Is this not too . . . daring?" Jane asked when she got closer to him. She felt exposed, what with most of her decolletage on display for public consumption. Was this dress not a mistake? He wanted his wife dressed as a whore for their first time out in public?

"For the opera?" His tone was imperious, disdainful even.

She knew he thought her barely above an imbecile, but the gown was frightfully low. Aunt Diana would never approve.

Mr. Vernon held out her cape, and she slipped into it, embarrassed to give the older man a full view of her bosom. The butler said nothing, of course, and held the door for them as they exited to where the coachman held open the carriage doors.

Jane didn't mean to seek her servants' approval, yet she couldn't help but watch the expression on Vasily Nikoleavich's face when her cape flapped open, exposing one side of her gown, showcasing her left breast. His eyes widened, and though she couldn't see the twist of his mouth beneath his black beard, she knew he was shocked.

She was right. This dress was well beyond respectable, so why did her husband insist that she wear it? The dress she had ordered from the modiste was a merry spring green with gold thread, high-necked and long-sleeved for the winter months. While her husband gave her the impression of choice, he had clearly made other arrangements. She thought of how he'd dangled the country houses in front of her before snapping them away.

"It would just take a moment for me to change," she said to Andrepont, pulling away.

He stopped cold, as if she had just accused him of murder. His dark eyes turned to her, and it unnerved her how very violent they seemed. "There is no time."

She licked her lips and pulled at her hand, which was tucked in his arm. "But it truly cannot be appropriate if I feel so ill at ease in this frock."

He clamped his other hand over hers. "Jane. Get in the carriage."

"But—" She wasn't thinking anymore, just protesting. Her mind went blank and she tugged on her arm again.

He backhanded her. The slap resounded in the marble entry, and the sting on her cheek was hot and painful. She knew it wasn't hard, a slap that an errant child might earn for petulance. Still, tears sprang to her eyes. Instinctively, she knew he would deliver worse if she tried to flee back into the house. There was only one way forward, and that was to get into the carriage, regardless of what she wore or how she felt.

She stole a look at her husband, dark-eyed and imperious. His face was like marble, harsh and forbidding, unmovable. He would not tolerate her impertinence, her opinion, her preferences. Cold dread settled in her stomach, her cheek still hot from the slap, when she realized the time for negotiation had passed as soon as she stepped in front of the bishop who married them.

"Into the carriage, Jane. Now."

She nodded, allowing herself to be handed up the steps into the vehicle. She sniffled, unable to keep a tear or two from falling even though she was afraid it would make him angry.

He followed her into the carriage, taking the opposite seat. He rolled his eyes and made a show of taking out his handkerchief and handing it to her. "Stop crying," he commanded, but his tone didn't seem as serious as the one that pushed her into the carriage.

She dried her eyes, trying to think of something other than her stinging cheek. Mrs. Houseman. Her watercolors. The feel of picking a mushroom, where there was resistance and then a sudden give as she plucked it from the ground. The smell of garden dirt. Her sister's hand in hers.

A hole opened in her chest, one her dress would never be able to reveal. She missed Emma. Where was her big sister now that Jane really needed her? Had she known Andrepont was like this? Was that why she ran away?

They arrived at the opera house, and Jane took Andrepont's hand as she stepped down from the carriage. It was a very large building, Jane could say as much with certainty. It was . . . yes. Very busy as well.

There were so many eyes to see her, so many eyes to witness her low dress and her shame. Andrepont took her inside, where the crowded room overflowed with new fashionable confections. Brocade ran along every gentleman's coat, polished gold and silver buttons and buckles gleamed in the candlelight. The women's dresses were luxurious pieces of finery, the skirts wide and adorned with patterns and ruching in every dazzling color. Gleaming gems and opulent pearls dangled from ears and sat snug against bosoms. It almost made her forget her own adornment until she was forced to remove her cloak.

As soon as the cloak was gone, every eye seemed magnetized to her bosom. She breathed shallowly, her breasts pushed tightly together, held in place by a fragile red ribbon that trailed along the scandalous neckline. She glanced up at Andrepont, who didn't seem at all perturbed by the number of men staring directly at her decolletage. He offered his arm, which she took, hating the weight of the stares that followed her.

It was the first time in her life that she was grateful for the wide panniers under her skirts. At least no other part of her body was on display in this way. Even her hair was disguised with powder. Hope had not been able to pin a wig on Jane that she was willing to wear. She needed one thing to feel proud of that night, even if it was her hair.

An older man appeared in front of them, a young woman about Jane's age on his arm. "Lord Andrepont, how very nice to see you," the man said, his mouth showing teeth yellowed from tobacco.

"Lord Highbrook," Andrepont said. In comparison to this man, Jane's husband looked especially handsome. At least she didn't have to watch this man's mouth at dinner every night.

"Will you introduce me to your companion?" Lord

Highbrook made no attempt to disguise his lascivious gaze. He clearly did not think she was Andrepont's wife—rather, he assumed she was a lady of the evening, as his companion must be.

His young lady did not seem interested in their conversation, but she did give Andrepont a pointed wink. Her husband didn't respond, but Jane was livid. He allowed this man to treat her like this? To introduce her to courtesans? Aunt Diana would have a fit.

"No, I don't believe I will. Excuse us." Andrepont gave the barest head tilt of recognition—Jane had no idea of Lord Highbrook's rank—and they turned away. A thrill of satisfaction at her husband's curt response coursed through Jane.

Lord Highbrook was clearly insulted, but he didn't pursue the introduction, which was a relief. She and Andrepont didn't make it but a few steps before another man blocked their path. "Ho, ho, Matthew," he said. "Who is this delectable young lady?"

This man was younger than Andrepont but older than Jane. His hands were clasped in front of him, but his fingers continued to drum, as if they were worms that could not be contained. His clothes were dark, but enough of the style that he did not stand out. He was thin, and the breeches and stockings made it clear that his knees were the largest portion of his build.

Jane had assumed the rich were always more ample than the poor. But the cut of the man's coat and the shine on his buckled shoes made it clear he had money despite the gaunt cast of his cheeks.

Andrepont gave the man a cool look. Was it because he'd used Andrepont's Christian name and didn't have leave to do so? Or was it because he'd called her delectable, which was so grotesque Jane couldn't even shiver?

"Lady Andrepont, this is Lord Denby. He is a friend to me, and a man with whom I spend a great deal of time. Lord Denby, this is Lady Andrepont, my wife."

Denby's eyes almost popped out of his head. He sputtered until he finally managed to make a bow of courtesy. "My lady."

Jane did her best not to frown as she returned his courtesy with her own brief bend of the knees. If he was a friend, then why had he not known Andrepont had married? It was no secret. There had been a notice in the papers and gossip columns. Even a sketch of her had accompanied it, though it was not a terribly accurate likeness.

"My lord," she said in turn. Hopefully this man was not going to damage her reputation. Goodness, listen to her, thinking like Aunt Diana. Still, her stomach turned at the thought of these men believing they might have a chance to bed her, as they would if she were a courtesan. How terrifying to have no choice but to let them touch her.

Thankfully, Andrepont whisked her away from everyone, striding with purpose through the opulent passages, red carpet beneath them, gilded sconces on the walls lighting their way. He ushered her to seats directly on the balcony, overlooking the general audience.

"Is this our own box?" Jane asked, completely awed by the view. They could see everyone. The stage, the audience, the other opera boxes. But then she noticed the opera glasses turning towards her from below and from across.

"Yes. We've always maintained a private box."

A servant appeared with two glasses of hay-colored liquid. Unsure of propriety, and not knowing what to do, Jane took the glass. It smelled sweet and sour all at once. She decided to just hold it for a while and pretend at drinking it.

She hadn't had spirits before. Emma had, but Jane had always been careful about what she ate. There were tastes she didn't like, ones that soured in her stomach afterwards. The smell of this wine—for it was wine, wasn't it? she wasn't sure—was cloying. All of her work with Mrs. Houseman had made her even more aware of the effects of different foods.

"Do you not like it?" Andrepont asked, looking directly at her for the first time since they arrived.

She was afraid to displease him, but even a polite lie seemed dangerous. "I haven't tried it yet."

He looked amused, as if she were a child that had just performed an awkward dance. "Whyever not?"

A spider, she thought. Before, she'd compared him to a predator, some animal that was brutal and ripping. But no, he wasn't that. Her husband was far more calculating, like a spider, entrapping, waiting, knowing that no matter what happened, he would win in the end.

"The wine smelled . . . strange." Those opera glasses were all still trained upon her. Somehow, it made her nervous even though they were so far away.

His mouth quirked in amusement. "Do you think it's poisoned?"

Her mouth dropped open in shock. It took her a moment to compose herself. "Of course not! I only mean that I'm not accustomed to wine."

He sipped his own glass and looked down at the sea of opera glasses trained up at him. "No time like the present. But do please be discreet if you don't like it."

"Oh, I mean—"

"Don't get flustered," he said from behind his wine. "You are being watched by every important set of eyes in London. It would behoove you to control yourself."

Blush crept up her neck and she cast her eyes down. No, wait. At her wine. She sipped it. The hay-colored liquid was sweet and musty all at the same time, and she hated it. But she gave her husband a doting smile. "Better?"

He glanced over at her expression. "You are quick to learn."

She tipped the glass to her lips but did not imbibe anymore, just let it touch her lips. The charade wasn't believable for much longer, but hopefully the opera would begin soon and put her out of her misery. "I've always been an excellent student."

Intrigue flared in his dark eyes. "Indeed. I shall bear that in mind."

CHAPTER 7

"You summoned me?" Vasya rumbled as he entered the drawing room. The light was fading, and Jane knew she shouldn't have done this. She was selfish and hurt, wanting an explanation where she had no right to ask for one. He should be downstairs taking his meal with the other servants or going to his home, where his *wife* might have food waiting. Instead, Jane had called him, placing her needs above his.

Jane hated how the low growl of his voice flowed through her body like a fast-moving stream. She was angry with him. Oh, so angry with him. She sat by the fire sewing as loudly as Aunt Diana used to do. She couldn't bring herself to lift her eyes to him, so she left him standing in the middle of the room like a schoolboy who had been taken to the headmaster.

It couldn't be any worse than his interrogation by the coroner. Or any worse than dumping her husband's body into the Thames. Or any number of other indignities he had no doubt suffered over the years. But this time, she was inflicting it. Her. She was causing the pain, not just feeling it. "I understand felicitations are in order."

Jane hated darning. Why was she darning? She shoved the needle through the stocking she was mending with far more force than needed and pricked her finger. She shoved the offending digit into her mouth.

He came to her shockingly fast. He knelt on the floor in front of her, gently pulling at her arm until she surrendered. He took her finger, examined the injury, and then placed it in his mouth.

Her eyes flickered as she allowed the feeling to take over in a way she never had before. He had held her plenty of times, dabbing at injuries or applying poultices. But never like this. Oh God, never like this. She felt his tongue swirl around her finger under the pretext of blood, but it meant so much more than that.

It was hard for Jane to feel in her heart the way she felt in her body—Matthew had robbed her of that. But here, with Vasya, her steady, ever-present Vasya, she felt it. Her liquid core, the warmth in knowing she was safe with him. He sucked and she was ready to swoon. He licked at her, and she wanted more. She wanted everything.

To finally cross that line. To finally lavish affection on him, to caress him, to bare herself to him and him to her. She was ready to rend her own bodice in the drawing room when her mind returned, and with it, the knowledge that Vasya was a married man.

She gently tugged her hand away, and he allowed her to separate. There was so much she wanted from him, so much she wanted to demand. She wanted for him to slowly work his way up her silk-stockinged legs with his mouth. To love her in his gentle, complete way, which left her feeling cocooned and drugged. A way that she had never felt, only dreamed of.

But he could not give her that.

Because they'd killed her husband and he needed an alibi. So he married someone else to prove his innocence. Her heart fell through her chest, plummeting into the floor and then the ground beneath, pulling every veneer she'd created in the last decades, leaving her a barren, smooth rock. Nothing to hold onto. Nothing to feel.

Vasya's great dark head was bowed, his forehead moving slowly to touch her knee. "I'm sorry," he whispered.

This was when she wanted tears. She wanted the rage she saw in James's face, even in her niece Lydia's, now that the poor girl was emerging from the shock of the damage she'd endured at Matthew's hands. Jane wanted to rant and scream. But she could not. She was empty.

She couldn't even tell Vasya she loved him. Couldn't say what he meant to her, that she couldn't live without him. That the few gleaming moments of joy and light in her life had been because of him. She touched his hair, something she had never done. She'd never caressed in return, for fear it would push them both past what restraint they had. Her pale fingers threaded through unexpected softness. His hair wasn't as coarse as her husband's had been. Vasya's was softer and fuller; it made her body thrum in sweet pain.

Because of course Vasya's hair was softer than Matthew's. Everything about him was better. She stroked his head, and he rested more fully against her. Why had the events of her life happened this way? Why could they not have gone some other way, where Matthew was killed long before they'd met him? Where her father had never known him? Where Aunt Diana understood that nobility was a social class and not a moral virtue?

And Jane was to blame as well. She'd accepted and acquiesced. Now, she couldn't even remember why. Why had she married so terrifyingly young? Why had no one protected her?

She removed her hands and Vasya lifted his head, his warm, brown eyes questioning her. If there was ever a time when she could have pledged her love, she could have here. But it was not the time. Perhaps there would never be the time.

Jane was tired of scheming. Her entire marriage had been one plot or another to evade Matthew's excesses and cruelty, to let another maid whom he'd fixated on leave London without his knowledge. Jane deserved to live simply, didn't she? A life where the day held nothing but a few meals, some hours in the garden, luncheon with her sister or perhaps Mrs. Foraker, and readying for bed blissfully alone.

No one—because she'd refused to authorize such an event—put a notice in the paper of her husband's death, but even so, the *ton* found out. Calling cards piled up on the door, and she received stacks of carefully folded letters of condolences. She set about returning these missives with notes of thanks, carefully reading between what was actually said and what was meant. The notes from the men were, by and large, notes of polite regret. Some were sincere, as Matthew had been, to a certain type of Corinthian, a guide to the rougher parts of pleasure in London. The condolences from these men's wives could not be disputed, and they also sent invitations for her— when her mourning was over—to call upon them if she desired. Invitations that had not been issued while Matthew was alive.

She didn't blame the Society matrons for not wanting her about. Matthew was a danger to all he encountered. The ones with skirts knew it better than the ones without. To invite Jane was to establish a sinister thread to their young daughters, which was not worth the risk.

With Matthew gone, there was freedom all around. Except she didn't feel free. Not when Vasya was beholden to another. She hadn't gone to these lengths for Vasya alone; there had been many factors, many people to protect. But her heart was broken. So many decades spent pining for him. So many daydreams and desires kept carefully locked away.

"I must explain—"

She held up her hand. It was why she'd asked him here, but now, she found it nothing but poison. "Please. I cannot hear it now."

Vasya nodded and pulled away. She immediately missed the sensation of his nearness. Of all the times Matthew had sweated and grunted above her, pulling climaxes from her in a way that felt unwilling yet pleasurable, how she'd wished it had been Vasya above her. Loving her. Seeing her. Wanting her because he loved her, not because he wanted to make a point or punish her sister.

Vasya left the room, not looking back, and she watched him go. Her body was as thin as paper, her soul already torn in two.

BEFORE

Jane didn't always like her husband. She didn't always loathe him, either, and it confused her. Sometimes, he looked at her and she felt so wanted, it was thrilling. This handsome, erudite, worldly man was captivated by *her*. He'd married *her*.

When she pleased him by dressing the way he wanted her to, his sideways compliments sent pleasure shooting through her. She was almost desperate now for the painting lessons he'd promised before they were married because she wanted to show him she could be good at something other than looking like a courtesan.

Tonight was her hostessing debut in Society, their first ball. The party he'd promised her so many months ago. They'd invited everyone in the *ton*, apparently. Aunt Diana had helped with the invitations and the planning, which had thrilled her socially mobile relative. It was mostly Aunt Diana teaching Jane by example—what foods to serve, how many servants to have on hand for the night, how many dishes might be required, and how many barrels of wine. What Jane knew—and what Aunt Diana had tried to keep from her—was that the respectable echelons didn't wish to attend. Hope had told her that Aunt Diana had written sheaves of personal notes begging the highly regarded matrons for their company.

Hope listened when the other servants talked. Given how little Jane was told, either by her husband or the housekeeper, she needed Hope's ears. The house was like a nursery where she was sequestered and kept out of sight. That is, until her husband decided to dress her like a harlot on their public forays.

Society had noticed. That might be something that didn't matter in the French court, but this was England. She didn't want to be shunned, not by women who understood what it was to be part of the nobility. She had so much to learn, and she was also desperate for some kind of friendship outside of Aunt Diana, who told her to be grateful, and Hope, who was herself learning how to dress a great lady with the proper gowns and hairstyles.

But Jane knew there was more to being a viscountess than she was allowed to learn: charity work, helping tenants on her husband's estates—not that she'd ever seen them. Even her now-neglected botanical work could be beneficial. There was so much knowledge she could share with those who were ill or needed help. She let out a frustrated sigh and allowed Hope to lay a cool gold-and-ruby necklace on her chest, tying it in the back.

The necklace had been made for someone stouter than her, and it hung low, the ruby like a small pomegranate resting just above the cleft between her breasts. It would have everyone salivating—some for the jewel, some for her flesh.

She hated it. The ruby wore her, instead of the other way around. The ruby was the color of her husband's family, a stamp of his ownership. She'd wondered for a while if she could get the marriage annulled on the grounds of no consummation, but she knew Andrepont would bed her the second he got wind of it. Likely in an unpleasant manner.

Still, she was ignorant of her marital requirement, as she would remain for another year and some months. It was Aunt Diana's stipulation; she worried about Jane's slim frame delivering a child. Surprisingly, Andrepont had agreed to the condition of the contract and was in no danger of breaking his vow. He had not touched her, had not given her more than a chaste peck on the cheek. But the looks he'd given her had burned, which had made her wonder about the nature of passion.

Perhaps their relationship would sort itself out once that piece of their marriage was completed. It brought couples closer, she imagined, or at least, having a child would please him, as he would then have an heir. Given the looks he'd garnered from the loose women his friends brought to the opera, her husband wasn't keeping himself chaste for her. Not that she should expect that, no. It stung a little, and it made her feel even more like a child, but she didn't feel as if there was a choice in the matter. She was not quite seventeen. What was she supposed to do? Seduce him? How? She'd not even had a real kiss before. Her skills were nonexistent, and a man like Andrepont would laugh at her clumsy attempts.

Besides, she wasn't sure she was looking forward to the night when she became his wife. In truth, she was wary of his every move, never knowing which side of him she faced given how he alternately insulted and praised her.

"Finished," Hope announced, admiring Jane in the polished glass. "You look incredible."

Jane turned her head this way and that, her dark hair coiled in intricate curls and studded with dark red rubies. Her green eyes stood out against the blood red, making a striking contrast. She sighed. "Wonderful, Hope. Thank you."

Hope's sweet face fell at Jane's unimpressed tone, and that hurt Jane, too. "I'll be downstairs helping in the kitchen for tonight," Hope said, bobbing a curtsy and removing herself from Jane's dressing room.

Another heavy sigh left Jane's chest. While this might be a dream come true for some women, this life was surprisingly stifling for Jane. Without Emma, and without friends, what did she have other than expensive clothes?

She rose from her dressing table, trying to remember to glide. Aunt Diana had chastised her during her last visit, telling her that she walked like a horse, clomping about. Fine ladies slid across ballrooms as if they didn't have feet. Especially on a night like tonight, when she was the hostess of a ball with all the right people.

The house positively bustled with activity. Jane did her best to glide downstairs, going to meet her husband in his study. She passed maids doing last-minute polishing of sconces and candlesticks and footmen carrying bouquets of flowers in vases she didn't recognize. Every so often, the door to the servants' stair opened and a whiff of something delicious wafted out.

For a moment, all Jane could think was that she wanted to get some kind of disfiguring disease. Smallpox would do if she could survive the illness. It would irritate Andrepont to no end having an unattractive wife. It was tempting.

His study door was closed and the passageway was dark. She rested her forehead against the heavy oak door, not wanting to knock. Not wanting to face him and all his unknowable expectations. If she was pretty enough, would he let her paint? If she was elegant enough, could she have a garden? What would it take to get something she wanted?

"Come in, Jane," Andrepont called from behind the door. "I can hear you breathing out there like an asthmatic pig."

Jane winced but entered. His feet were up on his desk, and he was in his shirtsleeves. The picture of relaxed entitlement. He was handsome with his cravat undone, revealing an expanse of his chest. She should have wanted him, craved his touch, but she didn't. "Good evening, my lord."

"Good evening, Jane," he said, not looking up from his book. "Are you ready for this evening's entertainment?"

She stood in her finery, waiting for him to notice that she was indeed ready.

"Is your resounding silence a sign of a positive or a negative answer?" He still didn't look at her, leafing through pages so fast the book must have been illustrated.

Irritation clawed at her, but she didn't dare say anything, not even to mention that guests would arrive in less than an hour and he still hadn't bathed. "I believe I am ready for our first party."

Andrepont looked up, his thumb on the page, as if he could only spare his attention for a moment or two. She'd hoped he would look at her and gasp, tell her she was beautiful, for she knew that she was. It was the only thing she knew.

He burst out laughing. "You're wearing *that?*"

Her cheeks heated but she said nothing. There was nothing to say, only to wait for his criticism. She tried desperately to not cast her eyes down to the floor, but it was such a strong instinct she couldn't fight it.

He got up from his desk and went to her, chucking her under the chin to lift her eyes and make her look at him. "Let's find you something more appropriate." He purred the words as if he were doing her a great favor.

But if she let him dress her, she would look like a harlot, and she didn't want to look like she sold her body. She didn't want lustful stares from men and scornful gazes from women. She wanted to be a success in this other world—the other world that her husband mocked and scorned.

"Thank you, my lord, for your attentions. But I received many good opinions from the dressmaker and Aunt Diana, and I think I shall stay in my current gown. Aunt Diana has approved this one for our welcoming of respectable society."

He dropped his hand from her face. She waited for a slap or an insult, or even for him to tear the dress from her body. But it didn't come. He was studying her.

Finally, she had the courage to look him directly in the eye.

"There's that backbone your sister had."

Jane flushed hot and then cold, knowing he'd only

said that to goad her. "I am ready to meet our guests when they arrive. I should very much like it if you were by my side."

His expression shifted and changed, unreadable, until he settled into a snake-like smile. He leaned in and whispered in her ear. "I like your resistance, Jane. The months cannot pass quickly enough for me."

And then he left, Jane's heart beating fast, like a rabbit's as it skitters to safety. If she had more time, she would cry. But there wasn't enough emotion left in her, so instead, she smoothed her skirts and went to the ballroom to oversee the servants even though her hands wouldn't stop shaking.

⚜

Vasya watched. He listened to talk around the table in the servant's hall. It was perfunctory at best. None of the ribbing one might find amongst young footmen, and no flirting between them and the maids. Mrs. Renwood and Mr. Vernon were stern, as they should be given their positions, but not overly so.

Cook served a simple stew and bread with cheese for the early meal, given the bustle for the party above them. There was nothing but slurps and the clank of metal spoons against clay bowls in the darkened servants' hall. Another contingent of servants would appear soon, and Cook would give them the same stew and bread and cheese. After all the garlands were hung, tapers lit, and platters set, they would change into their nicest livery, wigs and all, to serve London's powerbrokers.

He would know many of the men gathered, given that he'd taken their winnings at gaming hells across London before coming into Andrepont's employ. Maybe it had been a mistake to try to protect Lady

Andrepont—what could he do as a servant? He barely caught glimpses of her, so how would he protect her? It didn't make sense. But every one of his instincts told him to stay, that Gareth needed him nearby as he could not protect his sister-in-law while he was across the Atlantic Ocean.

But Vasya was not doing very well. He barely saw her, and when they were together, he didn't dare interfere. Vasya had seen the man slap her—it hadn't sat well with him, but he had allowed it to happen. There hadn't been a choice. If he'd spoken up against his master, he would have been sacked immediately, and then how could he help her when she really needed him?

All the servants knew of the marital contract's terms, that Andrepont wasn't supposed to bed her. Given how little the servants here talked—wasn't the hallmark of a servant knowing the best gossip?— Vasya was surprised it was common knowledge downstairs. But everyone agreed that Andrepont was honoring the terms. The chambermaids who left after four months were proof that the master of the house was not slaking his bodily needs with his wife. But they'd also left with bruises peeking out beneath sleeves, angry handprints marring their necks, and one who'd been unable to move her right arm.

To think that soon Lady Andrepont would be the sole focus of that man's attention.

That was when she would need him most—after this portion of the marriage was over and the beddings began. It hurt like a knife to his gut to think of it, but this was just another thing to suffer, another circumstance he could not change, only endure.

The footmen were dispatched to the gardens to carry in huge floral arrangements and garlands for decorations. But Vasya's real work would happen when the carriages started arriving. He would need to make sure the horses were cared for, keep track of which carriages were staying and which were leaving, and direct the traffic as required. But for now, lifting heavy things sounded like the work he needed to put his mind off his lady, so he followed the young men out to the gardens.

The time passed quickly, and the evening sun warmed him as he hauled in potted orange trees, four-foot-tall vases bursting with greenery, and buckets of flowers still in water, all for the party arranger who had been hired by Lady Andrepont's aunt. He thought he caught a glimpse of Lady Andrepont's skirts once, twirling just out of the frame. He was glad she hadn't seen him; he wasn't a fit sight for a lady as he and the other footmen were in only their shirtsleeves, keeping their livery clean for the evening.

There was a burst of energy when the temporary servants arrived and new men joined their decorating brigade. After the heavy things were arranged in proper corners, Vasya and the other footmen were dismissed. He returned to his quarters for a quick rag bath before donning his livery for the evening. He checked in with the aged stablemaster, Mr. Dendrum, and then found his way to the front of the house where he waited with a footman for guests to arrive.

"You nervous, mate?" asked a footman. He was so young that his face was still smooth and spotted.

Vasya harrumphed. "Why? There is no reason for nerves."

"It's a big party, yeah? So many fancy people. This is where you might find opportunities." The man couldn't keep himself still, shifting from foot to foot.

Vasya shook his head. This was no opportunity for a servant. This was work. But he had no wish to burst the hope this young man possessed. He wondered if he had ever been that young. There had been so very little hope in his childhood, and by the time he was this footman's age, he'd already been a part of a failed rebellion and had blood on his hands.

The evening was fading into full night. Another footman came out to light the sconces so the guests wouldn't descend in darkness. The door opened, but Vasya paid no attention. None of the traffic that went by appeared to be diverting into their semicircular drive. The first few carriages would be easy to manage. The fifteenth or twentieth? Mayhem.

"Is everything shaping up out here?" Lady Andrepont's soft voice was unmistakable.

Vasya whirled around, barely managing to secure his jaw. She was a vision. Her dress sported a higher square neckline than the gowns she'd worn while out with her husband, which undoubtedly made her feel more comfortable. But her hair sparkled, curled around jewels, with tendrils falling to her collarbone, making her seem more like a lady from a fable than a flesh-and-blood woman standing in front of him. The heavy ruby that dangled from her neck and nestled between her small breasts made it difficult for Vasya to keep his gaze above her collarbone.

"Yes, my lady," Vasya managed to say. The footman standing next to him was useless. Young men were easily the stupidest creatures. Older men, well . . . Vasya didn't feel like he was doing that much better at keeping himself together. He cleared his throat. "We are but waiting for guests to arrive."

"Excellent," she said, her gaze sweeping the grounds. She chewed her lip before catching herself at the habit. "I suppose I would better greet my guests inside. Excuse me."

Vasya and the footman both bowed as she left them, but the footman stared after her like a stray dog, so Vasya cuffed him on the shoulder. "Show some respect," he growled.

The boy rubbed his arm as if it had hurt. "I was."

Vasya eyed him, realizing now the difference in speaking about women that he hadn't understood during his conversations with Gareth. When a woman was his—not that he owned her or marked her, but needed to protect her—one did not stand by to hear those vulgar thoughts of other men. "She's your employer. Besides, Andrepont will have your balls if he finds out you're slobbering after his wife."

The thought of that seemed to be the bucket of cold water the boy needed. Fortunately, the first carriage arrived. Vasya breathed a sigh of relief. Work would take his mind off the place where that large red jewel had hung.

Hours passed quickly as Vasya guided carriages to waiting spots, fetched water, and made conversation with the coachmen from various estates. The network of gossip was not isolated to the servants below stairs. Here, with the carriages, there was plenty of talk.

The smell of the straw and the horses in the night air comforted Vasya, as did the conversations. He heard from many of the men that their masters and mistresses would not ordinarily attend a private ball thrown by Lord Andrepont, whose disreputable activities were widely known by the men of the *beau monde*. They had come because the invitations were followed by notes from Mrs. Fraser, Lady Andrepont's aunt. Finally, Lord Andrepont's choice of an unknown child bride was clear: here was the social cache required for Andrepont's future children.

Finally, Lady Andrepont was showing her worth, which pleased Vasya. However, the coachmen weren't as kind in their assessments of Lady Andrepont's person. Her bosom was discussed in great detail, urged by one driver in particular, until Vasya could get to the other side of the horses and put his fist in the man's mouth.

Vasya wasn't seeing red with outrage; rather, his disdain was crystal-clear and cold. He would happily beat any man who disrespected her. Who couldn't see her worth. She had already borne so much, and she was barely more than a child. He put his other fist in the man's belly.

The outcry was immediate. Another coachman came between Vasya and the man with the filthy, bloody mouth.

"What's this, what's this?" The coachman said, wearing not livery but plain clothes. He put his arm out to keep Vasya from continuing to pummel the other driver.

"He needs to watch his mouth," Vasya said, fairly salivating over the violence. The sight of the man panting and spitting blood riled him. It had been too long since he'd bloodied his fists, and the surge of his pulse thrumming in his ears was a sweet melody. He would fight all night, happily so.

"Too right, sir, too right. The young men don't know when to keep it to themselves. Those are ladies in there, lad, and you don't speak of them," the coachman said to Vasya's victim and the others who had joined in on the banter and speculation. Then he said to Vasya, "I know a man must protect his household, and fair play to you, sir, for doing your diligence. But might you cool off in some part of the garden for a moment?"

Vasya snarled, placated that the man recognized his authority and his righteousness but unhappy to be told to take a walk. He was also angry with himself for losing his temper. He was not a man made for servitude. He stalked off, finding the gardener's doorway to the back, hidden as it was by ivy.

The gardeners had made hedgerows, clipped and

tidy, coming only to Vasya's midthighs. They were stout enough that he could not just tromp through them as he wished. No, he had to move this way, then that way, making him more frustrated—he only wanted to stride through to the bench that sat between the tall, thin Italian cypresses. It gave a full view of the ballroom but remained hidden in shadow. He'd sat there often enough watching Lady Andrepont, Mrs. Fraser, and whichever hired hand make plans for the ball.

He accidentally kicked an animal as he waded through the shrubbery. A cat, a rat, who cared? It went skittering through the underbrush. His temper ebbed. Young men talked about women. Vasya knew this. Many men his age still spoke in that vulgarity. But he'd known young women with just as much fire, just as much violence and rebellion in their hearts as he'd had. Women who were tired of the yolk of the noblemen, ready to bloody themselves for freedom.

When a man comes to realize that and sees that women fight their wars, too, there's no need to talk of them without the respect one might show another warrior. He was ashamed that it had only now occurred to him. He trudged through the small yard between the hedges and cypresses, pulling up short when he saw a figure already on the bench.

The shadow was small, almost a heap of fabric in the low light that spilled from the house. He lightened his steps, approaching as one might approach a rabid dog. "Miss, are you well?" he called, doing his best to smooth out his accent. He knew it made English women uncomfortable.

There was a hiccup of surprise, and the woman shot to her feet. It was then that he recognized Lady Andrepont. He quickly bowed.

"My lady, I beg your pardon. I didn't mean to disturb you."

She sniffed in the dark, sounding as if she'd been crying. "No, no. You surprised me. I was only taking some air away from . . . from . . ." She waved her hands towards the ballroom.

"Yes. The house seems . . ." He momentarily forgot how to speak English. "Stifling." He put his hands behind his back, as if this might make him smaller. It did not.

Lady Andrepont sighed and plopped herself down on the stone bench in a childlike manner. She might hold the titles of viscountess and wife, but she was nothing but a girl not quite seven and ten. Vasya sat carefully on the other edge of the bench, balancing so that one massive thigh hung off, giving her plenty of room.

"This is not what I expected."

Vasya grunted, not knowing what to say in return. But she seemed like she needed a friendly ear, and he could at least help her in that way, so he waited. She would either return to the party or continue to talk. Either way was well within his ability.

"What am I saying?" She sighed. "I didn't know what to expect. I thought they would be well-behaved. Noblemen, they're called. Noble. That should mean something, shouldn't it?"

Vasya said nothing, but he couldn't help but agree. He dared not tell her what he had done when he'd felt the same way.

"I suppose I'm one of them now, a *lady*." She didn't seem pleased by her elevation. "But I'm not a lady, I'm not. Nothing changed for me but a name. I'm still me on the inside. Still just Jane who would much rather sift through dirt than throw expensive parties and listen to everyone's sordid stories, smelling their rotting teeth from up close." She slumped forward like a petulant child, her elbows on her knees, her smooth chin balanced on her fists.

"I've done what was asked of me. I've fulfilled my end of the bargain. How have I not gotten a single thing I've wanted?"

Vasya frowned. This he did not like. "What did you want?"

"My sister. But she's in the colonies, so that can't be helped. But after that, a greenhouse. A place to grow plants and flowers, to keep studying the herbcraft I had wanted to devote my life to back in Chilton. I studied very hard. I'm quite smart, you know, when I put my mind to it."

"I believe you," Vasya said. He quickly riffled through what would be needed for a greenhouse. It would take some time to find glass panes, and he'd need to figure out the best builders. And then there was the money. Well, it was something for him to think about.

"It's just . . . once I became somebody, the more nobody I became." Jane sat up as Lord Andrepont came into view through the ballroom window. She pulled herself back into the shadows. "You know, I thought he'd come to like me. Tolerate me, even. I'm not so bad—not near as pretty as Emma, I know, but I have other things to recommend me. I've been told I have beautiful eyes. That's something, is it not?"

To say her eyes were beautiful was to call the sea big. The fact was true, but hardly enough. Her eyes were a luminous, bright green. Easily the most beguiling color he'd ever seen, even throughout all his travels. "Yes" was all he could say.

"I think he hates me." She pulled her light-colored skirts away from the streaks of light, concealing herself further.

"I think he hates everyone. Including himself." Vasya hadn't thought much on it before, but as he spoke the words, they rang of truth. The man was nothing but ill will and brinkmanship. A man of honor did not need those tools as they rotted the soul from the inside as well as the outside.

"Nothing I do will ever be enough, will it?" she whispered.

Vasya's great chest heaved with grief for her future. No one deserved this. "No," he agreed.

But instead of bursting into tears as he expected her to do, she narrowed her eyes as she gazed at her husband through the glass. "Then there's no point in trying."

Vasya's heart skipped. He wanted to warn her of what violence might come if she displeased him. What he might try to bend her into line. But this, too, was not his place. He didn't have a place from which to advise. Besides, what expertise did he have? He had nothing. He'd started with nothing and he was still, twenty-eight years on, with nothing. He had his body. His strength. The forbidding black beard that seemed to stop everyone in London mid-stride. "If you or anyone in the house needs protection, come find me. I will do my best."

She looked over at him in surprise. It was the first time he'd felt her gaze land fully on his face. She didn't appear scared, merely pleased, perhaps surprised. "Thank you, Vasily Nikolaevich."

Warmth coursed through him as she said his name, and he grunted, willing himself to control his emotions. He was surprised she remembered his name. Surprised that she could say it so smoothly, the syllables dancing out of her mouth, instead of tumbling like a rockslide. "I should return to my duties with the carriages."

"Oh," she said, seeming to shake herself. "And I ought to return to mine. These old lechers are disgusting. But someday I'll want them on my side, I'm sure."

Vasya wanted to squeeze her hand for reassurance.

"In my experience, men say such things because they believe no one will chastise them for it. Make them feel a cad, and perhaps they will stop."

She stood and bestowed a dazzling smile on him. It was as if a horse had kicked him square in the chest. "Excellent advice, sir. I shall maintain my dignity at all costs."

"Goodnight, my lady. Good luck." He bowed to her, and for the first time when performing the gesture, he meant it. He meant it in the old ways of bowing—respect, fidelity, honor.

"Thank you. And Godspeed to you, as well, Vasily Nikolaevich." She melted into the light as she made her way through the garden, her dress shimmering as she went.

CHAPTER 8

"Come," Andrepont commanded as he pushed into the drawing room.

He startled her. Jane was working on her watercolors and wore an apron over her day dress. The brush skipped across the page, marring the white space with a dab of the yellow she'd been using for highlights. She blinked first at the page and then at him. Was he here to finally give her the art lesson he'd promised?

Then she noticed his riding clothes. Of course not.

"You don't ride your horse enough. Come." Andrepont extended his arm and gestured at her as if she were a willful child. Given the riding whip already in his hand, she didn't dare disobey or ask for time to clean up her project. She dropped the brush into the small pot of water and removed her apron.

As soon as she crossed the threshold, his arm was around her, guiding her up the stairs to her bedroom. Hope was laying out her riding habit—a wine-red skirt lined with a gold military-style waistcoat and dark green jacket with gold brocade work. It was beautiful work, so feminine despite the masculine cut of the dress.

Both Jane and Hope looked to Andrepont to leave, but he merely sat down on the vanity stool. He leaned back, his long legs stretched out and crossed at the ankle. He gestured at the women as if they were a performance.

Jane felt something hard gather in her throat. "My lord, if you would please excuse us?"

"Why? I own this room. I own you. And I pay you," he said, gesturing with the horsewhip. The sound of it slicing through the air put Jane on edge.

Hope looked to Jane, clearly willing to protest this trespass. But that whip in his hand made Jane nervous. She didn't like how he looked so at ease wielding it in the house. Pointing it at her. Though she had no doubt Hope would feel the brunt of it long before Jane would. But Jane would have to watch because Andrepont knew how much his wife loved and depended on her lady's maid.

"Help me with these buttons," Jane whispered, turning her back so that Hope could begin undressing her.

Andrepont said nothing but watched them carefully, as if he thought they were there to steal the silver. Jane stepped out of her day dress, trying very hard to not feel exposed as her husband perused her figure in her shift and short stays.

The shift was of fine linen, and there was no doubt that he could see every bump of gooseflesh on her legs.

"It's cold today. You'll probably need to change into a woolen shift to keep warm," Andrepont said.

Hope looked at Jane again, her eyes pleading to protest. Changing shifts would mean the stays would come off. She would be bared completely. Jane hesitated. This felt wrong. But he held that horsewhip for a reason.

Andrepont gestured at them to continue, his face expectant and bored. He slashed through the air, making both Jane and Hope jump.

"Yes, my lord," Jane whispered. Hope's hands were shaking as she started to undo the laces of Jane's stays.

A knock at the door startled them all. "My lord," came the gruff and unmistakably accented voice of Vasily Nikolaevich. "There is an issue with your mount for today. You'll need to come attend to it."

Andrepont stood but huffed in annoyance, the horsewhip swishing through the air, its menace quiet and constant. Jane held her breath.

"I'll see you down there," he said, leaving the room with long, heavy strides. When the door closed behind him, both women sagged in relief.

"Hurry," Jane said, pulling the strings of her stays, wanting to change to the woolen shift before he might think up a way to return while she was still dressing.

They rushed, both of them moving, deft fingers tying and pinning. Hope spun and asked, "Wig?"

It was customary for women to wear big powdered wigs on which to perch the flat bonnets, letting colored ribbons lay against the white-gray background of the false hair. Jane nodded. It would be faster to pin the wig on than attempt a suitable hairstyle. Jane sat on the stool, still warm from Andrepont's occupancy, and tried to compose herself.

She reminded herself that Andrepont had done nothing. He had not belittled her, and he had not harmed her. Everyone was safe. So why was she terrified?

Once readied, she donned her bonnet and gloves in the foyer and exited the house, finding her horse paired with her husband's, saddled and waiting. Vasily Nikolaevich held the horses, but he watched her.

She wished she could thank him for pulling her husband from her room, but knew she could not. She willed it in her mind, for him to know what a service he had done for her, that she was grateful for his interference.

It was with disappointment that she noted a different groom would be following them out on their ride today. The young man was already mounted, waiting for them. Andrepont checked his own mount's saddle and fussed. "I don't see what the problem is. Everything is perfectly well. If you can't figure that out, you haven't the knowledge you claim and I ought to sack you." His dark eyes narrowed at Vasily Nikolaevich.

"My apologies, my lord. It must have been bloat." The large man never wavered in his confidence.

"Pay better attention next time." Andrepont swung himself up on his horse, and then Jane stepped up the mounting block herself.

She was not an accomplished rider and this horse made her nervous. It was still a bit wild, and its eyes would roll back every so often, spooking her. This horse seemed to delight in scaring her, just as her own husband did.

"Do you require assistance, my lady?" Vasily Nikolaevich rumbled, tying off her horse's reins and coming around to her.

"No," Jane said, her voice barely above a whisper. "I can do this." She settled into the sidesaddle, her knee hooking hard as she spread her skirts out. She was a lady. She was a viscountess. She was proper. She was regal. She exhaled heavily and nodded her readiness.

Vasily Nikolaevich bowed his head to her, untying her horse's reins and handing them to her. Her hands were clammy inside her thick riding gloves. She took the reins, trying to remember just how she was supposed to hold them, but Andrepont's lessons were hard to recall as she'd been so afraid during them.

Andrepont shook his head, annoyed, and clicked his horse to begin walking. Jane's horse peeled off behind him, the great beast's saunter jarring her. Fear rose in her, but she tamped it down.

She heard the groom's horse behind her.

By the time they arrived at Rotten Row, she'd grown almost confident. As long as they did no more than walk, she could handle the horse. She leaned forward, petting the beast's beautiful dark mane, wanting to create a bond with the animal like the ones she'd read about in novels. Some young ladies were horse-mad, but she was not one of them. She wished to be, but her fear was difficult to overcome.

Before Jane could sit up, a rough step caused her to fall forward and lose her balance on her seat. The groom swiftly rode up, but Andrepont merely snorted at her foolishness. Jane righted herself, her cheeks coloring.

"Ah, Andrepont!" A man called from atop another horse.

As they approached and stopped to chat, Jane recognized the man—the young Lord Denby. He gave her merely a cursory glance, his distaste clear from his sneer. She didn't know if it was distaste for her, her position, or her clothing, which revealed nothing.

"I assume you've heard the news." Denby's skeletal face held a ghoulish smile.

Jane shivered.

"Percy, Lord Aberscomb, has perished." Denby gave a mocking frown. "The heir to that wretched house succumbed to some kind of sickness."

Jane's hand went to her mouth with a gasp. "What illness was it?"

Denby waved his hand, annoyed that she'd spoken. He didn't look at her. "Le grippe, pleurisy, who cares?"

Andrepont didn't say much, allowing Denby to talk at length about his dislike of the man and his family. The family that now included Jane's sister. Oh dear. She remembered her Debrett's. This meant Captain Somerset was now the heir to an earldom. He had become the new Lord Aberscomb, meaning Emma was now a viscountess, just like her.

Jane slid her gaze to her husband. The muscle in his jaw worked. He could be annoyed by the realization that Emma would now be a viscountess. Or perhaps her speaking had annoyed him. Or Denby's loquaciousness annoyed him. Jane stared off at the other promenading groups, all in high fashion, all stopping to discuss the gossip of the day. No doubt the death would be a popular topic.

And then she wondered if this was why Andrepont had hauled her out here. He'd never asked her to ride with him before. Was this his way of torturing her? Taunting her with the news that Lord Aberscomb was dead? Who knew why her husband did what he did? She'd never believe he did things to help her, to make her happy. And so why should she fret about the mysterious why?

She recalled the conversation she'd had with Vasily Nikolaevich on the garden bench the night of the party. The large man with the kind voice had convinced her that nothing she could do for Andrepont would ever be correct. It sounded petulant, childlike, but it was true. And once again, she thought, why should she worry over it?

The only praise he ever gave her was that she resembled her sister in some way.

A faint hope speared her. Would Aberscomb's passing mean Captain Somerset would leave the war and return to England now that he was the heir to an earldom? The longing for her sister echoed through her bones.

"I want to go home," she told the groom quietly. She didn't ask for permission as she should have. She didn't say a word to her husband. Another man had arrived on horseback, and Andrepont had angled even further away from her.

"Of course, my lady."

The groom escorted her home—slowly—and without incident. She'd likely get a reprimand of some sort for this. But she didn't care. Her sister would return to her. She only needed to bide her time. It would be months, of course. Sea travel wasn't fast, and certainly not in the middle of a war.

⊱✦⊰

A BOY POUNDED ON THE BACK DOOR, ASKING FOR Vasya during the servant's evening meal. Vasya stood, under the watchful gaze of the rest of the staff, and wisely closed the door so that none could overhear.

"I'm to tell you the news, sir," the boy said breathlessly, taking his cap off to wipe his forehead. His fair hair was greasy with soot, its light color peering from beneath the dirt.

Vasya eyed the slender boy, wishing he had a bit of cake or bread for him. He was nothing but skin and bones. But Vasya didn't dare go back into the servant's hall before hearing this message. Instead, he guided the boy over to the pump and got him a cup of water.

The boy gulped it down. "I come from Lord Aberscomb's place."

Vasya frowned. He'd heard the man had died some weeks back.

"His wife is returned." The boy burped loudly.

"Lord Aberscomb didn't have a wife." That was common knowledge. Was someone who trying to impersonate his widow to gain access to money? It was a bold move, but not original.

"No, no, not that Lord Aberscomb. The next one. The brother, fighting in the colonies."

Vasya nodded, understanding dawning. The nobility and their titles. Easy to forget when names changed so quickly. So Mrs. Somerset had returned. He wanted to see her, but he wouldn't have a moment until the following Sunday, when he got his half-day. And where was Gareth?

"She wants to see her sister but is afraid of sending word. Afraid that her sister might not receive the message."

"She said those words?" Vasya asked.

"Those are the words I was bid to say," the boy clarified.

Vasya rumbled his understanding. Interesting that the boy didn't say "her ladyship" or "viscountess." Perhaps Lady Aberscomb kept her own counsel and didn't want it to be known who her sister was. Or didn't want to acknowledge it. And she was likely right. Andrepont received all missives and then doled out that which was allowed to pass his censorship. A missive from Lady Aberscomb would not be welcome.

"Thank you," Vasya said, clapping a hand on the boy's shoulder. He fished in his pocket for a ha'penny and handed it over. "I will get you some food."

"Your horseback riding lesson is all arranged," Hope said, bustling in with a freshly pressed gown. The smile on her face was genuine and sly. "If I'd known sooner, I would have pressed the green riding habit, but as it is, the blue one is the least creased."

Jane sat at her dressing table, brushing out her hair. She knew nothing of a riding lesson. Had Andrepont seen how terrified she'd been after their ride in the park? He'd not seen her since she left him without a word. She'd expected some kind of punishment for that, but perhaps he'd understood and forgiven her. That didn't seem like him at all. Likely something else had taken his attention, or perhaps he was concocting even more discomfort for her. "What is in your hands then?"

Hope waved away her concern. "This is your morning dress for calling. I didn't know your plans, but in case you'd decided to go out, this would be suitable. But it isn't at all good for riding. It's far too fussy, and the ribbons would catch something frightful." Hope went to the wardrobe and stowed it away, work to be resumed at a later time.

"Perhaps when I'm done with my riding lesson." Jane frowned, suddenly thinking about calling on new acquaintances. She'd honestly been thinking only of continuing her watercolors. "I do have some new friends I'd like to visit."

Since the ball they'd hosted, Jane had managed to make acquaintances with a few young women. All of them were married to men who were much older and had little in common with them. Aunt Diana had introduced this small cadre of wives who needed friends. Now that Hope mentioned it, it might be nice to see Lady Haglund today. She seemed kind and vibrant in a way that Jane felt drawn to. Jane herself had always been so steady and Emma so serious. It was interesting to be around a woman so bright.

"As you wish. I'll have it ready for you. I'm supposed to tell you that Vasily Nikoleavich will be ready for you out front at half past."

Jane felt her eyebrow raise of its own volition. It was her tell, and she knew it, but goodness knew she couldn't stop it. Vasily Nikoleavich was to be her riding tutor? The man who had saved her from Andrepont's lechery. The man who'd given her such kind words during her garden break at the party. She tried to keep her small smile to herself. Warmth skittered through her at the thought of his kind attentions. "Then we must hurry, Hope."

When Jane walked out the townhome's front door, there were two horses tied to the post in front, her gloriously imposing chestnut and a smaller dappled mare that looked sweet and inviting.

"Good morning, Vasily Nikolaevich," she greeted, daring to pet the small, dappled mare.

"Good morning, my lady," he said. "I have brought you an easier mount to learn upon."

"Thank you," she said, and she meant it. The chestnut was too tall for her by half and had an aggressive temperament that she didn't know how to control.

Vasily helped her onto the dappled mare, and while she arranged her skirts, he mounted the chestnut. Jane was content to follow him on an easy canter down whatever path he preferred. In the beginning, she rode behind him, both herself and the mare happily led. But by the time they arrived at the wide thoroughfares of Rotten Row, she went abreast of him. This was so different from the terror she'd felt yesterday with her husband.

Vasily glanced at her, sizing up her seat, her hand position. "You do well," he said. "Your posture is good. Try to move more with the horse. It will keep you from sore muscles later."

She nodded at his advice, beaming at his compliment. Still, she felt as if she were doing something illicit, riding with a groom instead of with her husband, even though it was perfectly common and respectable. But somehow, being with Vasily Nikolaevich, it felt different. Bolder. Better. "Did Andrepont arrange this?"

"No," he said with equal frankness, but he did not elaborate.

Silence fell between them as Jane searched for the correct question to ask, hoping the taciturn Russian might answer of his own volition. But that was not her luck. "Is my riding so terrible that I need this lesson? Or is this a new horse that I need to get to know?" She liked this sweet mare.

Vasily Nikolaevich gave her an amused glance. "You looked uncomfortable yesterday. If you wish to accompany your husband, you must practice your riding."

Jane nodded, patting the mare, not losing her seat because this horse fit her size so much better. She smiled at it.

"Do you like that mount?" he asked, noticing her affection.

Jane nodded. "She fits me better. I don't feel like I'll fall off of her. What's her name?"

"Whatever you wish it to be. She is yours." Vasily was in profile to her, but still, Jane thought she saw a satisfied smirk on his face.

"Where did she come from? Did Andrepont want her for me because of yesterday?"

The groom frowned. "The stablemaster is the man who oversees his lordship's stock. This mare lived in the country until recently."

Jane looked around, taking in the trees, longing

again for the countryside. She and this mare definitely had something in common. No wonder she felt so at ease with her. "So you had her moved into Town for me?"

Vasily Nikolaevich nodded. "I did. Some weeks back."

Jane's cheeks heated. He'd known she wasn't a confident rider. Did he see her? Know she needed something different than what Andrepont wanted for her? That warmth spread through her again, but she stopped it. No, he was a groomsman, her husband's driver. This was his job. And a good servant anticipated his employer's needs and wants. She wasn't special to him, she convinced herself, despite desperately wishing to be special to someone. But she looked at his face again. He wore a look of soft amusement. The look of someone who had another surprise. "What is it?"

"What is what, my lady?" He gave her a quirked grin that made him look almost boyish despite his jet-black beard.

"You look very satisfied with yourself, sir."

He looked at her in surprise with her added teasing honorific. But his smile grew. "I have some very good news for you."

"Good news is always welcome." Jane looked around, noticing they had changed direction and were heading to another neighborhood. He had a plan indeed.

"I received word that your sister is back in London and eager to see you."

The words hit her as if she'd fallen from her mare. "Emma? Is in London? Why did you not tell me sooner?" Jane was ready to kick the mare to a fast cantor when Vasily Nikolaevich shot his arm out to block her.

"Because your husband should not know. He will

not be happy for you to see her. You must be careful. So this is a riding lesson, and all of London will have seen you doing well at it."

Jane nodded, her heart still thumping and thrumming. Emma! "But riding faster could be a part of the lesson, could it not?"

He considered her. "Do you know how?"

Jane shook her head. "No. I'm not a terribly good horsewoman."

"We will change that. But we will get to our destination safely, and without attracting attention."

She bit her lip, impatient. Emma would have to have boarded a ship long before the previous Aberscomb's death. What could have prompted her to return so soon? She couldn't speak for the rest of the ride, pondering over Emma, wondering everything about her life. Jane still didn't know why Emma had run off with the Captain, as it was out of character for her to be so impulsive. Jane desperately wanted to talk to her sister, tell her about her own strange union, ask if she'd known about Andrepont's temperament.

Vasily Nikolaevich held the horses while Jane knocked on the door of the smart townhome. Compared to her own home, this townhouse was small, though both were grander than the home their father had rented.

The butler opened the door and bade Jane wait while he informed Emma of who was calling. Jane brushed off her skirts even though they had not ridden very far. Still, the dirt of London was pervasive.

As the minutes ticked on, Jane wanted to rush upstairs, calling Emma's name. Formalities be damned! This was her sister. The other half of her heart!

Finally, finally! Emma's face appeared at the top of

the stairs. She was rounder, her dark hair simply done, but her eyes shone. When her belly came into view, Jane froze.

Emma was pregnant. So very pregnant. Jane burst out laughing. And then, when Emma reached her, trying to pull her into a hug, Jane found herself crying. She buried herself in her sister's familiar scent, her hair, and let go of all the bits of herself she'd been holding back.

"You!" Emma said, pulling back to look at her.

The happiness in her sister's face was unmistakable. Jane wiped the tears from her cheeks, smiling so hard that even her ears hurt.

"Come, come up for tea or cake or whatever it is that I can serve you." Emma grasped her sister and Jane held her in return, as if neither wanted to let the other go.

"I have a man outside," Jane said, realizing as she spoke that Emma likely knew Vasily Nikolaevich.

"Invite him around back. There's a stable for your horses if you'd like to stay. I don't have a groom at the moment." Emma gave an odd smile.

Jane felt suddenly unsteady. "My groom is Vasily Nikolaevich."

Emma's face lit up. "Then he must come in!" She waddled past Jane and threw open the heavy front door. "Vasya!"

It took a moment for Jane to realize she'd called him something different. Something familiar. Something Jane had not been invited to do. She didn't like that it irked her, but she followed Emma out to the top step where she spoke to him.

Vasily Nikolaevich's face split into a wide grin when he saw her straining belly. Tears shone in his eyes. "I had heard, but I did not know for sure. Many congratulations to you, my lady."

"Pah," Emma scoffed, waving a hand. "I haven't

gotten used to that. I'm so sorry that I do need you to stable the horses, but please come in afterwards. I know Martha will be pleased to see you."

Another sharp poke. Jane did not like that there was a Martha who would be pleased to see him. Who might also call him Vasya. She cast her eyes down. It wasn't her business. She was a married woman, and barely more than a child. Vasily Nikoleavich was a full-grown man who had life experiences and had traveled the world. He surely had already taken lovers and maybe even a wife somewhere, while she was cloistered and small and knew nothing. Did not even know her own marriage bed. Her cheeks burned.

Emma led Jane upstairs to a light, spacious drawing room. Already fit for a lady, Emma was at ease in a space where she hadn't been but for hardly a moment.

"How long have you been back?" Jane asked.

Emma thought. "I'm so exhausted I could hardly tell you. Two days? Maybe three?"

Jane nodded, her ego petted that Emma had reached out to her quickly and quietly. "Have you contacted Papa or Aunt Diana? Papa is still in Town."

A line creased Emma's forehead. It made her seem matronly. "I haven't. I didn't want to have that kind of discontent during these last weeks." Emma traced a finger along the quick rise of her rotund belly.

Martha Foraker bustled in with an excellent spread of tea and sweets and buns. Between the two of them, Jane and Emma had a repast fit for Queen Marie Antoinette herself. But neither of them touched it.

Emma introduced Martha to Jane. She was not much older than Emma, Jane guessed, but flame-red hair escaped her cap, and her freckled face made it obvious that she was a ginger. Jane once again noted how different she was from this maid who would be pleased to see Vasily Nikolaevich.

They sat in the drawing room, Emma apologizing as she groaned and put her feet up on the chaise longue. Her feet were swollen and her slippers cut into the bulging white flesh.

"Mrs. Houseman always made this lovely warming oil for new mothers, massaging their feet when they became swollen like this."

"Bless Mrs. Houseman, wherever she may be. That woman was a miracle. I've wished for her many a time during this." Emma closed her eyes, her excitement momentarily erased by fatigue.

"I helped her plenty. I could make some for you," Jane said, already thinking about where she might find some of the ingredients. She wished she had a garden again. The kind like Mrs. Houseman had, near to the size of a small farm, with rows and rows of herbs and helpful plants.

Emma blindly put her hand out, and Jane immediately grasped it. They were together. It had been worth the ordeal. Here was Emma, bringing in new life. Jane's focus drifted out the window, thinking of other small comforts Mrs. Houseman would bring to pregnant women. Jane frowned. There had been a few concoctions that were not for women in the late stages of pregnancy. She would need to write Mrs. Houseman since there was no way Andrepont would allow her to go to the country to visit her.

"Oh!" Emma exclaimed, then smiled. "Look." Her belly jumped like a Punch and Judy show. "He's got the hiccups."

The bouncing baby belly made Jane laugh, and having such joy in the room relieved her. She hadn't known how long it had been since the last time she truly laughed. "You know it's a boy?"

"In here." Emma tapped her chest, over her heart.

"But I'm also carrying low, and that's what everyone says. But I know it's true, too."

Jane looked from the bouncing belly up to Emma's face, as if the belly was its own beast.

"Did you know that I am married?" Jane asked, her voice low.

"I'd heard." Emma rubbed her belly, not looking at Jane.

"I am a viscountess, just like you," Jane said. "Who would've thought the Laurent sisters worked so quickly?"

Emma's mouth lost its joy, and her jaw muscles hardened. "I'm sorry. I—"

Jane didn't want to hear any apology. "What's done is done, Em."

Emma glanced over. "He's not a good man."

Jane couldn't help but let out a rueful laugh. Emma didn't know the half of it. Jane suspected she didn't know either. "I know."

"Has he—" Emma winced, not continuing her question.

But Jane figured out what she wanted to know. "Aunt Diana insisted that he cannot visit my bed until I turn eighteen."

Emma sighed in relief, putting her hand over her eyes. "Small mercies." Then she reached over with her hand and grasped Jane again. Neither of them spoke.

Jane felt as if she should say something about the complex nature of Emma's life—her baby, the death of her husband's brother, her elevation to countess, what experiencing war had been like. Emma had lived for this past year, while Jane had merely survived.

Like always, her older sister beat her to it. "My father-in-law, Lord Lorian, has offered me a country house to stay in. I would have the baby there and spend the first few months there. He thinks the slower country pace would be better for me. The country air."

Jane's spirits lifted merely thinking about it. "The country? Where?"

"Not terribly far from Chilton, as it happens," Emma said. Jane could see her sister's mind whirring like gears in a clock. "I would like to have you there for the lying-in. Just in case."

"I haven't been to the country since we left home," Jane said. It had been almost two years since she'd last seen its wide spaces and old trees.

Tears welled up in Emma's eyes and she turned her head, trying to blink away the tears. "Pregnancy makes me such a ninny!"

"Oh Emma, that isn't fair. You've always been a ninny."

Emma gave her a playful slap on the arm. "Have a bun, you monster."

"Pour you a cup?" Jane asked. Already she was wondering how she could convince Andrepont to let her stay in the country with her sister.

"Please," Emma said. "If you can manage without overturning the entire tray."

Jane gave Emma the cool viscountess expression that she'd been practicing, then poured the tea.

"That was very graceful," Emma said, her compliment careful.

"It should be—I've practiced enough." Jane presented the cup to Emma, who rested it on her belly since it was large enough to be its own tray. Jane then poured her own cup and added sugar. She sat back in the settee and pushed away the old memories of her wedding morning with Andrepont, cleaning spilled tea and shattered porcelain from the floor of the drawing room. Jane's jaw clenched and unclenched.

Emma pushed the teacup handle around and

around her belly. "Why—what compelled you to marry him?"

Jane looked at her, knowing there were some things she might never share with her sister. Living with Andrepont compelled Jane to create a space inside her heart that no one could ever go to. Not even Emma. "There was a broken contract to mend. There are handsome stipulations attached. One of them being Papa's acceptance of your return." Jane dropped her eyes to her teacup.

There was nothing to say to that. Emma had broken the contract. This was Emma's fault. But Jane had said yes. Jane had walked down the aisle of that church. Jane had accepted the terms.

"If I had known—"

"Did he hit you? Is that why you ran off with Captain Somerset?" Jane asked, her expression mild, as if they were discussing the weather.

Emma's cheeks flushed. "I saw him choking and attempting to violate a maidservant at the ball, just before they were set to announce the engagement. I knew I couldn't marry a man like that. No woman should."

Jane nodded. "What happened to the servant?"

Emma shook her head. "She ran away. I hoped he couldn't find her again."

Jane looked at the banked fireplace, the day warm enough to not require it.

"Are you well?" Emma asked, trying to regain Jane's attention.

Jane smiled, but it wasn't a true one. The past year had been eye-opening. Trying. But she was stronger than people thought. "Perfectly well. Merely thinking about what I need to do in order to be in the country with you. I should be able to stay there until my next birthday, I believe."

Emma nodded. "I'm glad. Won't you miss London? Your friends?"

Jane snorted and rolled her eyes. Friends. Surely married women didn't have friends, did they? "No one will miss me." But it would take work to join Emma. She'd have to be very careful about how she handled it, because there was no other place she'd rather be. With Emma, in the countryside? It sounded like a dream.

CHAPTER 9

AFTER – DAY 3

"AMr. Eier," Mr. Afreé announced. Jane looked up from her letter. The balding man stepped into the room, his face tight.

Jane heaved the desk off her lap and stood, brushing her skirts free of whatever wrinkles might have creased. "Mr. Eier. Please, come in. I've been expecting you. Mr. Afreé, some refreshments, please." Jane invited him to sit in the chair across from her. His long stride ate the distance as he crossed the drawing room, every movement efficient. He bowed to her when he arrived at his seat.

"Lady Andrepont, thank you for seeing me." He waited until she sat, then mirrored the action.

"Of course, Mr. Eier. Do you have news?"

"I fear for your delicate condition. Perhaps you have someone you might call to bolster yourself?"

Jane could feel her eyebrow moving skyward. Someone to lean on in her time of need? No such person existed. She was more solid than Hadrian's Wall had ever been. "No need, Mr. Eier. Pray, continue." Jane was tired of making a show of her weakness. She was all iron and sinew these days.

He picked at a loose thread on the inseam of his pants. "Then I must apologize in advance for the trouble I'm about to cause."

Jane waited. She wasn't about to faint over a conversation.

"As you know, my duties as coroner bid me to be thorough. When I opened the body yesterday evening, I noticed that many of his internal organs seemed to be . . . not well."

Jane's stomach clenched. "What does that mean?"

"It means that I believe someone had been poisoning him for some time. Likely in his food. This puts your entire household under suspicion."

"Does it?" Jane asked mildly. "He typically took his meals at his club and in other households. He rarely ate at home in the last decade or so."

Mr. Eier slid his notebook out of his waistcoat pocket. "Is that a fact? Why did you not mention this earlier?"

"I doubt the discontent of my husband in our household was of any import when discussing highwaymen."

"I see your point, my lady, begging your pardon. Still, it behooves me to bring an inquest on behalf of the deceased." Mr. Eier returned the notebook to his pocket once he finished scribbling.

Jane sighed as if she were the bereaved and put-upon widow. Which, incidentally, she was, but not for the reasons he might believe. Gone was the biddable girl whom Andrepont had eaten up over the years. Her heart should be pounding. She should be afraid. But she was too angry for that. Too angry about her stolen decades. "But who will you charge with his murder?"

The man's mouth opened and closed like a fish. "I still have the rest of the evening."

She stared him down, and he at least had the

decency to squirm. "Mr. Eier. To be clear. You wish me to forego my mourning, the preparations for my husband's funeral, the letters I must write, the bills I must pay, so that I may sit in a cold office and testify that someone, of whom we have no idea, may have poisoned him, or may have stabbed him, or may have strangled him. An event that I did not witness, nor have I seen my husband since this unfortunate occurrence. Do you hear yourself speaking? Do you not see how absurd this is?"

There was a commotion downstairs but Jane ignored it. She was so furious that even Mr. Eier didn't dare look away from her.

"My husband is dead. He had responsibilities to the Crown, which will now fall to my young son, who is not prepared to hold the weight of a title. And you wish me to go withstand a gruesome inquest? To what end? Do you believe you will find the person who dumped his body in the Thames?"

"Lady Andrepont, I see that you are upset by the thought of justice, which, may I say, is not what I expected—"

James appeared in the doorway. He wore his traveling coat and looked far more grown than the last time she'd seen him. His shoulders were beginning to widen in a way that looked at odds with the rest of his young boy's body. She saw his open, vulnerable expression, and it viscerally hurt her. What had she done? She'd taken his father from him, the only person who could explain his position in the world, the expectations of his title, even if his father was a monster.

"Oh," Jane gasped.

"Mama?" His voice was still a boy's voice, and the way he called to her made her body ache as if he were still a babe. He was only twelve years old. Not near old enough to forego his mother's embrace.

Jane stood and he ran to her, stopping short of her embrace when he spied Mr. Eier. He couldn't be a little boy when confronted with a stranger. Jane understood. This was another moment that divided their lives into "before" and "after." This was the moment when James became a man—when James became the viscount in truth.

His shoulders straightened and he looked the man over coolly. "And you are?"

Jane heard his voice deepen, the cold shield of his title come down, and she mourned it. Mourned the thousands of things she wished she could have shielded him from. Her pride in his strength. Her fear that he might turn into his father. And how she felt all of these in the same instant, his eyebrow rising, a trait he'd inherited from her.

No, James was her boy. Creating him was her doing. Her hand formed a fist. The desire to keep control of this room filled her. But she would allow this disruption. If nothing else, it only bolstered her position that Mr. Eier could do nothing. His impotence was obvious. Because of James's title, Mr. Eier still had to defer. Jane smiled, and she knew it was a vicious one.

BEFORE

Vasya measured the footprint of the greenhouse he was planning. He stood thinking about it in the chill morning, early enough that he had no duties to attend. He stroked his fine beard, for despite the English avoidance of facial hair, he was proud of his and kept it trimmed and oiled.

He pictured the finished greenhouse, thinking about what kind of space the young Lady Andrepont needed. A place to work and replant, grow seedlings in the winter. He didn't know much about gardening, but he certainly could ask others.

"Thinking?" a voice asked.

Vasya jumped, startled that he hadn't heard footsteps behind him. It was the viscountess, catching him in the act. Fortunately, there was nothing yet to hide. "Yes."

She wore a simple day dress with a woolen bonnet and a woolen shawl draped over her. Still, she must be freezing in the early morning. A basket hung from her ungloved hands, her knuckles red in the cold.

"Why are you out so early, my lady?" Vasya cringed inwardly. As a servant, he should beg forgiveness for prying. They were not to ask questions. But Vasya still had trouble being humble enough for his station. He'd spent too much time with Gareth.

She gave him an unrestrained smile. He was so surprised he almost stumbled. She was stunning even when she didn't smile. But the happiness and glow on her face made her easily the most beautiful woman Vasya had ever seen. "I'm going to make a medicine for my sister. When I was younger, I helped our village's midwife. She had potions for everything and instructed me on how to make them. I believe I still remember this one."

Vasya couldn't speak for how very surprised he was. It was easy to dismiss a pretty girl as having no other talent than being pretty. Yet, she could remember medicines and tinctures that would help others. "That sounds very important."

Another beatific smile. "Once I make it, I'll know if I've remembered the ingredients and proportions correctly. And not to worry, it's only for the skin. It won't hurt the babe." She reached out to touch his arm, but suddenly drew back as if she'd thought better of it.

"There are many that would benefit from such a potion," Vasya said, not knowing what else to say, feeling cornered by her beauty even though there was an entire field he could retreat to. Her very being beckoned him but his life's experiences pushed him away. *Not for you, not for you,* chanted in his head.

Her eyes dropped to the ground. Vasya panicked, afraid he had done or said something wrong. But then she raised them again and closed their distance by another step. He almost took a step back to widen the distance between them, but willed himself to stand his ground. He'd been less terrified in actual skirmishes than he was standing here with young Lady Andrepont.

"I have a deep favor to ask of you, Vasily Nikolaevich." Her eyebrow arched up.

His stomach clenched, a river of roaring desire threatening to take over his mind and body. It was unexpected, unwelcome, yet still, it thundered. He calmed himself by taking a large breath, covering it up as if he were thoughtful. "Go ahead."

"Emma has invited me to the Lorian country house for her lying-in. I need to be there with her for the birth of her child. I need to be out of London. I can't . . ." She trailed off, gesturing widely to the brick walls that ran along the property. "But I need help figuring out a way that Andrepont will allow me to leave. I'm certain he won't of his own accord."

Vasya nodded, almost smelling the desperation on her. "What do you require of me?"

Jane looked around, as if the answer might pop out of a hedge. "A plan? I thought of telling everyone I knew that he was letting me attend, and how wonderful he was for doing so. But he loves to humiliate me so much, I'm afraid he'd tell everyone I was mad."

Vasya nodded. That outcome was likely. Andrepont was mercurial and vindictive, hard to predict.

"But if I don't leave London—if I can't be with Emma—I *will* go mad." Her red knuckles turned white as she gripped her basket handle even harder.

"Perhaps if I work to persuade him? He is a man who wants to be in charge. So naturally, the idea must be his. Perhaps when you ask him to go, you do not mention Emma."

"You would do that? You would help me?" Her wide green eyes, so sharp, so beguiling, shone on him. A beacon to his weary heart.

Vasya nodded. "Any way that I can."

When she put her hand on his forearm, grasping him, a heat passed between them. She might not have known it, but she branded him then. He was hers for however long she needed him. "Oh, thank you. I couldn't live here without you. You make it bearable."

Her cheeks colored. Or maybe it was the wind whipping across her face. But Vasya's throat went dry at her words. "Yes," he managed to say, although he didn't—couldn't—think of what she had just told him. That his presence was necessary to her. That her world was bearable only because of him. Those were words that bedeviled a man.

Her hand dropped away from him. "I need to go in and ask Cook for oil. And a mortar and pestle."

Vasya nodded once, simply. The viscountess turned away, taking a few steps before turning back. "I heard Emma call you Vasya."

"It is my name." Gareth's wife had leave to call him whatever she wished, frankly. And whatever it was, he would answer to it.

"May I call you Vasya?" she asked.

This woman was dangerous. So very dangerous. "For me, it is a name only my closest friends may call me. It is very informal. It is . . . not what an employer should say."

"I'm not your employer. My husband is."

If he was a Believer, now was when he would pray to God, or Jesus, or a Saint, or something to intervene, for he was not strong enough to resist this girl with her dark hair, green eyes, and surprising strength of spirit. "If you wish."

She gave him another one of those luminescent smiles. She might as well stab him through the heart. "Vasya."

His heart stopped in his chest. He couldn't breathe. He bowed to her. It was the only thing he could think to do. How she speared him. "My lady." He stood, and they locked eyes. He didn't know what it meant. He didn't know what would happen next.

She nodded and turned, walking into the house as if the entire land on which they stood hadn't shifted beneath their feet.

⚜

JANE WAS PLEASED WITH HERSELF. THE OIL WAS perfect, and good for Emma's swollen feet, belly, and hands. She'd commandeered the kitchen for the very first time. Cook was taken rather aback, but once she explained what she was doing, all the maids came to watch and help. They all spoke of knowing someone who needed such a potion, or would need it in the future. They all asked if Jane would make more, if she would charge money for it, or if she would barter.

That was pleasing, too, being thought of as good at something. And she felt so much like herself when she was grinding fresh herbs in a mortar and pestle. To smell the scents, to have her hands slick with oil as she decanted her mixture into a small bottle that once held a cherry cordial. She felt like Jane again. For so long, she had been not-her. Emma's sister, then Andrepont's wife. Now she was just Jane.

Just Jane was riding with Informal Vasya, and she couldn't stop smiling in the bright sun. Just Jane and Informal Vasya were visiting Emma, and Jane's heart was full for the first time in years. The former cherry cordial bottle was deep in her pocket, ready to gift and use on Emma. But Vasily—Vasya—wasn't speaking or looking at her. Had she done something to offend him? She was too happy right then to ruin it by asking.

When they arrived, Jane slid off her dappled gray mare, thinking she would end up on the mounting block. But her skirt pocket caught on the lower pommel with the cherry cordial bottle on one side, her body on the other. And forward she lurched.

Vasya was there in an instant. How had he moved so fast? One large arm wrapped around her waist as she fell onto his shoulder. His other hand flipped the extra fabric of her riding habit up over the pommel, rooting around to find the trouble. He smelled wonderful. Both of them had the scent of horses on them, yes, but he also had a smell of rosemary and sage. Perhaps because he'd been lurking in the gardens of late.

His bare neck was right there, his skin warm and clear. She wanted to kiss it. To claim it for herself, to taste it, to feel the texture of him on her tender lips. To show how important he was to her.

Vasya found the offending article, pushing the bottle up and over the pommel and guiding her down until her feet touched the mounting block. He backed away and held her hand as she descended to the ground. She felt almost dizzy.

They still hadn't spoken. Jane realized she had

made a grave error in asking to call him Vasya. Because he smelled of things she loved. Because he helped her. Saved her. She couldn't look at him. He escorted her to the door of Emma's townhouse, descending the steps as she was admitted.

She turned and looked back at him, retreating to the horses. Why wouldn't he look at her? She wanted him to lock eyes with her, confirm that he also felt what she felt. But he wouldn't, even though she knew he felt the weight of her gaze. She *knew* it.

Emma's butler was ushering her inside, but Jane couldn't tear her eyes from the large figure of Vasily Nikolaevich, strong and broad, checking the bridles of the horses he would care for while Jane visited Emma. So unlike her husband. So unlike any man she knew, though she knew precious few.

Was she being silly? Was this a girlish fancy, one that a man like him would dismiss? He'd helped her, been kind to her, but he was still a servant, paid to do so. Her cheeks burned in humiliation. Was she so starved for kindness that she'd fallen headlong after someone who'd been willing to extend himself for her?

Why, why was life like this?

VASYA BRUSHED DOWN LADY ANDREPONT'S GRAY mare, trying very hard not to think about the lady herself. The moment he'd held her in one arm, crushing her to him, had felt right. Not just right. Inevitable. Appropriate. Necessary.

But now the master came storming into the stable. Mr. Dendrum intercepted the viscount, who stomped in irritation.

"I'll speak to this groom, Dendrum. Move." Andrepont strode over, his black clothes impeccable.

Clearly, the man was not here for riding. He sized Vasya up as he walked, as if the lord was considering taking him on in a fistfight.

Vasya's ego wanted the violence, a way to hold his own against this spoiled arse. But it would not help Vasya, nor would it help Jane if he were to fight her husband. Instead, he schooled his expression into his very blandest English subservience and asked with his thickest accent, "You need me, my lord?"

"I saw you." Andrepont shoved his finger in the middle of Vasya's chest. The man came up a little past Vasya's shoulders, and he was solidly built. But it was no match for Vasya's sheer size. "Out on my wife's horse! While she was relegated to this insignificant beast. If I had my pistol on me, I'd shoot it right now."

Vasya ignored the threat. He concentrated on his thickened accent instead, not wanting to slip into his clear, British vowels. "My lady wanted a smaller mount."

"It isn't about what she wants," Andrepont snarled. "She rides the chestnut because it is regal, it is beautiful, it is powerful. That is what she needs to convey to the rest of the world."

Vasya shrugged as if he had no thoughts. Instead, his mind whirred quickly, trying to spin the conversation to his advantage. "The chestnut is very powerful. Very beautiful. Yes."

"I don't need your opinion, I need your obedience. My wife rides the chestnut. And I don't care if she doesn't want to. It's the only horse that will be saddled for her, do you understand?"

Vasya nodded. "In my country," he started, mentally fumbling for what he would say. "One might look at this gray mare and say, oh yes, fine horse, does well. But then, look at the chestnut and say, oh, magnificent horse! But they all know how one is normal, one is special, so there is no need to ask why it is so."

Andrepont stared at him, and Vasya wondered if he would take the bait. If not, he'd think his foreign groom was insane. "Why would they say that?"

"Because for powerful horses, strong horses, the mare is let run free for the weeks before stud. She run, she free with the earth and the grasses, and it becomes a strong womb for a strong stud. Horses like the gray, bred in a stable. It is fine. But not powerful. Not strong. Womb needs earth and wildness to root a strong seed." Mr. Dendrum stared at Vasya as he spoke. Perhaps because his accent was so thick, perhaps because what he was saying was utter shit.

Andrepont blinked at him, no expression on his face. "Fine. Do you understand my instructions?"

"*Da*," Vasya said, keeping up the ruse of his poor English. Which the servants all knew was fake. This could get him into trouble if someone told, but this was not a house where servants gossiped. Not even amongst each other.

The viscount turned on his heel and approached Mr. Dendrum, giving him the same instruction not to let Lady Andrepont ride any other horse than the chestnut. It made Vasya sad to know that this poor little gray mare would no longer get the love that the lady lavished upon it. But he hoped that his strange story of horses running free before rutting translated into what he'd hoped—that when Jane asked to go to the country, Andrepont would say yes.

⚜

Jane awoke with a start. The room was momentarily unfamiliar with cool, bright sunshine streaming in the east-facing window. The smell of fresh air permeated the room, despite the closed windows. She was at the Lorian estate. Flopping back down onto the pillow, Jane closed her eyes once again, savoring the dream.

The illicit dream. The dream she would tell no one, not even Emma. The dream in which she lay in a meadow with Vasya—as she'd called him in her dream. Vasya had his arm open, and she lay within its confines. They spoke about something—she couldn't remember what, it was all fading so fast. But he placed his finger on her chin, turning her face towards his. The searing look in his dark eyes was all she needed. She knew, like a thunderclap, that she loved him.

He pulled her on top of him, as if he were a horse, and pulled her down to kiss him. They kissed and they kissed, and his hands roamed her body, caressing her sides, cupping her face.

She supposed that dreams could be more illicit than that. But it was the feeling she had when she awoke. The aching in her belly, the want thrumming through her, all the way to her fingertips. She would luxuriate in those feelings. But in came a maid to lay the fire. So much for luxuriating.

"Oh," the maid said, shocked that Jane was awake. She bobbed a curtsy. "My apologies, my lady. I hope I did not wake you."

"No, I was already up." Jane looked at the window's light. The sun was different in the country. No buildings to hide behind here. No ash to blacken the windows. Jane threw back the blankets but found the air much colder than she anticipated. She flipped them back on, vowing to wait until the room warmed before she left her bed.

Christmas had passed and they had not celebrated it, which was fine by Jane. Their father was still livid with Emma and had said it would take him longer to reunite with his eldest daughter, and Aunt Diana wasn't sure she could associate with Emma until Captain Somerset, now Lord Aberscomb, returned and claimed in front of God and everyone that Emma was in truth his wife.

Aunt Diana was suspicious. As were many, according to one of the gossip columns, calling Emma's maneuvers a "coup d'etat" as she had been betrothed to a viscount but married the heir to an earldom. But Emma had never truly been engaged, not for more than a few minutes. Jane didn't care for the gossip columns and didn't care for Aunt Diana sharing them with her.

Once the maid was gone and the fire had warmed her small room, she put on her wrapper and slippers and wandered over to Emma's bedroom next door. Emma was still sleeping, her face swollen and exhausted, pillows and blankets arranged to support the absolutely huge belly she had grown.

Jane slipped in on the other side of the bed, keeping her wrapper on as she stole some blankets and rubbed Emma's back with a feather-light touch. Her body was hot with sleep and pregnancy. Jane closed her eyes and reveled in the comforting smell of her sister's bedclothes. She was so surprised and thankful to be here.

Andrepont had frowned at her when she initially asked to go to the country, but Jane kept her eyes downcast, a supplicant in front of her lord. Finally, a brisk "I don't care what you do. But on your eighteenth birthday, you're here."

The words had chilled her, but she was grateful that she could leave the confines of London. Whatever Vasya had said to him, it had worked. Jane had no idea what her husband would do with his own time—something awful, no doubt—but she didn't care. She was with Emma. Jane inhaled again, the familiar scent of her sister giving her drowsy comfort.

Without meaning to, but not having a reason to deprive herself, Jane fell back asleep, her palms flat on Emma's warm back.

⁂

Vasya finished unloading the trunks from the carriage, allowing Lord Carlisle's footmen to take possession of Andrepont's belongings. Andrepont was already inside, no doubt drinking fine port or claret, or whatever it was that they did.

As Andrepont's groom, Vasya was allowed to go round to the kitchens while the horses were watered so he could have a cup of warmed wine and a bit of bread and cheese for his troubles. The country estate was of moderate size and of moderate upkeep. Nothing overly done, but clearly from a generation or two back. Paint was peeling in certain places, a patina of age obvious in less-noticeable places.

Once he was admitted to the bustling kitchens, the maids eyed him.

"Ohh, I like you," one of them purred.

Vasya gave a terse smile at the odd compliment. But as another maid set down his small meal and mug of warmed wine, he noticed the low-cut nature of her uniform, showing off all her natural endowments. It was then that Vasya looked around and noticed every single servant was good-looking. He'd dismissed it when dealing with the footmen, because for many of the peerage, that was a requirement. Footmen were to be tall, well-built, and handsome as they were the first representation of the family they served.

Vasya smelled something burning. He leaned forward, looking past a wall to peer into the kitchen proper. A large, curvaceous woman, whose apron seductively strained at all her ample parts, scolded a young, willowy maid.

"I told you to watch yesself. Lucky it weren't the pie. Away wi' ye," the cook yelled.

She was, Vasya had to admit, the prettiest cook he'd ever seen, and if he hadn't been fairly certain the entire staff had also been hired for intimacies at guests' behest, Vasya might have tried for her attention.

As it was, the idea of staying here, waiting for whatever games might be played during this fortnight, Vasya didn't want to be a part of it. Perhaps it was a childhood spent watching the women of his village have no choice when it came to the noblemen's whims. He downed his warmed wine and took his bread and cheese outside to see to the horses.

The stables were even stranger. The grooms, who were brushing down other beasts, chuckled as Vasya's eyes widened at what hung on the walls of the stable. There were instruments and costumes and all sorts of whips that looked like they were not meant for horses. Vasya did not consider himself prudish, and certainly not inexperienced. He knew of many acts between a man and a woman, or a man and a man, or any number of people and combinations.

It was the horse mask that made him finally feel nervous. Perhaps because he'd once been told he was the size of a pony. He had no interest in acting as one. Before the horses were fully ready, he re-hitched the carriage and was on his way.

The horses wouldn't manage the ride all the way back to London, but he was not all that far from the Lorian estate, where he'd deposited Lady Andrepont a few days earlier. He decided to stop there to fully rest the horses.

As Vasya drove down the gravel drive, he saw a single horse being readied. The door opened and the housekeeper, Mrs. Thorne, practically pushed a footman out onto the drive.

"But my coat—" the footman protested.

Vasya slowed his carriage to a stop. "Is there something amiss?"

"We need Mrs. Houseman. From the village. Now. Now!" Mrs. Thorne pushed the young footman as he pulled on his overcoat.

"May I be of some assistance?" Vasya said, hopping down from his perch.

"And who ye be?" Mrs. Thorne scowled at him.

"I am Lady Andrepont's groom. I deposited her here a few days ago," Vasya explained. The footman struggled to get his other sleeve on. The boy did not seem to be very capable.

Mrs. Thorne cuffed the clumsy footman. "If your carriage can manage, get ye to the inn in town. Mrs. Houseman has been staying close by, waiting for such a moment. A carriage will be nicer than riding behind this nitwit. You'll stay on tonight?"

Vasya nodded. "If I may."

Mrs. Thorne nodded, as if his politeness had passed some kind of test. "Be off with ye, then. Lady Aberscomb needs her quickly."

CHAPTER 10

BEFORE

Emma sat up on the bed. "Who is it? Who has arrived? Is Mrs. Houseman here?"

Jane scurried over to the window to peer out. As the carriage slowed to a stop, she recognized Vasya. Her cheeks colored, as he had visited her dreams more than once in the past few days. But the presence of the stamped carriage made her stomach clench. Her hands shook at the thought of Andrepont here, with Emma so vulnerable.

"Well?" Emma hoisted herself from the bed, one hand on her belly as if it could steady her.

Jane waved her off, watching the scene play out below, relieved when Vasya spurred the horses down the drive once again. "It was Vasya. I think he's going to fetch Mrs. Houseman in our carriage."

Emma frowned. "What is he doing here?"

Jane shook her head, dreading whatever news he might bring. Had Andrepont changed his mind and sent a carriage to fetch her? She wouldn't go. She didn't care what punishment he might mete out. She was staying here through the birth of Emma's baby. "Naught to worry about now. How are you feeling?"

Emma relaxed against the pillows. "I suppose I'm fine now. It feels silly. One moment, I'm completely fine, the next, it feels like I'm being ripped apart. Very odd."

"We could walk in the rose garden, if you like. Maybe we can call for some broth and tea. You should have something to keep your strength up while we wait for Mrs. Houseman and the baby."

Emma nodded, so Jane found her wrapper and tried to help put slippers on her sister's swollen feet. From her experience with Mrs. Houseman, Jane knew they had hours before Emma's labor progressed, possibly an entire day. Best to keep company now, before Emma tired from the pain and the pushing.

They passed a few pleasant hours and were returning to the house just as Vasya pulled the carriage to the front. He locked eyes with Jane as he hopped down from the driver's perch. Still, he said nothing to her. Just looked. His eyes flicked to Emma as he lowered the carriage step and opened the door. Mrs. Houseman emerged, looking precisely the same.

Unexpected sadness whirled up from inside Jane. This woman had given her so much, yet Jane had vanished from her life. Even though it hadn't been Jane's choice, the lost time with her mentor overwhelmed her. But this wasn't about Jane.

Emma suddenly gripped Jane's hand hard. The weight of Emma's body sagged against her sister, and her squeeze became bone-crushing. "Mrs. Houseman!" Jane yelled.

All of Jane's attention locked on Emma, and she tried to keep her sister upright as a contraction wracked her. Jane murmured encouragement. Mrs. Houseman was on Emma's other side in moments. Emma let out a big breath as the contraction passed. With help, she stood up straight.

"There now," Mrs. Houseman said. "Now I can be helpful. Let's get ourselves upstairs and comfortable."

"I've already ordered tea and broth," Jane said.

Mrs. Houseman smiled at her, acknowledging her star pupil. "I'm so glad, dear. With the two of us, this baby will come into the world as smooth as butter."

"God willing," Emma murmured.

"Attend my bag, Jane?" Mrs. Houseman said as she escorted Emma inside.

Jane smiled. It was as if the years hadn't passed and she was once again simply Jane. An undeclared apprentice in the village.

"I will get the bag," Vasya said, stepping forward.

Jane jolted, realizing he was there still. She'd been so preoccupied with Emma that she'd forgotten him completely. "No, you have horses to care for. I can get it."

They both stepped up to the bag. They were closer to one another than they normally stood, both with arms extended. His hand brushed against hers. Their eyes locked. There were so many things she wanted to tell him. The memories of her dream—of being wrapped in his arms, of him kissing her— pressed on her mind.

She felt as if she should say something, but nothing would exit her mouth.

"Shall I take the horses?" A footman interrupted.

Jane shook her head as if she needed to wake up. Which she did. Being around Vasya made her feel drowsy, like too much sherry as the sun went down. Vasya turned away from her, and she admired the twist of his body, the breadth of his capable shoulders. He took the form of a man who could destroy whatever came in his path, but he treated her as gently as a butterfly.

"Please," Vasya called after the footman. "I shall attend the luggage." He turned back to Jane, searching her face for something. "I am at your service."

Jane's lips parted. "I can take this bag up to Mrs. Houseman." She knew she had to move quickly to avoid being once again held under his sway, so she snatched up the fabric bag and scurried inside, glancing over her shoulder to watch Vasya untie Mrs. Houseman's luggage from the back of the carriage. When his eyes met hers, Jane blushed. His expression was inscrutable.

঩

IT WAS THE MIDDLE OF THE NIGHT, BUT THE ENTIRE house was ablaze with candles. Lady Aberscomb's shrieks kept everyone up. Most of the servants sat at the communal table downstairs doing the small chores that occupied them in idle moments—darning, polishing. Cook was making another loaf of bread. Only the horses in the stables slept. And even they might be up.

Vasya recognized some of the servants from Aberscomb's London townhouse. No doubt because they were familiar with Lady Aberscomb and her preferences. The red-headed maid was here, Martha Foraker. He was about to ask her how she found the country but didn't get the chance.

"Rider coming!" Someone called downstairs.

Vasya exchanged looks with a footman. Who would be coming here now? In the middle of a cold winter night? Fear stung him—worry that Andrepont had somehow learned Vasya hadn't gone to London or knew that his young wife was with her sister. He bounded out the back door, hearing the hoofbeats on the long gravel drive. There was no snow, but the chill was below freezing. He wished for his heavier overcoat, but he wanted to have freedom of movement in case of a brigand.

When he rounded the outside of the house, his own feet crunching on the gravel, he almost doubled over in gratitude.

"Vasya!" Gareth shouted when he saw him.

Gareth was long-haired and long-whiskered, wearing a dirty oilskin overcoat and a tricorn hat pulled low. Vasya couldn't say anything; he just barreled toward the man and clutched his hand. The English were not much for embraces, so instead Vasya clapped him on the back.

"I came as fast as I could. I arrived in London yesterday and found everything upside down, but my father said that Emma was in her confinement here. Has it happened yet?" Gareth was short of breath, his face flushed, but he didn't look any worse for wear.

"No baby as of yet. Lady Andrepont is here with her."

Gareth blinked. "I'm sorry?"

He had not heard yet, then. "Your wife's sister."

The news set Gareth back a step. "Miss Laurent married . . .?"

Vasya nodded in confirmation. Gareth took off his hat and swept his brow, leaving a streak of pale forehead above the dirt on his face. He heaved a sigh, looked to the heavens, then shook his head. "No matter. That bastard is something to think about later. Can you have a bath set up for me? I'd like to see Emma."

Vasya whistled for one of the footmen to take the horse, then showed his friend up to where the women had taken refuge. He knew he wasn't the right person to do it, and Mrs. Thorne would have his head for entering in his boots, yet Vasya felt he must. He was Gareth's honor guard, and in this capacity, he was the master's friend, not a guest's servant. In a world where the lines between upstairs and downstairs were so strict, this felt very much as if he were inviting a whipping at the very least.

Vasya barked orders at the other footman to have a bath prepared for his lordship.

"My trunk is coming on a coach, but it won't be here for hours, I'm afraid," Gareth said. "I was in far too much of a hurry."

Mrs. Thorne appeared the moment Vasya stepped inside the house. She saw Gareth, the state of him, but still curtsied. "Lord Aberscomb, we are delighted you could be here."

Gareth's face contorted in pain for a moment, but he recovered quickly. "Thank you, Mrs. Thorne. I'm hoping for a bath, and perhaps some clean clothes that might have been left here at some point? My trunk hadn't made it off the ship when I turned the horse towards the country."

"Of course. Mr. Kuznetsov, I can escort his lordship." Her tone was exacting, with no room for argument. Fortunately, he wasn't the one making the argument.

"No need, Mrs. Thorne. Vasya is an old friend. I'd prefer he take me to my wife. We have much to catch up on."

Mrs. Thorne eyed Vasya with suspicion but nodded, letting them both pass up the stairs with dirty boots. Vasya would find a way to make it up to whichever maid had to clean the front stairs after them.

Lady Aberscomb had taken the mistress's bedchamber, leaving the adjoining master bedchamber available for anyone who might be attending to her if they needed rest. The hall carpet padded their steps, and they heard a low moan.

Gareth shot him an alarmed look. Vasya shrugged.

The low moans were better than the shrieks. Vasya knocked softly on the door.

"Enter," called Lady Aberscomb through audibly clenched teeth. No doubt she believed them to be servants returning with a request.

Vasya looked to Gareth to make sure he was prepared for what he might see, though Vasya had no idea what to expect, either. Gareth nodded, his expression grim. Indeed, Vasya would much rather enter a battlefield, for at least there, he had experience.

When they swung the door open, they saw the two ladies lying on the bed, fully clothed. Lady Andrepont's face was pinched with worry, and Lady Aberscomb's was a rictus of pain. They held hands, their white knuckles visible from the doorway.

Lady Andrepont noticed them first and gasped. Her sister then swung her gaze, her face relaxing, then melting into surprise.

Gareth seemed to suddenly remember his unkempt appearance and swept the tricorn off his head. He looked like a dog who had finally sighted his long-lost master.

Lady Aberscomb burst into tears. "You came!"

Gareth nodded but still didn't step into the room. "I'm here. I couldn't miss it. I wouldn't." He took a step forward, clouding the room with dust as he brushed against the doorframe.

Lady Andrepont was up in an instant. "No. Out. Bath first. Then a lovely reunion." She shooed them both, but Vasya caught her gaze, connecting with her in that moment.

He saw relief in her face, and more joy than he'd ever known her to experience. She was happy for her sister. Happy that Gareth had made it to his baby's birth. And that made Vasya happy, too.

JANE HAD NEVER WITNESSED A BIRTH THIS HORRID. The baby's head was bigger than she'd ever seen while attending births with Mrs. Houseman. The old woman wasn't perplexed or annoyed by any of the complications, but her instructions were curt and numerous. Jane had the oils. Martha returned periodically with broth and other food for Emma to keep her strength up. But when it happened, it was awful.

The sound that came out of Emma's mouth was one that shook Jane. Of all the screams she'd ever heard, this was the worst. Mrs. Houseman caught the baby, handed it off to Jane to clean, barked at Martha for more towels, and waited for the afterbirth. There was so much blood. Jane cleaned the baby roughly, clearing its nostrils until it began to cry.

Jane couldn't help herself; she began to cry as well, passing the baby to Emma, who was pale from lack of blood and exhaustion.

"Put the baby to your breast. That will help with the afterbirth," Mrs. Houseman instructed, though not for the first time.

Emma did as she was told, and soon, the afterbirth was out as well. Jane went back to the midwife to help, only to see the woman's expression was grim. A low, cold panic set in Jane's stomach.

"What can I do?" Jane asked.

"Fetch my bag," Mrs. Houseman said, saying words Jane knew from experience to signal a poor outcome. When Jane returned with it, Mrs. Houseman soothed. "It's not as bad as all that, girl."

The epithet made her feel better. Despite her elevation to viscountess, she'd always be *girl* to Mrs. Houseman. "Then what is it?" Women died from childbirth all the time. Whether it was the first baby or the ninth, each time was a new gamble.

"She's torn. Torn quite badly. Hold the rag to help stop the blood." Mrs. Houseman gestured for Jane to switch places with her, and when she did so, Jane could see the horrific tear the baby had caused. In times past, Mrs. Houseman had spoken of these kinds of tears. It could prevent future children.

Jane looked to her teacher and found a sympathetic friend. "You'll be with her, helping her heal," Mrs. Houseman said. "This won't be her only child."

Jane nodded, following instructions, helping Mrs. Houseman as she dabbed on new oils and helped staunch the bleeding.

There was a knock at the door and Gareth called through. "Is everything all right? The screaming stopped."

An exhausted laugh ran through the women.

"Don't you wish for us to clean up your wife before you come in, my lord?" Martha cried.

"No, I don't care. Please let me in," he said through the door. The anguish in his voice was obvious.

Jane looked to Emma, who stared at the door with longing even though she had her newborn babe at her breast.

"Please," Emma said, her voice hoarse.

Mrs. Houseman nodded, and Martha opened the door. Captain Somerset—er, Lord Aberscomb—stood there in his shirtsleeves, the most lovelorn look on his face.

"Emma," he said, stock-still until Martha motioned him in. Then he rushed to the bedside. He looked at the baby. "Is this . . . is this?"

Emma nodded, and a laugh gurgled out of her,

barely distinguishable from a sob. "Yes. Our son. Our beautiful baby boy."

Gareth sobbed.

Mrs. Houseman elbowed Jane. "Pay attention to the work, girl."

"Yes, ma'am." Jane began the cleaning process. She tidied up the dirty rags and tightened the lids on the jars of oils they'd used. Martha came bustling over.

"I cannot let you be doing that, my lady," she said, trying to wrestle an armload of bloody rags from Jane.

"Martha, this is what I did before I married. It's perfectly fine." Jane tried to hold on to the dirty bundle, but Martha was surprisingly strong.

"You weren't a viscountess then. You are now. I'll be taking care of the rags. You go do . . . other things." Martha bested Jane and hunched over with the rags. "You'll be needing at least some tea and a light repast. And a bath and a change of clothes, by the looks of it."

Jane looked over at Mrs. Houseman, who was pulling the blankets down, hiding a smile. "I don't actually care for tea all that much."

"Lady Aberscomb," Mrs. Houseman called. Emma stopped murmuring to her husband and baby.

"Yes, Mrs. Houseman?" Emma's voice betrayed her exhaustion.

"You'll be needing further care. Perhaps your husband could carry you to the bed next door so that we might change the linens on this one."

"I'll go turn down the bed," Jane volunteered, only to be stopped by Martha.

"It's already done," Martha said, holding open the adjoining door. "I'll fetch some refreshment for everyone." Her tone was firm, which Jane rather liked. "I'll bring tea up for Lord and Lady Aberscomb, and then a tray to the main drawing room for everyone else. The maids have already refreshed the washing basins in your rooms, so you may tidy up first, Lady Andrepont, Mrs. Houseman."

She was a capable woman, that Martha. The kind that Jane wouldn't mind having in her own house. Someone who might be loyal to her instead of her husband. Someone who could anticipate needs and wants, be efficient. Someone who might breathe life into the tomb-like feel of her home. Not that her husband would ever part with his ancient staff because he knew they wouldn't speak about his affairs. Or the pretty maids who rotated through the house. As if Jane wouldn't notice that.

Gareth scooped up Emma, who held tightly to the babe at her breast, and walked through the adjoining door to the other bedchamber. Jane moved to help strip the bed of the soiled and bloody linens, but Martha gave her such a look that she backed away.

"Away with you, then," Martha said. "Go clean up. You look affright."

Jane exchanged grins with Mrs. Houseman and they both retreated to their rooms—Jane's in the family wing of the house and Mrs. Houseman's on the other side of the staircase. They'd given her a room so that she might stay on for another day to help Emma mend. Normally Mrs. Houseman didn't accept such extravagances, but it was Emma, and it was far to travel back to Chilton in a single day. It was too late to even get back to the inn in the nearest town.

As Jane entered her room, she looked at her hands, with blood dried under her fingernails. There was a lovely lavender-scented soap next to the fresh water in the wash basin. Jane stripped off the pinafore and the dress underneath. She washed in the cool water, scrubbing all the way up her arms for good measure.

Refreshed from her ablutions, Jane donned

another dress, a nicer one that made her feel more like herself. She brushed out her hair and pinned it back into a simple low bun, as she had when she got up early to forage in the woods back when they lived in Chilton and she was nothing more than a girl digging in the dirt.

No one had yet arrived when she entered the drawing room. Next to the fireplace, Jane found a very much abandoned embroidery sampler. There was a harpsichord, which she could not play with any affinity, and the walls were hung with portraits of ancestors and mythical allegories.

Vasily Nikolaevich opened the door, stopping abruptly when he caught sight of her. "Lady Andrepont, I beg your pardon," he grumbled. He turned to leave.

"Did you need something?" Jane was exhausted, but she didn't want to be alone. Not then. Not after helping to bring her nephew into the world. She needed companionship, someone to help celebrate the joy of a new life.

"I was in search of Gareth." The big man shook his head. "I beg your pardon. Lord Aberscomb."

"You were friends, weren't you? Before, I mean?" Jane took a step forward.

A maid bustled in carrying a tray laden with tea and seedcakes, breads, and apricot preserves. She eyed Vasily Nikolaevich as she left the room.

"Yes," he conceded.

"Won't you join me and tell me all about it?" Jane asked, gesturing to the seat opposite her. She hoped she didn't sound too desperate. "Mrs. Houseman will be ages. And Gareth and Emma are together in her room. I would adore some company."

He stared at her long enough for heat to rise to her cheeks, but finally, he lumbered into the room and sat down. Jane hid her smile at her success.

"Cream or sugar?" Jane asked, assuming he would want a cup of tea.

"None," he said.

She handed him a teacup, which he seemed very uncomfortable with. Surely he'd held a teacup before. Or perhaps it was her. Maybe she made him uncomfortable. She fixed her own, continuing to stir, just to keep herself busy.

"When did you meet him? Lord Aberscomb, I mean." Jane bestowed a warm, encouraging smile, hoping that might help their conversation.

Her informality had the opposite effect. "Many years now." He drank the cup in one swallow. "I should go."

Jane hastily put her cup down to stop him. He was almost to the door before she caught up to him, putting her hand on his arm. He stopped, frozen in time. She felt as if she had put her hand in the fire but couldn't remove it. They both stared at where she touched him. Where she dared.

"Lady Andrepont," he said, his voice raking across her.

"Jane," she whispered. "My name is Jane. If you gave me leave to call you . . . Vasya . . . then you should call me Jane."

He shook his head, licking his lips as he did so. Jane had never paid such careful attention to anyone in her life. Every movement he made seemed like a code that she needed to decipher. "I cannot."

"I need—" she started, not knowing what she meant to say. She needed so much. She needed company, yes, but not just right then in the drawing room. She needed a life, friends, a world that was hers, and not the small cage her husband had confined her in.

His dark eyelashes fluttered as his gaze flitted across her features. "I know."

The flimsy webbing that had kept her together all those months fell apart in response. Of course he knew her plight. He lived there, he drove Andrepont, he saw everything. But did he see her?

His other hand came up and brushed an errant strand of hair from her face. His touch on her bare skin was brief, but so very welcome. She was starved for touch. Starved for admiration. And this man, she knew, was a good man. Not like her husband.

A throat clearing made them both jump apart. Martha Foraker, bless her efficiency, stood in the doorway. "Is all set here? Enough for everyone?"

"Yes, Martha, thank you. I appreciate your thoroughness. Is Mrs. Houseman taken care of? She has not come down yet. I fear she is not as young as she used to be."

Martha smiled at her worry. "Mrs. Houseman has already changed and checked on Lady Aberscomb. She is taking a more substantive repast in her room. She said she preferred the quiet after such an ado."

Jane smiled. "Of course. Thank you."

The maid turned to go, but Jane couldn't resist the urge to continue her boldness. Especially if the maid had seen Vasya's hand on her cheek. "And Martha? I know that my sister and her husband will need a place to live, and that house may have its own staff, but I would be honored if you would consider my household. I think we would work very well together."

Martha's freckled cheeks blushed. "Thank you, my lady. That is very kind. I shall keep your offer in mind." The maid left, leaving Jane alone with the Russian man once again.

He eyed Jane. "Did you make the offer because you feared her gossip or because you wish to replace Mrs. Renwood?"

"Are you trying to figure out how devious I am?" Jane asked, stepping back towards the sitting area.

He shook his dark head. "No. But I would welcome staff changes. Below stairs is most depressing."

Jane cocked her head. "How so? Are they not respectable?"

"No one speaks. Everyone has been beaten, whether in body or in spirit, I do not know."

"I will make some adjustments, then," Jane said. "Perhaps starting with Martha."

Vasya nodded and turned away to leave. Abruptly he stopped and turned back. "My lady?"

Jane's heart stopped. "Yes?"

"I like when you call me Vasya." He shoved his hands in the pockets of his coat.

A knot that felt golden and shining and wonderful cinched tight in her throat. "Then I will."

CHAPTER 11

J ane could see the shape of Emma's eyes in the baby's face. The baby boy looked so much like Emma that it was hard to imagine Gareth had anything to do with it at all. Later, the boy might grow into Gareth's nicely sharp jaw, but until that day, this baby was wholly her sister's. And Jane loved her beautiful nephew, volunteering to take care of little William while Emma bathed or rested.

The days were chilly, and while they strolled in the gardens with the babe, one big parade, they also lay on the rug in front of the fireplace in the library and stared at the sleeping baby's closed eyes. It was bliss. It was the strangest, loveliest, fullest Jane had ever felt. Gareth and Vasya rode horses while Jane wrote letters and Emma and the babe napped.

When the first note from Andrepont appeared, Jane was terrified. Her hiding place had been discovered. But she entered a new campaign of writing to everyone in London about how generous her husband was, letting her stay during her sister's recovery. And from then on, she threw every note from Andrepont into the fire and stopped worrying.

Eventually, a wet nurse came for the baby, and then Emma slept for what seemed an entire full day. Mrs. Houseman left them eventually, warning Gareth that he was not to seek Emma's bed for several months. Gareth seemed mortified that Mrs. Houseman would speak of such a thing, but it was important advice. Emma had torn—horrifically so—and she needed longer than usual to recover. Mrs. Houseman also warned them that Emma might not be able to carry another babe. But they would not know until the time came.

It put fear into Jane. She knew another babe would come eventually. All she had to do was look at how Gareth watched her sister. And her sister, despite her pain, exhaustion, and loss of blood, looked at Gareth the same way. They loved each other. It made Jane's chest ache. One night, after waking from yet another dream of herself and Vasya entangled on a blanket in the forest, love passing between them openly, she let herself cry into her pillow. She would be lonely in this life. And that was just her lot.

One afternoon, Andrepont finally succeeded in interrupting Jane's country idyll. Gareth wandered into the drawing room with a letter, finding the two sisters. A fine, freezing drizzle had surprised them on a walk. Jane's gown was muddy, but she was too cold to change. Instead, she bent over a book, as if to give Gareth privacy with his wife, who was embroidering yet another baby bonnet.

"Ladies," he greeted. "I have a note from Andrepont."

Jane did her best to school her face into a look of bland pleasantness. Despite her efforts, Gareth seemed to notice.

"What does he want?" Jane asked. She tried very hard to not let her stomach turn into a fist.

"He wants you in London. Although I don't know why he doesn't write you himself." Gareth sat down next to Emma, looking pleased with himself.

Jane made another face, but finally looked up. "He does. I threw his notes into the fire without reading them. I've written absolutely everyone in London, telling them how wonderfully generous he was in letting me come stay with my dear sister. How exceptional. How kind . . ."

Emma harrumphed. It was a noise she only made now that she was happy like this, comfortable in her skin and her space.

"It was the only way I could think of to let me stay away." Jane shrugged. "But I guess that can only last so long."

"Your birthday is coming up," Emma reminded her.

Jane paled. That was precisely what he'd told her. She could stay away as long as she returned for her eighteenth birthday. The one when he would find her bed. "Oh. That's what it is. I'd quite forgotten."

Gareth shook his head. "I'm sorry. I don't follow."

"It's not—" Emma started.

"Go on," Jane interrupted. Being surrounded by people she loved made her reckless. She wanted her brother-in-law to know what he'd saved Emma from. And to know what she suffered, for if there was any man who would ever have the power to intervene on her behalf, Gareth was the man. Someday, he would be an earl. "You may tell him."

Emma sighed and turned to Gareth. "In their marriage contract, it stipulated that there were to be no marital relations until Jane turned eighteen. Aunt Diana was worried after her health in the childbed since Jane is so very slender."

Gareth watched the two women, clearly

uncomfortable with this well-discussed topic. "Are you—"

"Amenable?" Jane slammed her book closed, sending the various leaves and clippings she'd laid out fluttering to the floor. "Yes. I have to be. That's the job description. I am the viscountess, there to give birth to the next generation of viscounts."

"You don't—" Gareth started, again, not sure what he meant to say entirely.

"Ah, but I do." Jane stood, agitated now. "I've seen now what he does to the maids." She sighed and stalked the edges of the room. She didn't like to admit or even think about the noises she'd gone to investigate, only to turn away. Shame had coursed through her in those moments—an unknowable, unspeakable shame that she couldn't identify.

Gareth glanced at Emma, who only gave him a quelling look.

"You were at war, weren't you, Captain?" Jane said, wanting to wrest the conversation back to herself. Her husband used to fill her with dread, but after this sojourn of comfort, he made her angry.

Gareth cleared his throat to answer her obvious question.

"You were compelled by your duty to the King. I'm sure there were dastardly actions called for, and you performed them because that was why you were there. Such is my lot." Jane's jaw clenched. "I shall get my things packed and return to London tomorrow. I doubt I have much longer until he will come after me himself."

"Do you want me to go with you?" Emma asked.

"No!" Gareth protested.

"God no," Jane said.

Emma looked chastened. "Only for support. I wouldn't stay with them."

"Do you not remember him breaking into your bedroom?" Gareth asked.

"He broke into your bedroom?" Jane asked. This was the first she'd heard of such an event. Why would Emma not tell her this? They'd been together a month now. There had been plenty of occasions to mention that her husband had harassed her sister. "When? Did he hurt you?"

"Yes, he did, and no he did not. Thanks to the former Lord Aberscomb, God rest his soul." Emma put down the mending. "Jane, I only want to help. Tell me what I can do. It's my fault that you've ended up where you are. I don't know how to make amends."

Jane shook her head. "I made my own decisions, Emma. I entered the marriage willingly. This is the consequence of my actions. Vasya will drive me back."

Gareth's eyes popped open wide. "Vasya?"

Jane nodded, pretending she didn't understand his surprise. She was done with apologizing. Vasya was the only good thing she could take with her. She didn't know when she might see Emma and the baby again. It might be years until the next time Andrepont let her out of his sight. She never knew how to predict him. "He drove me out here. Why would he not return to London?"

"I don't want you to go," Emma said.

If her sister looked at her one more minute, Jane would burst into tears. "I must go pack." She fled the room, dread dogging every step.

❦

"You think you're clever," Andrepont said, glancing at Jane over the newspaper he read at his desk in his office.

She had been called to the carpet as if she were an

unruly child, not his wife. She didn't care for it, but now that she was back under his roof, she wasn't willing to push his limits any further. "Not clever, my lord. I spoke the truth."

"You think me kind and generous?" he sneered.

"For a husband to allow his wife to help her sister with her lying-in, yes. For I will likely soon be in the same position, and it would behoove all of us for me to attend to her so that I might know what is in store for me."

Andrepont's eyes narrowed as she obliquely referenced their marital union. He snapped the paper and folded it in half. "Your birthday is coming. We should celebrate."

Jane kept her expression calm. She did not want to celebrate her birthday, as she knew every man invited would ogle her. The whispers would run like wildfire that her birthday night would be her first bedded night. "If you like."

He examined her thoroughly, as if trying to parse her opinion. Jane did not doubt that he would do the opposite of whatever he believed she wanted. Since she had no control over whatever may come, she surrendered herself to it. She was impervious to him.

"What would you say to a party rivaling the birthday celebration the King gave to Queen Charlotte? A cake as tall as you?"

"It would seem extravagant, but if that would please you, my lord, then we should speak to a baker very soon." With her birthday less than a week away, a party of that scale would be difficult to put together.

Andrepont hummed and walked close to her. "An evening out, just the two of us?"

"If you like," Jane said again. She hated going out on his arm, with men of all stripes ogling her.

He dragged his finger along her cheek, pulling back an errant hair. It was the same gesture Vasya had performed a thousand times in her dreams, thrilling her. But when Andrepont did it, she felt nothing. No spark, no desire. Only movement. "Something more intimate, then?"

"If you like," Jane repeated, her eyes downcast. He wanted to humiliate her, she could feel it. He wanted her to squirm, to cry, to plead, but she refused.

He let out a short grunt, and Jane smothered a grin. He was exasperated with her. Good. It made her feel like she was winning, the old goat. "Fine. Do as you wish. But be at the house before midnight." Andrepont returned to his desk and shook out the folded newspaper, staring her down. As if he were devising a very specific torture.

Jane curtsied and left, feeling triumphant. She knew it was a foolish emotion, unreal, because she had not known anyone to yet win against her husband. She certainly had not, yet his noise of frustration had been a triumph. Even if it would be likely short-lived. She needed to prove she could win sometimes.

AFTER – DAY THREE

"And you are?" James asked the coroner, already sounding imperious. His tone was not unlike his father's, and it chilled Jane. He wouldn't be like his father, she'd sworn it so many times, but she knew there was still work to see him become a fair-minded, generous man.

Mr. Eier had stood when Jane did, and now he sketched a bow. "My lord. I am Mr. Eier, the coroner.

I am here informing your mother of the developments regarding your father's death."

James turned and stood facing him fully, his body relaxing into a stance that echoed Matthew's. It turned Jane's stomach, but she willed herself to put Matthew out of her mind. His stance was in no way reflective of his father's behavior. "And what is the development? Have you found a cause?"

Mr. Eier colored. "That is the trouble, you see. The more I look into this, the more I find other causes."

"So you don't know," James said. His tone was withering, a man's confidence in the body of a twelve-year-old boy.

"It could be a number of things, you see. There is the violent aspect of it, of course, which is immediate."

"Violence is like that," James said drily.

Jane watched the debate between her son and the coroner with fascination. She still saw James as a child, but the rest of the world now saw him as what he would become—what he became the moment his father died: the next viscount.

"You see, my lord, on my initial examination, I thought the body was not bloody enough considering the location of the knife wound."

James narrowed his eyes at the man. "Did you not find the body in the Thames? Last I heard from the valet, cold water is excellent for a blood stain."

"Of course, my lord, that is a valid consideration."

Jane could barely refrain from rolling her eyes.

"But the assault didn't follow all the usual rules of a person being assaulted by highwaymen."

James folded his arms. "Do tell."

"While he was most assuredly robbed of his most precious items, the signet ring was still on his finger.

Many times, during an assault, the highwaymen will cut off a finger in order to relieve its owner of the jewelry."

"And this is every case?" James asked.

"Not every single one. Certainly, one could argue that the brigands didn't have enough time and needed to flee the scene swiftly to avoid discovery."

"Could that not be the case here?" James asked.

"It is a possibility. But then, when I opened the body, I found evidence of poisoning of his internal organs."

At this, James laughed. His bright boyish gaiety put both Jane and Mr. Eier aghast.

"This is not a laughing matter, James," Jane admonished her son.

He turned his green eyes on her, the telltale sign of her blood in his body. "Oh, but it is, dear Mama. It is." He turned back to Mr. Eier. "I know nothing of the circumstances. I know nothing of poisons or blood stains or robberies, but I do know one thing. Few are the people who have encountered my father who have not fantasized about killing him."

Mr. Eier shifted uncomfortably. "I would like to bring the case to the magistrate tomorrow. Testimony, of course, would be key in securing the hangman's noose for the culprit of this dastardly crime."

Another burst of laughter from James. "To what end? Who would accuse someone of such a crime? It sounds as if you need someone to burst into the magistrate's office and announce his guilt. Other than that, the population of London at large will warrant an accusation."

Mr. Eier stiffened. "Someone needs to hang for this offense. Justice needs to be pursued to the fullest extent of the law."

James folded his arms and narrowed his eyes. "And where has justice been?"

Jane winced. Her son referenced so much that she wanted to forget. The assaults on numerous housemaids over the years—some that she knew James had witnessed. But in the case of a lord assaulting a maid, justice would never take the side of a poor woman over a rich man. James knew that Matthew had hurt her at times, too—but again, justice turned a blind eye since Jane was his wife, to do with as he wished.

The only crime Matthew had committed that Justice might have cared about at all was when he'd hurt Jane's niece. She was not only a child but also an earl's daughter. Yet to expose that crime was to expose the girl, something none of them was willing to risk. Best to keep it under wraps. And Justice would be kept in the family.

"I'm sure I don't know what you mean." Mr. Eier cleared his throat. "But I will see you tomorrow morning at the inquest."

James gave him a sharp look. "As suspects or witnesses?"

Jane wanted to clamp her hand over his mouth. *Don't give him any ideas.*

BEFORE

Jane's hands shook.

Hope crooned a soothing lullaby as she dressed Jane's hair. Andrepont had gifted her a white frock laced with silver and gold thread. It was exquisite, but the dress turned Jane's stomach. She was meant to appear virginal on her eighteenth birthday. On the night their marriage was finalized. This was a show, and Jane knew it. The only thing she didn't know was who the show was for. Andrepont might intend to terrorize only her, but Jane doubted it. The man preferred elaborate theatre, knowing he was the puppet master, pulling strings.

Hope threaded pearls into Jane's hair. They contrasted beautifully with her thick, dark locks. "You look like something out of a French story," Hope said. "I wish more people could see it. You'd be the talk of London for weeks!"

Jane winced. She likely already was, and not in a way respectable ladies ought to be. "At least you and I will know that I've been beautiful," Jane said. And that's how she felt. Beauty wasn't hers, or anyone's. It was this other thing entirely, like another dress one slipped on. It might be hers, it might be someone else's. But it never belonged to one person alone.

Tonight, she'd pay for her respite in the country with Emma. She'd pay for any and all slights, intentional or otherwise, in whatever Andrepont had designed for her birthday.

"I'm sure . . ." Hope trailed off, finishing Jane's hair.

The tired old phrases that worked for other women took on new, uncomfortable meanings in this house. *I'm sure his lordship will like it* threatened violence. *His lordship would approve* was pure manipulation.

"I'm fine, Hope. It doesn't matter. Thank you for all your hard work." Jane was beginning to feel like Mary, Queen of Scots heading to the gallows in the only way she knew how: wearing a beautiful dress.

"Yes, my lady." Hope gave a stunted curtsy and quickly tidied the dressing table as Jane stood and smoothed her skirts. After one last fuss and straightening of fabric, Jane opened the door, ready for dinner. Or the gallows. Whichever came first.

⚜

AFTER – DAY THREE

Jane was still in the drawing room, about to go up and change for dinner, when her sister entered.

"I thought I might catch you before dinner," Emma said.

"You're in luck. I'm taking my time since James is finally home." Jane could hear the faint strains of his piano music all the way up here. She found it comforting to have her son home, have him close. Especially now, knowing that Matthew could no longer hurt him.

"I heard." Emma smiled. The pain lingering in her heart was obvious in her expression. Emma's boy would never come home from school. William was gone forever.

Jane stuck the needle in her mending. James had brought home shirts that were in terrible disrepair. "I swear, the boy must roll in thorn bushes to rip his clothes so thoroughly."

"Keeping yourself rather busy," Emma said.

"I'm trying to be left alone," Jane snapped. Her head hurt from all the machinations. She wanted to be safe and calm with her boy by her side. "I should like to go to bed and not get out for a fortnight. But there are too many affairs to be put to rights, and I cannot afford such a luxury now."

Emma sat back, her pale blue skirts rustling. She sighed. "You've not had an easy path."

"There are no easy paths," Jane said, letting her fingers massage her temples. "Even the easiest is fraught with grief and hardship."

Emma smiled. "You should read Gareth's texts about Buddha."

"Did he have a very hard life?" Jane asked.

"He had thoughts about the suffering of all peoples," Emma said. "It might give you solace."

"I'm not terribly interested in a man's pontifications on suffering." Jane suddenly felt the urge to cry, but of course, that was reserved for a time when she was alone. And even then, she was far too tired for actual tears to fall. She felt as if weeping was for the young. Endurance was for women of her age.

"If an apology for any of my actions was worth anything, I would do so another thousand times." Emma's voice was quiet as the old regret surfaced.

There had already been a thousand apologies, wishes for actions to be undone, promises of safety and protection that could never have been kept. Vasya had been the most concrete of those promises. And he had tried to keep her safe. But Vasya had never been able to predict Matthew. In fact, Jane hadn't, either, though she had been the best at managing expectations. What would soothe him, what would aggravate him. Yet his swings to violence, and who would suffer as a result, were as random as a lightning strike.

Emma put a hand on Jane's arm. "Go to bed, Jane. You look tired."

But Jane's head still buzzed with all her responsibilities. As she ticked down the list of her duties, she realized much of her chores were solely to mitigate Matthew's moods. Now that he was gone, Martha had the household under control. "But," she protested, more out of habit than anything else.

"Would you like me to take you to bed? Like when we were children?" Emma stood and held out her hand.

"I haven't had dinner," Jane protested.

"We'll have a tray sent up," Emma promised, shaking her hand as a second invitation.

"But James—"

"Doesn't need to be bothered while he's using music to work through his grief." Emma waggled her hand again, akin to a worm on a fishing hook.

Jane took it and sighed, letting her sister guide her to her rooms. Once there, Emma helped Jane out of her dress and stays, holding out the silk dressing gown for her arms. She then poured two tumblers of claret from the supply that Jane kept in her rooms. She sometimes needed it to help her sleep at night, knowing the door separating her rooms from Matthew's was no barrier to him.

The sisters didn't speak, just drank companionably while sitting on Jane's bed, Emma rubbing her sister's back. Once they emptied their tumblers, Emma put them both on the tray next to the claret decanter. Then she tucked Jane into bed.

"Not to worry. Gareth and I will come to support you and James. We can even pick you up in our carriage, if you like."

It would be better if they arrived in the carriage with the Andrepont crest on it. Let James have his entrance as a viscount, even if it was not yet confirmed.

"No, we'll take our own."

"Then it's settled. I will see you at the magistrate's in the morning. Do you still want that dinner tray?" Emma asked.

Jane shook her head.

"Wonderful. I'll tell Martha not to bother, and I'll let James know you've gone to bed as well."

Jane got back to her elbows. "What if he needs me?"

Emma smiled. "He might. But you need your rest if you are to answer questions in the morning. And he will as well. I'll remind him of that. Not to worry. Go to sleep."

Jane nodded, grateful, suddenly and once again, for her older sister. Sometimes, those with great burdens need someone else's permission to put those burdens aside for a small time. She melted down into the bed as Emma left, closing the door ever so quietly.

CHAPTER 12

J ane sat at the dinner table, her hands shaking despite clutching them in her lap. Men lined the table, and only men. They were her husband's friends and acquaintances. Men who had leered and ogled; gawked and taunted. There was one seat empty. Considering the degenerates who already graced her table, she couldn't begin to guess who would take the last place setting.

Until Gareth entered the room. She glanced over at her husband, who also noted Gareth's arrival. The spider-like gleam in Andrepont's eye deepened. This was another manipulation—for both her and her brother-in-law. He was her only lifeline of hope in whatever it was that her husband intended tonight. And this was a way to make Gareth complicit, for there was no way he could stop whatever Andrepont had planned. One man against so many others.

"Aberscomb! Sorry to hear of your brother," one man said to Gareth, pulling his attention away from Jane, who was seated to Andrepont's right at the head of the table. "Carringwell. Went to school with your uncle."

Gareth gave a slight bow. "Good evening, my lord. I didn't realize there would be such company for dinner."

Carringwell elbowed him as if they were in on the same joke. "Ah, you married the sister, didn't you? Lucky man. Well, we get to drink a toast to this one, anyway."

Gareth gave a wary nod and made his way deeper into the dining room, to the empty place setting. He looked confused, and Jane pitied him. He couldn't know the depths of her husband's cruelty.

There were sixteen men seated at the table now, eight on one side, seven on the other. Whatever was to happen would commence soon, as the men were all still talking. She answered questions politely when she was addressed, but she tried very hard to stay out of the conversations that surged around her. She strained to hear Gareth's conversation halfway down the table. On his left was Lord Denby.

Jane suppressed a shiver. He was so skeletal. His neck seemed to be one nod away from falling off, like an old, dried-out twig.

"Surprised to see you here, Aberscomb. Didn't think you went in for nights like this," Denby said, letting out a wracking cough into his napkin.

Gareth looked around. "Nights like what?"

Jane closed her eyes for a brief moment. *Nights like this.* There wasn't a word to express the amount of dread she felt.

A dark claret was poured for each guest, including her. She wanted to down it completely, but she refrained. She needed to maintain her dignity, whatever little she could keep intact tonight. Andrepont stood, his glass aloft, ready to make a speech. Jane made the mistake of glancing at Gareth. The horror on his face showed her that he'd figured out whatever it was that would happen to her tonight.

"As you are all aware, tonight we celebrate the birth of my bride, eighteen years ago today."

There was a low chuckle from the men that made the hair on the nape of her neck stand on end.

Gareth motioned to the footman, who balked. After a moment of holding his gaze, the younger man broke away, checked in with the butler, and then disappeared from the room. The butler frowned, looking at Gareth. Jane didn't dare to hope that whatever Gareth had said would help her. Save her.

"Jane has not been fully my wife up until now, as per the marriage contract I signed," Andrepont said.

Jane refused to give this pack of jackals an ounce of herself. Of course she caught that Andrepont used her first name with all of these men. Referencing their chaste marriage was either to humiliate her or titillate them.

"But tonight, no longer." Andrepont continued. "Tonight, I will take my marital privileges, and I invite you all to witness the event."

If she'd had any food in her belly, Jane might have cast up her accounts. Despite herself, she squeezed her eyes shut. This was the payment. This was his way of proving that he owned her. Her teeth began to chatter, so she clamped her jaw tight. Murmurs down the table made her eyes fly open.

"This was an old custom, and one I think we should restart. Don't you agree?" The room was full of applause and jokes and laughter. The wicked grin on Andrepont's face was unmistakable. He threw back the rest of his claret and leaned down. "I win," he whispered.

Jane swallowed involuntarily.

"I beg your pardon," Denby said, having the gall to sound offended. But his voice was not directed to the room. It was directed to one man. Jane's attention snapped down the table.

"Get out now." Gareth got to his feet. "Or I will snap your neck and enjoy doing so."

Denby threw his serviette onto the table.

Andrepont looked at Gareth, amused. "Have something to say, my lord?"

"This isn't happening," Gareth said, standing. "I advise all of you to get out now."

Jane tried so hard to look bland and even. She wasn't scared—she was absolutely terrified. She wouldn't show it. She wouldn't. Andrepont could not win. She wouldn't allow it.

"Lord Aberscomb, your display is admirable, and I understand you have the urge to defend your sister-in-law, but you may go home now and tell your dear *lady wife*"—he spat the words—"that you did your best. Run along."

"Anyone who doesn't wish to be pummeled by me personally should leave now." Gareth cast his gaze around the room, as now Jane did the same. She was grateful for his defense, but ultimately, there were fifteen of them and one of him. While many of the men were paunchy or weak, it was still not in his favor. Jane looked down. She should stand and protest. She should stand and submit. Let Gareth leave the house without harm.

"My staff knows that if they defy me, they will be out on their arses with no references. You have no allies here, Aberscomb."

Jane knew Andrepont was right. She sipped the ruby-colored claret, fortifying herself and readying to stand. To tell Gareth that he ought to go and leave her to her fate. But Gareth spoke before she could.

"Gentlemen. This is a lady. A viscountess. Would you have your own wives thus debased? She is no courtesan, paid to be relieved of her virtue. Do you believe for one moment she is choosing this? She's barely more than a child. Some of you, I know."

Gareth eyed them. No doubt he'd gone to school with them or belonged to whatever men's clubs they might frequent. "Men of honor do not shame a young woman of quality. No matter what her husband has promised you, this will only bring shame on yourselves."

There was a cough and a screech of a chair leg on the parquet flooring. Andrepont gave Gareth a smug grimace.

"Then shame will come because I will tell all of your wives." Gareth tried, but Jane knew that wouldn't mean a thing. These men either didn't have wives or didn't bother with their opinions. These were not men who respected women of any ilk.

There wasn't so much as an eye roll.

"And your mistresses. You'll not have a warm bed in the years to come," Gareth said.

Denby finally stood and stalked out without a word. Then Carringwell threw his serviette on his plate and stood. "I didn't come here to be heckled, Andrepont."

The two men started a vanguard, with the majority following them out of the dining room. As they filed out, Vasya's large frame filled the doorway. He said nothing and did nothing, but the rest of the men stood and wordlessly left their dinner seats.

Jane squeezed her eyes shut as Andrepont glared at Gareth. "You have no right!" he hissed.

Gareth said nothing, merely extended his hand to Jane. "You are welcome at my home."

"She stays here!" Andrepont growled.

She wanted to go. Oh, she did. But she also knew the retribution for such an abandonment would be cataclysmic. She didn't dare. Andrepont would not be denied his marital rights. She looked past Gareth to Vasya, his face inscrutable. He was hers. She would think of him tonight. Her dream Vasya come to life. That's what she would think.

Gareth glanced between Jane and Andrepont. Jane gave a small nod and mouthed the words *thank you*. She hoped he would leave. Vasya was here. He'd help. He would always help, she knew.

"I'm watching you, Andrepont." Gareth stared down his brother-in-law.

The viscount bared his teeth. "I don't forget things, Aberscomb. I won't forget this."

"Neither will I," Gareth said before stomping out of the room.

Jane didn't watch Gareth leave; instead, she kept her eyes on her wine. She didn't dare look at Vasya, either. If Andrepont guessed that Jane wished to be with Vasya, her *tendre* would become her weakness, and then even her dreams would no longer belong to her.

"Go eat in your room," Andrepont spat, waving at her. "But don't change. And don't snuff any candles. I'll be expecting my rights tonight. Finally." Andrepont tossed back another glass of wine.

Jane stood, grateful and shaking. She said nothing, not wanting to disturb whatever anger swirled in his breast. Tears were for another day. Regret was useless. Gratitude was all she could feel at that moment.

☙❦❧

THE YEARS FELL INTO A KIND OF PATTERN. Andrepont allowed his wife small freedoms in London—such as visiting her aunt or her sister—so long as he visited her bedchambers regularly. Because there was no heir forthcoming, Vasya couldn't help but wonder if those visits were for marital relations or for the purposes of humiliation. Neither would surprise him, and no one would ask, not even Hope.

Because Jane often walked, not needing a carriage to visit her relations, Vasya rarely saw her. It hurt to know she existed without his help, without his protection, but she was living as a viscountess would, and he had neither the privilege nor the experience to protest.

The couple never entertained and rarely went out, so the staff equally fell into their own easy rhythms. Maids still came and went, though they stayed longer than they used to before falling prey to the master's appetites. Lady Andrepont had to know—but never commented, never controlled. She floated from room to room, aloof, beautiful, surviving.

Sometimes Vasya would spy her in the gardens. Or when she went down to the kitchens to work on a lotion or a tonic. She had little jars lined up, bits of paper attached to them, describing their purpose. Cook swore by her oil for rheumatism, and one of the footman said her tonic helped with his upset bowels. It made him wonder if she had tonics to keep herself from becoming with child. But that didn't make sense to him since Andrepont would stop coming to her bed if she produced an heir. And that made Vasya wonder if Andrepont was a good lover—a thought that turned his stomach, so he stopped that line of thinking immediately.

The young woman Vasya had met so long ago on Rotten Row was gone. Now she was stoic, if not blandly pleasant, showing little reaction to any news. Whatever Andrepont was doing to Jane, it was working, and Vasya hated him for it.

Instead, Vasya focused on what he could do for Jane. It had taken him years to accomplish, but finally, he did. Not wanting to use money dictated by the viscount, Vasya had bargained and bartered his way into labor, building materials, and skills. He'd also won a few choice card games while waiting for

Andrepont in disreputable places. That had helped with the budget.

He'd discreetly received permission from Andrepont to build a greenhouse in the back garden, near the mews. Vasya had couched it as a more reliable kitchen garden for Cook, and Andrepont had stopped listening when he thought the request was for servants. He'd waited until Jane was visiting the country estate to begin the build, mustering every favor he could call in.

So it was with bitter pleasure one spring morning, when Lord Andrepont was away doing his actual duty at the House of Lords, that Vasya approached Jane in her drawing room. He knew he should still think of her as Lady Andrepont, and he didn't dare say her name aloud, but in his mind, he savored her short, simple name: Jane. She sat, as she often did, in the drawing room, working on her watercolors. On those mornings, she left the door open, gathering all available light for the room.

He knocked softly on the doorframe. She looked up and smiled when she saw it was him. "Yes, Vasya?"

When she said his name, it nearly brought him to his knees every time. She said it as if they had spoken yesterday and not months ago. He returned the smile as best as he was able.

"I have something for you." He held out his hand. "Will you come with me to see it?"

She eagerly stood, going to him as if their differences didn't matter. As if nothing mattered but the two of them.

Vasya loved the feel of her hand tucked in his elbow as he escorted her down the stairs, through the ballroom, and into the manicured gardens.

"Where are we going?" She laughed like a child, and it made him smile. She felt something. She wasn't that bleak, bland automaton. When they rounded the corner of the hedges, where the line of tall, thin cypresses gave way, she saw the building with its shining glass panels. She gasped. "Is that a—"

Vasya smiled. "A greenhouse. Built for you. To enjoy."

Jane rushed ahead of him, giving a small, undignified shriek. "How did you do this?" She stopped short and spun around. "Does *he* know about this?"

The *he* she referred to was unquestionably Andrepont. "Yes and no," Vasya said, wanting to reassure her that yes, his lordship had approved of the building and would hopefully not retaliate when he found that she had something she wanted. But also, Vasya wanted the credit for having organized and built such a wonder. "Andrepont approved the building."

Relief flooded her expression, but then a new wariness crept in. "*How* did he approve it? Not for me, surely."

Vasya shifted his weight onto his back foot. An old habit that he couldn't help whenever a confrontation brewed. "It is a kitchen garden, for Cook."

Jane shook her head. Finally, a smile cracked through. "You are a sneaky man, Vasya."

His breath caught. It had been worth every gamble, every shilling, every bead of sweat to hear his name on her lips. "Let me show you inside."

She glowed so brightly he could barely keep from tripping over his own feet. The glass panes covering the greenhouse were spotlessly clean. There was a long wooden table down the center of the structure, ready for anything she might desire. He had bought some clay pots for her, should she need them, and had arranged to get regular deliveries of good soil before it got sent north to the farming communities.

She took a deep breath. "Oh, I can already smell the dirt. It's perfect."

"I did not know what you would like to have, so I have no seeds for you." Vasya wished he had gotten something, an oversight he kicked himself for.

She looked at him, her eyes brimming with tears. Happy tears, he reassured himself. The day he brought her to sad tears, he would murder himself. Without warning, she threw her arms around his neck. It startled him and he stepped back, catching her about the waist.

The sensation of holding her felt perfect and terribly wrong all at once. She was small, fragile. He didn't want to hurt her. Yet the touch of her made him feel as if gallons of the finest liquor had been poured down his throat. She was soft, and she smelled of flowers and pastel colors. If he knew poetry, or any beautiful words, he would say them now as he buried his face in her hair.

She didn't know how she slayed him. If she wanted his life, she could have it. If she demanded he get to his knees so she could behead him, he would hand her the sword. He could cry for how much he cared. He closed his eyes, letting her guide the encounter. If she wanted more from him, he would give it, but not until she asked.

The greenhouse was already warm and humid, the smell of the soil loamy and rich and full of possibility. His heart kicked faster as he held this precious woman in his arms. Perhaps the only time it might ever happen. For they would never dance together, never lie together.

She pulled away, her arms sliding down his chest in a way that made the placket of his work trousers feel tight. He shifted, hoping to disguise the sudden reaction.

"I cannot thank you enough, Vasya. This is

incredible. I—" She broke off, tears beginning to fall down her cheeks. When she turned back to him, the redness of her eyes made the green of her irises glow bright, like a candle in a glass bottle. "Thank you."

Vasya nodded, not knowing what to say. How did you tell someone, *I would die for you, and it would make me happy to spend my life that way*. "I will leave you to get acquainted." He stumbled out of the building, not trusting himself to keep his mouth shut.

❧

JANE'S WORLD GREW SMALLER AS IT BECAME CLEAR that Andrepont's nightly visits weren't causing her to increase. She was relieved, at least, that he encouraged her daily walks and visits to her sister. Sometimes she and Emma would walk together or go out to the shops, but it made Jane more restless.

Emma was becoming someone amongst the London elites. She'd befriended the young Lady Haglund and tried to pull Jane in, but Jane didn't know how to tell her sister that she wasn't allowed to attend parties. She wasn't allowed to be seen by the world. Andrepont's possessiveness was the only thing increasing.

At first, his visits were taunting but pleasant enough. As she grew to understand her own body and the nature of pleasure, he would switch to perfunctory, purposeful copulating, which had its own humiliations. She knew he would find a maid beforehand, get himself worked into his illicit lather, and then come spend inside her for the chance of an heir. She would admit that it was painful and unwelcome. But she didn't have a choice.

She made herself tonics to help her conceive, but nothing worked. There were several times when Jane suspected she'd managed to conceive, but then, within a week or two, she would bleed and her hopes would be dashed. She was frustrated, and rightly so. Andrepont's visits would only cease if she were to become with child.

She even asked her sister for advice, but Emma shrugged, bewildered. Taking pity on her sister, Emma agreed to walk, leaving young William at home with the nanny.

"How is it that London is the biggest city in the world, yet I feel like I'm slowly being strangled?" Jane asked, throwing a rock in the Serpentine.

The day already smelled of rain, but at least it was warm. They had time before the rain arrived in the afternoon. Emma shook her head, not responding because the answer was always the same. It only made Jane feel more restless.

"Have you heard of The Dutchman?" Jane asked, wanting to know. She'd overheard the term in a conversation between Cook and a housemaid.

"What? Just any Dutchman?" Emma asked, giving Jane a careful look, as if she was afraid Jane's mind was going.

Jane laughed. "No, it's a place. I heard about it. Supposed to be interesting. I'd like something interesting. Everywhere we go, the shops are simple and boring and respectable."

"And safe," Emma added. "What does this Dutchman sell?"

Jane gave her a conspiratorial look. "Everything."

"That's impossible, Jane. One cannot sell everything." Emma folded her arms, forgetting she was in public.

"I heard that it was the first place all the mud larkers take their stuff to try to sell." At least, that was what she'd gleaned from the housemaid's contribution.

"So it's a smuggling den?"

Jane cast her eyes to the sky and huffed. "Let's just go look at things. Something. Anything. I don't care."

Emma sighed and looked around as if answers lurked in the bushes. "We need a carriage. And some kind of protection. Where is this place?" After much negotiation, Emma canceled her afternoon calls. Jane also convinced Emma that Gareth would feel much better having Vasya with them if they were going to a dangerous place. Emma questioned Jane about still calling him *Vasya* instead of his proper name, but Jane refused to answer. If Andrepont heard her, yes, they'd be in trouble. But she couldn't give up that one small piece, too.

"It isn't *that* dangerous," Jane insisted, no longer certain if they were discussing The Dutchman or Vasya. When Emma stared her down, Jane finally admitted, "We will be going through a dangerous area."

They returned to Jane's house, given that Andrepont was not at home, to ask for a carriage. Jane felt the addition of another footman was far more than they needed since Vasya was taking them. Vasya gave no hint of approval or disapproval as he loaded them into the carriage.

When he handed Jane into the carriage, she could have sworn he felt the same frisson she felt. As if lightning were passing between them. But he merely handed Emma up into the carriage after her, then closed the door. The carriage lurched forward as the horses pulled.

They passed through rough roads and fields before finally grinding to a halt. Jane caught Emma staring at her as if she could see that invisible gold thread that stretched between Vasya and Jane. But Emma said nothing—didn't say if she saw something that Andrepont would never tolerate.

They rocked as the Russian got down from his post and opened the door.

The large brick building had a plank of wood next to it on which someone had painted tulips using some kind of vegetable ink. The result was quaint. Inside, the building was dark despite its tall windows. No one had cleaned the glass in a long time.

There was a wooden countertop behind which stood a blue-eyed man with wispy white-blond hair and pink skin. He seemed pleased to see them, and not at all surprised. "Welcome to my humble shop."

Jane acknowledged the proprietor with a nod while Emma smiled politely and Vasya glowered.

"Are you the Dutchman? Or is this shop The Dutchman?" Jane asked. "Shop" was perhaps the wrong term. It was dirtier and vaster than any shop she'd ever been in.

"Both. Whatever you wish." The man's Dutch accent made the guessing far less troublesome. "What may I help you with today?"

"We are looking for something interesting. Unusual." Emma glanced at the rows of shelves and drawers that surrounded them.

Jane was drawn to the same kind of curious perusal. Who knew what kind of treasures lay inside such a place?

"Jewelry? Portraiture? Taxidermy?" the Dutchman suggested, looking between them.

Emma looked at Jane, her nose scrunched in distaste. "Not taxidermy."

Jane frowned. She had enough of her husband's dead relatives staring down at her. "Or portraiture."

"I have some excellent jewelry made from the teeth of condemned men—"

"No teeth, either, I'm afraid," Emma interrupted.

The Dutchman's vibrant expression dimmed. "Glassworks? Porcelain? Enamelware?"

"Teapots?" Jane suggested, looking at Emma. "You drink a dreadful amount of it."

The Dutchman's eyes lit up. "Yes! I have a great many teapots. Stay right here, please. I will fetch them."

The sisters exchanged another look. Who knew what this strange old man would bring out? They heard clanging and clinking and one disappointed *tsk* come from the depths of the building. Emma giggled, which pleased Jane. She still felt the invisible thread to Vasya, who stood behind them surveying the strangeness of the place. But here, the connection was one of safety and familiarity. She could laugh with her sister, relax with two people who cared for her.

A few minutes later, the Dutchman returned carrying an enormous tray filled with teapots. He set it on the counter and said, "I shall return. I have another tray." He disappeared into the maze of shelves again.

Stepping up to the display of teapots, Jane and Emma surveyed the lot. There were all sorts of teapots, some beautifully hand-painted but chipped in spots. Another one was square and looked like an elephant, with its trunk being the spout. Another was lacquered in gold and very garish, bone white glaring through nicks in several places. Yet another depicted a man and a woman twisted in a passionate embrace, and what looked to be—

"This is not for respectable ladies," Vasya said, reaching over their heads to grab the obscene teapot with one hand.

Jane smacked him lightly with the back of her hand. "That's not for you to say."

Emma watched the childish flirtation with her mouth buttoned shut and her eyes wide. Jane knew her sister could feel how the air between Jane and Vaysa thickened in the warehouse's cool air.

"A shopkeeper should know better than to show these things to fine ladies," Vasya said, his Russian accent noticeably thicker.

"But it's here, and you are not our chaperone. We're married ladies now. We get to see whatever we want," Jane said.

"No," Vasya said, reaching around Jane's waist for the teapot, his subtle teasing smile clear as day.

Jane made a grab for the teapot, which put Emma's eyebrows up to her forehead. The two were acting like children in the schoolroom, but Jane liked it. Vasya held the teapot over his head, where Jane could only jump for it—something more childish than she was willing to do. Emma turned back to the teapots, examining the rest of the unusual collection as if she weren't witnessing a flirtation between a viscountess and her groom.

They heard a crash, followed by a string of foreign words that were most likely Dutch curses. The unfortunate accident at least snapped Jane out of behaving like a naughty schoolgirl.

"Are you quite well?" Emma called.

The Dutchman appeared, looking sheepish. "I apologize. I was so eager to bring the next tray out that I tripped, and they all went—" The Dutchman made a gesture with his hands of things flying into the air.

"I'm so sorry," Jane said, wincing. She hoped he wouldn't blame them for coming in. In fact, Jane resolved to buy something from the poor man to make up for it. She scanned the tray of dishes. There was one that was quite simple, a clay teapot that looked wretched next to the dazzling gilt and painted pieces. "Tell me about this one."

"Very discerning eye," The Dutchman said, shaking his finger at her. "It may not look like much on the outside, but this one is very special. It is called . . ." He stopped, looking amongst them as if he had a secret. "The Assassin's Teapot!"

Jane, appropriately, gasped. The Dutchman seemed pleased with her reaction. Vasya, however, harrumphed.

Emma appeared amused. "How is this a teapot for an assassin?"

The Dutchman picked up the teapot and lifted the lid. Inside, there was a wall dividing the pot into two. "In one side, you have good tea. In the other, poison. But you pour only out of one teapot! It fools the victim into a false sense of safety."

"Or you can drink regular tea and I can drink my herbal blends," Jane suggested.

Emma shuddered. Ever since Jane's greenhouse had started flourishing, her herbal tea concoctions had grown increasingly exploratory. Emma claimed the tisanes smelled like rotting mushrooms and tasted like death. Jane tried to explain all the health benefits, but Emma only scoffed.

"How much?" Jane asked, determined to buy something.

"One pound," The Dutchman said.

Vasya scoffed loudly from behind them. Jane knew he didn't mean to be menacing, but it certainly sounded that way.

"You cannot be serious," Emma said. "One pound for a teapot is outrageous."

"It is not a teapot," the Dutchman insisted. "It is a lethal weapon."

Emma rolled her eyes. "Two crowns."

"Two crowns and three shillings." The Dutchman countered.

"Two crowns, two shillings." Jane held the man's eye.

"Done," The Dutchman said. "I will wrap your purchase for you, madame."

Emma elbowed her sister as Jane fished her coin purse from her skirt pockets and counted out the coins. Jane gave Emma a triumphant smile, scooping the teapot out from underneath her sister's gaze. This was the kind of good-natured competition she liked to have with her sister. It was the kind of sibling rivalry that she missed living apart.

❧

"How does this even work?" Emma said, exasperated already with Jane's purchase.

Jane lifted the teapot lid and examined it closely. "There are holes in the handle. Maybe that's how?"

Emma leaned over to look. Jane felt curiously light. As if her daily life had receded into nothing but noise, like walking away from a raucous fair in the middle of Town. "I don't see how that would do anything."

"What if it's like a flute? Covering the holes changes things?" Jane suggested.

"That's for sound," Emma protested.

Jane looked at her. "Then we might as well try it and find out. Put the tea in one compartment and sherry in the other."

Her sister looked scandalized, as if she had suggested they swim naked in the Serpentine. "Sherry? In a teapot?"

"Just do it," Jane insisted, reaching for the tea in the perfectly normal, regular, everyday, non-lethal teapot.

Emma grumbled, but she stood and fumbled with the keys on her chatelaine to open the sherry tumbler in the corner.

Once the liquids were in their proper chambers, obvious in their color differences, Jane was eager to pour. "Get your cup over here."

Emma rolled her eyes but obeyed.

"I'm not covering any holes," Jane announced, then poured. A mixture of darkly brewed tea and the red-tinted sherry came out. They both frowned.

"Well, that looks revolting," Emma said. "Another cup."

"I'm covering the first hole in the handle now," Jane announced. Both sisters peered into the cup as she poured. They saw darkly brewed tea, which had been in the teapot's forward chamber.

Emma looked closely, picked up the cup, and sniffed. "Huh."

"Taste it," Jane urged.

Emma sipped. "Lovely, malty tea. No sherry that I can tell. Here, do the second one." She quickly got a new cup.

"Covering only the second hole," Jane announced again, and as she had hoped, the pretty, reddish sherry splashed into the cup.

"How intriguing," Emma said, picking up the second cup and sniffing it. She sipped. "Definitely sherry."

"Only you would find a covert way to drink liquor intriguing," Jane teased.

Emma lifted one shoulder. "You're the one with the teapot. Pour yourself a cup."

Jane did. They laughed with each other like they used to, and it felt like this was a life they could both live. More children would come along, and they would have pleasant afternoons together.

"I think you should practice with it so you may drink your horrid concoctions and serve normal, delicious tea to any visitors," Emma said. "We'll wash it out and wrap it up again."

"Emma," Jane protested. She'd thought they might share the teapot, rotate it back and forth, a game for them to play.

"You clearly need it more than me," Emma said, giving a mocking shiver. "No one else should be subjected to your brews."

Jane looked down, hoping Emma didn't realize she never had visitors. The only person who might call on her was Emma, but she didn't for fear of Andrepont's retaliation. There was too much that Jane kept to herself. She didn't need to keep the teapot as well. But she didn't want to tell her sister that. Emma didn't need any more burdens.

CHAPTER 13

"Wake up, Vasya," a woman said. The voice was soft and feminine and familiar, but he couldn't quite place it. When he opened his eyes, heavy from sleep, the face he saw was not one he immediately recognized.

Ah. His wife.

"The inquest is today. I've made you porridge and laid out your clothes," she said.

Vasya rubbed his eyes and stretched out, feeling cramped in this bed with another person. The ropes creaked and squeaked as he moved. "You did not have to do so."

She smiled at him, nothing but kindness in her pale gray eyes. "I'm your wife. It's my job." She busied herself, whisking herself into the next room, her rough-spun skirts swaying around her thin frame.

He smiled back at her, a gentleness coming over him. She was a sweet woman, this newly minted Mrs. Kuznetsov. She was the niece of the old housekeeper and had briefly worked as a maid in the household before Andrepont could get his hands on her. She was sweet and slow-moving, not of a temperament for service.

She was the opposite of sharp and incisive Jane, who had been honed like a whittled spear. But the knife who had harried her was gone now. Would she become a different woman?

Vasya shook his head and sat up. The bed was of decent quality, the ropes having been tightened when he bought it from the previous owner. It would take time to adjust to the noise. Mrs. Kuznetsov smiled at him once more through the doorway to the main room. She had a fire going in the small stove, a kettle steaming on top of it. On the wooden table sat two bowls, the aforementioned porridge, no doubt. Vasya rubbed his face again and tugged at his dark black beard, hoping it wasn't wild and terrifying.

He knew white hairs were coming soon, which would soften the look of his face, but he didn't look forward to it. Much of his life in England had been to intimidate. Could one instill abject obedience in other men if those men did not fear for their lives?

He stood, his white shirt falling to his thighs. On other men's shirts fell to knee length, but getting a tailor in London to accommodate him was not worth the effort. There were other big men that roamed the streets, and they all seemed to catch sight of one another, acknowledge one another. *I don't have to strain my neck to speak with you*, they all implied.

Vasya washed his face and dressed in the clothes his wife had laid out for him, already pressed. She must have gotten up much earlier than he had. "You've worked hard this morning," he said, hoping she heard it as a compliment.

"Nervous energy, I suppose. Sit," she said, gesturing to a chair. He did, and she settled across from him. She watched him, and he knew it was to see if he liked the porridge she'd made. Obligingly, he took a bite, only to find that it was delicious. "Did you put molasses in here?"

Pride stretched across her face. "I did. Bartered for it with some of my sewing skills. Do you like it?"

"Very much so," he said, gobbling two more bites before he willed himself to slow down. He looked over at her bowl, whose portion was considerably smaller than his, and paler. "Did you not add any to yours?"

"Oh, it doesn't sit well with me," she said, and he couldn't tell if she meant it or if it was an excuse. She lifted her spoon and picked at the porridge. Her thinness was not a girlish figure or a fit of fashion. He'd known before they married that she couldn't eat much.

"I was thinking that I might accompany you to the inquest," she said.

Vasya immediately shook his head. There would be nothing but terrible outcomes if she was present. He didn't want Jane to see her. He hadn't wanted Jane to know that he'd married, even though she'd found out. The hurt in her eyes. He couldn't inflict it further.

"You'll be called to witness," she said. "And they'll want a witness to your being home with me the night it happened. I can honestly tell them you were. I can help." When she laid her hand on his, his fingers retreated, curling around his palm.

"It will be a strain on your health," he said, knowing it sounded ridiculous.

"I might save your life," she said. "That's all I care to do."

Shame swept through him. He was the worst of men, hiding behind a woman. He squeezed his eyes shut. "Then you will go with me. Together."

"Husband and wife," she amended. "That no man shall tear asunder."

A lump formed in his throat. He was the worst of men. Then he thought of Andrepont as he'd last seen him, floating face down in the Thames. Perhaps the second worst.

BEFORE

Jane panted as the pain receded. Beyond her bedroom door, Mrs. Houseman argued with the physician. At least, the man was supposed to be a physician. Matthew had hired him to help Jane get through the birth of the Andrepont heir. Mrs. Houseman believed the man to be an idiot and told him so to his face. When he didn't budge, Jane yelled at the man as well. He now had the decency to stand outside of her room and argue.

Jane didn't know what Matthew would do when he realized his man was no longer there to spy on her. Matthew. Was Jane really going to start calling her husband by his given name? She ought to, given it was his fault that she felt like her pelvis was going to rip into two separate pieces. She roared as the pain returned.

Mrs. Houseman was by her side again, talking, squeezing her hand, lifting the white sheet now stained with sweat and some kind of fluid. Jane knew she shouldn't be ashamed of anything, that childbirth was natural and as right as could be.

"I need to stand up," Jane panted.

Mrs. Houseman nodded, and together, they stood Jane upright. Something dripped down the back of Jane's knee, tickling, then itching. She wished once again for Emma, but Matthew had forbidden her sister from being present at the birth. He didn't trust

Emma near his heirs, he said. As if Emma might switch the child or some nonsense.

Hope entered the room with fresh water and bread slathered with butter and honey. Her eyes widened, but she didn't shrink from Jane's predicament. The maid claimed she had been present for other births, so Mrs. Houseman allowed her to stay.

Jane thought of Emma's labor, of William's birth. Of Gareth arriving, rain dripping from his tricorn hat onto the carpet, insistent that he see his wife and child. As far as Jane knew, Matthew wasn't even at home.

"My mama always listed the things she loved when she was in labor. Said it helped with the pain to think of it." Hope glanced over to Mrs. Houseman for approval, and the midwife nodded in acceptance. So Jane tried it.

"Emma," she gritted out. "My mother. My father."

"No," Hope said. "Things you really love. Not just your family."

The pain receded. Jane caught her breath.

"Let me look," Mrs. Houseman said, pulling up Jane's flimsy shift. "There's a head. We'll make our way back to the bed so I can catch it before it falls on the ground."

Jane breathed deeply as they turned. It felt almost like having her menstrual rags bunched up between her legs at night. But much, much more pain. "Emma," she said, huffing to catch her breath.

"Yes, dear Emma," Mrs. Houseman echoed. "What else?"

"Walking barefoot on cool grass in the for—" Pain gripped her again, but she was close enough to the bed to lean on a post. Her fingernails dug into the wood. Matthew would be furious if he knew. But he'd never notice. Her jaw clenched so tightly that she thought her teeth might crack.

Mrs. Houseman was down on her knees. "A little more, girl. A little more. Get me a clean towel."

Hope bumbled around the room.

Jane took a breath, feeling dizzy and almost out of her mind. "Vasyaaaaaaa—"

And there was a baby.

❦

EMMA CAME THE DAY AFTER JAMES WAS BORN. JANE was exhausted. Mrs. Houseman was gone—staying at the nearby inn. The midwife's instincts were perfect. She'd taken one look at the pristine house and shivered. She knew that evil lurked there.

Hope doted on Jane, and a new woman had joined the staff—a nursemaid for James. Because she grew up as a village girl, Jane had assumed she would nurse her own babes, but Matthew had scoffed when she made mention of it. So here was a nurse, a plump woman with ample milk available.

Jane barely remembered Emma's visit—what they talked about, what they'd eaten—but Emma had sat in a chair next to Jane's bed. Hope had brought in a tray. Jane had prepared her own herbal concoctions months ago in preparation for after the baby was born to help her heal and stop the bleeding. Emma had scrunched her nose at the smell. That was all Jane remembered in her fatigue.

Matthew was incensed by Emma's presence. That night, he burst into Jane's room, throwing her perfumes and salves to the floor, ripping apart every letter, every pamphlet, every book he could find in her room. Jane was half-convinced that he would rip her apart with his very hands. She was too tired to be afraid, and Matthew didn't like that at all.

Matthew roared, his words unintelligible. She caught words like "her" and "whore," but his sentences were incoherent. His normally beautiful face was red and then purple, his dark eyes bottomless. After destroying her room, he merely turned to Jane, who was lying in the bed bleeding, exhausted, and vulnerable. He shook with rage. "You," he sputtered.

And then he left.

The front door slammed, and the house echoed in the silent wake of Matthew's anger. Sometime later, ten minutes or perhaps an hour, the house came to life again. Hope crept into Jane's room, cleaning and tidying. When the maid noticed Jane was awake, she checked on her.

"Did he hurt you? Do you need anything?" The worry in the maid's charming face was obvious.

Jane shook her head. "All thunder this time."

Hope looked pained and closed her eyes. "I can't believe I'm going to say what I'm about to say, so I beg your forgiveness in advance."

Jane expected the girl to tell her to leave the house or tender her resignation. She guarded against the disappointment both comments would bring. But Hope had always been a surprise: her kindness, her quiet strength.

"Molly is about to leave. She's been the focus of his attentions the last few months. She's not with child, she just can't stand it anymore. But everyone knows his lordship is going to find his entertainment below stairs. I've been protected because of my status as your lady's maid, but I think . . . I think—" Hope sniffled, her eyes shining, full of tears.

Jane began to guess what Hope was about to offer and she shook her head.

"But my lady, it's only going to get worse. He has his heir. He'll want another from you, but he needn't treat you so well. He'll hurt you like he's hurt Molly, and she never could figure out how to make him stop, and I . . . I . . . think I know how to."

Tired as she was, Jane felt her eyebrows rise up as far as they could stretch. "Hope, no one can control him. That's the reason behind his cruelty. There's no stopping him."

Hope furrowed her brow and her eyes cleared. "It isn't that I think I can make him stop, but I can make him stop hurting you."

Jane pitied her if she thought anyone could make that happen. "Hope, thank you for offering, but—"

"Because I'd let him hurt me."

Jane's jaw dropped. "Absolutely not. Hope. No."

"But you see, it's fine because it's happened before. I don't mind it." A perfect blonde curl escaped from her cap.

"That's ridiculous. No." Jane turned her head, hoping that would end the conversation.

"My father would beat me, you see, if my mother garnered attention, which I've already told you she did. But what I never told him was that the beatings didn't matter to me. I don't feel bruises the way others do. It isn't that bad. It really isn't. I can feign pain, of course, that will likely be necessary, but I don't really mind that much."

"Hope!" Jane wanted her to stop talking. To stop whatever this nonsense was that would get her killed.

"My only request is that you help me prevent a babe. And if there is one, that you pledge to protect it. That's all."

"Hope!" Jane said again. "I can't accept an offer like this. It's absurd."

"Think it over. He'll come after me sooner or later. If there's a plan, if I'm willing, it will help everyone." Hope curtsied and left, promising to return and sweep up the broken glass scattered on the rug from Matthew's rampage.

⁂

VASYA SWEATED THE NIGHT THE ANDREPONT HEIR was born. Stingy as Andrepont was, he'd allowed the staff to have wine to celebrate, and then again when he found out the babe was a boy.

Secretly, Vasya had hoped Jane might have a girl. A sweet, beautiful girl that he might be allowed to dandle on his knee. One to sneak trinkets and gifts to whenever he could. A boy—the heir—was meant for greater things and would be watched. An heir would not spend time with servants and would be shipped off to the best schools as early as possible. If nothing else, the viscount was obsessed with rank. His child would uphold his duty.

A few weeks after the boy's birth, the elderly housekeeper, Mrs. Renwood, fell. She broke a bone and could no longer walk. Andrepont set her up in a flat nearby and found a physician to tend to her. But a new position was open, and when Martha Foraker walked through the door, Vasya smiled under his great black beard.

Two Jane loyalists in the house.

Between Martha and the wet nurse, the new staff breathed a little life into the house. It felt less dusty, less morose. And when Jane resumed her visits to the greenhouse, Vasya did his best to find excuses to carry supplies nearby.

One day, Hope pulled his arm as he was about to step outside. "Be careful."

He frowned.

Hope glanced around as if she were worried about being overheard. "I know how you feel about each other."

"Who?" he asked. And indeed, she could be speaking about anyone. It was not uncommon to have women's names tied to his, many of whom he'd never so much as spoken with. His size made him an object of scrutiny, especially by women.

"During her labor, she screamed your name."

The sound of a water droplet falling from the outside pump seemed as loud as a gunshot. "There is no—we have not—"

Hope shook her head. "It doesn't matter what has happened. Only what it looks like. You must know that."

Vasya nodded, glancing at the other servants milling about downstairs, the constant list of tasks addressed. None seemed to pay attention to them whispering by the door, but that did not mean it was not marked. There were very few secrets in a big house like this. At least amongst the servants.

He pushed out the back door onto the slate step, watching Jane move in the greenhouse, her watery form obscured by the sun's glare and the thriving herbs and plants. Hope still stood in the doorway, her expression a pitying one. He knew she was right. Vasya could not be so obvious. Always appearing at the greenhouse.

But Vasya had already stayed away for so long that he ached for Jane's gaze. Even a word wasn't necessary, just her awareness of him. She was busy in her greenhouse, drying herbs and moving about in there, busy like a squirrel preparing for winter.

He opened the door, memorizing how she looked with her dirtied apron tied around her waist, the small watch pinned to her breast, her hair spilling out of its pins and curling in the humid air. She glanced up, surprised, her brilliant green eyes pinning him.

"Do you need anything?" he asked.

It seemed like a thousand expressions crossed her

face. Since having the babe, she was different, yet the same. Vasya couldn't explain it. She was more *her* than she'd ever been, and it snared him deeper.

She glanced over her shoulder at a big pot of something green. "Can you move that over here, to the light? I'm afraid it doesn't like being on that side of the greenhouse."

He knew it was busy work and the plant didn't care. But he happily tucked an apron over his clothes and moved the very heavy plant. Once he delivered it, they stood side by side. Vasya turned the pot, rotating the plant as if he knew what to do with it.

"What else do you need?" Vasya asked.

"Advice," Jane said, her hands moving. She trimmed crispy leaves from dried stems, measuring them on a heavy silver scale. There was a receipt book open on the other side of the bench, a pencil at the ready.

"I am happy to help. Always."

"Hope has offered to place herself in the path of my husband." She said it without malice or any hint of agitation.

Vasya frowned. Hope was a smart girl, but offering her mistress to have an affair with the master seemed strange. "Why would she say such a thing to you?"

"To help me. To save me from Matthew's violence."

Vasya startled. She'd called her husband by his first name. He'd never heard her do that before, and unwarranted jealousy coursed through him.

"Should I allow her to do it? I'm making her a preventative tonic right now. That's why I'm making such a large batch. For she needs to be meticulous in her taking of it. Every morning, without fail, at the same time. And she must start before he comes to her. If not, it will be too late."

Vasya watched as Jane's movements became fiercer, leaves starting to crumble as she picked. He said, "Are you angry at her, at his lordship, or yourself?"

Her hands quieted, and she braced against the wooden table. "I don't know," she whispered. "I hate him so much, Vasya. I hate him so much that it's far past a sin. Far past anything of the earth."

Vasya nodded. "And Hope?"

Jane shook her head, more hair falling loose from the pins. "I love her. She's been a constant for me since I arrived in this dreadful house. She's sacrificing herself for my sake, and I can't allow it."

Vasya thought on the problem. He'd met many people in his travels, all very different from one another. There was no rhyme or reason to any person. But he had been at a gaming hell in Paris that sat at the bottom of a very specific type of brothel. To even call it a brothel was wrong. The women there were of a different ilk. So were the customers. And they employed men as well. When he asked after it, one gentleman carefully explained that for some, pain was pleasure. For some, the intricacies of intimacy had different rules, and the events that happened there were voluntary.

"Perhaps," Vasya said slowly, not wanting to offend Jane or offer ideas she might not want in her head. "Perhaps the kind of intimacy that she has seen between his lordship and the other maids is not terrible to Hope."

Jane sighed. Vasya wanted to sigh as well. He did not wish to speak of others' intimacies with her. Especially not the type that brought pain.

"She said as much."

"She did?" Vasya could barely get out the words, but these women spoke so candidly? He'd often heard that women were very different when men were not present. Perhaps this was one of those things.

"Molly is gone. You are recovered. He will be coming to you and looking for an avenue to cause you pain. Hope could fulfill both of those roles for you. He will go to her eventually. Why not now, when she is ready for it?" Vasya hated that his thoughts strayed a step farther: if his lordship was preoccupied with Hope, could not Jane be with Vasya? "And perhaps you would be free as well."

Jane flashed him an angry look. "I would be free? Vasya. The only time I will be free will be when he's dead." She threw down the stems and put her hands on her hips.

He shouldn't have said it. It was an irresponsible and selfish thing to say, but he'd done it anyway. She tilted her head back, looking at the ceiling. She blinked rapidly, and he realized she was trying not to cry. The idea that he'd made her cry ripped through him. He'd rather take a musket ball in the face. "I will take my leave."

As he passed behind Jane, she exhaled loudly, and he paused, hoping she would speak more. He hung his head and hurried out, feeling like a misbehaved dog.

❦

As long as Jane didn't think too hard, life was good. She had her son, her greenhouse, and her sister. Though Emma had not returned since her afternoon visit when James was first born. Jane understood. It took time to learn Matthew's moods and motives. And she had believed for a long time that she had him figured out. But she was wrong.

Ever since Emma's visit, Matthew had redoubled his efforts to make her life miserable. Jane knew he did it so that she might complain to Emma, and thus agitate her. So Jane said nothing. Matthew thought she was still a weak child, not realizing she had grown into a woman, understood his motivations, and had begun maneuvering herself accordingly. She was a mother now. She was a healer for her staff. She was a woman who longed for something greater but understood she would never get it.

Martha Foraker was now housekeeper, and soon Jane could replace the increasingly decrepit Mr. Vernon. Matthew was holding on to the man for as long as possible, knowing he was losing control over his house. Matthew wanted the old ways—a staff that would never question his actions and never speak to someone outside the household. The secret keepers. But Jane didn't want secret keepers. She knew she had allies in her staff, those who would help thwart the viscount when he was in one of his moods.

Still. Even with Martha and Hope and Vasya, it wasn't enough.

Jane made her elixir for Hope, a tea to drink every morning at the same time, without fail. Hope had to refuse Matthew's advances until her cycle began. But the time passed quickly, and Hope reported every approach, every lingering stare. It turned Jane's stomach, but what was she to do?

Having had a child seemed to make Jane less appealing in Matthew's eyes. She'd lost all the weight she'd gained, but her body was decidedly different. Her hips were slightly wider, but her waist was trimmer than ever. She had a hard time eating, knowing that every time Hope and Matthew were out of sight, he could be hurting her friend.

When Hope began a torrid affair with Matthew, Jane didn't need any spies in her staff to tell her so. Matthew dropped sneering comments about it at every opportunity. He also went to great lengths to gift Hope trinkets while Jane stood there, no doubt hoping that Jane would feel inadequate. Jane tried to act the part, as did Hope. Matthew was wrapped up in his own world and never noticed either woman's dreadful acting abilities.

And time went on. Jane was safe, James was safe, and Hope received special gifts that she could later sell if needed. Matthew was most often away from the house; when he was gone, that was as close to peace as they might find. With Hope secured as an in-house mistress, Jane took James for extended stays with Emma, letting sweet William dote on his younger cousin and teach him all the important things, like the feel of a flower petal on one's face. How to run faster. How a slingshot worked. The best way to catch a bug, and what to do with it after: let it be free.

Emma and Jane would sit, often without talking, watching the boys play in the expansive lawns of whichever Lorian country house they were currently visiting. Emma was increasing again, past the quickening—a milestone she hadn't hit in the years she'd been hoping for a child. Dreams were thick in the air. Jane believed she could live this life. It wasn't ideal, but there was happiness to be found.

Jane never knew exactly how it happened, but perhaps the strain of Parliament's political machinations annoyed Matthew. The situation in France was unstable at best, and Britain's nobility flapped about, divided on how best to take advantage of their closest rival's evolution in governance.

Or perhaps it was merely Matthew. His obsession with his own reputation, his perception of his power, his extreme vanity.

Jane was in the drawing room—the only place Matthew allowed her to be, aside from her bedchamber, which came with its own perils, given its adjoining door to his bedchamber. Sometimes he had Hope in his bed, ordering her to express her pleasure or her pain—whatever pleased him that day—to ensure Jane would hear.

Matthew stomped into the drawing room, interrupting her work on her herbal receipts.

"All this time?" His voice wasn't overly loud, but his fury was evidenced by the vein in his forehead and the tendon straining in his neck. "Is James even mine?"

Jane put aside her writing desk, capping the ink pot carefully. She stood, purposely moving slowly and gracefully. She tried to exude calmness, hoping that, like a wild animal, her demeanor might influence his. But it seemed only to infuriate him further. She might ask the same of all the dark-haired orphans in London.

"Am I to be a cuckold? The most hated of creatures? Pathetic, pitiful." He spat the words at her.

"I don't know what you mean," Jane said. "I've never lain with anyone but you."

"I know the coachman is your man! I saw him with that devil Aberscomb today. I should have known when he came round. He's a spy for you!"

Jane was accustomed to Matthew's conspiracy plots, leaping from one idea to the next, his logic never connecting for anyone but him. Even still, she wasn't sure what accusation she needed to address. "I had not known the man until our wedding day when I was introduced to all the staff. I swear to you."

Had she seen him before? Yes. But that was not the question. She certainly had not let him into her bed, even if she had thought about it, had wondered if Vasya was a considerate lover and what it would be like to have someone who wanted her to feel adored, loved, worshipped. His heavy weight hovering over her, his strength controlled and gentle. What would such an act be like?

"What a fool I've been to trust a succubus like you. Such a whore, traipsing about the house as if it belongs to you. Manipulating me into marriage. How clever you must think yourself."

Jane folded her hands in front of her. She might as well wait until his tirade was over. This was not a new trick of his, though it had lessened when Hope stepped in.

"The coachman is sacked! As of this instant! Does that please you, Jane? To know your lover is out on his arse?" Matthew sneered, and even as handsome as he was, the sneer deformed his features.

"His isn't my lover."

And then, for the second time in their marriage, he slapped her. It was a shock, yes. But worse when he didn't stop there. He pulled the knife he kept in his boot, holding it close to her face. He said nothing, slicing a lock of her hair to prove it's edge. Jane tried to keep her eyes on the dagger, but couldn't. She was relieved when she heard it clatter to the floor, and Matthew set about applying his fists.

Jane didn't know how much later it was when Martha came to her. Then Vasya. The two of them dabbed on the poultices Jane had made from the herbs in the greenhouse, the ratios defined in the receipt book she'd been working on when Matthew had interrupted.

"I'm here," Vasya said, the low rumble in his chest the most beautiful sound Jane had ever heard.

"He says you're out," Jane managed. Her lip was swollen and it hurt to talk.

"No," Vasya said. "Hope has convinced him that it is far more torture for me to stay on and see you, knowing I could be out on the street at any moment."

"Hope," Jane whispered. "So brave."

"You are also brave," he rumbled. "So many years you have been with him. The child you have borne him."

Jane looked at him, her eyes clearing to see him. The strong length of his nose, the dark eyes, the strong jaw hidden by the trimmed black beard. So handsome. She reached up and touched his cheek. "My Vasya. I'm not brave."

He kissed her hair, and they both inhaled sharply at the touch. The touch they both wanted to be more. But it couldn't.

CHAPTER 14

The inn's dining room, where the inquest convened, was cleaner than what Jane had expected. She wasn't sure why she'd thought there would be a formal courtroom for this inquest, with a bewigged judge and barristers, but she had. The inn itself had been scrubbed, out of habit or respect, she didn't know. There was no sooty window from coal smoke, and the smells of wood polish and wax filled her nose.

Gareth and Emma were already seated in the arranged chairs, looking handsome. Gareth appeared ready for Parliament, and Emma was smartly dressed in somber black, edged with simple gray velvet ribbons. Jane wanted to wear yellow or red, or a frothy pink celebratory gown. Which was out of the question, of course.

Jane was in mourning, as was James. He escorted his mother with all the gravitas of a grown man. He was as tall as her now, growing quickly. She thought back to William, Emma's boy, at that age. He'd been small at twelve, not blossoming until around fourteen, when he seemed to grow overnight. James was steadier, gaining inches and broadness too early, in Jane's opinion. He still couldn't grow whiskers, for which Jane was glad, but his dark hair and hard features echoed his father's in the most disconcerting way. Paternity was never in question, outside of Matthew's rages, and if it truly had been, one look at James would have cleared that thought away.

Jane's silk had been dyed black, and she wore a black bonnet with a dark veil, hiding her eyes. She had cried—though not in mourning for Matthew. She'd cried in relief. In mourning for all the things that could have been or should never have happened. For Emma and her years of his looming anger. For Lydia. Poor Lydia. Who didn't deserve to inherit the Matthew's wrath at Emma.

Jane and James sat next to Emma and Gareth, a family united. Jane had wanted to spare James this experience, but he got a hard look in his eyes when she suggested that he stay at home during the inquest.

"I'm the viscount. If I'm to be called by his name, I'm going," he had said, looking so grown up and so like Emma that Jane couldn't dissuade him.

As they settled in, the door creaked open behind them. Jane knew she shouldn't look, but she did. It hit her as if she'd taken a musket ball to the stomach.

Vasya walked in, tidily dressed and looking devastatingly competent. His beard was neatly trimmed, his back straight, his demeanor calm. No matter the calamity, this was the man to sort the aftermath. And on his arm was his wife. Jane didn't remember her, though Martha had said she'd once worked in the house as a maid, ever so briefly. She was thin, frail-looking but beautiful in that waifish sort of way, with large gray eyes and blonde hair peeking out of her bonnet.

Jane looked at her gloved hands. Then she looked

over at James, resisting the urge to touch him, grab his hand, run her fingers through his hair. He was no longer a child, despite the number of his years. But he would still finish his schooling, and there were estate managers for the rest of the wide fortunes Matthew had accumulated and squandered.

Jane and James could handle the estates together. Anything was better than what life had been.

Emma caught Jane's eye and gave her a worried look. She knew that seeing Vasya had rattled Jane. Or, rather, seeing Vasya's wife. The woman he'd married to protect Jane. Jane wanted to cast up her accounts, heave and scream and writhe on the floor with the injustice of it all. But she sat there. Docile. Domesticated, but feeling feral all the way up to the edge of her skin.

BEFORE

Stories of the executions in France were everywhere. Jane's chest hurt and heaved with each new account that was printed in daily newspapers. Entire families run off their land, rounded up like wayward sheep and led to slaughter. Just when it seemed to end, another wave of unrest in Paris carried more terrified French refugees to England's shores.

At one point, Jane sought Matthew out, hoping she could persuade him to open some of the country houses to let the lost French nobility recover. Matthew narrowed his eyes at her. "You reap what you sow," he said, utterly without irony.

Jane called on Emma, hoping for more information, more comfort, knowing her sister would have learned more from Gareth. But much to Emma's dismay, Gareth had regained his military commission, enlisting Vasya as well. The French had declared war, not just on Britain and Spain but on the very idea of monarchy.

The thought of a guillotine set up in London, taking its tolls from the aristocratic families, gave Jane nightmares. Images of her standing there clutching young James in his short pants, gripping Emma's hand with the other, wrested her from sleep on more than one occasion.

The panic that gripped her was irrational and inconstant. While she was sorry to see Gareth and Vasya go to war, she believed in them. Gareth had gone to war before, and Vasya was the most capable man she knew. If anyone could protect her, protect England, it was Vasya. She prayed for their safety—the first real prayers she'd said since leaving her father's house.

Every so often, Matthew would entertain male guests in his study, and she overheard them talking about the Coalition War. In her mind, she urged him to purchase a commission and seek glory on the battlefield. Torment other men for a while since he'd certainly terrorized London's female population for long enough.

On those nights, she'd scoop up young James and the two of them would hie over to Emma's house for a grand mamas dinner in the nursery with her sister, baby Lydia, and sweet, growing William, who was almost off to school. At least they could bring joy to their children. The smallness of everyday tasks made it seem all the more real. Peeling an orange for James. Blowing in Lydia's face as a game. Listening to William's stories about the horses. She'd look at Emma—the strain around her eyes from knowing that Gareth was gone.

Jane had a pit in her stomach knowing that Vasya might not return. But she refused to think about it.

And she suffered no illusions that her fear for Vasya was anything like Emma's fear for Gareth. Gareth was not only the father of her children but also a partner. Gareth and Emma worked together, ate together, loved their children together. Jane could not say the same of Vasya.

"Jane?" Emma asked one evening as William began playing a stacking game with James, much to Lydia's fascination.

Jane dragged her eyes away from the children.

"Why don't you move in here? With us?" Emma's face was soft and open and vulnerable.

Fear gripped Jane at the thought of Matthew following them over here.

"I've thought about it," Emma said. "And as long as we stay in London, I don't see why not. You said that you don't even catch sight of him most days. Why don't we try it? Come stay for a week here. The children will adore having James in the nursery full time." Emma looked at him fondly. "He's such a polite boy."

Jane looked at James; his eyes were lit up, and he was happy in a way she rarely saw at home. Her stomach clenched. Would Matthew allow it? If she started slow, a few days here, a week there, perhaps it would work. "We have to stay in London."

Emma nodded, a smile growing on her face. "Of course."

"And we start with only overnight. Then go to two nights, then three."

"Whatever works best."

Jane rubbed her hand across the flat of her stomacher. "James?"

The boy turned around in a flash, eager for her attention. "Mama?"

"How would you like to stay the night here, with

your cousins?" Jane bent down to him, talking almost nose to nose.

His eyes lit up. "Yes! Yes! Stay!"

Jane straightened, exchanging glances with Emma. "Then we're settled."

Days were much more enjoyable spent in her sister's company. Matthew, preoccupied with the French, with Hope, with drowning cats, or with whatever it was he did in his free time, either did not notice Jane and James's absence or did not care. When Jane was finally bold enough to stay at Emma's for two weeks, she found Matthew had hied himself off to some kind of house party in Kent when she returned to the Andrepont townhome.

So Jane moved them in with Emma full-time. Their days were lovely no matter the weather. Emma taught James a pretty melody on the piano. James taught Lydia how to jump. William taught James how to gallop. And Jane taught William Latin.

The French were forgotten, as were the men. Weeks passed, then months. They lived in a singular bubble, women and children, free from politics and war. Jane knew it was a fragile dream. But she reveled in her happiness, sealing it away each night in a jar, keeping it safe on a shelf inside of her. Ready to be opened when the need arose.

AFTER – DAY FOUR

Mr. Eier shuffled forth. Vasya watched him carefully. The man was not much for vices—Vasya had checked. He walked with a slight limp, but it had been consistent, which meant it was an old injury. He hid it well. He'd probably been in the wars that had plagued Britain for so long. That could be why he revered the ruling class so much—he'd had an excellent commander, the hierarchical rankings working in his favor.

Vasya wondered if Mr. Eier knew that Andrepont had not fought in any of the wars. Not that any man would be compelled to outside of a press-gang, but if it would change Eier's opinion of the viscount he was attempting to defend, it might bear mentioning. For was that not what Eier sought justice for? To say that monster had a right to continue hurting others? To stomp on those less fortunate—which was nearly everyone in that man's life?

"The coroner may present his case," the magistrate intoned.

The men speaking wore wigs, a style that was already waning, for which Vasya was thankful. He didn't have time for that sort of pretense, and the idea of powdering his hair wasn't worth it. Would he smell better? Yes. Would the lice be more likely to leave him alone? Yes. But he was proud of his thick black hair, and he'd be damned if the English took that sign of virility from him.

The coroner, whom Vasya knew was bald underneath that wig, stood and cleared his throat. "I have clear evidence that the viscount Andrepont was murdered on or around September 15, likely in the early morning hours. Not only are knife wounds to the chest and stomach evident, upon an autopsy, I also found internal changes consistent with prolonged arsenic intake."

Vasya felt his bowels go watery. Indeed, he didn't know if Jane had poisoned the man, or Cook, or Martha Foraker. He suspected Jane first and foremost, but he had not wanted to ask questions. It was safer for no one to know.

The magistrate nodded. "And have you suspects to charge in this heinous crime?"

Mr. Eier cleared his throat, but he glanced at Jane. Vasya wanted to rip his throat out. "I have no certain suspects, but I have witnesses who would testify to their beliefs of who might be the culprit."

The wrinkled mass of skin that made up the magistrate's face contorted. "Inquests are to determine a trial, Mr. Eier. If you do not have one of the components necessary, namely an accused, then what are we here for?"

"It is strange, I admit," Mr. Eier said, twisting his body to turn and look at the crowd assembled. "But I believe that when I bring forth the nobleman who has knowledge of Lord Andrepont's final hours, a suspect will become clear from this assembled party. Perhaps amongst the ladies in this room."

The magistrate's face rearranged into one resembling a mask of exasperation. "You are wasting the time of all these good people. Surely, you don't expect me to believe that either the viscountess or the countess"—he gestured at Jane and then her sister —"stabbed a man much larger and stronger than them and then dumped him in the water?"

"They could be the parties responsible for the poison," Mr. Eier said.

"Did the poison kill him or the knife?" the magistrate demanded.

Mr. Eier shook his head. "I could not be certain."

"The body is available for viewing?" The magistrate asked.

"Yes. I have replaced his lordship's clothing, and he is laid out in the next room, should his body need to be viewed." Mr. Eier kept his gaze downcast.

Vasya willed himself to stop sweating. His wife held onto his arm even more tightly, giving him her support. She was a good woman, and she didn't deserve any of this. She shouldn't even be here. Vasya felt Jane's heavy gaze, and he couldn't help it. He looked at her, wondering if she could feel the longing he'd felt for her over the nearly two decades.

But her expression was unreadable. She'd become an expert at that, which always made him sad. For she hadn't started out that way.

BEFORE

The years moved like mouse feet: skittering and quick, surprising and sharp. War was a constant refrain for the English, but the immensity of this war seemed different somehow. The French not only fought against the monarchies, they also fought themselves. Seemingly beloved war commanders could be guillotined just as easily as a minor nobleman.

Emma received irregular missives from Gareth while other women in Town seemed to receive near-daily notices from their husbands or sons. Jane heard nothing from Vasya. The men were not together, either, as Gareth was an officer, but sometimes he would include news of the Russian man amongst British troops.

It was troubling to feel ignored, but Jane understood. Vasya could not write to her directly. And there would be rumors should he write to Emma; Matthew would hear of it once again, and Jane would no longer be allowed to stay with Emma. He might even try to take James from her, a hell Jane was unwilling to risk.

Together, Jane and Emma tried to follow the troop movements and battles, but Jane found that every time she tried to remember which regiment Gareth was in, her mind went smooth and placid, like a lake before a storm. Emma didn't seem much better.

Something about the conflict and the danger it posed to her husband made her incapable of discussing it. But they knew one thing: the French seemed to be winning, and that scared them.

Jane and Emma were acutely aware of the French calls for noblemen's deaths. The refrain from that song—its Revolutionary lyrics—flew out of taverns and mean-hearted singers on streets: *Ah! It'll be fine, it'll be fine, it'll be fine / Aristocrats to the lamppost / Ah! It'll be fine, it'll be fine, it'll be fine / The aristocrats, we'll hang them! / If we don't hang them / We'll break them / If we don't break them / We'll burn them / Ah! It'll be fine, it'll be fine, it'll be fine / Aristocrats to the lamppost / Ah! It'll be fine, it'll be fine, it'll be fine / The aristocrats, we'll hang them!*

Jane could think only of the children when she heard the tune, terrified, wondering how to protect them. Emma gripped her hand tightly, both of them white-knuckled as they crept past. With so many able-bodied men gone, Jane felt undefended at Emma's house, but even more so at her own. Matthew would be far likelier to offer Jane up to an angry mob than defend her.

After too many nights of expressing their unresolvable worries by the fireside, Jane and Emma finally made a decision. The decision alone made them feel better even if it did nothing to alleviate the risks of a French invasion. They made medicines. Jane kept her stores well-stocked below stairs at her home, as she was gaining a reputation for having inexpensive remedies for all sorts of things that the servant class didn't dare approach an apothecary for.

During Andrepont's journeys to the country, Jane likewise retreated to the country with Emma. They spent months doing rounds for the tenant farmers, making medicines from Jane's receipt book on request, delivering what goods they had to spare amongst the people on Gareth's lands.

When Emma received notice that Gareth would return home shortly after the New Year of 1794, she was giddy. Jane wished she had news of Vasya. Even wished she was capable of feeling the fizzy excitement that followed Emma's every step. Baby Lydia was three and wouldn't recognize the man who was her father. William was at school, homesick and desperate for both his mother and his father. James was the only one who didn't seem affected by the war. The more his father was absent, the better off he was.

Emma planned a country assembly, inviting all the tenants and their families for a day to explore the grounds and enjoy their food. Jane was enlisted to help, of course, and together the sisters prepared an event where the people of the country would be able to shake the hand of Gareth, who was once again fighting for the British against the evil French. She invited families from the area, planning a ball at the end of a hectic but happy week amongst friends.

The household was in a frantic but enthusiastic kind of clamor. Flowers were shipped in from hothouses around the countryside and London alike. The January dark seemed unimportant when coming up against party preparations for February. Even the children were excited at the prospect of a party, as they'd been promised special tea for that evening.

Although she hadn't meant for it to become so highly anticipated, Emma's country party was the most talked-about off-Season event. Soon, her mornings were flooded with missives from acquaintances wanting to be included. Not seeing why she needed to be exclusive, she invited them along as well. Jane smiled at the stack of her sister's correspondence, happy to help copy out invitations when needed. Perhaps this would give Jane a wider circle. Matthew had relaxed his grip on her, and she wanted to take advantage of that.

Jane and Emma spent hours every night upstairs in the nursery, giving good-night cuddles to Lydia and James, and even William, who was on a break from school. He pretended he didn't want the attention, but he most definitely needed it.

William was a sensitive boy, and the break was much needed. Despite his instructors admonishing that he needed to be disciplined more heavily and saying he required punishing physical exercise to stiffen his spine, Emma took the opposite tack. Staying up later than James and Lydia, the three of them snuggled deep under blankets, each of them reading an adventure novel. William would find an exciting part and read it aloud so they could all enjoy the characters' derring-do.

William was growing fast and should have had his own room by then, but James, seven years younger, pleaded so hard for him to stay in the nursery that William did. Despite William's status as the next Lorian heir, Emma did not require him to do any studying while he was home. Jane assumed William would get plenty of that from Gareth later on, and she wasn't about to ruin the dreamy enjoyment of their joint-family cocoon.

Gareth arrived home three days early. They'd heard reports from the inns that he was riding with a companion, whom Jane desperately hoped was Vasya. She sat by the windows all day, waiting, promising the children she would be the lookout while they played.

Towards afternoon, two men rode up on horseback, hats battered and tugged low against the icy winds. Spying down from the nursery window, Jane watched as Gareth removed his cap to identify himself. The second man, tall but not nearly as large as she remembered Vasya, did not remove his hat. Jane fidgeted, wanting to know who this second man could be. Finally, Mrs. Thorne allowed the fatigued travelers to cross the threshold, and when they did, the whole house seemed to break loose in chaos.

William was first to hear his father's voice and went thundering down the nursery stairs. James went next, running on his much shorter little boy legs, leaving Emma and Jane staring at each other while three-year-old Lydia cried at the sudden shift in mood.

Easily placated, Emma scooped Lydia up and they moved cautiously downstairs as well, the governess behind Jane, having likewise been roused by the commotion. Jane reached the first-floor balcony seconds after Emma and saw the scene below: Gareth holding William, scooped into his arms as easily as if he were years younger. Emma handed Lydia off to the governess without tearing her eyes off her husband.

Gareth caught sight of her at the same time, and he let William go, the boy's body sliding down until his feet touched the floor. Gareth stepped forward, anticipating Emma's arrival on the bottom step. He whisked her off her feet, hugging her close.

Jane crept forward, not seeing the other man, trying to find him in the clutter of servants and children. Then she spied him caring for the sodden garments both he and Gareth had worn, giving directions to the footmen about their luggage and the horses. Bareheaded, with water dripping from the tendrils of his over-long black hair, he looked up at her. His eyes were dark and wide, taking her in as if he had been in the desert and she was the only water. She stared back, heart thudding, almost sick with relief. Vasya was much thinner than he'd been when he'd left. Not gaunt, but thin. She did her best to not run down the stairs. After all, she was a lady—a viscountess—married to another man.

But as she approached him, her hands shook. He wiped his wet, dirty hands on his wet, dirty pants, but she didn't care. He took her hands, neither of them daring to go so far as to embrace. Without meaning to, her hands crept up to his elbows, and he allowed her in closer, moving together, letting her catch the wild scent of him: rain and horses, and the sharp metallic scents of gunpowder and blood. But he was here. He was alive. He was healthy.

Vasya held no obligation to her, no need to return. But he was here, for her.

"Jane." His voice cracked.

She couldn't speak. The world had shrunk to the two of them. Then she heard his stomach grumble. Before leaving Gareth's arms, Emma sprang to action, barking orders, the mistress of the estates as she had been these last few years.

"Two baths need to be prepared, please. One to the master bedchamber and the other to the third guest room in the east wing. No, no, Vasily Nikolaevich is a war hero and will not be housed in servant quarters—I will not hear of it any other way. Mrs. Thorne, please have Cook send up two trays, one to each room. Please include decent wine for each."

As Emma turned her attention to Vasya, Jane dropped her hands, discreetly stepping away. "Should we call the physician in for either of you?"

"No need, Lady Aberscomb." Vasya's voice sounded weary.

"We haven't slept," Gareth explained. "We got fresh horses and rode through the night. Neither of us could wait to be home."

James found Jane's skirts and hid behind them. Jane bent down and pointed out Gareth as his uncle and Vasya as a friend.

In response, Vasya squatted down to the ground so he would be more at James's level. "I have been gone for a long time," he said. "I am your good friend,

Vasya. I am the friend that will teach you hunting and riding, if you wish."

James nodded eagerly, not looking away. Jane reached for James's small hand, and in that tableau, the Russian soldier seemed like he could have been James's father. The trio would have been happier if that were true.

"I have quite the week planned, so you both should head upstairs, get cleaned, and get rested. I will take care of everything," Emma said, putting hands on both of the men. She squeezed their arms. "You cannot imagine how grateful we are to have you back. Even if it is just a short while."

The men's leave was a week-long celebration. Jane imagined that Emma slept intertwined with Gareth every night, not thinking of the next day, focused only on the feel of his rough skin against hers. Jane wished for the same with Vasya, knowing it was impossible. The closer he was, the more she ached.

⁂

VASYA PREFERRED TO BE IN MOTION NOW. Whereas before he had been perfectly content to be still, something about this war had compelled him to move. He felt Jane's green eyes on him no matter where he was. She haunted him, and he welcomed it. The ballroom was open to all, decorated with evergreens, and there were tables full of meat pies, seedcakes, honeyed fruit. Footmen doled out cups of spiced wine and apple cider.

"Take a turn around the room with me?" It took more courage for Vasya to ask Jane to walk with him than it did to bayonet a man.

Jane stopped fluffing an arrangement of snowdrops that required no attention. She looked him in the eye, but she did not smile. Not even the polite one she offered to these strangers. When she nodded, he offered his arm, and she took it.

"How has it been? Are you hurt?" Vasya knew it was far too abrupt to ask such questions, but he couldn't help himself. On his worst nights, he'd dreamt of Andrepont abusing Jane as he'd witnessed soldiers doing in war. He awoke fiercer, meaner. Ready for battle.

"I'm not hurt," she said, and it was a blessing to hear her voice. It seemed to have more steel in it, more command. He was glad. "James and I have been staying mostly with Emma and the children. It's been quite peaceful, actually."

Vasya blinked in surprise. "And his lordship allows this?"

"At first, it was Hope's doing. And then, I think he forgot about me. He's very caught up in himself. And what with Emma being elevated to countess, it can't hurt to raise James with a future earl."

Vasya grunted, knowing that Jane would see what others could not.

"And you? Are you hurt?" Jane turned to him as if she could see through his shirt to the saber scar, hear the throbbing of the arm that he should keep wrapped—but his pride wouldn't allow it in front of Jane.

"I was wounded, but I am healed." It wasn't precisely a lie.

She frowned at him, knowing there was more. "I have heard that war changes a man. That he might see things, do things, that are beyond his moral comprehension."

"I don't regret what I've done," Vasya grunted. "I regret that I had to leave you unprotected while I did it."

"There have been sacrifices all around. You've come back alive. Baby Lydia doesn't even know her father," Jane said. The child had wailed when she was placed in Gareth's arms, everything about him foreign and unfamiliar.

"And what have you sacrificed?" Vasya wished he could unsay it. She had sacrificed her happiness, her body, her child. She had very little left.

Jane stiffened but did not retract her arm. "You already know what I've sacrificed, and it was not demanded of me because of war but because of womanhood."

"It shouldn't have been asked of you," Vasya growled.

"But it was. And I made my choice."

They stopped their promenade. She turned and looked at him square-on with her firm shoulders, her proud neck. "You're different," he said.

"As are you."

"That is the way of all things, is it not?" Vasya asked, admiring this new woman, no longer a bold, funny girl but a steely, incisive viscountess. "Not just war—time also changes and shifts perspectives and priorities."

"Are we strangers now?" Jane asked, her expression thoroughly unreadable except for that one thin, black eyebrow, arched high.

"Were we ever not?" Vasya countered, his longing for her a visceral pain, not unlike the saber that left the scar.

She contemplated him for a long moment, long enough that he wanted to squirm. But he held her gaze, willing her to find every one of his weaknesses. To know him. To see him. Then she curtsied to him, deep, unexpected, her head low. She rose, looked him in the eye, and said, "Thank you."

Then she was gone. And the emptiness he felt made him long for the battlefield.

CHAPTER 15

J ane never regretted her sudden coldness to Vasya that night, nor the distance she kept over the next years whenever he returned for leave with Gareth. She saw in his face his feelings of recklessness and his recognition of her growth. She could also see that he wasn't afraid of Matthew. But she still had too much to lose by risking a kiss from Vasya in some winter garden. There was no such thing as privacy for her, and though she could not prove it, she believed her husband had someone on Emma's staff to whisper the goings-on in the household.

But every time Vasya came home, his eyes colder and more distant, she got as close as she dared, taking his hands, letting hers run over his forearms, stepping that much closer. Because she wanted to know him. She wanted what Emma and Gareth had. The way they stayed up late talking, catching up about the house, the children, the war, other people, themselves.

Despite Napoleon's best efforts, the war years passed. Some men returned without limbs, and others never returned. Widows clogged the streets, begging for alms from parishes that could not support them all. Orphaned children became chimney sweeps, pickpockets, and matchgirls.

England grew accustomed to going without its luxuries, and styles changed. Emma kept throwing her yearly parties, and coinciding with Gareth's leave, it led to the birth of baby Agnes. Matthew continued to sulk, now in the arms of an Italian opera singer and sometimes Hope, who attended Jane only when she was home, which was rare.

While Jane had attended Emma during her delivery of Agnes, just weeks later, Hope's daughter Margaret was born. Hope had cried when she told Jane of her increasing, saying that she'd always taken the tea. She was scared Matthew had switched it out on her to be cruel, but Jane soothed her. She would do her best to take care of baby Margaret, whose dark hair and eyes made the paternity obvious.

Margaret's birth meant that Matthew stopped taking Hope to bed. And Jane worried there would be an end to the idyll she'd had during the war. Strange that so many had suffered and died during her best years, yet Jane suffered when the country was at peace.

And then the army came home while the navy stayed at war. As soon as news came of Gareth's imminent arrival, implying Vasya's, Matthew summoned Jane and James home.

❧

VASYA STAYED AT GARETH'S AS A GUEST UNTIL HE'D put on more weight, filling out as he had before, caring for the horses and playing with the children for lack of anything productive to do. He knew he should find employment, do something with himself. But

Gareth said to wait, to take time. Both of them were nursing visible and invisible wounds.

Vasya found himself riding in the park often and riding past the Andrepont estate daily. He watched for Jane on Bond Street, in the park—any sign of her. He didn't dare ask the staff or Emma if she'd come to call recently, and so he waited impatiently during the times Emma took visitors, waiting to hear Jane's voice, disappointed by the various ladies of regard.

When the family decided to go to the country, Emma insisted Vasya go, too. He had not gone back to London's gaming hells. But during the war years, he'd taken plenty of coin from officers and enlisted men alike.

The country was pleasant enough for a time. Until the worst came.

"William's coming," Gareth announced, looking up from the note he'd received on a tray. But his face wasn't full of joy as Vasya had expected. Instead, he was tight around the eyes.

Later, Vasya would wonder why, in all the years he had known what a monster Andrepont was, he hadn't stormed Andrepont's front steps, kicked in his door, and strangled him with his bare hands.

William was delivered in a carriage, pale and feverish, by another boy his same age, a friend from school. Vasya offered to fetch anyone Emma might require, and together, they called on every healer she could find in a twenty-mile radius. When none of them had better remedies for fever or the wet cough William soon developed, Emma moved to a fifty-mile radius. Vasya knew Emma needed Jane.

But Jane wouldn't come. Couldn't come. She was shut in a tower like the French stories of Rapunzel.

The notes that made their way from London were frantically scribbled, as if she were worried she might be found out while writing.

Emma kept Lydia and Agnes away from William's room, terrified they would get sick as well, so Vasya would take the girls out walking, letting them climb trees or pick grass and weeds. Whether it was a mother's need or divine Providence, Emma spent every waking moment she could with William, never taking ill.

Gareth came and went from the sick room, losing weight, his face tight and his shoulders tense. He and Vasya drank together in the evenings.

Gareth both ridiculed and marveled at his wife's dedication to her son. "She's so intent on William, it's like she thinks she can heal him through sheer force of will."

Vasya considered it. He knew nothing of physicking and nothing of motherhood, but Emma was strong. If anyone could, it would be her. But she needed Jane in order to have that full strength. Together, the sisters were a force of nature.

But Jane didn't arrive, and William didn't improve. The cough worsened. His skin swelled as if he were drowning from the inside out. Gareth whispered of the boy's devastation at night as he stared into the fire. He described the boy's swollen fingers, which were so unlike his usual strong, bony hands.

As maids changed the boy's sheets daily, Vasya would listen in the passageway. William's breathing was wet and congested, noisy and disturbing. Vasya would stand still, not breathing, listening hard, waiting for some kind of break, some kind of clearing. Some kind of proof that the war would be won.

But that relief didn't come. William waged battles in his own body. But he didn't win the war. Emma was there when he stopped breathing. Gareth was not. He was in the study with Vasya. They heard the wail, low and animal-like, rise to a keening. Gareth's glass slipped from his hand and he ran to his son's room, but there was nothing he could do. Vasya felt bereft that William was gone but grateful that the boy no longer hurt.

Gareth crumpled, a man who'd withstood battle, commanded men in the mud. Bled while he saved his soldiers. But here, where there was no enemy—only loss—the pain was unbearable. Vasya couldn't imagine a worse world.

❦

THE FAMILY WENT FOR THE FUNERAL, AS THAT WAS what families did. Jane was shocked when Matthew acknowledged they were family, but she supposed he wanted to revel in Emma and Gareth's pain and flaunt their living son.

James hadn't spoken since Jane told him William had died. He'd idolized his cousin. Jane hadn't thought about how James might first encounter real death, how he might handle losing the first person to die whom he'd really loved. He was twelve, come home for the summer holiday, dreading his father's company, and then this.

With bags packed full of clothes freshly dyed black, they headed to Emma and Gareth's country house. Jane was anxious to see her sister and the girls but dreaded what Matthew might say at any given moment. In the carriage, the three of them were closer than they'd ever been in any other setting. Matthew had never traveled with them before.

There was a second carriage behind them. Riding in it alongside Matthew's valet were Hope and her daughter, Margaret. As she'd grown, the girl's resemblance to Matthew and James became even more plain. Jane didn't mind a bit, and in fact, she welcomed the little one. She was a playmate for Agnes, as they were the same age. With Hope in tow, Jane didn't worry about Matthew making untoward advances on any women present, including herself. Hope had an uncanny ability to redirect Matthew's attentions, even still.

Jane had Debrett's on her lap, but the swaying of the carriage made it difficult to read. A summer storm had befallen the countryside the night before, leaving the roads rutted and muddy. James stared out the window, his face a frozen mask of anguish, while Matthew sat contentedly surveying his captives and the countryside.

Matthew caught Jane's eye and smiled as if this were any family holiday and they were some other family, one whose members tolerated each other. Jane was tempted to say something, but she didn't know how Matthew would respond, and James needed his parents to be calm. For her son, Jane could do anything. Including studying the damned Debrett's, which Matthew insisted she do now that James was getting older. She needed to understand family connections so they could match James properly.

They arrived at the small family chapel that was on the grounds of the Lorian estate. The prior lord had been buried here not long ago. The chapel itself was old, dating back to the fourteenth century, but had been updated since to be less Catholic. Consecrated ground was holy, no matter which priest or bishop blessed it.

Gareth greeted guests outside the chapel, and when he saw the unasked question on Jane's face, he teared up. "She's inside. Front row. She hasn't left him."

Jane nodded, gripping James's clammy hand

harder than was necessary. She didn't listen to see if Matthew was polite or antagonistic to Gareth; she didn't care. Her sister needed her. The girls were in the back stone pews with their governess. They wore black, and their big blue eyes seemed scared and shocked. Lydia was already ten, precociously pretty, as if she were readying for her debut, while Agnes was only five, still with that delightfully smooth chubbiness children had.

James squeezed his mother's hand to get her attention. He pulled his head in the direction of the girls, and Jane nodded. Sweet boy to comfort his cousins. Jane's emotions were pulled so taut that she didn't think she could cry. She didn't want to—she wanted to be strong for Emma. She sat next to her sister in the front row. The coffin was made of beautiful wood, polished and shining and perfect. Beeswax candles were lit throughout the chapel, and the stained glass windows let in red- and blue-tinted light.

Jane placed her hand on the bench, palm up, and without speaking, Emma put her hand in it. They held hands as everyone filed in and also through the service. When it was over and they were supposed to go outside, Emma whispered "no" as the pallbearers picked up the coffin.

Jane moved her hand, now using it to support Emma's elbow. They stood, but Emma's feet wouldn't move. "No," she whispered again. Her eyes had been dry until then. She squeezed them shut, and Jane waited. This was a nightmare, and Jane knew something about those.

"Come," Jane whispered, and they began a slow shuffle behind the coffin, allowing everyone else to follow them out to the small churchyard where William would be buried near his grandfather.

They stood outside, and when the coffin was

lowered into the ground with ropes, Emma collapsed. Jane tried to hold her up but only succeeded in not letting her sister hit the ground very hard. Gareth was by her side in an instant. A guest produced smelling salts, but Emma couldn't be roused long enough to stand.

Gareth disappeared into the house with Emma, flanked by the housekeeper and two footmen. The service continued, and Jane took over the hostess duties. Some guests departed immediately, but others stayed on. Jane presided when tea was served in the drawing room. Matthew puffed his chest out as if he himself were lord of the manor, making rounds amongst the remaining crowd as if he'd spent any time at all with young William.

Jane spoke with the vicar. She also spoke with the tenants who filed through the room, all looking as devastated as if William were one of their own. And he was, in a way.

Matthew strayed over, glaring at her. Then she remembered that she'd touched a young farmer's shoulder as a comfort to him. He had a young son, and the very idea of William passing away had shaken him to the core. Jane glared back at her husband, eyebrow raised. He was ridiculous. There wasn't a formula yet devised to calculate how much she loathed him.

And then she stopped breathing.

After years without seeing Vasya, he was here, in this room. She'd been so focused on Emma at the chapel that she hadn't noticed him. He looked older, as did she. He was as big as a wagon once again, black hair thick and full, sporting his highly unfashionable beard. He wore the clothes of a tradesman, good quality but nothing ornate. He spotted her immediately.

Matthew came over and placed a hand on Jane's

shoulder, his fingers digging into her flesh. The warning was clear to everyone. He might as well have growled like a dog over a bone.

"Possessiveness doesn't become you," Jane snapped at Matthew.

"Whoreishness doesn't become you," Matthew retorted.

She wanted to scream that it wasn't a word, that she'd never slept with any other man, that by all the measures of Society, she was perfect. She'd given him a son. He sought his pleasure elsewhere with her blessing. She could pine for another man in her own thoughts. That was allowed.

For one moment, she wished she hadn't pushed Vasya away that night at Emma's party, so many years ago now. She wished she'd pulled him into the winter gardens herself, told him how she loved his gentleness and attentiveness, and then kissed him, just to see what it was like to kiss a man she admired.

⛦

VASYA HAD BEEN WATCHING JANE SINCE THE moment she got out of the carriage. She was regal, carrying herself with a straight spine, clutching her son's hand, her closeness to him obvious. Andrepont, the filth, slunk out of the carriage, looking about as if he were going to buy the place. With the amount of money he was winning on his bets, he probably could.

Vasya stayed out of Jane's eyeline, not wanting to intrude on this hurtful, awful time. But now he had to make an appearance. He was too close to the family, too close to some of these farmers, to miss a reception to remember William. So Vasya walked into the drawing room after that painful ceremony—after seeing a mother collapse while watching her son's body lowered into the ground—and there Jane stood, perfect in her black crepe, her green eyes clear and cutting. It was the first time he'd felt at home since the fighting in Flanders.

Andrepont stepped closer to Jane and placed his hand on her shoulder as if he were a dragon protecting a horde. That's what these English believed in, wasn't it? Dragons? They were like that, men like Andrepont. Greedy monsters, hell-bent on claiming what wasn't theirs.

The viscount's knuckles went white as he ground them into Jane's shoulder, and Vasya clenched his teeth so hard he might lose a molar. The image of Jane, beaten soundly one afternoon, returned to his mind's eye. He didn't want to return to service, but he would if it meant he could protect Jane.

How he could convince Andrepont to rehire him, he didn't know. But a fierce desire to be near Jane crowded his brain like hunger could. He took a step to the side, hoping he could talk to someone—anyone —to disguise the fact that he would not, could not, stop watching Jane's smallest movements. She was a ballet that compelled him.

Thankfully, Gareth appeared in the room. His face was drawn and pale, and he looked like an old man. Vasya remembered how Gareth's father had responded to Gareth's brother's death. Vasya hoped Gareth could see he needed to be a father to his little girls, who still needed him.

And if Gareth struggled, Vasya would be happy to step in. He loved those little girls. Quick and bright, they were shiny beacons of frippery to any magpie. Their games were flooded with laughter, a high tinkling that reminded Vasya of rows of tiny silver bells. He loved how bold they were with him, climbing on him as if he were a pile of apple boxes or a gnarled old tree. That was love, he knew. He loved those girls. He loved this family. And he loved Jane.

There was little he could do to help them now except mourn when they were sad and protect them so they might feel safe.

⚜

THE IN-BETWEEN TIME

Vasya didn't like that Andrepont was staying in the house. When he questioned Gareth about the decision, Gareth had given him a baleful look and said, "They're family."

So Vasya patrolled the passageways just as he had patrolled the camp during the war. He wouldn't let the viscount hurt anyone while he could help it. But as he headed to the door to begin his nightly rounds, he heard noises coming from the library. It sounded, in fact, an awful lot like a gaming hell. When he investigated, he found, indeed, a party: Andrepont and four men who had not been invited to Gareth's home.

Vasya recognized each of the men, none of whom any decent man wanted to spend any amount of time with. Lords Hackett and Denby were Andrepont's hangers-on, and Vasya knew far too much about each of them. Not just where they drank, but that the skeletal Denby's cock had a swerve in it, which was likely why he still had no heirs. He knew Hackett made all his money from the slave trade and bribed members of the House of Commons to vote against bills that might hamper or abolish it.

Those men drank what Andrepont told them to drink, invested where he bid them to put their money, and visited brothels where he told them which girls to tup. They could do nothing on their own accord, so enthralled were they. The other two, Lords Beecher and Tottingham, were ne'er-do-wells of their own accord. They were the type of men who truly believed they were ordained by God to be superior to other men.

In France, they would have been the first nobles beheaded. Vasya gave a low chuckle, realizing this was an instance where he agreed with the French. It was certainly not the first time Vasya had believed that aristocrats were not as deserving as they pretended to be. The men sat in Gareth's library, smoking Gareth's cigars and drinking Gareth's port, playing cards.

"What are you doing here?" Vasya asked.

Andrepont looked up. "Card game. Have to make rusticating interesting, after all." He eyed Vasya, evaluating him as he looked him up and down. "Care to join the next hand?"

"No," Vasya answered, stepping in closer. "What are you all doing here? This is a house in mourning."

"I'm aware," Andrepont answered coolly. "But the village has a wonderful brothel they all wanted to see since they came out to pay their respects. I figured we would go after this hand. Country beauties, you know, seem downright exotic after all the visits to London's demimonde. It'll be a wonder if any of them actually speak the King's English."

It was a classist dig about the country dialect most people spoke here, one that Vasya had heard in his native language more than once. Despite his nonexistent rank, Vasya wanted the men gone. "Get. Out." He bit out the words.

Lords Beecher and Tottingham had manners enough to look cowed and set down their cards. They still drained their glasses, though. Lord Hackett sneered at Vasya.

Andrepont looked around, gauging the room. "Fine." He drained his almost-full glass of port in one gulp. The glutton. "Let's go see what sort of buxom milkmaids await us." He stood, and so did the other men. Denby drained his glass, unable to meet Vasya's eyes as he practically ran out of the room.

Vasya followed them out of the library and found Gareth on the first landing, coming down the stairs. Gareth had to admit that he didn't mind the reinforcement his friend lent. His status as an earl should keep the miscreants out. Maybe not Hackett, but it would keep out Denby. The man skittered about, nervous as a rat.

The butler retrieved their hats and gloves. As the door closed behind them and Andrepont's carriage was brought about on the gravel drive, the entire house seemed to sigh in relief. Vasya narrowed his eyes, knowing that tonight's capitulation was only a ploy to buy time. Andrepont would not take an insult from a commoner, and a foreigner at that.

The next night was barely improved. Andrepont appeared in Gareth's study after the dinner hour, making bold claims about "owing" him card players since all but Lord Hackett had left.

"You made them feel unwelcome," Andrepont said, pacing the study where Gareth worked and Vasya pretended to read.

"They were," Gareth said, closing the ledger he'd been studying. "Unwelcome."

Vasya did his best not to snort, happy that Gareth stood his ground. Andrepont was older and had carried his title longer. But Gareth was now an earl, responsible for estates more extensive than the viscount's. Gareth had gone to war while Andrepont had lounged in England, pursuing whatever hedonistic idea occurred to him.

"It's unspeakably rude, you know," Andrepont continued, as if he hadn't heard Gareth.

"It's unspeakably rude to show up uninvited to a house of mourning," Gareth said.

Vasya felt a sharp pain at the reminder of

William's death, and he wondered if Gareth's grief felt sharp and acute or if it was a black shroud that came over him, sudden and complete.

"Hackett is still nearby, the dear friend. You and that Russian horse of yours make four." Andrepont chucked a thumb at Vasya. "Whist? Faro? Name your game."

"Will it make you go away?" Gareth asked.

"Only if you win," Andrepont smiled like a snake. Vasya kept his expression neutral, not that anyone looked at him. This was a power struggle between the two nobles. But Vasya was happy to take Andrepont's money. No matter how good the viscount thought he was, Vasya knew he was better. He'd played against more opponents, seen more hands. Experience gave him an edge that Andrepont lacked.

"Done. Give me thirty minutes. We'll meet you in the library," Gareth said. For the first time that evening, his eyes slid to Vasya.

Vasya gave him a subtle, approving nod.

The viscount strolled away, grinning. Was he that arrogant, or did he have some cheat up his sleeve that made him think he could get one better over Vasya?

Gareth put away his work and tidied his desk, locking his important papers away in a desk drawer. Vasya stowed the book he'd pretended to read while watching Gareth and then Andrepont over its pages. Gareth suddenly braced his arms against the desk.

"What am I doing, Vasya?" His voice was low, as if he were keeping in a sob. "Entertaining that snake while William—my son—" Gareth's voice cracked.

Vasya waited. There was no clarity in grief. Grief was a dream. It adhered to its own rules and could not be governed.

"I raced back to England to see him brought into this world, practically killing a horse to get here in time. He was so small. So red!" Gareth shook his head, lost in the happiness of the day he became a father.

Vasya kept silent, knowing there was more to come. Gareth was deep in the throes of pain. By God, if he could get Andrepont out of this house, that would be something. He balled his fists, feeling that sudden urge to rip apart the world with his bare hands. Cards. He'd take all their money and laugh as he kicked Andrepont out in the rain.

Once Gareth collected himself, they strolled together into the library, where cold cuts sat on ready platters and beautiful dark red claret glimmered in the crystal carafes. This was at Andrepont's orders, not Gareth's. Vasya took offense on his friend's behalf.

Did the viscount know that Gareth and Vasya had been friends for more than twenty years? That each other's tells were as obvious as screaming a clue out loud? They'd met in a dissolute gambling hell on the Continent, though Gareth now preferred to say they'd served together in Flanders. It was true, but it didn't encompass the breadth of their connection.

Vasya would happily take everything Andrepont was worth. He'd love nothing more than to see this arrogant arse broken.

❦

EMMA WOKE EARLY. THE LAUDANUM MUST HAVE worn off. She was exhausted. Her whole world felt gray and meaningless. Still, she dressed herself. The fires hadn't yet been lit, but the early summer sun was beginning to lighten the black night sky to a dark blue.

Her room felt unfamiliar, but there were her slippers. Her wrapper. A candle. She lit it and slid on the slippers, tossing the wrapper over her shoulders.

She needed to walk. Not outside, but movement seemed somehow necessary. She didn't know what day it was. How long it had been since they'd buried William. She felt numb.

As she crept down the large staircase, she thought she heard a knocking sound. No, a tapping sound. No, maybe it was raining? The laudanum still clouded her mind, but she thought walking would help clear things up. She followed the sound into Gareth's study. The study was dark, the room tidy, just as Gareth liked things to be. Apparently, it was something being in the King's service had drilled into him, and Emma wouldn't complain. She went to the windows and hefted the curtain open. There were droplets on the window, proof that it had rained at some point in the night. She pulled the cord, opening the curtains wider. She sat on the settee near the banked fireplace, staring out the window, her feet curled under her.

Perhaps she slept. But suddenly she heard a sound, a footstep, and thinking it was the maid coming to light the fire, she sat up, straightening her hair and her wrapper, trying to seem more put together than she actually was. But it was no maid.

Andrepont wobbled on his feet, turning as she caught his attention.

"What are you doing here?" she asked. The worst had already happened to her, so she no longer felt the dread and fear she'd once had when meeting him. It was as if William's death had robbed her of all sense of danger. Because it no longer mattered what happened to her. There was nothing Andrepont could do that would hurt her more than she already had been.

"What are you doing awake, Lady Lorian? Skulking about the house in your nightclothes?" Andrepont sneered and came toward her. "Hoping for an assignation?"

Emma rolled her eyes. "Certainly not with you."

"Oh," he feigned surprise, still approaching. "Is there a footman here you fancy? Or perhaps that hulking Russian has a thing for sisters."

"You're drunk," she said, getting to her feet. "I'm sure there's water in your room. I suggest you drink something besides claret before you sleep."

"I've had your sister you know," he said, casually.

Emma blinked at him. Even with the laudanum fogging her mind, she still recognized a drunk's mid-conversation topic switch. This must have been on his mind for a long time. "I'm aware. James is the very image of you. How pleased you must be."

"I am. Sour boy, but nothing that can't be beaten out of him."

Again, Emma rolled her eyes. This time, Andrepont narrowed his eyes at her, his nostrils flaring. "I hate it when you do that. Your petty eye trick. I know what it means; I know why you do that. You think you can dismiss me? I could have had you, you know. I could have."

Emma sidestepped him as he tried to grab her arm. "Clearly, you couldn't. You tried, and you failed. Good night, Andrepont."

She walked away, but he caught her in two steps, hauling her off her feet until she hit the wall. His forearm against her neck kept her head raised. "You little bitch," he snarled.

A second elongated in Emma's clouded mind. She had choices here. She could let him have his way, let him beat her, take her, hurt her. She didn't feel like she cared that much. But another child was always a roll of dice for her. She might not live through another birth. And to have one fathered by this monster was more than she could bear.

So she started kicking. It was difficult at first; her body felt weak and disconnected. But while she missed the bollocks region the first time, she landed the second kick before he could drop her on the floor.

He removed his arm to shield his prick, and she brought her elbow to his crouching form as hard as she could. She hoped for the face but wasn't entirely sure where she connected. Then she pushed him to the floor with one great shove and ran away.

She cackled as she ran upstairs. That devil-arsed man trying something on her! Wait until she told Gareth. No, Gareth would call him out. If there was a chance Andrepont could hurt him, she wouldn't risk it. She'd keep it to herself and smile every time she saw him, knowing he'd wake with a sore prick.

CHAPTER 16

When Jane went down to breakfast, she was surprised to see Emma dressed and drinking a pot of tea. It flushed her with warmth to see her sister there, able to meet the day. Her face was wan and her dress hung from her thin shoulders, but she was there. Awake.

Before she helped herself to the platters laid out for them, Jane brushed her hand along Emma's shoulders. "I'm glad to see you."

Emma smiled in return, a pale echo of her usual brilliant, face-spanning grin, but it was genuine. Jane would take every milestone.

The door opened behind Jane as Gareth and Vasya entered. They both looked as if they'd imbibed too much, but frankly, that was to be expected.

"Coffee," Gareth said as he stared at the tea. "This won't do."

Vasya grunted behind him, so very much a bear that Jane had the urge to kiss him on his grumpy cheek despite the distance she'd promised both him and herself. The butler disappeared for a few seconds before returning to tell Gareth that coffee would be served in minutes. Jane retrieved a cup and poured from Emma's teapot, sitting to watch the men lumber down the line of food.

"My lady," Gareth croaked, realizing Jane had been there first.

"I would prefer to wait," she said, hiding her smile with her teacup. There was something about the two of them that reminded her of naughty schoolboys.

More grunts followed. She looked to Emma to see if she was enjoying their misery, and when their eyes met, a mischievous gleam sparkled there.

"Has Andrepont already come down?" Gareth asked the butler.

"His lordships Andrepont and Hackett left early this morning, my lord. The footmen carried their suitcases. Doubtless they do not mean to return."

Jane's husband had left without rousing her and James to leave as well? What fortune was this? Jane's hand snaked over to cover Emma's, and her sister squeezed back. "Good riddance," Jane whispered.

"His humiliation was complete," Gareth said, sitting down at the table with a plate so full of food it spilled off as he set it down.

Emma looked up sharply, a motion Jane caught but not Gareth or Vasya.

Vasya looked directly at Jane and said, "I will return to his employ."

"That's his humiliation?" Jane asked. "Rehiring a coachman?"

Gareth smiled. "I'd already taken all his money. He didn't have much to bet with."

Jane noticed that Emma's spine relaxed as she sank back into her chair. Something else was afoot, but Jane could speak to her sister later.

The governess appeared in the room, her normally sweet and calm demeanor clouded. "Lady Lorian? I need to speak to you."

"Of course," Emma said, rising from the table.

Gareth quickly wiped his napkin across his face, clearing the grease from the ham steak. "Perhaps I could take care of it instead?"

The governess considered him. "No, my lord. I'm quite sure Lady Lorian needs to attend to this particular matter."

⁂

VASYA DID NOT WANT TO KNOW THE SPECIFICS. THE villain Andrepont had accosted Emma. His humiliation at cards had not been complete enough. When Emma also handily dispatched him, he sought the only other innocent he knew he could best. Poor Lydia. The idea of it made him want to wretch. When Emma told them, he'd had to open the window, not wanting to cast up his accounts on the rug.

But it was not his place to be a part of their conversation, to be a part of the blames. He should have protected the girl. He'd tried. He'd thought the card game enough. His glowering enough. His decades-long presence enough. But Andrepont had been pushed too far. And now he was gone. As were his cronies.

Vasya caught James skulking outside the study as Gareth and Emma yelled at one another. Neither of them blamed the other, but there was too much grief, anger, and betrayal in the house to speak civilly.

"Come," Vasya said to the young man. Already, he looked chillingly like his father. Thankfully, he wore his mother's emerald green eyes instead of the octopus-ink black depths of his father.

"Where are we going?" James asked, his voice in that late stage of puberty where he no longer sounded like a boy but not yet like a man.

"Out," Vasya said, not knowing himself. He didn't

want to bother the stablemen or risk James wandering back inside as they readied horses, so instead, they walked. They walked for miles, in the woods, through fields, across pastures.

The few people they encountered knew them both by sight and exchanged pleasantries, offering condolences on William's loss. James accepted these with the air of a nobleman while Vasya watched. That's all he felt he could do. Steady the boy. He needed calmness, for he was entering the storm of manhood that his father had never recovered from. The boasting, the affairs of honor, the need to always be in the right, to be superior. In Andrepont, it was pathological. If Vasya could do anything, he would do his best to ensure it would only be a phase for Andrepont's heir.

"Do you know what's going on?" James asked five miles in with no other person in sight.

"No," Vasya lied.

"But you're Uncle Gareth's best mate. You went to *war* together."

"I don't know," Vasya said. He glanced over at the boy, whose frustration was as evident as the dandelion seeds floating on the wind.

"Lydia is saying that my father snuck into the nursery last night and—" James broke off. "I think I might vomit."

Vasya slowed his pace, allowing for the body's needs. James dry heaved into the sweetgrass.

"Could it be possible? Or is she lying?" James shook his head. "I didn't mean lying. Lydia wouldn't lie. I mean, perhaps she had a dream and thought it was real?"

"That would be a strange dream for a young girl to have, raised as she has been."

James screwed his face into a strange expression. "What does that mean?"

"How did you learn of the relations between a man and a woman?" Vasya asked, knowing very well that he might not receive the truth.

James looked away. "Some boys at school."

"Your sisters have not gone away to school. There is no one to instruct them. I doubt very much Lydia knows what happens with a man. She is far too young."

"Does that mean my father did *that* with a ten-year-old girl?"

Vasya didn't want to answer. He had failed. He was supposed to protect this family, but a little girl had suffered because he'd drank too much while playing cards.

They resumed their earlier pace, and James was quiet as they trudged. Finally, he stopped, his troubled face screwed up almost as if he might cry. "Why aren't you my father? You're so much better than he is. In every way."

Vasya permitted himself a wistful smile. "I will say this truthfully: I often wish I was."

❧

JANE SAT IN A CORNER, FROZEN IN HER POLITENESS, her face a cool piece of stone, while Gareth paced the rug near the fireplace. Emma was a lump on the leather chair, a shawl draped over her bony shoulders.

Jane's insides were a whirlwind, not understanding, not wanting to believe. "I am truly sorry—"

Both Emma and Gareth waved her off.

"But if I didn't insist on coming—"

"You didn't do it," Gareth said over her, his most blunt expressions coming under stress.

"It doesn't matter now," Emma said at the same time.

Jane recoiled. Lydia had been hurt by Matthew, and that was it? They allowed him to carry on hurting them, one at a time?

Gareth looked at Emma, his eyes popping out with incredulity. He said, "That's your belief, is it? What's done is done?"

"Well, I can't *fix* it," Emma said. "I can only deal with the aftermath. And we know who did it—Andrepont. So I can do my best to help Lydia, and after that, murder Andrepont. It seems quite straightforward, honestly."

"I can make her some teas," Jane suggested quietly. "I've been caring for my entire staff in that way for years."

"She hasn't bled yet," Emma said, staggered by the impact of Jane's implication. "She shouldn't have the risk."

"Just in case," Gareth said firmly.

"It won't hurt her," Jane said. "It might make her tummy hurt for an hour, but it's easier if she nibbles on something while she drinks it."

Emma pulled herself up straight, looking like herself for the first time that morning. She spoke with her fundraiser voice, the one that organized the best parties. "Jane, yes. Please look after Lydia's body."

They all shuddered. "And I will kill Andrepont," Gareth said.

"No one can know," Emma whispered.

Jane wasn't sure if her sister meant no one could know Gareth had thought of killing her husband or if no one could know what Matthew had done to Lydia.

"I'm an earl. I can do what I please." Gareth stopped pacing and puffed his chest out.

Jane wondered if his posturing was a part of himself that he kept hidden—if all noblemen had that strutting nature. Or maybe he was putting it on like a silly hat, worn only for the appropriate occasion. "Now you sound like him," Jane said.

"Don't," Gareth warned.

"Stop. I don't understand how he could have done this," Emma said.

"I'm not shocked." Jane knew she should be shocked. That even this—the rape of a young girl—was out of bounds for Matthew. But Jane knew it wasn't. Some of the kitchen maids they'd hired over the years were barely older, and looked just as young. Because it didn't matter to Matthew. His victims weren't people to him. They were objects. And with that realization, a door closed inside of her. The door that had held her back from her own dark impulses. The door that kept her in the house. The door that allowed Hope to take the abuse that should have been Jane's.

It was her turn to reach a point of no return. Matthew wanted to inflict a pain beyond all others? He knew it only worked when there was someone else to care about. So Jane, knowing Matthew cared for no one else, would eliminate Matthew completely. Erase him. Make it as if he never existed. Nor any of the men who considered themselves friends. Their power was at an end.

"He's a monster," Gareth added.

"He couldn't have done it," Emma insisted. They both looked at her as if she had grown a second head. "He couldn't. I couldn't sleep. I came down early in the morning and he was in here, prowling about. I didn't know what time it was, and so I thought it might be a maid to light a fire."

"It's summer. They aren't lighting fires," Gareth said flatly.

"I've taken a great deal of laudanum, Gareth. You

take that much and tell me how clear-headed you are," she snapped.

"Go on," urged Jane.

"He attacked me."

"Where did he hurt you?" Gareth roared, his face going red.

"Nowhere. I defended myself and left *him* hurting."

Jane laughed at the thought of Matthew's humiliation, pleasure genuine and clear. She was glad that Matthew had been bested by Emma. Again. And so viscerally.

"How did you do that?" Gareth asked, plainly disbelieving.

"You think the only thing I did in New York was clean that house with Mrs. Bantam? She'd lived through many a raid and war. She taught me tricks for if any overzealous soldiers found me on market day."

The idea of her sweet, polite sister with the knowledge of putting highwaymen in their place. It was a small comfort in this horrid conversation.

"What?" Gareth exploded. "Why didn't you tell me you were doing this?"

"It was none of your business! Besides, I remember being quite distracted by other things when you came home." Emma's cheeks colored hot and red, and she knew it.

"Everything is my business!" Gareth said, stomping around the rug again.

"No, my lord. It is not." Jane stood. She couldn't take any more of his pretentious posturing. It reminded her too much of Matthew, and that made her feel responsible for bringing him here. As if she could have stopped him. The guilt of it hung around her neck like a millstone, and she knew she would carry it for life. But to watch Gareth pretend he had some kind of authority in this moment was too much.

"If you'll excuse me, I'm going to go attend to your garden to make sure I get the correct herbs."

Jane found Lydia curled up in the passageway outside the study door. She was quiet as a mouse, a little rumpled thing in her yellow dress, tracks of tears evident on her cheeks.

"Mama doesn't believe me," Lydia whispered as Jane scooped her up. The girl was so light in her arms. James had been so heavy by age five that Jane couldn't indulge herself and carry him to bed.

Jane tutted. "That's not true. Your mama believes you."

"It wasn't a dream," Lydia said with tearful conviction.

"I know it wasn't, dearest." Jane squeezed her tight, cheek to cheek. "You are safe now. And I will do my very, very best to make sure nothing like that happens to you ever, ever again. And do you know what?"

Lydia looked at her with her beautiful dark blue eyes and shook her head solemnly.

"I always keep my promises."

⁂

AFTER – DAY FOUR

The magistrate heaved a sigh that flapped his jowls. "Sir. If the widow does not wish to pursue an inquest due to lack of a suspect, and the heir does not wish to, on whose desire are we gathered?"

Mr. Eier fidgeted. "Lord Andrepont was a powerful and important man, and his friends demand justice. I would like to call Lord Hackett to speak."

An aristocrat changed the magistrate's posture. Jane stared with naked disgust at Lord Hackett as he made his way past her and into the box where he was to speak. She hated that man. How he'd leered at her while she was on Matthew's arm. She was hardly more than a child at the time. He'd gained weight since then, no doubt due to his significant indulgences.

The magistrate held up his hand to silence Mr. Eier, addressing the aristocrat instead. "Why do *you* wish to pursue this case, my lord?"

"Sir, anyone would want to pursue justice for a good man." Hackett shifted in the wooden chair as if he were lying. Because he was lying. Neither Matthew nor this man was good. Or decent.

Beside Jane, Gareth snorted, but when eyes darted to where the sound had been made, no one could pinpoint the noise. Lord Hackett shifted his portly frame.

"And who is the suspect that we should pursue? Who should hang for this crime?"

"I think we must start with his wife!" Hackett speared her with his small eyes.

Jane didn't react. She knew the accusation was a matter of time. He hated her for standing up to Matthew. For not allowing Hackett to slither his hands on her during her eighteenth birthday celebration when he'd wanted to see her vulnerable and abused.

The magistrate examined her with a shrewd glance. "And to what would drive a viscountess to murder?"

Lord Hackett blustered, his face turning red. Anything he said might incriminate himself. Jane knew they had visited brothels together, lured unfortunate young women to his home. "She was a jealous woman!"

The magistrate nodded thoughtfully and glanced down at the paper on his desk. "And I am to believe that Lady Andrepont accosted her husband in the middle of the night, stabbed him several times, robbed him, and threw him in the Thames. Is that your assessment?"

Jane had never been so grateful for her slight frame in her life. The idea that she could have stood up to broad-shouldered Matthew was absurd. Even in his altered states, she hadn't ever raised her hand to him. Not like Emma. She wanted to smile thinking of Emma kicking and elbowing him.

Mr. Eier had the decency to be red-faced while Lord Hackett spluttered more. "She poisoned him! She's known to be a witch, dispensing medicines out of the servants' entrance at her house."

The magistrate nodded thoughtfully. "Lady Andrepont, would you please stand?"

Jane let go of James's hand and stood. "Yes, your lordship."

The honorific appeased the magistrate, and she could see his face softening as he looked over her widow's weeds. "Please remove your veil so that we may see your face."

Reluctantly, Jane lifted the veil and tidied it back. Her face was drawn and pale. She hadn't slept well, thinking of Vasya in bed with his wife. Worrying for Vasya.

"Are you a witch?"

The crowd murmured as if this could be a possibility. Witches were not anything a modern person was afraid of anymore. Not in this time of the new, the changing world around them. "No, my lord. I am not a witch."

"But you dispense medicines."

"Yes, my lord. As a lady of a great house, that is what I am tasked to do. I care for my household, and that includes minor physicking. Ask any woman of rank."

The magistrate nodded, an approving expression on his face. "You may sit."

Jane heard the lack of honorific in his mouth. He clearly didn't think she was a threat. Turning back to Hackett, he said, "And if there was not a poisoning, who would you accuse of being the hands of death? The one that stabbed the man and threw him in the river?"

Hackett squirmed again. "The coachman. Andrepont didn't want to rehire him, but he lost a game of cards to him and was forced to!"

"The coachman. And that would be Mr. Kuznetsov?" The magistrate stumbled over Vasya's name.

"Yes. That big Russian fellow over there."

Jane felt warm all over as Lord Hackett pointed at Vasya, sitting proudly in his well-pressed coat. A lump formed in her throat as she remembered who had readied his clothes for him. His wife.

The magistrate consulted his paper. "Mr. Eier has confirmed that Mr. Kuznetsov had married earlier in the day and was at home with his new bride that night."

"That's a ruse!" Lord Hackett alleged. "Andrepont suspected long ago that the driver was in love with his wife!"

Jane's stomach tumbled to hear the words spoken aloud. She'd long hoped that Vasya loved her. Because that would make one person who did, and even if she could not act on such a revelation, it would mean something. It would mean that one man could love her even if her husband could not.

"Has there been any proof of such a matter?" The magistrate asked. "Or indeed, any recent rumor?"

Hackett stuttered. "No. He'd been at war for the past few years."

"And by 'he,' you mean Lord Andrepont?" the magistrate pressed.

"No, no. The Russian."

"Is Mrs. Kuznetsov present?" The magistrate asked.

Jane didn't want to turn and look, but she did because that was what was expected of her. The woman in question raised her hand to shoulder height, wincing as she did so.

"Something wrong?" The magistrate asked.

The woman answered, but her voice was drowned out by the noise of boots shuffling and throats clearing.

The magistrate frowned and waved his hand at her. "Come forward so I may hear you, madam."

She looked at Vasya, as if for permission, and Jane's throat constricted. By all accounts, it was clear she adored him. She was his wife. They slept in the same bed. She'd taken his name. Jane closed her eyes. *Oh God. She was young enough to have his children.*

"Are you in pain?" The magistrate asked.

She nodded.

"Did he beat you? Your husband? Were you coerced into this marriage?"

Vasya's wife laughed, a pretty sound, clear and fine. The crowd echoed her with nervous chuckles. "No. I've wanted to marry him for a very long time. I was not coerced."

"What is a very long time?" The magistrate pressed.

She looked back at him, smiling. "Perhaps fourteen years?"

Jane felt her admission like a knife. Of course other women wanted him. And why shouldn't he have them? Why should he have saved himself for her when she had been so cold to him, so closed off, so unavailable?

"That is a long time. Is that when you met for the first time?"

"Yes, sir. I was taken into service by Lady

Andrepont's former housekeeper, who was also my father's cousin."

"Fine. All well and good. Was your husband at home on the night Lord Andrepont was murdered?"

The woman nodded, blushing even, and Jane thought her fingernails might break the skin of her palm.

"We had a lovely dinner, and then we . . . er . . . we went to bed."

A bawdy murmur went through the assembled crowd, and the magistrate gave a cross look all around. "I'm satisfied. Mrs. Kuznetsov, you may go back to your husband. Thank you. And felicitations."

The crowd parted for her to return to Vasya, smiling. Jane realized the woman had never answered why she was in pain. Why was Vasya's new bride hurting? She was too young to have rheumatism or some other ache. But if the magistrate was satisfied, so must she be.

The magistrate turned back to Lord Hackett. "Have you any more wild accusations? Any more respectable ladies in the audience?"

Lord Hackett looked sour. "Andrepont didn't murder himself."

"That he did not," the magistrate agreed. "Lord Hackett, thank you for your concern, but you may return to your seat. Mr. Eier?"

"Have you examined the body, my lord?" Mr. Eier stood once more, his head bowed, looking abject.

"I have, Mr. Eier. But that does not bring me closer to knowing who might have done this. To me, it looks like any other highwayman, of which many plague London. Especially in that area. Please, give me another witness, another name, and I will be happy to hear more and pass this to a jury."

Mr. Eier did not look up, and his shoulders bunched up around his ears. "I have no one, sir. I had hoped something might be illuminated during this proceeding."

The magistrate looked about the room as if waiting for someone to come forward, to confess. But no one did. Silence reigned. "Since we have no one brought forward, and I cannot put an idea to the hangman's noose, I find—"

Hackett stood and pointed a finger at Vasya. "It's this man. This man here. Vasily Nicholas Krushen."

Jane raised her brow at Hackett's butchering of Vasya's name. The magistrate looked annoyed.

"Mr. Eier, would you like to revisit Mr. Kutznetsov's alibi?" The magistrate folded his arms.

"No, my lord." Mr. Eier sat down, chastened. Hackett's face was purple with rage.

The magistrate clapped his hands and sighed. "It seems that all you have successfully done is waste my time and cause pain to the family. If that was your aim, well done, sir." The magistrate's jowls seemed to flap freely of their own accord, but Jane didn't mind. This man was more objective than most, and she was grateful the matter was done. "I will not recommend that this case continue to a jury, and in fact, I dismiss it entirely. God be with you, Lady Andrepont. We are sorry for your loss."

❧

AFTER THE AFTER

Vasya stayed in Lady Andrepont's employ. Mr. Dendrum retired, and Vasya took over as stablemaster. Even old Mr. Vernon, the decrepit butler who knew Andrepont's sordid secrets, was persuaded to leave service with an ample pension. As months passed, Vasya expected the house to change, to enliven, to become a place of hope and happiness.

But while Jane didn't appear to mourn for

Andrepont, she still mourned. She received notice that Mrs. Houseman had died from the illness that kept her from attending to William. If that caused her melancholy, it didn't matter much. There were no callers, no women with bonnets and ribbons crowding the drawing room. There were no plans for dinner parties or elaborate afternoon soirees. Vasya sat at the servants' dining table polishing his boots as he listened to Martha Foraker talk with Hope and the other maids. Hope's daughter, Margaret, Andrepont's bastard child, occupied the nursery, and the nanny was kept on staff for her. She was cared for, as promised.

Aside from the calm, nothing seemed to change. It felt not like the master was dead, but rather like he had stepped out and was soon to return. Vasya shifted in his seat. Had they done all this for nothing? Could Jane not move on in her life?

At the end of each day, Vasya returned to his home. Mary would have a meal ready for him, and she would mend his shirts or darn his socks while she listened to all the gossip he could relay. He kissed her cheeks. She once asked for more, and he'd tried. He'd kissed her lips, wanting to feel the desire that had been so ready during his younger decades. The kind that wasn't all that discerning.

"I want to be your wife in all the ways, Vasya," Mary said.

Vasya knew she was ill. It could hardly be a secret, given the lumps on her breasts that had begun to spill over onto her skin. She kept her shift on, and he let her slide on top of him until her release. He tried so hard not to think of Jane. To not stop his wife at the unfairness of his disloyal mind.

She fell asleep nestled in his arm, her hand threaded through the dark hair on his chest. It felt like treason. She was a lovely woman, a competent homemaker, and a good cook. She deserved a good man. A man who loved her for all her excellent qualities. Instead, she had Vasya. Instead, she had a wasting disease that ate her from the inside out. More proof that life wasn't fair, and no one got what was coming to them.

CHAPTER 17

As the months passed, Jane kept the drawing room permanently set up with her paints. She worked hard on her book of herbal receipts. While she no longer had Mrs. Houseman to correspond with, she ordered books and pamphlets, which helped her gather the knowledge she wanted for her personal book. Every great lady ought to have one.

The greenhouse was full and much more productive as well. Now that she didn't have to tiptoe around Matthew, it was far easier to commandeer a small room downstairs to keep tinctures and teas at the ready for any needy soul. She was pleased every time a new young woman found her way to the kitchen door.

Now, she could freely tell whoever knocked that they might tell other girls in need. Some women wanted to pay, which wasn't necessary, but Jane always welcomed information as barter. She liked keeping tabs on certain members. Like Hackett. Denby. The men who had associated with Matthew.

In some ways, Jane was just as powerful now as Matthew had ever been. She knew plenty of secrets because she handed out potions for keeping babies at bay and others for helping them arrive. She had other medicines for rashes and acne, headaches, toothaches, and flashes of heat for older women. She enjoyed the power, but mostly, she enjoyed her work. She was useful. She helped. And that was more than she'd ever been able to do while married.

Emma now came for tea at least weekly. Sometimes she brought the girls, but mostly not. She was still fragile, still mourning William.

Today was a cold, gray day with a drizzle marking the windows. Emma stared at the long marks streaking the glass as Jane poured. Not from the Assassin's Teapot but from a pretty lemon-yellow one she'd bought after Matthew's death.

"Lydia has nightmares every single night now." Dark circles ringed Emma's eyes, evidence bolstering her statement. "Doesn't trust the nanny to protect her. I go in and sleep with her, but even that isn't enough. I don't understand. She'd seemed to be improving, and now this."

Jane frowned. She didn't know what to say, other than that she understood. She understood the monster Matthew was, and if she could have stopped him, she would have. There was no point in telling her sister how sorry she was that he hadn't died sooner.

A low voice grumbled from the doorway. Jane struggled against the small panic that still flared at the sound of a masculine voice. But it was Vasya. Not Matthew.

"I'm sorry to overhear," Vasya said, bowing stiffly to them.

"Oh, Vasya," Emma said. "The girls miss you and send their regards."

Jane watched with too much interest as he smiled in response. He loved those girls like they were his own. His expression held all that grace and loyalty, and Jane felt as if she didn't deserve to even witness it. What he'd done for them—for all of them—made her chest ache.

"I would not mind sitting with her," he said, "if it would help the nightmares."

Emma practically melted in her seat. "I'm sure Lydia would adore it. At least we could try. That is, if you can take a break from your duties here." Emma looked at Jane.

Jane didn't know how Vasya occupied himself. She rarely left the house. Rarely needed a carriage. She'd instructed Vasya to sell the racing horses as they were unnecessary. There were still outstanding debts, she'd found, from Matthew's excesses. She was determined to pay them all. That wasn't something James should worry about when he returned home from school during his breaks.

Jane shook her head. "I have no objections. Perhaps you would be better served in a different position."

He stared at her, and she stared back. That golden thread that tethered them still stretched, ever so thin. But she was taking her sewing shears to it. Their decades-long affair-that-wasn't-an-affair was at an end. She no longer required protection. And he had a wife. They were not meant to be. It was all for naught.

Vasya bowed his head. "As you wish. I can provide a list of names to Mrs. Foraker for my replacement as stablemaster."

The lump in Jane's throat—hot inside of her—grew so large she couldn't swallow. So she nodded in agreement.

"Well," Emma said. "I'll tell Lydia you shall be joining us to protect her. I'm sure she'll be much comforted."

MARY DIED. VASYA BURIED HER IN THE churchyard and shook the hands of her family members, people he'd barely known. He paid for a tombstone that read "Devoted Wife." Because she was. If he got a tombstone, it would not say "Devoted Husband." Because he wasn't. He was a liar.

He moved from the flat he'd shared with Mary into the Lorian manor home in Town. They never went to the country anymore, which was a shame. It sent Emma into cold shivers when Gareth mentioned it, so they stayed in London.

Vasya had foolishly believed his tenure with Gareth's family would be short. A year, perhaps, until Lydia's nightmares vanished. But they didn't. So he stayed on. And then Lydia grew reckless and angry as she got older. Every tutor imaginable was brought in to curb her sharp tongue and willingness to slap and hit whoever was in front of her. She had dancing instructors, Latin tutors. She played piano and sewed. None of it calmed her.

For a month, Agnes and Lydia were sent to visit their aunt. And Vasya went with them. It was the first time he'd seen Jane in four years. Mr Afreé, the butler, admitted them and instructed them to go straight to the greenhouse. After Vasya took care of the carriage and horses, he joined them.

Walking through the garden, now overflowing with almost hedge-high shrubs of lavender, sage, and rosemary, Vasya saw the women's watery silhouettes through the greenhouse glass; Jane was instructing her nieces in weeding and repotting. He noticed the pile of fertilizing soil near the mews. Without asking, he found the shovel and wheelbarrow in front of the greenhouse. He left his coat and waistcoat draped over the mews gate, rolled up his sleeves, and set to work.

While he shoveled and transported, he wondered

what Jane would make of a land where it was easy to grow plants. Where the sun shone more often than the clouds shrouded the land. His homeland, for instance, grew fruits and grains, harvests virtually guaranteed.

When he finished shoveling, he went to the greenhouse. Should he knock? No, Jane knew he was here. It was expected that he should enter and ask to assist further. Wasn't it?

JANE WAS SO VERY AWARE OF THE MAN WHO FILLED the doorway of her greenhouse. When Vasya finally opened the door and revealed himself in his shirtsleeves, cuffs rolled up, exposing powerful forearms, her knees threatened to buckle. He had a streak of gray at his temple that only made him more handsome than the last time she'd seen him.

He bowed his head in deference to her, as if he needed to perform such formalities. As if he were not everything to their family, occupying some strange space between guardian and dear friend.

She still thought of him. Often. Wondered if he'd taken a lover. Another wife. Wondered if he thought of her or if she was just another wish he'd made that hadn't come true. The dream of sharing a bed with him kept her up at night.

"You—" She wasn't able to get the words out. She'd wanted to say, *You look well*.

"Have you any other work that needs to be done, my lady?" he asked.

Again, he was formal, putting distance between them. She looked at his hands, so large and capable, and wondered ever so briefly what it might feel like for his hands to rove her body. How well she might fit that palm. Thoughts that shouldn't be aired. Couldn't be aired. "No, thank you, sir. I'm sure Mrs. Foraker can provide you with a cup of tea and some refreshment."

The words sounded cold even to her, her tone icy and distant. Why had she done that? Because the girls were here?

She watched the man she loved stroll through her garden to retrieve his coat. Regret ate at her as he slid on the clothing. She should have invited him to stay. Or at least thanked him for moving the fertilizer closer. She only managed one wheelbarrow load at a time, taking only what she needed for the day.

Vasya disappeared through the kitchen door, and that was when she felt that golden thread snap of its own accord. She'd done it. And she'd likely never get another chance. But that was something to think about a different time. Right now, Lydia was plucking leaves from plants and Agnes was squishing dirt clods between her fingers.

And it was then that Jane realized that her part of this story, the part where Matthew's inflicted pains were no longer hers. They were not even Emma's. They were Lydia's. Jane had meant to hurt Matthew's friends. That hated circle of entitled greed. But her own needs, Emma's needs, James's and Lydia's and Agnes's needs, superseded that other vow of revenge.

"Lydia?" She called. The girl sulked and came over. And Jane told her. Not everything, and nothing in detail. The girl's memory was hazy and some details weren't correct, but it was enough.

She told Lydia enough about Denby and Hackett that should the girl choose to carry out some kind of retribution, it would be on her own terms. That she had ways to obtain information on them, should Lydia need it. And that whatever she chose to do, Jane would always be there to support her actions. Even the most outrageous ones.

No one had told Vasya that young women were insufferable. He would have rather pulled James out of every gaming hell in London than deal with Lydia's polite sniping. It was never directed at him, of course; he was her favorite, and they both knew it. But one more snipe at Agnes and he was ready to pull Lydia aside to box her ears.

When James was preparing for his upcoming Grand Tour, he suggested that Lydia try boxing as an exercise. It seemed to be the only pursuit they had not yet considered for the girl, and to Vasya's surprise, it wasn't Emma who protested—it was Gareth. But his protests didn't amount to much, and before long, a lady boxer came regularly to train the girl, arriving through the servant's entrance. The woman refused Vasya's services to drive her home. Soon, Vasya began to wonder if his place as Lydia's favorite was being threatened by this Miss Bess Abbott. She certainly was an impressive force.

At one point, he received a note from Mrs. Foraker to retrieve James from a gaming hell. He did, delivering the son home just as he'd delivered the father so many years ago. He kept looking for Jane somewhere in the house, but she was nowhere to be found. Was it because of him? Or was it too much for her to see her son in the same state she'd so often seen her husband in?

The house smelled the same. It felt the same. And he knew in his bones that it had become a mausoleum of sorts. A place where the terror had ceased but was still remembered. Vasya couldn't live like this, always in the past, always haunted by something that could have been. It was no way to exist.

Vasya saw himself out, wondering how many

times James would repeat his father's mistakes. Wondering if the boy had taken over his father's traits in other ways as well. He hoped for Jane's sake that he was gentle. Kind. But he also knew the boy couldn't be. He wasn't yet old enough to be kind.

It was time for Vasya to put away the hope he'd had. That small ember he'd left burning for her. Pining for her. A love that could never be returned.

LATER – 1814

Frost fairs were rare, but they brought out all of London to enjoy ice skating on the Thames, hot food in the snow, and whatever amusements royalty bid. Whether it was a parading elephant or bear baiting or giving away mufflers and coats to the poor, there was something to be gained by attending.

It was rare for Jane to go out, but she felt as if something had shaken loose this year. She wasn't sure what it was. As if her poor soul had finally broken through the soil of despair. The time had come for her to grow even more. To be fully in herself and in her own power. She was a formidable woman, cowed by no man. It was time to enjoy herself again, not just work.

So at this frost fair, Jane was determined to ice skate. She'd done it on the frozen pond when she was a girl. Part of finding joy was regaining that sense of freedom she'd felt when she slid through the frozen reeds that sprung through the ice. Even if no such boundaries were present here, it didn't matter. The snow had been brushed to the side, and water had been poured and smoothed over with brooms.

There was already a crowd in the circular area, men and women both, of all classes. Their colorful skirts and mufflers flared and waved underneath heavy woolen coats, and Jane had the urge to clap for them all.

James had chosen not to come. He was somewhere doing whatever young men of leisure did. At five and twenty, he didn't answer to his mother, but whenever he returned home with a black eye and his knuckles torn and bruised, she made her poultices and healing tisanes. He fussed and protested, but she did it no matter what and was happy to write out the receipt when he said he had a friend who might benefit from it as well.

Jane's heart turned over when Emma and Gareth joined her on the snow. Emma snuggled deep into Gareth's arm. They did not often display their closeness in public, but since everyone was smothered in large woolen overcoats, there was an element of anonymity at a distance. And fairs were meant for doing the unusual, for pursuing a romantic fancy.

"Will you join me?" Jane asked, her brow raised.

Emma shook her head. "I'd break my ankle."

"Or worse," Gareth said.

"Then I suppose I shall venture forth alone," Jane announced.

"Oh, Jane, not alone," Emma said, stopping Jane midstride.

"I'm a widow, Emma. Everything I do is alone. And I'm quite happy for it, I assure you." Jane meant it. Her life had meaning over and beyond her title and her son. Her teas and poultices helped women from across London. She had an entire trade operating out of the mews with young women who were in trouble, seeking help. Her teas were not effective past a certain date of pregnancy, but she did have teas that could prevent a child with surprising accuracy.

She cared for women of all walks and listened to

their tales of love or tales of woe. Most of her clients were women in service who couldn't start a family at the risk of losing their places. Typically, they were involved with a handsome footman, but sometimes it was a grasping son-of-the-manor, or even the master himself.

Once the women trusted her for that type of care, they'd come for other reasons as well. Jane had finally become the type of healer she'd wanted to be. Like Mrs. Houseman, she helped those who had been abandoned by the bespectacled men who didn't listen to a housemaid, or, if they did, judged her harshly for the position she found herself in, never bothering to understand how that position came about.

Ice skating alone was not something Jane would trouble herself about. She wanted to fly across the ice, and so she would, listening to that delightful scrape of a blade carving its way underneath, opening a path that had been previously closed.

Emma smiled at her sister. "Have fun skating, then. I think we might go warm up with some cider."

"Are the girls here?" Jane asked.

Gareth nodded. "Terrorizing everyone, no doubt."

"Perhaps they'd like to skate," Jane suggested.

"I don't want to give Lydia anything sharp," Emma said. "Or let her make a greater spectacle of herself. Every mama in the *ton* is angry with me for not getting her married off already. She's taking all the attention from the other girls and still not marrying any of the men panting after her."

Jane laughed, tickled to hear that Lydia was such a hoyden. "Good. I'm glad she's not marrying. No woman in her right mind would."

Emma gave her an indulgent smile. But Gareth frowned. "Marriage would calm her down, make her less angry."

Jane raised her brow at her brother-in-law. "Would

it, now? I was a perfectly mild girl, and look what marriage did to me."

Emma reached out and squeezed Jane's hand. "You are lovely the way you are. An absolute delight."

"Spoken like a highly biased sister."

"If you would like to get back into the market, several fine gentlemen have approached me about you—"

Jane held up her hand, shushing Gareth's speech. "I'm never marrying again. That's final. And as for dalliances, I'm not interested in a gentleman's tepid thrusting."

"Jane!" Emma said, blushing furiously.

Gareth barked out a laugh. "And not so tepid ones?"

"Those I might consider," Jane said with a smile. "Excuse me, I need to put on some skates."

When they parted company, Jane outfitted her skates and took to the ice. She wobbled at first, but once she found the strength in her ankles and the balance with her arms, the sensations all came back to her. The familiar icy wind on her face, her cheeks flushed both with blood and with cold from the frost.

"My lady," came a grumbling from next to her.

Jane's stomach flipped. They hadn't spoken in years. She had only seen Vasya at a distance on the few occasions when the girls visited her house. After she'd dismissed him that day in her greenhouse, it had never felt right to approach him. Or even inquire after him. Still, Martha kept her abreast of all the news, even if Jane hadn't specifically asked. Because Martha was loyal. And Jane was not. She didn't know how to be.

"Vasily Nikolaevich. How lovely to see you." She slowed her pace, but he clearly had no trouble keeping up. For such a big man, he was surprisingly agile. She took an extra second to look him over. He'd put on a little weight, as had everyone in the last few years, but he wore it well. He was still imposing and strong with an impenetrable black beard, bits of gray peppered in. Handsome, capable, and looking at her in a way that made her melt.

"You glide like you are born to the ice and snow," he said, his accent suddenly thick.

Jane couldn't help but give him a strange look. He'd been in England for over thirty years. How could his accent be thicker now than it had been years ago?

"Sorry," he said, returning to the voice Jane recognized. "I find that women like the exotic sounds."

She harrumphed. "Too late for that with me. Have you been having much success with women?"

They skated in silence for a moment, him not answering. "Only because I do not try."

"Oh?" Jane feigned indifference. "Whyever not? You have long been a widower."

When his wife had died less than a year into their marriage, Jane finally understood. Martha Foraker was the one who explained that the woman had long been aware of tumors on her breast. Knowing what some thought of women who had those bulges, she'd been grateful to have gentle Vasily Nikolaevich to take care of her in what she knew to be the last months of her life. She had more than a roof over her head—she had a warm home, with someone to check on her and keep her safe. She had provided an alibi, and he had provided her comfort and protection.

"May I call you Jane?" he asked, his voice low.

A thrill ran through her, and she looked about to see how close the other skaters were. It felt as if they were alone even though the world around them was a vivid, crowded blur.

"You have before," she reminded him.

"I would not assume any closeness," he said. "But I would be most grateful if you once again called me Vasya. As you once did."

Quite against her will, her heart beat faster. She felt silly fluttering over his attentions. Vasya's attentions. "Then I shall, Vasya. And you may address me as Jane."

He smiled, and how gentle and warm he looked when he smiled. "How have you been these past years, Jane?"

She raised her eyebrow at him. "Do you not know? Haven't you gotten every slice of gossip from Martha?"

He grinned and looked away. "It isn't the same if it doesn't come from your lips."

Dear lord, her lips tingled at his mention of them. She caught her breath, and he opened his mouth and closed it again without speaking. This was a moment that she could repair. The loose gold thread between them could be tied back together. Their rend could be repaired like a rip in a shirt.

"Would you like to have dinner with me, Vasya?" Her heart pounded in her chest. She kept her face impassive, but she'd never been this nervous in her life. Not even when Hackett had stared her down in front of the magistrate and accused her of murder.

"I beg your pardon?" he asked.

It was a bold move, and from his perspective, likely unexpected. With his official position as groom for the Lorian estate, he was entirely below her station. But Jane wasn't looking for a man to marry. She was looking for a kind man. One who knew what she had already lived through. Why there were doors that would never be opened in her house. Why she might never marry. Why she didn't like guests or parties. Why she didn't leave London, even on the smelliest, hottest days.

"I'd like to show you what has become of the greenhouse you built me. Do you remember it?"

"How could I not?"

"I'll have Martha pack me a dinner picnic and we'll dine in the warm greenhouse. Perhaps tomorrow night, if you can get loose of your charges?"

Vasya shook his great head with an indulgent smile. "The girls are . . ."

She smiled back, knowing intimately what handfuls her nieces were, in two very different ways.

"I will be there before the dinner bell." He offered his arm to her.

She contemplated it, but then she took it, feeling the warmth of his arm through his coat. And she decided that as long as the warmth was meant to support and not subsume, it was time for her to learn the difference.

⁂

THE LAST NIGHT OF LORD ANDREPONT

Martha delivered the tea tray, the house keys swinging at her waist. Jane noted the Assassin's Teapot on the tray and looked the housekeeper in the eye to confirm. Martha blinked, then curtsied and left without a word.

Matthew stood at the window, surveying his kingdom. Quickly, Jane opened the lid, checking to see which chamber contained which tea. Matthew's sense of smell was not good—damaged, no doubt, from some of his more hedonistic pursuits. Both compartments held peppermint tea. But one compartment had a smell. A terrible one, actually. Jane wasn't sure he would drink.

He ambled over to her, his fine black clothes indicating that he planned to spend the night with a woman. Not her. Not Hope. Matthew preened when he noticed the attention she gave him. She took stock of him as he did so. The boot knife glinted as he posed. It was the knife he'd held to Hope's throat once. The knife he'd used when he threatened to slit her wrist and watch her blood pool on the floor. Jane hated that knife.

"Are you jealous, Jane?" He enjoyed this ritual of his. Keeping her here while he ventured out. Making sure she was unhappy while he indulged himself.

She kept her mouth tight, as she always did. This was a test of endurance and survival. And she would pass it. He sat as she poured. Smoothly, she covered one hole and then the other. Passing his cup to him, she took hers.

But he made a face as he sipped. "This isn't tea. What have you done?"

She'd anticipated this. She knew it would happen. "I've been having some digestive troubles. I thought perhaps you had them as well, considering Cook has been—"

He cut her off with a raise of his hand. "Fine. But dear God, Jane. Make sure we have some decent tea brought up for me."

One cup was enough for hallucinations and a pleasant, loose feeling in his limbs. He needed another cup for the full dose. "Of course." Jane rose and pulled the bell. As she sat down, she poured him another cup as she sipped her own.

"Do you not find it dreadful?" Matthew made another face, yet he kept drinking.

Jane shrugged. "I find it therapeutic. Excellent regenerative qualities, as well as helping with the digestion. A side effect is found . . . well. Anyway." Jane looked away, baiting him. Waiting for him. He didn't let her down.

His wolfish smile took over. "What kind of side effects, Jane?"

She shook her head, eyes averted. No, no, she was meek. She was mild. She couldn't possibly say something vulgar. He reached across the divide where the tea tray lay, grabbing her chin, hauling her forward.

"Look at me."

She did. Her heart thundered. This was it. She could do this.

He purred, "What is the side effect?" Another woman might find his smooth voice and dark eyes seductive. "Jane. Answer me."

"Prolonged . . . tumescence." She struggled with the words.

He let go of her chin and sat back, looking impressed. "You've done well, then. I'll need that tonight." He winked at her and threw back the second cup of tea.

I've got you now, you bastard, she thought. But she didn't dare smile. If he vomited, the effects would likely not be lethal. He'd just go to sleep. He couldn't know. So she looked ashamed. Small.

"Perhaps I'll find three women tonight. And I'll tell them all how you helped me service them."

She hated him. Martha arrived, curtsied, and averted eyes. "Yes, my lady?"

"His lordship would prefer the Ceylon tea. Here is the key to the tea chest. Please brew it and return the key to me." Jane unhooked the key from her own chatelaine and handed it to Martha.

"Of course, my lady." Martha bobbed another curtsy just as someone knocked on the door.

Martha's eyes met Jane's, both in terror. Emma wasn't supposed to arrive yet. She and Gareth were only to arrive after Matthew left, to ensure they all had alibis.

Mr. Vernon's voice swam up from below, his words unintelligible. At least the ancient butler would take his time escorting a guest up from the foyer.

"Expecting someone?" Matthew asked, his eyes narrowing.

Jane shook her head. Emma would complicate things. Matthew had perhaps twenty minutes before he would feel the effects. He had to get into the carriage right away—the carriage Vasya had waiting— so he could get to Denby's, where he would collapse. A sudden heart attack. So tragic. So unexpected. So young.

He tapped his empty teacup. "Why not more of your side effect tea, Jane? Perhaps I can come home and plant a spare in you."

She tamped her look of pure hatred and poured him another cup. This was death. She was the angel of death.

Emma appeared at the doorway, a perplexed Mr. Vernon behind her and noticeably out of breath. Seeing Matthew idly sipping a cup of tea made Emma's spine snap to attention. "Lord Andrepont." Her tone was anything but respectful.

"Lady Lorian." He didn't bother standing or bowing even though she outranked him.

They stared each other down, the hatred palpable.

"You're looking well, considering," Matthew said.

Emma didn't take the bait.

"I meant to congratulate you at your son's funeral. How well you managed to do for yourself despite running from a viscount."

Emma didn't bat an eye. "A countess outranks a viscount."

He cocked his head as if he was amused by her politeness. "Oh, no. That isn't true. A countess outranks a viscountess. Regardless, you'll never be a man. But come to think of it, your line will end now that William is dead." He prodded Emma's grief, waiting for an outburst. He didn't get one. Emma stood stock still, her pale face wan, her fists balled.

Martha arrived with another pot of tea, placing it on the tray.

"Lady Lorian, would you like to stay for tea?" Matthew gestured to the new pot. "We are family, after all. Too bad your son couldn't be as healthy as my son. Really, it's too bad they couldn't be one and the same."

Jane's blood boiled with all the insults contained in that sentence.

"What amazes me after all this time," Emma said, taking a step forward. *Would she actually stay for tea?* "Is that no matter what you say, you sound like nothing more than a snake in the grass."

Vasya appeared at the door to the drawing room, no doubt because he'd seen Emma's arrival. He noted the second teapot and connected his gaze with Jane's. "Your carriage, my lord."

Matthew stood, narrowing his eyes at Emma, his cold smile threaded with pity. "Your mistake, Emma, is your naivete. You don't understand how long life truly is."

Jane thought she might cast up her accounts. Her heart pounded in her throat, and she felt lightheaded. Did he know? Would he cast up his accounts, aware of the poison doing its work? But Matthew glided out of the room, steady as could be.

"Don't mind him," Jane said smoothly, as if Matthew had not been as horrid as possible. She couldn't interfere. Vasya had a timetable and he knew it. He had to get Matthew to Denby's, and time was running short.

There was the sound of a stumble on the stairs. Jane shot to her feet, running to the door. Matthew clung to the banister, recovering his footing. That was from the third cup. She shouldn't have given him so much, but she didn't want him to grow suspicious.

Vasya gave Jane a worried glance. She shrugged. He said, "My lord, may I help?"

Matthew slapped Vasya's hand away, continuing down the stairs, where Mr. Vernon had Matthew's coat, gloves, and hat ready. He was unsteady on his feet as the aged butler assisted him.

Emma shouldered past Jane. "I'm not letting anything go to chance."

Jane shooed Vasya out the door with her hands as Emma picked up her skirts and ran down the stairs, nimble as a deer. Vasya slammed the door shut, and Jane was on Emma's heels, hissing her name. She couldn't shout their plans. Some of the servants were still Matthew's creatures and couldn't be trusted.

Emma flung the front door open, Jane right behind her. Vasya had the carriage door open, and Matthew's body was sprawled on the seat. He was losing muscle control. It was too soon. He couldn't arrive at Denby's like that. He'd likely die in the carriage on the way over. This wasn't the plan. This wasn't good. Emma stalked up to the carriage, finding Matthew's boot hanging out, not yet contained, the door unable to latch. Still advancing, she said, "Move, Vasya." Her voice was commanding, one that no one would question.

Vasya did as he was told.

In one swift movement, Emma removed the boot knife that had long menaced Jane and drove it hard into Matthew's chest.

Jane swayed on her feet. Almost fell.

"Rot in hell, you fucking devil." Emma shoved Matthew's black-booted foot into the carriage and slammed the door shut.

Vasya looked to Jane. Jane shook her head in disbelief. This wasn't the plan. This wasn't how it was supposed to go. "Just drive. Drive around London for as long as you can."

"But Lord Hackett expects—" Vasya protested.

"Park somewhere with him inside, go about your business, and return later," Emma said, fury so overflowing that it leaked from her. Blood spray dotted her face and hair. Matthew's body had blocked her dress from it. That, and the henbane in his tea had given him exceptionally low blood pressure. He'd drank three cups. She'd only planned on two.

"We'll figure it out," Jane said dully, though her mind felt diamond-sharp. He had a knife in his chest. His own knife. "Be obvious about the carriage in rougher neighborhoods. Then throw him in the Thames."

"I'll have to be late indeed to do that unseen," Vasya said.

"Be safe," Jane said. "You are—" She couldn't finish her sentence for she didn't know what to say. She grabbed ahold of Emma's shoulders, wanting to guide her inside to clean her off before the servants saw her.

Vasya nodded, and they parted ways. This was the beginning of Jane's new life. A new life that could include Vasya.

⚶

LATER - 1814

Vasya felt like an unwhiskered boy. He debated finding flowers for Jane. Or wine. Or some kind of trinket. But nothing felt right. They'd known each other for decades, been through what had at times felt like a war.

He wasn't certain if he should go to the front door as a guest or around back like a servant. Or a secret lover. But if she'd wanted to hide him, she wouldn't have taken his arm in public. He'd arrived on a horse, so he secured the animal in the stable himself, finding it odd that Garcia, his personal recommendation for Jane's replacement stablemaster, was not available to take the beast. That didn't bode well for the man. Vasya went round to the front of the house to make himself known. She didn't mean to hide him. He would woo her as a suitor and enter the house as any gentleman might.

Vasya was expecting Mr. Afreé, the butler. Instead, Jane herself greeted him, outfitted in a magnificent dark green dress lined with white fur that made her look mouthwateringly beautiful. He swallowed, attempted to speak, but failed miserably. Her green eyes bored into him, and he had no defense. She was exquisite.

"Welcome," Jane said. "I gave the servants a night off and extra coal. Most of them are snuggled up in their rooms, but the footmen all went out. Young men." She shook her head, which Vasya took to mean that James was also out of the house.

"Leave your coat on," she said as he crossed the threshold. "We'll go straight out to the gardens."

Vasya nodded, still unable to speak. The house was both intimately familiar and strange all at once. He'd trod these floors before, but instead of exuding that feeling of swimming in a sea of angst and poison and control, it felt oddly empty. The air was different than before, but still tomb-like.

She walked him down the passage to the ballroom —a place that no longer resembled the room as it had been in Vasya's time. Instead of the waxed dancefloor, there was a boxing ring with a straw bag, towels, and marks on the dulled floor. Vasya was shocked Martha Foraker didn't have an apoplexy at the very sight of this room.

"What—" he began.

"James," Jane said as both an explanation and an apology. "He's . . . lost."

Vasya grunted. The boy had been born lost. How could a decent child grow to be a man when his only role model was *that* man? Vasya cursed himself for leaving Jane's service. He should have stayed here. But the girls had needed him for protection and guidance. Emma had needed him for peace of mind, and Gareth had needed him for reassurance. There had been no right answer for him.

Snow blanketed the garden. The familiar cypress trees stood taller and wider than they had before. He smiled at the stone bench that still sat between them. It was there that Vasya had fallen completely in love with Jane so long ago. She'd been so young then. His eyes strayed to her body once again. She looked older, of course, but her beauty was still obvious. The tilt of her head was elegant and refined, her cheeks still angled. But instead of a mischievous elfin demeanor, she had a regal one.

He wondered how she felt about time's effects on him. He was no longer the young, strong buck he'd once been. His knees hurt, and he'd done something to his shoulder a few months back while saddling Lydia's horse that still bothered him. He wasn't the dashing soldier or the successful gambler. He was an old man who followed around headstrong girls, keeping them from trouble. Well, too much trouble.

When Jane opened the greenhouse door, a blast of warm air hit him in the face. The smell of rich soil and humid life was overwhelming. A blanket and pillows had been laid out on the floor at the far end. The pathways were swept clean, and in fact, the whole building had the air of being on its best behavior. The last time he'd been in here, he'd asked

Jane for more work and she'd dismissed him. It had hurt. He'd felt the rejection keenly.

Under Jane's care, the building overflowed with greenery of all kinds, some even flowering. Different scents flowed past as he walked towards the back: lemon, mint, basil, thyme, pepper, jasmine—it was almost overwhelming.

She knelt on the blanket, her green skirts flowing all around her.

He got to the edge of the blanket and faltered. He removed his hat and gloves and put them on the table beside them. "Should I remove my shoes?"

She laughed. "That was perhaps the most forward thing you've ever said to me."

"You make me forget myself," he muttered. Unbuttoning his overcoat, he shrugged it off and sat uncomfortably on the ground across from her.

"How strange," she said, studying him. "You're the only person who ever makes me feel like me."

He felt breathless, as if he'd been punched square in the chest. "Jane, I—" He cut himself off. There was a basket on the ground filled with a rough round of bread, a bottle of wine, and other shapes he couldn't make out at a glance. They should eat first. Of course. One did not confess their soul before a meal.

"I've loved you for a very long time," she said, her expression solemn.

Or not. He was glad she'd said it, even if it made him feel as if he had a bird's heart, fluttering quick and fragile just below the surface of his skin.

"It kept me afloat in my marriage to Matthew. No matter what he did, I clung to the idea of you, and that was enough. You kept me alive." She reached out and grasped his hand. "If nothing else, thank you for that."

Vasya cleared his throat, afraid that his hands

might start shaking. "Do you remember the night of your first ball here?"

"Of course," she said, her hand warm and heavy on his. He waited for her to remove it, but she didn't.

"One of the guests' coachmen maligned you. I was half in love with you already, and I was told to take a break before I beat the man senseless for what he'd said."

Jane looked nonplussed, but rather, amused.

"I found you on the bench, outside of the party."

"I remember," she said, her expression softening.

"You talked about him, his lord—"

"You don't need to speak of him," Jane protested.

"And you said you wanted one thing that was yours. It was then that you talked of the greenhouse. It took me years of bribes and card games and half-truths to get you this. But it was the only way I knew to tell you how I loved you. How I would do anything for you."

Tears shone in her eyes. She scooted closer to him. "And have your feelings changed?"

"I know I've changed. I'm not that same impulsive, violent, melancholy young man. But every glimpse of you makes me feel that same way all over again. As if I've run so far I can't catch my breath."

He looked at her hand on his, the paler of the two, calloused from her work in the garden. There was dirt under her fingernails, and he smiled. Who would think of a viscountess with indelible soil marks? "And you?" he asked, dreading her answer. "Have you changed?"

She sat back. "Of course. I'm stronger now. More set in my ways. But happy. I know my worth and my value. And it isn't connected to my husband or my title, or my son for that matter. So yes, I've changed. I'm my own woman, and that is an entirely different creature than the one you fell in love with."

"No," Vasya said, pleased with her blindness. "I fell in love with the girl who was only starting to realize her strength."

She removed her hand, letting it fall to her lap. He felt the loss. "Vasya." She sighed and looked up at the beams that supported the roof. Beams he'd helped place with his own hands. "I'm not unaware that men prefer biddable women. I'm telling you right now that I'm not biddable. I won't marry again for any reason. I refuse to give up my autonomy, and I'm not moving away from what I've built for myself."

Vasya frowned. She'd said many words, and she clearly meant every single one of them. Why it should trouble him, he didn't understand. So he echoed her, hoping to make things clear. "You say you are not a biddable woman now."

She snorted, drawing further away.

"But I have never known you to be biddable."

A genuine grin split her face. He felt pride for making it appear.

"You say you refuse to give up your autonomy, but I watched your marriage closer than anyone. You never gave it up. He caged you the best he could, but you ran him in circles, frustrating him at every turn. None of what you say is new. You have always been thus."

He plucked her hand from her lap and placed it in his. "And that, Jane, is why I have loved you for thirty years."

Her eyes shone and she half-hiccupped. "Gracious, has it been so long?"

"May I?" he asked, tugging more firmly on her hand.

Her mouth opened slightly, her tongue darting out, and even though he was not a young man, he went stiff as a soldier. She nodded, and he pulled her onto his lap. He dwarfed her, but having her in his lap was the most exquisite torture. She leaned her forehead to his, and if he'd died right in that moment, he would have felt like the greatest man who'd ever lived.

"Should I kiss you?" she whispered.

"Every part of me is for you," he said. When she said nothing and didn't move, he felt his cock twitch and hoped it hadn't offended her. "Some parts more than others."

She laughed, full-throated, tossing her head back, and he admired that smooth column. She was beautiful. And he was the lucky arsehole who got to hold her. Finally.

"Vasya," she said. "How I've missed you."

He cradled her cheek and drew her lips to his. Soft and knowing, neither of them shy but both cautious, they let themselves be known in light pressure and cool exploration. She slid her hands around his neck and into his hair, and by God, if there was a better feeling, Vasya didn't know it.

She deepened their kiss and pulled at her skirts until they were above her thighs, then turned and straddled him. Oh. No, that felt better indeed. She ground herself in his lap, and he let out an involuntary grunt. He needed to stop thinking about what could feel better before he spent himself in his trousers.

"Would you think it too fast if I bedded you?" Jane asked, breathless.

"It's been thirty years," he protested. "How much slower do you need to go? We'll be dead."

She laughed again, and he found himself enjoying his ability to make her laugh even more the second time. He also wondered what it would take to make her cry out in a different way.

"Undo your trousers," she said, pulling herself away from him.

"You might outrank me, my lady, but I'm not here for your bidding." He gave her a look that he dearly hoped was as seductive as he felt.

Her eyebrow popped up. He was going to kiss that expressive brow ridge as she shuddered around him, he decided. But first. "Are you not, sir?"

"Lay down," he growled, pulling a pillow over for her head. He didn't want her to be uncomfortable. He pushed up the folds of the pretty green dress with the white fur trim until it was near her navel, exposing that beautiful flower of a woman's center. Her lips trembled. "Are you still wanting me?" he asked, concerned.

"Very, very much so," she said, her eyes wide and serious.

He slid his hand up her leg, skating past the stocking, then the garter ribbon, and finally to bare skin. He kneaded her thigh, getting her used to his touch. "I can be gentle."

"I don't need gentle, Vasya. I just need you."

He moved his hands to her apex, furred with downy dark hair. One casual swipe of his finger and he felt her wetness, relieving the burden of his mind. He was terrified that she hadn't been telling him the truth, that she was allowing him favors and didn't really want him. But this was true. He watched his fingers play in her wetness, swirling, causing her to spread her legs wider, to arch in pleasure. He looked at her face, beautiful and honest, no mask right now. No cool assessment. Just pleasure, and all for him.

He slid one of his thick fingers inside of her, slowly, to see how she responded. She ground down on his hand, and he couldn't help but glory in it. His cock strained against his trousers, and he didn't look forward to having them cleaned, so he willed himself to keep control a little longer. He wanted to see pretty Jane come.

Her wetness overwhelmed his senses in the humid greenhouse, already rich and heady. He lowered his head, ready to fully immerse his sensations. He withdrew his finger from inside her, spread the lips of her sex apart, and licked that small, shining, hard bud.

Jane sprung up to sitting, but he pushed her back down. "Holy . . ." she muttered, nothing but gibberish after that first intelligible word.

He dared another lick, and she spread her legs even wider. He chuckled, happy that her pleasure was so obvious and clear. He continued on, sucking and licking until her thighs clamped on either side of his head and she came hard.

She sagged into limpness. He wiped his face and beard on the blanket. Her green eyes followed him as he came to lie beside her.

"I never knew what the beard was for," she said. "It was so out of fashion. Now. I. Know."

It was his turn to laugh. Her smell wouldn't be out of his beard without proper soap and a washing. Until then, its scent would arouse him mercilessly.

"Now," she said, clearing her throat. "I believe I have a request pending."

It was his turn to raise his eyebrows. "Oh?"

"After thirty years, I would very much like to see your cock."

For fuck's sake. At those words, he was painfully erect. He said, "I'm certain I can oblige."

He unbuttoned his trousers, shoving them downwards. His prick strained and leaked. He really wasn't going to last long at this rate. She took him in hand. "Jane, I—"

"You had your turn. Let me have mine," she said, looking at him with those green eyes, which were very persuasive. As was her hand.

"Why aren't you naked?" he growled, suddenly irritated that he couldn't see her. He wanted to see the slope of her breasts as she frigged him. How they fell together when she was on her side.

"Why aren't you?" she challenged.

Even with her hand on his cock, he unbuttoned his coat and waistcoat as quickly as possible, his fingers nimble and well-exercised. Even the fabric-covered buttons would smell of her wetness, he thought. He might never wash the garments again. He pulled the white lawn shirt over his head.

She laughed. "I'm afraid my garments are more intricate than that."

"Are they?" he asked, thinking of how absolutely flimsy they seemed in comparison to his desire.

"Yes, I have my stays and my—"

He interrupted her protests by grabbing the neckline of her gown and pulling it low, the corset straining and folding over in the wake of his strength. Her pert breasts popped into display and he was on them, unwilling to wait any longer. He sucked on their pink tips, alternating one and then the other.

"Sit up," she commanded, and he'd be damned if he didn't obey.

He sat up and she climbed on him again, straddling as she had before, but with him now sucking on her beautiful, firm breasts the size of a perfect melon and twice as sweet. He felt her position him, the soft, warm wetness swiping across the tip of his cock. It strained and pulled, wanting satisfaction. Until, mercifully, she gave it, sliding down him, letting him enter her warmth, gripping him as he desperately wrestled himself for control.

"I control the pace," she whispered, her voice firm as she moved up and down on him, slowly, ever so slowly. Her breasts dangled tantalizingly in Vasya's face. He caught one hard peak in his mouth and she came, hard and fast, all over again. Her silky cunt clutched his cock, pushing him closer and closer to the edge, but he wanted more than this. It had been thirty long goddamned years.

"You've had your turn. I want control," Vasya growled in her ear, and she shuddered again, the climax clutching at his cock with exquisite pleasure.

"Then do it," she managed, breathless.

He lifted her just enough to lay her down, placing pillows around her, never withdrawing from her as he built her a comfortable nest. He could feel her passage shift and change as he moved.

"This is quite the cushioning," she said.

"You said you didn't need gentle," Vasya said, hoping he'd understood correctly.

Her eyes darkened. "I don't."

He grunted as he thrust in short bursts, reclaiming control over himself, though his prick argued. Building up speed and strength, Jane made noises that she hadn't made during her other two crises. She wrapped her legs around his waist and he buried himself deeper and deeper until he could no longer call himself master of his body. He thrust blindly, hard and insistent, and it felt better than anything he'd ever felt in his life. He came, spilling himself in her, and she clutched him tight with her legs, back arched in abandon.

He braced himself above her, not wanting to crush her. She found his gaze, questioning. He nodded at her, brushing a kiss across her lips, then pulling out, falling to his back. They both lay there, panting.

"Do you still feel the same about me?" she asked.

He glanced over at her. "Of course not." He placed his hand on her cheek. "I have always said I would die for you. I would kill for you. But now I can say that I love you, out loud, to your face."

She laughed and took his hand, cradling it.

"I did try to kill for you, but the bastard was already dead when I got him."

Jane shrugged. "Too many people wanted the honors. I had been working on it for years. I wasn't about to let anyone step in front of me."

Vasya frowned and turned on his side. "What do you mean, years?"

She sighed. "Every so often, Matthew would come into my drawing room for tea. Why? I don't know. Part of his ego, proving to himself that he'd somehow beaten me. And I served tea with a pinch of arsenic. Not enough to kill him outright, just enough to shorten his life. A year here, a decade there. It made me feel better."

Vasya shook his head. "How could you have known when he would visit? And how could he not be suspicious?"

"He never thought much of me. I was the little sister. His weak little toy." Jane shrugged. "He was always so caught up with Emma that he never paid attention to me. Even when I was sitting right in front of him."

"I don't know how," Vasya confessed. "You are the blazing sun that lights my world." He kissed her hand, hoping she understood that he was hers forever.

EPILOGUE

Jane closed the door to the rooms at the back of the house, where she had built a space for herself and Vasya. It was closer to her medicine room, and it was cozy and private. It was something that was all hers. Vasya had taken rooms at Lydia's house, but slipped away to be with Jane.

"What did you do?" he asked, his head cocked, attempting to look stern while secretly amused by her.

"Me?" she asked in feigned innocence. "Nothing except try to help my son along in his wedded bliss."

Vasya exhaled. "Let the children alone. They'll figure it out."

Jane put her hands on her hips. "That boy has never figured anything out. Not once. I just put some . . . added pressure."

Vasya groaned and sat down on the bed, which was covered in a simple quilt. She liked to keep this room simple, not opulent. She wanted to feel like she was in a cottage, like where she'd grown up. She didn't want to be a viscountess in this room. She wanted to be Just Jane. With her Informal Vasya. "What did you do?"

She bit her lip and climbed onto his lap. "I may have been adding a few extra ingredients to the dinner menu."

"Aphrodisiacs?" Vasya growled.

"Well," Jane said, looking everywhere but his beautiful dark brown eyes. "Some might call them that."

"Let them be," he repeated.

"If I let them be, it might take them thirty years to figure out they could be happy together. I can't allow that," Jane protested, wrapping her arms around Vasya's neck. She smoothed down his beard.

He stretched up and kissed her. "You meddling harpy."

"Not just me," Jane protested. "What about you? You meddled with Lydia, and with Agnes. Are there more, you great hairy cupid?"

Vasya chuckled, which Jane only recognized as a chuckle and not a grunt because she knew him so well.

"Besides." Jane sighed, playing with the soft hair that curled at the nape of his neck. "This house has been joyless for so long."

"Only because you prefer coupling out of doors," Vasya grumbled.

"That's not true," she protested. But once she thought about it, yes, they'd been in the greenhouse much of the time before she'd set up these rooms near the servant's quarters. They had once been silver closets, but Jane had repurposed them for herself. After all, it had been her home for so long. It was time to make something just for herself. And the man she loved. "Well, maybe it's a little true," she said. "But you like it."

"I like knowing that we're both happy," he said, reaching up for another kiss. "We've waited long enough for it."

HISTORICAL NOTE

One of the reasons I wanted to write <u>A Lady's Resilience</u> is because I have two family members who were victims of men like Matthew Wallingford, the viscount Andrepont. The men in their lives employed manipulation tactics, physical violence, and intimidation to take advantage of these women physically, emotionally, and financially. Even in the modern world, these monsters excel at isolation and control, though it is harder than what it would have been for a nobleman in the late 1700s. One of my family members got out of her situation. The other thought she had gotten out, but my cousin Julie was murdered by her ex-husband in 2017. Her killer is in prison.

The rise of "Dark Romance" as a subgenre has made the bad boy redemption arc very appealing to many people. And while I have no intention of "yucking someone's yum," I very much wanted to put out into the world a tale where the villain is *not* redeemable. Where he is, simply put, a monster.

As someone who watched from the outside of these abusive relationships, there was no amount of making the victim "see" what the abuser was. Shutting them out, or getting frustrated with them only helped the abuser in the long run. I don't have a right answer, nor am I an expert. But I love both of those strong, independent women, and watching them hurt was the worst. It is not a flaw to be strong *and* empathetic, but that is what their abusers preyed upon.

The National Domestic Violence Hotline is 800-799-7233, or 800-799-SAFE. Every state has its own system of shelters, but help is there. I know it's hard to ask for help. I know it's hard to speak out. But it might save your life, or someone else's.

Onto the historical aspects.

In the past, there were many cases where a marriage between a young, underage girl would be legally married with understanding and provisions made that intercourse would be delayed until she matured. These legal weddings were done because of familial/political alliances, while acknowledging that childbirth in a girl too young would result in her death and/or being unable to carry a child later on. Because women's lives are often reduced to significant dates in history books, such as birthdate, death date, and marriage date, we don't get the real sense of how they lived. A marriage date for the aristocracy did not necessarily mean a wedding night the way we think of it today. Sometimes yes, but sometimes no. For the purposes of fiction, I liked how it ramped up tension.

The timeline of this book starts in 1780, where the first Queen's Ball took place. If you have watched the Bridgerton spin-off Queen Charlotte, then you know that I am referencing that queen. Queen Charlotte and her husband, King George, were affectionate, and this is the first ball for her birthday, which became an annual charity event. This evolved into the tradition of the debutante ball.

Interestingly enough, while the American Revolution was happening in the colonies, London was obsessed with a bigamy trial of a woman. They were so distracted by the salacious details of her secret marriage, secret baby, friendships with powerful women in other countries and her absolutely extravagant spending (she built herself a custom yacht), that the public sort of "forgot" about the war. Some posit that this might be another reason the Americans won: the British upper class thought too much about this woman's sex life and not enough about money and weapons to fight a revolution. Read The Duchess Countess by Catherine Ostler for a riveting and eye-popping non-fiction look at this phenomenon of a woman who pissed off a LOT of people.

I also mention the French Revolution. It was a preoccupation of aristocrats in England, as there were revolutionary forces at work there too. Jane's vision of standing at the guillotine is not a work of fancy, but of real concern for women of the time. The song quoted is real, sung by the revolutionaries in France and England. French revolutionaries wanted to dismantle a system, but the system was so engrained, the belief of superiority of certain bloodlines, that some (not all) encouraged the murder of hundreds of thousands of people. I've read more than one book that quoted the eye witness account of the streets of Paris literally running with blood. While Jane is concerned with her life and her family's lives, many other English politicians tried to figure out the political advantage of their oldest rival existing in chaos.

To pivot away from revolutions, I'd also like to address the herbwoman, Mrs. Houseman. She is obviously a work of fiction, but it is a counterpoint of how medicine was practiced in those days. A woman of a great house, as Jane becomes, was the "mother" figure to the household. She was expected to have a receipt book (which we now call a recipe book), for all manner of cures. From abortifacients to cleaning solutions, these books can be found in Google books and in blogs. The lady of the house would administer cures or at least direct them for her family and for her servants. A woman like Mrs. Houseman would be known as a midwife, but since she is more than just there for births, she had a larger role: an herbwoman. Knowledgeable about plant life and their purposes, she was invaluable to a community. In contrast, an educated physician in London, would not touch a patient. They believed in the balances of humors, and an intellectual approach. The male surgeon-apothecaries were the general practitioners in the country. Not as well educated as a physician, they dispensed medicine and performed basic procedures (lancing a boil, etc). Not surprisingly, an herbwoman was associated with "country life" and a physician would be a more sophisticated practitioner, located in London.

That said, the childbed was a "woman's" place, and when Mrs. Houseman argues with the male physician, she wins. Jane's admiration of Mrs. Houseman is clear—this is a woman who holds great power. And while I try to not make Jane's character arc too obvious, her transformation into an herbwoman in her own right gives her the strength and inherent power to take action against Matthew.

Onto the Assassin's Teapot. This was really a thing. Not typically in the West, but poisons were common place all over. Not only did I want to showcase this very cool teapot that uses the physics of liquid dynamics to pour two separate liquids from one teapot, I also wanted to show how women have taken recourse on the abusers with poison. While I was writing this, I listened to the interview on the podcast Vulgar History with author Nikki M. Taylor, who wrote <u>Brooding Over Bloody Revenge: Enslaved Women's Lethal Resistance</u>. Much to my shame, I have not yet read this book, but she speaks on how enslaved women used covert forms of resistance to protect themselves, including poisoning. Of course, we only know of the ones who were caught. But when facing a system that does not believe in one's own agency, one's right to one's body, the route is necessarily a lethal one.

A note on the Georgian English legal system: I did my best. There were no police forces during this time, as it would have seemed extremely intrusive to the people of the day. A coroner was the one to deal with bodies, and since there is no refrigeration techniques, any murder trial would have three days to come to a suspect. The jury would be able to view the body in order to help understand the evidence. The reason that any suspicion would never fall on Jane was due to her status. As a lady, she would be deemed too delicate to commit murder. Vasily, on the other hand, would be instantly suspected. The anti-immigration sentiment was huge, and as a foreigner, he would be thought to have inherent violence in his soul. I tried to make clear what he would be facing through Jane's musings about Mr. Eier, the coroner. Hopefully it came across.

I love the Georgian era for all its quirks and oddities. It doesn't sell as well as Regency, which is a shame. So much of Georgian history is strange and hilarious and unregulated. The English bureaucracy began to flourish at the turn of the 19th century, and so much of the honest-to-goodness weirdery was legislated out of existence. Perhaps someday I will write books about the women's footraces that occurred in the 17th century. You never know.

ACKNOWLEDGMENTS

I would like to thank the Paper Lantern Writers for their support and enthusiasm for my work. Ana Brazil, especially, for advocating for Vasily on several occasions. It's been five years of publishing, and five years of us! Also thanks to Jillianne Hamilton for always asking (very quietly), *are you able to fit this into your schedule?*

Thank you to my kiddo for understanding (finally!), that my "computer time" is when I'm writing books. You should not read Mama's books until you are very old and I am very dead. Thank you to my amazing husband, Andy, without whom... everything. We've been partners for almost two decades, and I adore that you do the dishes, the laundry, make lunches, and chop down trees. You are an ungendered domestic role partner's dreamboat. Which is my dreamboat.

Thanks to my mom, for letting me know that when she reads these books, she doesn't think of them as mine. It makes it easier to write the steamy stuff.

As always, my dream team of Anya at Touchstone Editing, Signe at Jorgenson Editorial Services, and Fiona at Fiona Jayde Media, you guys make these books interesting, deep, and beautiful.

Lastly, thank you to everyone who has read my books. While I am obviously deeply embarrassed when someone tells me they like my work, it keeps me going. So please leave a review somewhere that I might find it. Or tell a friend. Or take a picture on social media. It's the one time I don't mind being talked about.

HELP AN AUTHOR OUT!

Did you enjoy this book? Please consider leaving a review for this book or others in this series. Reviews help get the word out about a book you enjoyed. It means a lot. Consider reviewing on sites like Bookbub, Goodreads, or BookDNA.

Thank you!

ABOUT THE AUTHOR

Edie Cay writes award-winning historical romances. Her five-book Regency series *When the Blood Is Up* focuses on the history of women's boxing and themes of misfits and found family.

The Ladies Alpine Society is a four-book series is set in the Victorian era, following four women who are determined to summit the Matterhorn against all odds.

Look for upcoming releases, including THE LYON'S LAST CHANCE, from Dragonblade Publishing, and the upcoming cozy queer historical SCOTTISH BREAKFAST.

As a speaker, she has presented at many international conferences both in-person and online, including Historical Novel Society, Regency Fiction Writers, Chicago-North Spring Fling, and the Toronto Romance Writers conference. She regularly contributes to the HNS quarterly journal. She is a member of HNS, The Regency Fiction Writers, and a founding member of Paper Lantern Writers. Follow her on social media @authorEdieCay.

Sign up for her newsletter at ediecay.com for free books, promotions, and book recommendations.

Shorts available by Edie Cay

In Her Element

contemporary romance novelette

A Soldier's Medal

Flash Historical Fiction in *Kindle Unlimited*

Hand-in-Hand Pies

Bess Abbott origin story

A Rarefied Gift

When the Blood Is Up Short Story

Non-Fiction

Crafting Stories from the Past: A How-To Guide for Writing Historical Fiction